THE STRANGE BIRTH, SHORT LIFE, AND SUDDEN DEATH OF

JUSTICE GIRL

Julian David Stone

Copyright © 2013 Julian David Stone
Cover designed by Greg Szimonisz
www.juliandavidstone.com

All rights reserved.
ISBN-10: 0989831507
ISBN-13: 9780989831505
Library Congress Control Number: 2013948414
For The Duration Press, Los Angeles, California

For Mom, Dad, Summer, and Archie

Episode Ninety - Seven

HERMIE'S HENHOUSE

"HAVE I GOT A DEAL FOR YOU"

Sunday, March 20, 1955

As amazing as it may seem, especially to the close friends, slight acquaintances, or even complete strangers who had the extreme misfortune to debate, argue, or shout, or scream through clenched teeth at Jonny Dirby, he never really considered himself a difficult person. Even when confronted with the obvious fact that he seemed to relish pushing even the most trivial confrontation to just shy of flying fists, he emphatically denied it. Not that he would claim for a moment that he didn't like a good tussle; Jonny savored them almost as much as when he wrote a piercing line in a play or, as was his current lot, a sharp joke in a comedy sketch. Rather, he would forcefully state, with flailing arms and flapping palms, that his strong reaction to the disagreeable situation at hand was entirely appropriate, whether it related to politics ("The New Deal saved this country from fascism!"), to a story point in a sketch he was helping to write ("If it's faster, it's funnier!"), or even to the quickest cab route to the West Village to see a friend's play ("Only an idiot would take a cab. Take the 2 train—half the time and a tenth the cost!"). Despite being only a tick over twenty-five years of age, Jonny carried with him the acute confidence that he was always right, and that is precisely how he would have defended his seemingly extreme behavior on the evening of Sunday, March 20, 1955. To him, standing alone atop the beaten-oak boardroom table that dominated the empty writers' room of the popular Sunday night television show *Hermie's Henhouse* with a baseball bat in hand, ready to swing at the spinning overhead fan, was completely understandable, because just ten minutes earlier he'd been fired from his job as one of the show's writers. Or at least it was ten minutes earlier when he finally believed his boss was serious about his termination.

As Jonny stared up at the four-bladed wooden fan spinning just two feet above his head, he seethed. He despised that fan with as much passion as any non-psychotic was capable of hating an inanimate object. To him, the fan perfectly symbolized his frustrations of the last eighteen months as one of the staff writers on the one-hour comedy review. *Hermie's Henhouse*, starring aging veteran performer Herman Fox, currently filled the 8:00 p.m. Sunday slot on the Regal Television Network. The show was transmitted live every week from the Crestview Theatre, a former burlesque house, located on Broadway just north of Times Square in Manhattan.

The writers' room, perched in the upper eastern corner of the theatre and more than a hundred feet above the gleaming sidewalk, was a dank, dark, dingy place, permanently reeking of cheap cigarettes, cheaper coffee, and still cheaper cigars. The filthy walls displayed evidence of at least three different stages of wallpapering with only one thing in common: they were all peeling. There was barely enough room to hold four full-grown adults, so it was miserably crowded when there were six, and downright intolerable when all eight of the writers who made up the current staff were in attendance. But to Jonny, the worst thing in the room was the "piece of shit" overhead fan. Installed at some point over the years by a good-hearted soul in a vain attempt to make the room more livable, it only made things worse—at least as far as Jonny was concerned. In the winter, when everyone sat around trying to be creative while wrapped in heavy wool overcoats because the theatre's anemic heating system didn't extend to the top floor, the fan created a most unwelcome and unneeded breeze. In the summer, when the room's one sad window could be squeezed open only a mere six inches because of forty years of sagging and settling, the fan blew the heavy stale air around the stifling room and into the writers' mouths as they spoke, forcing them to taste four decades of decay. And to make matters worse, no one could figure out how to turn the damn thing off. Jonny pestered anyone and everyone for a solution but to no avail. Ultimately, from stagehand to writer to producer to network executive, they were all far more concerned

PROLOGUE

In this age of DVDs, downloads, and digital recorders, it is hard to imagine a world before recordable media, when any and all aspects of television had to be performed live. But from the 1930s until the late 1950s, that's the way it was. Complex dramas, boisterous comedies, tense thrillers, convincing commercials, and informative news were watched in homes across America at the very same instant they were being created in some faraway studio. To viewers of that era, everything seemed calm and controlled as the images flashed across their screens in pristine black and white. But nothing could have been further from the truth. Every moment was a true high-wire act, filled with chaos, confusion, fear, and the constant dance across the razor's edge between complete disaster and unparalleled success. It was amid this combustible cocktail—and because of it—that Justice Girl first came to life. And was live.

with getting the show on the air. What finally drove Jonny over the edge, however, was the one thing the network executives did have time for that was *not* directly related to putting on the show: hounding him to sign a loyalty oath to the United States of America.

One month ago, an edict had come down from the new president of the Regal Television Network, Hogart Daniels, demanding that every staff member of every show, from the lowliest production assistant to the most senior executive producer, sign a loyalty oath, stating unequivocally an undying allegiance to the United States. Immediately, almost everyone working on *Hermie's Henhouse* lined up and signed. They were happy to do so, because they knew if they didn't, the same thing they had seen happen to thousands of others—many of them colleagues and friends—might happen to them: they could be blacklisted.

Slithering over the entire entertainment industry like the oozing spill from an oil tanker, the blacklist had claimed the careers of thousands of actors, writers, directors, musicians, and stagehands. Virtually no end of the business had been untouched by its ever-growing reach. Any association with Communism, from "full party member" to "just curious" to "went to a meeting because I wanted to fuck a girl who was a member" was enough to get someone's name on the list. And any attempt to clear a name was practically pointless—not for the obvious reason of being David against the massive entertainment industry's Goliath, but for a more insidious reason. No one would admit that the list even existed. When pressed, any industry executive would dismissively answer that it was merely a rumor, a work of fiction, the product of the sick mind of an agitator.

That thing that "didn't exist" had claimed the careers of at least a dozen people working on *Hermie's Henhouse*, including three of Jonny's fellow writers. A year or two earlier, during the most fevered period of the Communist witch hunt, they had simply showed up for work one day and learned they no longer had jobs. Partly in solidarity to them, and partly because Jonny felt he had nothing to prove when it came to his loyalty, he refused to sign the oath. How dare they question his Americanism! He was as patriotic as they came—his older brother had served in the army and had been repeatedly decorated, and his sister had died, both in support of the great crusade to crush the Nazis. Wasn't that enough? Wasn't his signature on some half-assed loyalty oath unnecessary?

For weeks, he put off signing the damn thing, even when some of the show's staffers, while sympathetic to his steadfastness, chased him down in search of his elusive signature. Until today, he had successfully evaded them, always dashing away because he was late for a rehearsal, or a sketch needed a big rewrite, or he had to get notes from the director or from the producer or from Hermie himself—anything to avoid signing the damn thing.

This morning, when he stepped into the writers' room—always the first one through the door—a plain, white business envelope (his name boldly typed on it) was on the table. Jonny opened it, read its contents, and rolled his eyes. It was a letter of termination signed by Charles Fox, Hermie's oldest son and the show's producer. Charles had thrown in "dereliction of duties" for good measure, but Jonny knew it was actually a blacklist threat. His termination was effective immediately, and it ordered Jonny to leave the premises upon receipt of his severance pay, which, the letter went on to say, would be delivered shortly. Sighing, Jonny crushed the letter in his hands and tossed the crumpled ball toward a nearby trash can, missing the receptacle by several feet. He reached into the worn leather satchel he always carried and began to search. Amid a scattered collection of debris, including a crumpled newspaper, some scribbled sketch ideas, a toothbrush, a couple of pens, a receipt for a shirt he'd been meaning to return, and a take-out menu (he loved Indian, but no one else in the room did, so when the take-out menu for Curry Palace kept conveniently disappearing, he started carrying his own copy), he found what he was looking for. Jonny pulled out a single piece of creased paper that was the loyalty oath—somewhere along the way, one of the numerous copies that had been shoved under his nose had made it into his satchel. Jonny scanned it with his beleaguered eyes.

I, the undersigned, swear and affirm that I do not advise, advocate, or teach the overthrow, by force, violence, or other unlawful means, of the government of the United States of America, and that I am not now, nor have I ever been a member of or affiliated with any group, society, association, organization, or party that advises, advocates, or teaches, or has advocated or taught the overthrow, by force, violence, or other unlawful means, of the government of the United States of America.

The oath went on for several more paragraphs, but Jonny couldn't read any farther. The words still angered him as much as the first time he had read them. But he forced the anger to subside, realizing that at this moment, the words were no longer the issue. He had taken his soft protest as far as he could and had made his point, sticking up for his friends, even if it had gone largely unnoticed. With a heavy hand, he quickly signed the oath and then marched down the two flights to Charles's office.

"Is he in?" Jonny asked the clearly startled secretary.

"No," she quickly offered back.

Jonny handed her the signed loyalty oath. "He'll be happy to see this. See that he gets it right away," he said flatly and then headed back to the writers' room.

The rest of the day was consumed with the usual show-day activities: final tweaking of the sketches, the full-dress run-through, the post-full-dress run-through tongue-lashing from Hermie, some more tweaking of the sketches, and then, finally, the late-afternoon meal in a nearby restaurant before returning to the theatre for the actual live broadcast.

Stepping back into the writers' room before taking his usual position behind the audience for the broadcast, Jonny found yet another letter waiting for him, his name once again typed boldly across the ivory-white front. Jonny ripped it open, and a single bluish rectangle flittered to the floor. He picked it up and, to his astonishment, discovered it was a severance check. He marched out the door and down to Charles's office.

"I need to see him!" Jonny ordered the now even-more-startled secretary.

"He's not available," she hurriedly offered back.

"Bullshit!" Jonny shot past her, heading for the door to Charles's office. Before he reached it, a uniformed guard appeared, blocking his way.

"Mr. Dirby," the guard said, glowering down at Jonny, his eyes at least a foot above Jonny's head, "we really need you to leave. If you would please gather all your belongings and immediately exit the building, we would be most appreciative."

Jonny wanted to fight, but he knew that if he did, the guard's fake politeness would dissipate into real anger. And given the fact that Jonny possessed the insignificant build of a man who sat on his ass for a living, he knew he would lose badly. Besides, the guard was obviously there in anticipation of Jonny's reaction, and his presence made it clear to Jonny that Charles was dead serious. Jonny turned around and headed back to the writers room.

Furious, he gathered his belongings. They had really gone and done it. They had fired him, and he knew if he tried to get work elsewhere, no one would hire him. He was blacklisted. The last personal item Jonny grabbed was the bat. It was a beautifully grained Louisville Slugger with Jonny's name etched into the thick end. Hermie had given similar bats to each member of the writing staff at the end of the last season as a gift for "hitting it out of the park." Jonny's never made it home with him, becoming, instead, a permanent fixture of the writers' room. Various writers had used it at one time or another to make their points by jabbing it at the air, to stretch their muscles by placing it across their backs and bending over, to lean on as a comical cane, or simply to relive a Mickey Mantle home run.

As he held it in his hand, feeling its weight and girth, Jonny got the idea of how he might let go of some of his anger and settle the score, if only just a tiny bit. It was to be his parting statement, a little coup de grâce. So, he climbed up on top of the rickety oak table, the bat held tightly in his stacked hands, and stared up at his spinning nemesis. It was a noisy piece of ancient machinery, taunting him with its incessant wobbling. Jonny focused on the whirring blades and took a swing. He missed. Sports—or anything physical—had never been his strong suit, let alone baseball. Verbal sparring—now that was something in which he could hit a home run! Jonny redoubled his grip on the bat, tightened his eyes, and bobbed his head, pacing the fan blades in an attempt to get in rhythm with them. He swung again. He missed again.

Sadly, he knew what would work. Somewhat defeated—after all, this wasn't quite the manly pounding he'd envisioned—he gripped the bat in one hand and held it straight up into the path of the slicing blades.

Shards of mahogany exploded in all directions and rained down, as the fan was defanged and quickly turned into nothing more than a pathetic spinning nub. His work done, Jonny jumped off the table but momentarily lost his balance as he landed on a rather large chunk of mahogany. As he kicked it away, he took in the sight of the room covered in broken wood. Maybe the method had not been the one of choice, but there was no doubt it felt good to have finally destroyed the damn thing.

Plus, the thought of his pending unemployment gave him a sudden, unexpected lift. Now he could concentrate full time on what he really wanted to do: write dramatic teleplays. There was great work being done in this new and charismatic medium of television. Paddy Chayefsky, Reginald Rose, Rod Serling—these were creative writers doing exciting work, penetrating work, work that didn't involve monologue jokes, punch lines, seltzer bottles, cream pies, silly costumes, preposterous wigs, or any of the rest of Hermie's cartoonish arsenal. They were creating piercing stories that were striking at the very heart of what it was to be an American in the middle decade of the twentieth century. And they weren't pulling any punches. What they'd seen in the jungles of Okinawa, on the beaches of France, or among the trees of Belgium made it a genetic impossibility for them to be any other way. Though not a veteran, Jonny, too, had seen his world turned upside by the great conflict. He longed to be among these uncompromising men, as week after week they took their blunt scalpel to the post-war American dream on shows like *Studio One*, *Kraft Television Theatre*, and *Alcoa Playhouse*, where their original teleplays created searing indictments of what had happened, what was happening, and most important, what *could* happen.

So strong was Jonny's desire to join their ranks and, to some degree, to keep from putting a pistol in his mouth while writing the inane jokes and ridiculous sketches necessary for receiving a paycheck, that despite his impossibly busy schedule, he had found the time to take his play, *The Road to Damascus*—a soaring epic in five acts about a Jewish family coming to

America—and cut, trim, slice, and slash it down into a one-hour teleplay. Quite pleased with the results, he confidently submitted the snappy seventy-five pages to the Regal Television Network show *American Stories*. He'd heard through a producer he'd met at the network Christmas party that the one-hour anthology series, which occupied the 10:00 p.m. slot on Monday nights, was always desperate for material.

Apparently, as he found out, not desperate enough.

The network unceremoniously rejected it. "Thank you, Mr. Dirby," the form letter had perfunctorily begun, "for your recent submission. While the work shows great promise, at this time it does not fit with the type of material we are looking for at *American Stories*. Please keep us in mind should you write anything new. Best of luck." There was no signature.

The brusque rejection letter had come just days before the demand that everyone sign loyalty oaths. If Jonny had been in the habit of admitting his faults, which he most certainly wasn't, he might have acknowledged that part of his evasiveness in not signing the oath was the need to throw a bit of a "fuck you" in the general direction of the network. Now that his obligation to the Regal Television Network had been severed, he was free to submit the teleplay to other networks, which was exactly what he planned to do. And while he awaited the responses, he'd start on new ones, breaking into his stash of scribbled story notes that lay dormant in the back of his nightstand drawer.

Unemployment won't be so bad, Jonny thought. He'd saved up a few dollars, and he knew he could coast for a few months and really sink his teeth into something: writing about real people with real problems, not sitting in this stifling dungeon, shouting out one-liners for someone who, ten years ago, couldn't even get work in the Catskills.

Jonny looked around the room, taking it in for what he knew was the last time. He grabbed his satchel and sport coat and, still holding the bat, headed for the door. Halfway there, he stopped.

It wasn't quite enough. The triumphant euphoria was fading, and he needed more. After all, they had fired him over nothing, after eighteen months of good and solid service. He had to make a bigger statement before he left.

But what to do?

On the corner of the table, amid a chaotic scramble of pens, pencils, note pads, discarded script pages, half-eaten food containers, and overflowing ashtrays, he spotted the final draft of a sketch he had written: "At Home with Justice Man."

It was a fun idea, a parody of the current Superman craze that had swept the nation since the premiere of the *Superman* television show just over a year ago. Simply put, it showed what the home life of a superhero would be, placing him in a decidedly middle-class apartment and portraying him as a simple working guy, just trying to drink a beer, read the paper, and enjoy a ballgame after a hard day's work, while his wife nagged him to do chores. It was a perfect sketch for Hermie. It would give him a chance to wear a silly costume, something he almost never turned down, and the chance to wear a silly wig on his baldhead, another thing he almost never turned down. But what guaranteed that the sketch would get on the air was when Jonny added a third character to the end of the sketch. Just as Justice Man and his wife are about to sit down to dinner, he gets a call from his trusty assistant, and as much as he wants to stay and enjoy his wife's traditional Thursday night meatloaf, he must depart—after all, duty calls. Justice Man then leaves the apartment and steps into the hallway, where a beautiful young woman—his trusty assistant, dressed in a female version of the Justice Man costume—awaits him. She apologizes for the interruption and promises that it won't take them long. He stoically shoots back, "However long it takes does not matter, as long as justice is served!" And then, with a wink to the audience (a Hermie specialty), Justice Man walks off arm in arm, with the beautiful young sidekick.

The chance to act with a pretty girl—or more important, to rehearse with one privately at his penthouse apartment—was also something Hermie never turned down. As soon as Jonny had figured out that little fact—put a pretty girl in the sketch for Hermie to seduce—the number of Jonny's sketches that made it to air had gone through the roof.

The actress chosen to play Justice Girl was just the type Hermie liked. Tall. Dark haired. Blue eyed. Gorgeous. Jonny found himself ogling her

11

during rehearsals and could have sworn, especially today, that she was returning his attention. As he thought about her— her tall, curvaceous figure and the splay of her thick, black hair spilling over her succulent shoulders— his breath began to speed up. Yes, she really was stunning, but ultimately, it was more than that. She was dramatic. Truly born to play a superhero.

Suddenly, Jonny held his breath, and his eyes darted back and forth as a plan formed in his mind. It came to him—whole, complete, ready to be born. It was so simple and yet so right. He was a writer, right? Shouldn't he get revenge with words? He quickly sank into one of the crooked chairs and fished a pen out from under a soiled container of sweet-and-sour pork. But just as his pen touched the sketch, he paused. Yes, in the preshow chaos, he could easily sneak on to the set and do what needed to be done. That was the easy part. Getting someone to say the new lines he was about to write—that was a whole other thing. Ultimately, it came down to one simple question: would the tall, dark-haired, blue-eyed, gorgeous actress help him?

He couldn't be sure. Maybe it'd be best not to tell her exactly what he was up to. Anyway, it was a moot point unless he wrote something, and with only five minutes to air, he'd have to write fast. Hunching over the page, Jonny went to work, writing like a man on a mission.

A man on a mission, seeking justice.

...

Two floors below Jonny, in her sardine-can dressing room, the tall, dark-haired, blue-eyed, gorgeous actress paced. Though her sketch was toward the end of the show, she was already dressed in her full Justice Girl costume. The heels of her shiny, red, knee-high boots added to the dark river of scuff marks crisscrossing the tile floor. With each turn, the crinoline lining of her short blue skirt spun roughly against her nylon stockings, so that, as her nervousness mounted and she paced faster and faster, she began to sound like a charging locomotive. Felicity Anders Kensington knew she looked ridiculous in this cheap, Superman-inspired parody of a costume, but that was not the source of her nervousness. In fact, she was thankful for the ill-fitting mess she was forced to wear, especially the scratchy blonde wig, because it made anyone she knew who happened to watch the broadcast—an unlikely scenario, considering the far more refined tastes of her friends—virtually incapable of identifying her. Being caught, even though she was on an important mission, would be a disaster.

She was a Kensington, and the Kensingtons of Greenwich, Connecticut, did not involve themselves in the tawdry and unsavory world of entertainment. They were doctors and lawyers and bankers and board members and charity-ball organizers and trustees, not (she could hear the gasp) *actresses*. But despite a Southern cousin who once playfully remarked, "Sugar, you got the kind of body that makes young men forget their ambitions and old men forget their families," Felicity knew her appearance was safe from exposure. The true shape of her figure and the richness of her hair were safely hidden under unflattering piles of nylon and rayon. Certainly no one would fault her if she were a bit nervous when she was about to make her first appearance on television. Even the most composed twenty-six-year-old, which her Wellesleyan boarding-school upbringing had made her, would find a maiden performance, broadcast live to fifty million viewers, a daunting prospect.

But this was not the source of her anxiety.

Felicity had auditioned for and gotten the tiny role on *Hermie's Henhouse* with absolutely no concern for an acting career. In fact, she had absolutely no interest in being an actress, now or ever. Spending the last five days in this world, with its petty ambitions and diverse inhabitants, had been hard enough, and the notion of being around these people for one day, one hour, one minute, or even one second longer than she needed to be nauseated her. But she would stay as long as was necessary to achieve her goal. Felicity was a soldier fighting for a great cause, with nothing less than the security, safety, and survival of the United States on the line.

There was a war raging across America, a war to defeat Communism and all of its clever and evasive minions. Felicity and other like-minded patriotic Americans were on the front lines of the battle; the enemy was everywhere, deeply burrowed into every nook and cranny of the country—cab drivers, dock workers, window washers, politicians, athletes, businessmen, financiers. Nowhere was safe from them. The horror of Communism spread its totalitarian tentacles into every aspect of American life.

But no place was it more deeply rooted than in the world of television. The Commies were a clever lot—no one ever denied them that—and they knew the best way to disseminate their dangerous propaganda was through the airwaves that poured unchecked into every living room across America. Fortunately—and this gave Felicity some relief—great people like her father had sought out some of the worst offenders and put their names on lists that were then provided to the networks to help them keep those trouble-makers off the networks' payrolls and their anti-American rantings off the air. The system was working well; hundreds of dangerous individuals who wanted nothing less than the overthrow of the government of the United States had been banned, or "blacklisted," as it had become known.

Unfortunately, with success had come complacency. Thinking the worst of the wannabe traitors had already been banished, and with the election to the presidency of the war hero General Dwight Eisenhower over three years ago, some who had been gallant warriors in the past now felt assured that the country was in safe hands and had moved on to other things—or worse, had turned their backs on the movement.

But not her father.

Franklin Scott Kensington was a truly great man, and he made damn sure—not that Felicity needed any reminding—that she knew exactly how it worked. Lull you into a stupor, thinking you're safe, while their evil beliefs, masked behind such seemingly benign catchphrases as "civil rights" or "social justice," metastasized throughout the entire country. Scott Kensington recognized that the threat was more dangerous than ten Pearl Harbors or a hundred Nazi blitzkriegs—those had been enemies you could easily find and attack. This was much, much tougher; they were hidden everywhere. And just because a few hundred Commies had been found out and put out of business didn't mean there weren't a few hundred, maybe even a few thousand, more out there, working feverishly to spread their malevolence.

Felicity knew that her father was right and always felt that he needed to be more than just the overseer of a list. He needed to be on the national stage, where his patriotic message could reach even more *real* Americans before it was too late.

And that was when the hand of God once again revealed that he was firmly on their side.

Out of the blue, Eustice Cummings, the five-term Republican senator from Connecticut, died of a heart attack. Some said it was because of his age—he was over seventy, after all. Others said it was the stress of the job, and still others, in gossipy circles, said it was the result of a young mistress. It was all pointless speculation to Felicity, because she knew the truth. It was so obvious; how could they not see it? It was God punishing Eustice for turning his back on the movement. Once one of the greatest Commie hunters in Congress, Eustice had slowly backed away from organizations like her father's. The final insult had been several months earlier, when he had voted along with most of the Senate to censure one of the greatest men in the country, Joseph McCarthy. Clearly, that was too much for God, and he called Eustice home.

More importantly and more presciently, it created an opening in the Senate. What better platform for her father's views than serving in the Congress of the United States? As per the state constitution, the governor called a special election for that fall, and Felicity decided to do everything she could to help her father with his campaign. She would make sure he became the next senator from their home state of Connecticut.

Unfortunately, two other men besides her father were vying to be the Republican nominee. So far, even with all the great work her father had done in compiling, maintaining, and helping to enforce the blacklist, he wasn't getting any real attention. It was clear that the party leaders were deciding between his two opponents, with her father barely more than an afterthought. Something had to be done to change that.

That's when Felicity got her idea.

It was a crazy scheme—she knew that—but it could work, and given how desperate the situation was, she decided to give it a try. The other two candidates weren't concerned with Communism. They were against it, naturally, but their campaigns were centered around economic issues.

Something had to be done to remind them of the true threat and of just how insidious it was. The way to do this, as well as to give a wake-up call to those who had gotten soft, was for her to go behind enemy lines and find the proof herself. And once she found it, she would naturally pass the information on to her father, who would then release it to the public, and thusly be known for uncovering this evil plot to undermine America. Then the state party leaders would take notice and surely pick him as their candidate. It couldn't fail.

It started with a tip that had been passed on to her father's organization from one of the congressional committees investigating Communist influence in entertainment. In closed-door testimony, a former Communist trying to clear his name had testified of a rumor that someone on the writing staff of *Hermie's Henhouse* had been fronting for blacklisted writers. The congressional committee had heard some scattered word of this practice— writers with clean records were putting their names on the work of those on the blacklist so that the scripts could then be sold to the networks without complaints from organizations like her father's. This clean writer, or front, would then collect the money and give it to his Commie friend. As her father always told her, they were a clever bunch. Unfortunately, the committee had its hands full investigating known Communists and couldn't be bothered with tracking down these fronts.

Hearing about the committee's lack of interest had at first incensed Felicity and her father. But as her father raged, Felicity saw a great opportunity. This nefarious activity had to be exposed, and she was just the person to do it. With the mission laid out before her, Felicity left the pastoral purity of her family's estate and traveled to Manhattan, sinking into its sleaze. Using a fake name—Denise Yarnell, which sounded common enough for someone who wanted to be a part of this disgusting world—she worked her way into an audition for *Hermie's Henhouse*. As it turned out, her cultivated patrician looks were exactly what they were looking for.

She got the job.

The small walk-on role had no lines, so she had spent every spare moment trying to dig deeper, to find the evil that she knew was there. At the first read-through, when the entire cast of the show got together at the beginning of the week to read the script for the next show, she sat at the end of the table—closest to the pack of what she was sure were the writers. But she found it very difficult to uncover anything useful. They were too busy arguing with each other over new lines for the sketches and speaking in a shorthand she couldn't understand. At her costume fitting, she asked careful questions of the harried seamstress, who grunted back useless answers through her pin-holding clenched teeth. Without being too obvious, Felicity tried prying information from cameramen, lighting people, script assistants, anyone she thought could be helpful, all with the same result. Nothing.

Finally, this very morning, she had hit pay dirt. As she purposely lingered by the small table of doughnuts, Danish, and coffee that was set up for the cast and crew in a back corner of the theatre, she overheard a pair of girlish secretaries gossiping. "Guess who finally got around to signing his loyalty oath?" one said. *Finally got around to signing.* Bingo! Felicity tried to get the name of this obvious Communist, but neither one said it before skittering back to her desk.

Now she had something to go on. By noon, she had a name, and by four o'clock that afternoon, when the writers had gathered around Hermie at the end of the final run-through so he could yell at them about their "jokes my own mom wouldn't laugh at," she had a face.

Though she would admit it was convenient hindsight, Jonny Dirby was definitely someone she'd had her eyes on. From the first time she saw him at the read-through, to the subsequent rehearsals, he seemed a little edgy. He was always rocking back and forth on his heels, anxiously mouthing the words as the scenes were performed, always scribbling notes—definitely the behavior of someone with something to hide. The more she thought about it, she was sure she'd found her man. With his kinky, unkempt hair; big nose; and sharp, confrontational eyes surrounded by saggy, dark circles, he was just the type of wiry Jew to be fronting for blacklisted writers.

Now, she paced quicker and quicker in her dressing room, wanting desperately to get the broadcast over with so she could move on to the afterparty. That was where she was going to make her full-court press on Jonny

Dirby. She was confident that anyone who would refuse, for even a second, to sign a loyalty oath must be the one illegally fronting.

A knock on the door froze her in her tracks.

"Yes?" Felicity asked, whirling around toward the sound.

"Miss Yarnell, I would like to speak with you," the muffled voice came through the door.

"Okay. Come in," she finally said, forcing herself to remain calm. It wasn't easy, because when the door opened, Jonny Dirby was standing right in front of her. Felicity almost jumped back at the sight of him—his hair even wilder and his brow more than a bit shiny with sweat.

"I just wanted to see if you had any questions about the new scene," Jonny said sincerely.

"What new scene?" Felicity asked, genuinely surprised.

Jonny rolled his eyes and sighed dramatically. "This happens every time." Shaking his head, he pulled several pages of script from under his arm and handed them over to Felicity.

She glanced at the new pages and, almost white with fear, looked up at Jonny. "I'm not supposed to be in this scene. My scene is much later in the show."

"Oh, yeah," Jonny said nonchalantly. "We've decided to add you to the first sketch. But don't worry; you're playing the same character."

"But...but we've never rehearsed it."

"That's okay. We do this all the time on live television. You're working with pros." Jonny tapped the pages with his finger. "Just do what it says you're supposed to do, and they'll go right along with you. Piece of cake."

Felicity's full lashes fluttered nervously as she quickly eyed the new scene again. "This part here," she said, pointing at a block of text on the script, "where I'm supposed to show my super-human strength..."

"Right, right," Jonny answered. "It's all been taken care of. Just do what it says to do in the description, and it will all work out just fine." He turned to leave.

"But...but...my character has lines. Lots of them!" Felicity said, almost trembling. "I...I didn't have any lines before."

"Yes, you'll have to learn them fast," Jonny called over his shoulder. "Consider this your lucky day." Jonny smiled as he walked away.

Felicity's heart suddenly became a jackhammer. She shut the door behind Jonny and wanted to collapse against the wooden surface, but it was disgustingly grimy. She fought the urge to go limp and collapse to the floor—it, too, was filthy. She wasn't the least bit worried about dirtying her costume; she just wanted to minimize her contact with the overall seediness of the room. She steeled herself and forced her legs to take her across the room, where she carefully sat down, easing as little of her rear as possible toward the edge of the disintegrating club chair.

Hunched forward, she stared down at the pages Jonny had given her. Lines. There were lines. Lots of them. The new pages were overflowing with them, and most of them were hers! This was not part of her plan; she was not prepared for this—not even close. But then she remembered she was engaged in a great battle, and she had to adapt. After all, she was after an elusive foe. But *lines*? Well, if that's what it took, so be it. All for the cause. And on the bright side, she certainly had a good conversation-starter to engage the wiry Jew at the after-party.

...

As in almost every other home in America, the family of Hogart Daniels, not surprisingly, spent their Sunday nights firmly planted in their living room in front of their television. But unlike the vast majority of other families, this bright family of four did not spend their evening switching the dial, jumping from one network to the next. Instead, they chose to spend the entire night with the dial firmly locked on the Regal Television Network. It was the way Hogart wanted it, and for reasons that went beyond the fact that he was the natural head of the family, there was no resistance to his desire. His son and daughter were too young to understand about the other stations that were available, and his wife knew better than to complain. After all, Hogart was the president of the network, and the Regal Television Network was the reason the roof over their heads covered three thousand square feet of a practically brand-new home.

So as the opening credits of *Hermie's Henhouse* finished playing on their grainy fifteen-inch black-and-white television screen, and Hermie himself, in his trademark striped pants, checkered jacket, and thatched fedora, stepped out and began his opening monologue, the family was ensconced in their familiar Sunday night positions. Hogart's five-year-old son, Tommy, and seven-year-old daughter, Becky, were planted on the luxuriously carpeted floor in front of the television, fighting over a board game that required a stern admonishment about every ten minutes from either Hogart or his cheery wife, Trudy. Trudy had taken over one of two matching floral-print couches, as she did every Sunday, covering it with a half-dozen catalogs. Redesigning was her passion, and each one of the catalogs had dozens of paper clips on the edges of pages containing items she wanted. Given that they were scheduled to move into a new house of almost four thousand square feet in the next month or two, a stack of another ten catalogs was piled at her feet, awaiting paper clips.

Overlooking them all from his perch at the perfectly polished dining room table—the living room being several feet below him since Trudy had a contractor dig into the foundation and create a large, sunken space shortly after they moved in two years ago—was Hogart. Now age thirty-eight, Hogart Daniels had made an unprecedented climb from camera assistant to senior network executive in just over ten years. He had been propelled by hard work, a borderline telepathic understanding of the TV audience, an almost fetishistic enjoyment of the new metrics, the willingness to fight tenaciously for what he thought would work, and the exit of top executives to other companies that had sped up as the Regal Television Network's ratings had gone down. Finally, nine months earlier, when the previous president departed—some would say "left the sinking ship"—to head New Product Development at General Motors, Hogart became head of the network.

The promotion had come from Clarence Regal himself, the namesake and founder of the network. With very little fanfare, on the day after the previous president departed, Regal showed up at the network offices for the first time in almost five years. He just walked into Hogart's office, his seventy-five years slowing his walk but clearly not his mind, and told Hogart that he was the new president. Then he vanished once again, returning to his Long Island home and his basement laboratory, where the network had been born twenty-five years earlier—not borne of his desire to be in the entertainment business but of the necessity to have something to show on the televisions that he had developed.

This personal nod from Regal had filled Hogart with immense pride, for he truly admired Clarence Regal. Here was a man who, in his tiny home laboratory and with no more than a handful of assistants, had taken a fledgling technology that allowed visual images to transmit through the air and built the first television that the public could easily use. Regal saw what was most important: the audience. Regal televisions were the first to be purchased in large quantities by the general public—not because of their superior visual quality, not because of their crisper sound, and not because of their high-grain oak boxes, but because their tuners worked the best. Other televisions on the market at the time were hard to tune, and when viewers finally found their channels and got pictures, the images would often slowly fade to fuzz as the signals were lost. Then viewers had to leave the comfort of their couches and tune them in yet again.

Not so with a Regal.

Its revolutionary push-button tuning required only the punching of one of a series of buttons at the bottom of the console to jump from channel to channel, and once on a channel, it stayed on that channel.

Frustratingly, especially for Hogart, this was where the common ground between Regal and Hogart ended. Regal believed television should be used to illuminate the masses, to increase their knowledge of culture, the world, and current events, not just to entertain them. This worked fine in the early days, right after the war, when television was the exclusive pet of large, mostly East Coast cities. But now, with the networks reaching coast to coast and almost everywhere in between, programs had to be designed to reach a larger audience. Less high-brow. More accessible.

Clarence Regal was very resistant to the changes, and the weekly schedule, much to Hogart's dismay, was still full of shows left over from the days when Regal was more directly involved in the network's content—shows like *Opera News*, *New York University Forum*, and *Ask the Elderly*, all of which were just profitable enough to break even but, as a whole, were destroying the network.

Now that Hogart was president, he was doing everything he could to move the Regal Television Network away from that type of erudite programming and lift it up to the level of the other three more successful networks: NBC, CBS, and ABC. His plan had actually started three years earlier, when Regal began to loosen his personal grip on the network, and Hogart had reached the programming department on his climb up. Hogart set about wooing and finally seduced Herman Fox away from CBS, with the promise of more money and a better time slot. Now, with even more control, Hogart was after newer and fresher shows. Shows that would grab audiences, scintillate them, enthrall them, and make them come back week after week.

He also set about changing another part of the Regal Broadcasting Network, or RBN, situation. For years, RBN had, at Regal's insistence, stayed out of the blacklist game. What people did in their private lives was none of his business, Regal felt. As long as their personal political agendas were kept to themselves, he didn't care what they did away from work.

But not Hogart.

Not that he was particularly political; it was just that what he was trying to do was hard enough without having to fight off claims that the network was being soft on Communism. He didn't want any trouble that would create bad press of a political sort, which could discourage talent from coming to the network. To squelch any rumors of subversive influence on their programming, he had let the producers of each show quietly remove anyone they felt was troublesome. And those who were allowed to remain were required to sign a loyalty oath. Anyone refusing to sign would be fired on the spot. Absolutely no exceptions.

But even with all the changes he'd made, things were not improving as quickly as he had hoped. Sitting at his dining room table, ignoring Hermie's monologue jokes because he was in no mood to laugh, Hogart intently went over the annual report that he was due to present to his hostile board of directors in three weeks. He had spent the last week with the network accountants, desperately trying to move the figures and numbers around in an attempt to cover up what was the undeniable truth: things were not good at the Regal Television Network. Ratings were down, audience share was shrinking, and ad revenue was plunging. They didn't have a single show on the schedule that had won its time slot; only one, *Tea with Audrey*, an afternoon chat show, had managed to finish second. It was so bad that in some time slots, it was cheaper to put no show on the air than to air a show that would lose money. The weekly schedule had come to resemble an unfinished crossword puzzle; there was not a single night without at least half an hour when the network went dark, with nothing more than a test pattern spilling into the home of anyone who had bothered to tune in on the way to a far healthier channel.

It was a desperate situation, and Hogart knew time was running out. An offer to buy the company—a generous offer, all things considered—was on the table, and Hogart knew that short of a miracle, the board would vote to take it. Worthington Camera and Instruments, a Syosset, New York-based technology company, specializing in building high-end optics like microscopes and telescopes, was hoping to expand and wanted RBN in the worst way. They weren't the least bit interested in running a television network; rather, they were interested in the laboratory and research divisions of the Regal Broadcasting Network and, most enticingly, the plethora of ingenious patents that they felt were not being exploited to their full potential. This was something Hogart was sure was true, if those divisions were run anything like the entertainment division had been run before he took over. Combining high-end optics with a way of delivering the gathered precise images over a long distance would be quite attractive to the government and would lead to lucrative military contracts. Once it acquired the network, Worthington would absorb what it wanted and then immediately shut down the entertainment division. The Regal Television Network would cease to exist. Poof! Gone. Like it never existed.

With all this hanging over his head, Hogart searched through the report for anything he might have missed during the week—a miracle, that shred of good news on which he could hang his last-ditch final pitch to the board. He looked for something that would sway them to turn down the deal and give him the time he needed to turn the Regal Television Network into the powerhouse he knew it could be. Still not finding it, he reached for a supplemental report that he had been waiting for all week, only to have it arrive at 5:00 p.m. on Friday as he was heading out the door. Opening it and expecting salvation, what he saw instead made his face tighten, and he threw the folder on the table. "Goddamn affiliates!" he yelled.

"Hogart!" his wife scolded him.

"Sorry. Sorry."

"You should be." She then returned her attention to the television, relieved that their two children had been so engrossed in their antics, they hadn't heard their father's cursing.

Hogart put his head in his hands. He had asked for the latest ratings numbers coming out of their Pittsburgh affiliate—their strongest—figuring there might be something in there that he could highlight. He'd been given the numbers for Philadelphia, all right...but from three weeks ago. He'd been given the wrong report.

And sadly, it didn't surprise him.

Making matters worse, his top executives—a group that should have been in there with him, thinking up creative ways to show the network's potential—were completely useless to him. Sensing that the end was near, almost all of their time was spent planning and plotting for their next job. So the result was that their work had become careless and sloppy, manifesting itself in a total lack of focus and a complete nadir of vision, along with deadlines missed and lateness to meetings commonplace. Hogart gladly would have canned several of them, but that would have created even more instability at the network, and that was the last thing he needed right now. Instead, Hogart reveled in his disgust and grew such a disdain for them as a group that when he thought about them, he refused to use their names, instead referring to them in his mind by the departments they headed:

Programming, Affiliates, Advertising, Personnel, Legal. That was all they meant to him. They weren't people; they were positions.

On the television, the monologue was over and the first sketch of the show had begun. In it, Hermie played one of his recurring characters, "Oscar Von Pimpleman, used car salesman." It was a great role for Hermie, allowing him to dress and perform at his borscht belt best as a pathological liar bent on doing absolutely anything and everything to sell a used car. It was one of Hogart's favorite characters. And despite his focus on finding something, *anything*, to work with for the upcoming board meeting, one of Hermie's lines—touting the amazing attributes of an obvious lemon—caused Hogart to push out a much-needed chuckle, lightening his mood. But just as quickly, his mood darkened again.

And maybe even got a bit darker.

This was exactly the problem Hogart was battling as he tried to save the network. Hermie was funny when he wanted to be funny, and he currently wanted to be funny because he was going through yet another divorce—he badly needed the extra money from the lucrative nightclub dates he could book because of his success on television. His ratings were decent—at least by RBN standards—but he, like the entire Sunday night lineup, was getting killed because they had a lousy lead-in. At 7:00 p.m., they aired *Square Dance Round-Up*. At 7:30 p.m., up until two weeks ago, they had aired *Johns Hopkins Science Review*, but they couldn't get a sponsor for the show. The few ads they did sell were all from small local stores, so *Johns Hopkins Science Review* ended up hemorrhaging cash, and they finally just pulled the plug on it. Because of the weak show at seven o'clock and nothing at all at seven-thirty, by the time Hermie came on at eight, nobody was watching, even though he had a full hour of really great comedy. This malaise carried over to the rest of the evening, to the point that there was talk of going dark again at ten o'clock to save even more money.

The sound of laughter made Hogart lose his place among the rows of depressing numbers. But as he tried to regain his focus, the laughter grew even louder. Hogart gave up; he could use a break anyway, so he turned toward the television set.

What he saw astonished him.

Hogart's wife and two children, as well as the studio audience, were the source of the uproarious laughter. With delight splashed across their faces, his family was glued to the action on the screen, the board game and catalogs suddenly forgotten. *Hermie is really killing tonight*, Hogart thought. *I need to send a memo to make sure he does Oscar Von Pimpleman more often.* But when he looked closer at the screen, he saw more than just Hermie and the unsuspecting car buyers in his private office, with stunned looks on their faces as they peered toward the office door, where a new character stood heroically before them. Justice Girl had just burst in and stood majestically before them, her hands on her hips and her head held high, a true beacon of hope, dignity, and justice.

Confused, Hogart stepped away from the dining room table, pausing briefly for his right leg to come back to life. Some days, depending on the weather or stress or myriad other factors, it stiffened up to the point of giving him a pronounced limp—a little reminder of his service in the Second World War. Now sufficiently loosened up but limping slightly, he moved into the living room and closer to the television set. He thought he recognized the new character; he had been in the theatre during an early rehearsal, but he was positive she was supposed to be in a different sketch.

On the screen, Hermie was no less confused. "Who are you?" he asked, with big, terrified eyes.

"I am Justice Girl!" Felicity answered back assuredly.

Hogart watched as Hermie's eyes darted offstage, past the camera, to a crew member, as he searched for an answer as to what the hell was going on. Clearly not getting one, Hermie turned back to Justice Girl. "What are you doing?"

"I want…," Felicity began, ignoring Hermie's question and following her own script, "you to stop ripping off your customers."

Hermie's eyes shifted back and forth. "Okay."

"I want you to start telling the truth!" she continued.

"The truth?"

"About the car you're selling them."

"Right, the truth…," Hermie said, struggling to keep up.

"Well, I'm waiting," Felicity commanded, indicating the unsuspecting couple.

"I…uh," Hermie stammered.

"Go ahead. Tell them," Felicity interjected. "Tell them, 'The car I was about to sell you is a piece of junk, a real lemon.'"

Hermie, pleased to have lines, did as he was told. "The car I was about to sell you is a piece of junk, a real lemon."

"And that you're very sorry."

"I'm very sorry."

"And that you'll be happy to show them a car that runs perfectly."

"I'll be happy to show you a car that runs perfectly," Hermie parroted.

"For a very affordable price."

"For a very affordable price."

"Good," Felicity intoned, pleased. "Now, that's how I expect you to treat all of your customers from now on. Got it?"

Hermie, still confused, nodded enthusiastically.

"Just to be sure, I'll be around to keep an eye on you. And so you know I'm a force to be reckoned with, here's a little taste of what will happen if you don't stay on the path of good." Felicity reached out and lightly tapped Von Pimpleman's desk with her foot. It instantly collapsed, as if run over by a dozen hulking linebackers. Hermie and the unsuspecting couple jumped to their feet, genuinely shocked.

Calmly, Felicity turned toward the camera and peered straight into the lens. "And to anyone else out there who treats others poorly, I have my eye on you, too. Let that be a warning. You cannot hide from Justice Girl."

Felicity took a step even closer to the camera. As if on cue, the camera moved in, going straight for her face. Felicity stared forward defiantly, her face growing larger by the second as the camera grew closer. "To the guy who takes advantage of the innocent, you cannot hide." Her face filled half of the screen. "To the man who profits from others' suffering, you cannot hide."

Her face filled three-quarters of the screen. "To the person who falsely accuses, you cannot hide." Finally, Justice Girl's face filled the entire screen of Hogart's television. "To the citizen who denies others their rights, you cannot hide!"

Felicity took a step back, and once again, as if cued, the camera pulled back, revealing Justice Girl from head to toe. "Remember all of you, whenever you see me," she said, sweeping her arm through the air. "Justice is served!" Felicity then turned and rushed out the door, her billowy cape flapping majestically behind her.

Hogart's two children and his wife broke into spontaneous applause. "I am Justice Girl!" his daughter proudly shouted as she jumped to her feet. "And justice is served!

"Justice is served!" his son echoed as he, too, jumped to his feet.

Not wanting to be left out, his wife was on her feet, too. "Justice is served!" she shouted, joining in the fun.

Astonished by what he had just seen on his television and what had just happened in his living room, Hogart's mind exploded with a fireball of excited thoughts. "I…I need to go into the office." was all he could get out.

...

Jonny wasn't sure if the loud knocking he heard was on the door of the room or just in his head. In fact, as he slowly slid back to consciousness, he wasn't entirely sure where he was at all. He forced open a single heavy eyelid and then slowly and painfully focused on Mel Ott's smiling face. He happily slammed his eye shut again, relieved. He was in his own bedroom, face down on his bed, safely in the apartment where he was still called Jacob Drabinowitz instead of his chosen professional name, Jonny Dirby. It was the only home he'd every known in his entire twenty-five years. He'd spent part of it with an older brother and sister, and all of it with his father, Samuel, a stamp dealer in Lower Manhattan, and his mother, Lena, a housewife. Around him, the walls of his bedroom were an archeological excavation of the varied interests of his short existence. A World War II enemy aircraft spotting chart, a map of the 1939 World's Fair, several felt pennants for a variety of New York professional and college sports teams, a pin-up of Barbara

Stanwyck that he had cut out of one of his sister's celebrity magazines (that had hailed the arrival of his adolescence), and finally, the 1933 newspaper clipping of the New York Giants winning the World Series. Mel Ott's beaming face dominated the photo of celebrating ballplayers that he had taped to his headboard and somehow had survived there since he was four years old.

The pounding returned—louder, more aggressive—and his relief turned to annoyance. *"What?"* he managed through gluey lips.

"Phone call!" Jonny's mother yelled through the door, too loudly for this time of the morning—or any time of day, considering the state he was in.

"Who is it?"

"What is this, the Ritz?"

"You couldn't ask?"

"I could, but I didn't. Get up. Your breakfast is almost ready." Then, he heard the scrape of her slippers as she turned and walked away.

Jonny forced his weary body into a sitting position, with his cloudy head hanging heavily to one side. As he tried to straighten his neck, he realized it wasn't just his head that hurt but also his jaw. It was killing him, throbbing incessantly. *Why my jaw?* he wondered as he struggled to remember the night before. Nothing came through the thick fog. Why he couldn't remember was answered as soon as he took his first deep breath, and his nose filled with the reek of too much alcohol and too many cigarettes. *So I really tied one on last night,* he thought. That explained his head but not his jaw. But before he could answer any other questions, the giant claw of sleep pulled him back down to the bedspread. He closed his eyes and blissfully drifted off to sleep again.

This time the pounding came from above.

As both eyes flashed open, Jonny was reminded yet again that they lived on the fifth floor of their six-story apartment building. As she did every morning, little Debbie Kirsch practiced her tap dancing before joining the rest of the children in the building as they stomped down the stairs to the street, joining the river of kids on the sidewalk on their way to PS 127. But on this morning, it sounded more like she was practicing dribbling...with a bowling ball.

Realizing sleep was impossible, at least for the next half hour or so, Jonny returned to his sitting position. Mustering all the strength he could in his hungover body, Jonny made it to his feet. As he took an unsteady moment to gain his balance, the haze finally began to dissipate, and a horrible fact came rushing straight at him like the headlight of a runaway locomotive.

I've been fired! I've been blacklisted!

Now he really wanted to curl up in a ball and go back to sleep for at least a month or two. But between the stomping from above and the clatter from the kitchen, he knew this was impossible. Using the phone call as motivation, he stiffly and painfully struggled toward the door. Each step brought a new agony, which in turn brought more and more clarity to his mind, which brought back more and more of the night before.

Fired. He'd been fired. That he remembered clearly. Then there was the exploding fan and its ensuing emptiness. The quick writing of the sketch, the pitch to the gorgeous actress, sneaking on stage to mess with the desk, watching the sketch go out live from a corner of the studio, the big laughs, and the even bigger applause. Hurrying out of the theatre before the guards caught him. Being caught not by the guards but by the actress. Her fury at him for her being made a fool of, his retort that it had all been in fun, her retort back, which had come in the form of a slap across the face.

Aha!

That explained the sore jaw! Then he was in the little bar that was attached to the side of the theatre. Lots and lots and lots of free drinks from Albert the bartender, from some people who worked on the show, from complete strangers. Now things got even hazier. There was toasting to his suddenly abundant free time, to the health of the Regal Television Network (with more than a touch of sarcasm), to Chayefsky, Rose, and Serling, and after more drinks, "Serbling," and after even more drinks, "Serewilbiling." There was the 4:00 a.m. stagger from the bar and Albert pouring him into a cab, with a cabbie who apparently knew Chinese, because that was the closest to the language he was speaking at that point. Hitting his head against the window three times as he dozed off on the ride uptown to Washington Heights. His shock at the bill for the cab ride "Two dollars and twenty-five cents! What did you do? Drive around Columbus Circle for fifteen minutes?" he had yelled.

He remembered handing over three dollar bills, one of which had inexplicably been rolled up into the size of a marble. The cabbie driving away before Jonny had a chance to tell him to keep a quarter and give him back the rest. The ride up in the elevator to the fifth floor. Realizing he had gotten off on the fourth and taking the stairs up the final flight, happy that at least they didn't live on the sixth floor. Creeping through the living room where his father was asleep in his chair, as usual with an open copy of *Linn's Stamp News* across his lap. And finally, as the rising sun blued the sky outside his window, collapsing on his bed where, obviously caused by the copious amounts of alcohol he had consumed, he could have sworn he heard, among the piercing clatter of the first kids playing on the street below, shouts of "Justice is served! Justice is served! Justice is served!"

He opened his bedroom door to the sizzle and snap of his breakfast on the stove. Wearily, he crossed the faded Oriental rug-covered floor and, upon reaching the symphony of brown that was the modest living room, he grabbed the displaced phone receiver off an end table.

"Hello," he managed.

"Jonny, this is Charles," the cultured voice at the other end declared.

"Oh." Jonny flinched, snapping quickly out of his daze. Charles Fox had just fired him twelve hours earlier. The man was quite possibly the last person on earth Jonny expected a call from. "Yes?"

"Can you be at Hogart's office at ten thirty?"

Why would he want to see me? Jonny thought. "I could if I wanted to," Jonny shot back, his annoyance getting the best of his curiosity.

"Well, *want* to."

"Why?"

"Just be there."

Jonny shook his head. There was no chance in hell he would be there. They'd fired him. He owed them nothing. They could all go take a flying leap. "I'm busy."

Charles sighed. What came next clearly was not easy for him. "Please?"

Please? Did he actually say please? Yesterday, he'd been fired; today, it was *please.* "Charles, what is going on?" Jonny asked.

"Just be there."

"Fine. Okay," Jonny said flatly.

Without another word, Charles hung up. Jonny stood holding the receiver for a long moment and then slowly eased it back onto the cradle. Like popcorn kernels over a flame, thoughts burst through his mind: *Why did he say please? Why did he ask me to come to Hogart's office? What could the head of the entire network want with a lowly comedy writer? A fired, blacklisted one at that? Are they going to arrest me for what I did?* Before Jonny could reach even the outskirts of a conclusion, the vibrant scent of fried eggs instantly overwhelmed him. Still shaky on his rubbery legs, he dashed for the bathroom.

Wiping his mouth with a coarse towel, he pulled the toilet seat cover down, flushed, and sat on it. There was absolutely no reason he had to listen to Charles and rush to Hogart's office. So what if he had agreed to come? He no longer worked there. He was fired. He was blacklisted. As far as Jonny was concerned, that meant he was a free man and could change his mind. Yes, he was going to change his mind. Today was the first day of his liberation, and he was going to spend it working. He was going to sift through that pile of story ideas in the back of his night-table drawer, find the one begging to be brought to life, and get to work. He would do ten, fifteen, maybe even twenty pages of good solid work today. He could feel it. His fingers tingled and began to twitch, aching for the rounded keys of his sturdy metal typewriter. *I won't even shower,* he thought as he reached over and turned off the spigot. He'd get right down to it, working in his alcohol- and smoke-covered clothes. Let the stink and filth fill his nose. That's what the real world was. Let the stench motivate him.

But then, just as quickly as his questions had been interrupted by the dash for the toilet, they all came tumbling back with one in particular repeating over and over in his brain. *Why did he say please? Why did he say please? Why did he say please?*

Resigned, Jonny turned the shower back on. He knew he had to make the trip downtown to Hogart's office. It would cost him half a day of writing, but there was no way he could write the sharp, crisp, cutting work he longed to do with so many unanswered questions swirling around his brain. Whatever they wanted with him had to be resolved. The sooner the better, so he could get to work. Besides, judging by the aggressiveness of the call, if he didn't show up, he knew they would probably come find him.

All through his shower, his begging off of his Mother's undercooked breakfast, his picking up a fried egg sandwich at the diner, his hurried walk to the 178th Street subway station, and his jiggling his way downtown on the 2 train, the question continued to haunt him: *Please? Why did he say please?* It was almost a begging "Please?" —plaintive, with a hint of desperation, like if Jonny didn't show up, Charles would somehow be in trouble. But why? They had fired him. It had been clean, simple, and he hadn't put up much of a fuss. Just a broken ceiling fan and a silly disruption to the show. And not much of a disruption at that. Hermie had come out of vaudeville. He knew how to roll with the punches, and he had. The sketch had elicited laughs. Big laughs. So what could be the problem?

As the train slipped farther and farther downtown, Jonny's confusion melted into worry. What if he had broken some law? Some law to keep people from doing what he had just done—disrupt a live broadcast. Maybe they were going to arrest him, and maybe Charles's pleading was all about saving his own ass. If he couldn't get Jonny to come in and take the fall, they would take Charles down instead. After all, he was the show's producer and, as such, was responsible for what went on the air.

As the train pulled into the 66th Street station, Jonny's forehead suddenly polka-dotted with sweat, and he shifted uneasily. He could take whatever the network had to give. Screw 'em; he didn't work there anymore. But maybe—just maybe—this had become a matter that was out of their control. A matter for the law.

Jonny sighed. *Should I bring my brother into this?* he wondered. *After all, this really is his area of expertise. On the other hand, with all he's been dealing with lately, would it be a good idea?* The saddest part was that until recently, Jonny wouldn't have had even the slightest hesitation. Finally, Jonny concluded, *He's still my brother, and even if he's been a bit off, he's still family, and it would be good to have someone I can trust in there with me.*

So, as the subway doors began to close, even though the Regal Television Network offices were still two stops away on 49th Street, Jonny pushed himself off the cushioned seat and slipped through the closing doors and out onto the platform.

Two at a time, he rushed up the steps leading out of the station and on to the street. He was in a hurry and began to sprint. Jonny needed a lawyer, and he knew just where to get one.

...

The main offices of the Regal Television Network occupied the top five floors of a twenty-seven-story, pre-Depression-era, marble-and-limestone office building on Park Avenue, several blocks north of Grand Central Station. Crammed in with a carload of people in the back of an elevator, Jonny implored it to rise faster. It was almost a quarter to eleven, and he was late to his meeting. But the elevator went about its work, unaware, rumbling upward one floor at a time. Finally, on the sixth floor, after it once again had opened, spit out two riders, sucked in four new ones, and then lurched up only one floor to the seventh, Jonny had had enough.

"For the love of God, do you have to stop at every floor?" Jonny wailed as he was smashed against ornate gold molding by a new and very overweight passenger.

With the car full again, the elevator operator turned around to stare drolly at Jonny, his droopy face sagged from extreme boredom. "Next time," he suggested, "take the express."

Jonny sighed and would have stamped his foot in exasperation, but that would have meant stepping on the toes of three other passengers. At the rate they were going, they wouldn't make it to the twenty-sixth floor, where Hogart had his office, until almost eleven.

As if reading Jonny's mind, his brother, Mitchell, standing behind him, put an oversized hand on Jonny's tense shoulder and said assuredly, "Relax. We'll get there when we get there."

Jonny turned and opened his mouth to say something but instead just nodded. It wasn't worth the time to explain to his brother that his anxiousness was not fear but excitement. With Mitchell at his side, Jonny couldn't wait to get in there and get into it with them.

It was as if the strangeness Jonny had seen in Mitchell over the last year or so had never happened. Today, Mitchell was spot on, returned to the form Jonny loved. Almost ten years Jonny's senior, Mitchell Drabinowitz was a ridiculously impressive character, bordering on almost comical perfection. Outfitted precisely in a tailored, dark-blue suit, he easily earned double-takes from women—and even a few men. Even though he was eight years removed from the service, where he had reached the rarified rank of full colonel, he still carried himself with a ramrod-straight posture that made him appear to tower over anyone near him, even when he wasn't the tallest person in the room. Adding to his appeal was his innate goodness. Even with the endless opportunities with women that came with being a powerfully handsome veteran, especially with the added aphrodisiac of having received numerous medals, Mitchell was a dedicated family man, with a wife he worshipped and three children he would gladly take a bullet for. Everything about him, from his mirror-polished shoes and perennially pressed attire to his impossibly broad shoulders and perfectly cut right-angle jawline, reeked of calm, focus, and confidence. As children, when their sister, Rachel, was still alive, they would often play games after school with the kids in the neighborhood. Whenever they played superheroes, Mitchell was always chosen to play Superman. Now, fifteen years later, as if they still played the game, Jonny saw no reason for it to be any different.

Despite his initial hesitation, Jonny was aware of how lucky he had been to get his brother to come along on what normally would have been a busy Monday morning for Mitchell. During the war, Mitchell had followed General Bennington Darcy as his chief of staff, who led a division of Patton's Third Army across France and eventually into Germany. After the war, Mitchell followed Gen. Darcy into the private sector where, after becoming a lawyer through the GI Bill, he helped the general set up a private consulting firm, Bennington Industries, and then went to work for him. Essentially, he had the same job as he'd had during the war, handling all of the general's affairs, but swapping the rank of colonel for vice president—and making a hell of a lot more money. The general's services were in great demand. He was asked to serve on dozens of corporate boards and to attend an endless stream of product launches, factory openings, shareholder meetings, and luncheons in his honor, all of which he happily did for a healthy fee.

Just the day before, Mitchell had driven the general to La Guardia and watched him board a DC-4 for an overnight flight to California so that he could attend the Hughes Aircraft Company's unveiling of its brand new constellation airliner. With his boss on the West Coast, and after Jonny had burst into their plush offices babbling in a panic about his fear of being arrested, Mitchell was able to dash out and make the quick trip thirteen blocks downtown to join his brother for his unexpected and still unexplained meeting.

Eventually, Jonny and Mitchell were the only two passengers left with the chronically bored elevator operator, and finally, after five eternities, the elevator doors parted, revealing the twenty-sixth floor. They stepped out onto the polished marble floor and, guided by the metallic munch of several typewriters being put to serious use, headed toward the office of Hogart Daniels. Jonny had never been on this floor, but his excitement was slightly tempered by his roving eyes, as he searched for any police who might be hiding behind one of the many pillars. Mitchell noticed and laughed slightly. "I told you; you did nothing that was illegal. Stupid, yes. But illegal? No."

"Then why do they want to see me?"

Mitchell shrugged. "If I could see the future, I'd be on the phone with my broker."

When they reached the pack of busy secretaries who lined the entrance to Hogart's office, Jonny and Mitchell were immediately led to his door by the oldest one. Mrs. Decosta, an officious woman of sixty, opened the door, announced Jonny and Mitchell, and then stepped aside, letting them enter.

Still a bit wary, Jonny poked his head in and again searched for any cops. Not seeing one in sight, he entered the office. As expected of the head of a network, the office was quite large, with the requisite high-priced furniture, lights, and adornments. A dozen paintings, all depicting nineteenth-century cattle rangers and cowboys, covered the gray walls. *Is Hogart from the Southwest?* Jonny wondered. It didn't jibe with what he had heard about him. But then he remembered the previous network president had been a big, boisterous Texan, and the artwork must have been purchased on his behalf. Hogart had merely kept what was already there when he moved in. The one modification he did make, however, which already was the stuff of legend to the employees of the network, was the single most dominant feature in the entire room. Four televisions had been mounted onto the wall, directly across from his desk. They were turned on all day long, each one tuned to a different network. Three of the sets hung in a horizontal row showing ABC, CBS, and NBC; the single television placed above them played the Regal Television Network.

Jonny had only met Hogart on one other occasion. At the beginning of each season of *Hermie's Henhouse*, a party was held at the theatre after the first show aired. Traditionally, the head of the network gave a speech, and with Hogart having just attained the position a few months previous, the responsibility fell on him. Jonny sort of remembered the speech—lots of clichés and platitudes about how this could be the best season yet if we'd all pull together and work as a team, etc., etc., etc. But what Jonny definitely did remember was Hogart's suit. It was a faded-brown, rumpled mess that looked as if it had never been pressed. Jonny was astonished to see the head of a network dressed like that—not that he should talk, considering his perennially casual attire, but on the other hand, he wasn't an executive. He came away from the encounter with the impression that this man cared very little for outward appearances.

As Hogart crossed the small room toward him, Jonny could have sworn Hogart was wearing the same suit...and it still hadn't been pressed. Hogart was limping, something Jonny also had heard about him but hadn't noticed at their one previous meeting. Hogart met him in the middle of the room with an outstretched hand. "Thank you for coming in on such short notice."

"No problem," Jonny politely answered as they shook hands.

Charles Fox, Hermie's son and the producer of *Hermie's Henhouse*, was the only other person in the room, and he hung back by the large desk. Unlike his father's penchant for loud clothes featuring mismatched patterns, Charles was dressed in a refined double-breasted wool suit, complete with kerchief in his chest pocket and a perfectly tied ascot. On some occasions, though he was barely thirty years old, Charles had been known to add a cane to his ensemble, a look that Jonny and some of the other writers would make fun of endlessly in the writers' room—they imagined him as a dandy, strutting through downtown London in the time of Dickens. But even under all that finely woven wool, Charles couldn't hide the squat, lumpy build he'd inherited from his father, nor could his morning regimen of a barbershop shave and haircut hide another gift from his father: a face like a puffy balloon and a rapidly receding hairline.

Charles gave Jonny a smile. Jonny replied with a short nod, which, as far as Jonny was concerned, was more than Charles deserved. Jonny quickly introduced Mitchell, and after more handshakes and inane chitchat, the pause they all knew was coming finally descended. It was time to get down to business.

"I wanted to talk about last night," Hogart said, without the slightest hint that he was stating the obvious.

Jonny rumpled his brow, as if trying to recall. "Let's see…let's see. Last night? Ah, yes, I remember it well. It was a clear, crisp night with the chill of winter finally giving way to the warmth of spring and the promise of a hot summer," Jonny said, mockingly poetic. "Oh, yeah. And I was blacklisted."

"There is no such thing as a blacklist," Charles offered, still standing at the desk.

"I see. So after eighteen months and countless sketches getting on the air, you suddenly woke up yesterday morning and discovered I was not a good writer."

Charles thought for a moment. "It was a bit more complicated than that."

"Illuminate me. I've got the time. After all, I'm currently unemployed."

Hogart waved a weathered and hairy-knuckled hand through the air. "Let's not dwell on the past. I want to talk about the future."

Jonny winced. *The future?* What possible future could he have with these two? They could debate the existence of the blacklist all they wanted, but one thing was irrefutable. "But you fired me," he said.

Hogart's leathery palm again swiped the air. "I told you; I want to talk about the future." He looked closely into Jonny's face. "As in, this coming Sunday at 7:30 p.m. That's when I want to see the first episode of *Justice Girl* air on my network."

"Excuse me?" Jonny asked, stunned.

"This Sunday at 7:30 p.m. *Justice Girl* premieres on the Regal Television Network," Hogart repeated, as if it were no more important than reading a grocery list.

"*Justice Girl*?" Jonny asked, still stunned. "As in, the character in the sketch last night?"

"Precisely."

"You want to make a series out of that character?" Jonny asked, with dripping incredulity. "And you want the first episode to air this Sunday. Six days from now?"

"I'm glad we're on the same page."

Still in shock, Jonny's gaze shot around the room. Hogart and Charles met his eyes straight on. "You're serious," Jonny finally said, though still in disbelief.

Hogart nodded. "Yes."

"That's impossible."

"Why?"

"Because there's no story, there's no script, there's…there's…there's… nothing," Jonny said, punctuating his last word by showing his open palms.

"And I know just the writer to turn that nothing into something." Hogart turned to Charles. "When would you need the script?"

Finally free to join the conversation, Charles stepped forward quickly and flipped open a folder he was holding. "If we got it by early Thursday, we could cast that same day, build and read-through on Friday, rehearse on set on Saturday, and then camera rehearse early Sunday before going out live that night."

They turned to look at Jonny, whose brow was peaked with dismissive amusement. "Come on. You guys aren't serious."

Charles nodded. "A thousand-dollars-a-week serious."

"For me?"

"Plus a hundred per episode royalty fee for however long the show runs, even if you're no longer involved."

"That's pretty serious." Jonny tilted his head, unsure of what to do. "Why are you being so generous?" he asked, not even trying to hide his suspiciousness.

Charles smiled brightly. "Because we like you."

"Bullshit."

Charles dropped his smile, relieved to drop the pretense. He almost charged at Jonny. "How dare you come in here and speak that way in front of Mr. Daniels!"

"I can speak any way I want," Jonny shot back. "I don't work here anymore."

Charles inhaled deeply, ready to go at Jonny again, but Hogart cut him off.

"That's enough of that," Hogart said flatly. Charles sighed and then retreated behind Hogart. Jonny relaxed.

Ignoring the tension in the room, Hogart began, "Mr. Dirby, last night I saw something on my television screen that I've never quite seen before. It pulled me away from my review of our annual report and made me get up and walk to the TV. Not only that, I saw it also stop my two children from throwing Monopoly pieces at each other, and it made my wife close her copy of the Sears catalog. In over ten years of being in the television business, I have never seen anything with that sort of across-the-board appeal."

Jonny nodded, as if to indicate that was what he'd intended all along.

"But what I've also learned from being in this business," Hogart continued, "is that it's not only *what* you put on the air that's important but *when*. A show's success is not only driven by the content but also by the timing. You look at a *Hermie's Henhouse*, the show on which your talents have been sorely wasted these last eighteen months."

He's really working the flattery, Jonny thought.

"Ten years ago Herman Fox was headed to the scrap heap of history—a washed-up vaudevillian playing to half-empty theatres during the last gasp of a dying art form. Then…boom! Along comes television, and suddenly all those old jokes, stupid gags, and silly characters of his are born again, fresh to millions of viewers who wouldn't pay a dime to see him in person but now can't wait to tune in each week in the comfort of their own homes." He pointed his finger for emphasis. "Timing." Hogart took a step closer to Jonny. "Right now is the time for *Justice Girl*. Two, three, four weeks from now it could still be, but I am not willing to take that chance."

Jonny nodded calmly. He exhaled, his face a thoughtful mask of deep consideration. But inside, he was riding a runaway horse that kicked and bucked in every direction. This was a whole lot to take, and it was all happening so fast. Too fast. He was being offered the opportunity of a lifetime. His own show. From his own creation. And they were offering more money a week than he currently made in two months. Yes—he should just say yes. "Give me a second," Jonny finally uttered, fighting to keep in the saddle.

"Take your time," Hogart answered calmly.

Jonny slipped over next to Mitchell and leaned in close. "What do you make of this?" he whispered.

Mitchell shook his head warily. "I don't know. Something's not right."

"For a thousand bucks a week, I can handle 'not right,'" Jonny shot back, his voice rising as his mind reeled at what he could do with all that money.

"Well, at least get more money," Mitchell encouraged, realizing his brother had already made his decision.

Jonny gave a sharp nod in agreement and stepped toward the other two. "I want twelve hundred a week, a one hundred and fifty dollar royalty per episode, *and* complete control of all content and casting."

Hogart shifted his jaw, considering. "Fine," he sighed. "You can have the money. But the content and casting are mine."

"But—"

"That part is not open to negotiation," Hogart answered strongly.

Jonny looked closely at the man and knew that was as far as he would go. He smiled softly. "Okay."

"Terrific!" Hogart nodded back. He turned to Charles, who pulled out a single piece of paper and handed it to Hogart. "This is a simple agreement." Hogart grabbed a pen from his desk. "I'll just amend it to go along with the terms we discussed." Leaning over his desk, Hogart wrote on the document and then held out the pen for Jonny. "And now, if you'll just give a quick signature, you can get started."

Jonny stared at the pen as it hung in the air, beckoning to him with the promise of a new life, one he couldn't even have dreamed of twenty-four hours earlier. It was real. It was actually happening. It was there for the taking. One quick signature and he would have his own show. A show created and written by Jonny Dirby.

He started to step forward when, once again, he felt Mitchell's large hand on his shoulder. Instead of saying something soothing in his ear, Mitchell moved quickly past him.

"How about thirteen hundred a week?" Mitchell said firmly, stopping just a few feet in front of Hogart.

Oh, my God, what's he doing? Jonny thought.

Hogart took Mitchell's presence without a flinch. He stared calmly at the towering figure. "Sure."

"Fourteen hundred," Mitchell shot back.

Holy crap, he's blowing it for me, Johnny thought, beginning to panic. *My first instinct was right. I should never have brought him.*

But again, Hogart remained calm. He merely blinked a few times before finally saying, "Okay. But that's as far as I go. You're pushing it."

Hogart offered the pen again. Jonny moved for it, but Mitchell stopped him and didn't bother being discreet. "I need to speak to you. Outside."

"But—"

"Now."

The office door shut behind them, and Jonny fought as Mitchell quickly pulled him past the hive of buzzing secretaries, into the hallway, and behind a polished marble column. "You're supposed to help me, and now you're blowing the whole thing," Jonny seethed at his brother. This close, he could notice details that fulfilled what he feared—that his brother really wasn't his old self: n unbuttoned button on his shirt collar, a couple of errant unshaved whiskers near his ears, a tiny stain on his tie. Small, seemingly insignificant details, but combined with Mitchell's current behavior, they were a sad confirmation of Jonny's fears.

"Just calm down," Mitchell said. Jonny didn't, so Mitchell forced him onto a nearby bench. "Just breathe." After some perfunctory thrashing, Jonny gave in, took several breaths, and slowly eased up. "Good. Now, listen to me. Something's definitely not right. Hogart's too willing to deal. I must have missed something. Now go through it all again, slowly, with every detail."

After an exaggerated eye roll and an over-the-top sigh, Jonny did, even as he prayed that he could get back in there and sign before it all went away. Mitchell listened intently, and when Jonny finished telling the story of the last twelve hours yet again, Mitchell smiled broadly.

Jonny glowered at his brother. "What? What?"

Mitchell answered him, very slowly and specifically. When he was done, Jonny, too, was smiling. He had been so, so wrong; his brother was doing just fine. And for the second time in his life, Mitchell had saved Jonny from making a huge mistake.

The doors to the office flew open, and Hogart and Charles, still standing where the brothers had last left them, recoiled.

"I want fifteen hundred a week, with a two hundred dollar per episode royalty, *and* complete control of content and casting—that last part is non-negotiable," Jonny spewed as he marched straight at them, with Mitchell struggling to keep up.

Hogart shook his head, disappointed. "Now you've gone too far."

"Oh, I could go a lot farther." Jonny took a deep breath; he was going to enjoy this. "Like all the way to another network." He practically jutted out his chest and said proudly, "You don't own the character. I do."

Charles gave his best confident laugh, but it was too confident. "What in the world are you talking about? You created the character while a staff writer for *Hermie's Henhouse*. It, like everything else you write, belongs to the Regal Television Network."

Jonny shook his head. "I rewrote the sketch after I was fired. Therefore, everything new in it, including Justice Girl, belongs to me."

"That's ridiculous," Charles said dismissively.

Mitchell stepped up next to Jonny and joined the fun. "In fact, we could sue you for exploiting a character you didn't have the rights to."

"If this ends up in court, we'd chop you to pieces," Charles sneered.

"Maybe; maybe not," Jonny answered brightly. "But one thing's for certain; it will take time. Lots of time." Jonny looked Hogart straight in the eyes. "Two, three, four weeks, a few months, maybe even years."

The shot hit its mark. Hogart clasped his hands and then bounced them off his chin, thinking. Clearly, things were not going according to his script. Finally, he lowered his hands and slowly unclasped them. "The money is fine, and you can have the content, but I control the casting. I won't budge on that. Even if it means the show doesn't go on the air."

So that's the final line Hogart won't cross, Jonny thought. *Very well. There's another thing I want, more than any of the other things.* "Okay, I'll give you the casting," Jonny began but then took a moment, because he knew he was about to dip his foot into a whole new pool—a new pool infested with sharks and alligators and crocodiles and piranhas. "But I get to decide who writes the show with me"—and now the full plunge—"and if I deem it necessary, I can hire whichever writers I like, even if they've been…accused of things." So there it was, hung out for all of them to see.

Charles practically exploded. "You would risk all of our careers by using blacklisted writers?"

"How can there be a risk from something that doesn't exist?"

"Don't be a smart-ass."

Jonny held his arms out reassuringly. "I will only use them if I deem it absolutely necessary, which I'm sure I won't, but I don't want anything to get in the way of producing the best possible show."

Charles was seething. "No way, not—"

Hogart raised his big paw yet again, stopping Charles in his tracks. "Mr. Dirby, what goes on within the walls of the studio concerns me. What goes on outside of them is none of my business."

Jonny gave a slight knowing nod. This was exactly what he was counting on—that in the end, Hogart was a true pragmatist. If Jonny chose to go that route, if he did indeed deem it "absolutely necessary," Hogart would look the other way—as long as the offending writers were never seen. Jonny could work with that. "It appears," Jonny said, extending his hand, "we have a deal."

They shook hands, and then Hogart grabbed the original deal memo and ripped it in half. "I'll have a new one drawn up to incorporate everything we've agreed upon."

"Send it to my office when it's done," Mitchell said, handing over his business card.

"Will do," Hogart answered. He then looked over to Charles, who opened his folder again, pulled out another slip of paper, and handed it to Jonny.

"What's this?" Jonny asked.

"Just a few ideas I had for some episodes," Hogart said nonchalantly. Jonny opened his mouth to object, but Hogart raised his hand. "I understand our deal. Use them; don't use them—it's up to you. I just thought you should see them."

Satisfied, Jonny nodded and then folded the paper and slipped it into his pocket.

Hogart glanced from person to person around the room. "Well, that's it for now. I think we all have a lot of work to do."

After another round of handshakes and farewells, Jonny headed for the door. "Step one: find an office without a fuckin' overhead fan!" he said to no one in particular.

Episode One

JUSTICE GIRL

"A STITCH IN CRIME"

March 27, 1955

They'd been riding for hours, over gently sloping hills and shady dirt trails, through lazy streams and sparsely treed forests. The air was cool, not cold, and by noon, Felicity had taken off her coat. The sun felt warm and comforting on her skin. Spring filled her eyes and nose with succulent rebirth—a perfect day for riding, yet Felicity was miserable.

It wasn't working.

No matter how far they rode—they'd already covered at least thirty miles on horseback—Felicity knew she could not outrun her fate. She would have to tell her father that her plan had failed and that she had discovered nothing. No Communists, no blacklisted writers, no plots to overthrow the government. She knew they were there—they had to be. After all, it was the world of television, and her father had already helped remove hundreds of known threats from the airwaves. But even with the tip and at a time when it was essential to expose the threat, she had come up with nothing, except even less desire to ever set foot in Manhattan again.

So severe was her dread that, if she'd been on her own, Felicity might have ridden on for a few more hours, maybe even forever, but her companion had to be back at his stable.

Felicity pulled her horse to a stop on a rocky bluff that overlooked the back of her house and out across the fluffy, green blanket that was Greenwich, Connecticut, all the way to the hazy blue of the distant ocean.

"Can we talk now?" Braeden Talbot, her riding companion asked, pulling himself and his horse to a clean stop next to her. An expert horseman at twenty-nine, he and his horse appeared to move as one.

Felicity slumped; she'd known this was coming. She took several silent breaths and flexed her sore right hand. It still hurt from the slap she had delivered to the face of that Commie writer who had made a fool of her last night. She sighed again. With all that had happened, there was also *this* to deal with. She knew she couldn't avoid the conversation yet again as she had done for the last few months. After all, she had been the one to show up at Braeden's stable just before dawn and finally take him up on his offer of an early morning ride. She couldn't tell him the truth—that she didn't really want to ride horses or even see him. Not because she didn't genuinely like him. She loved him. Their four years as a couple had been wonderful. She just desperately needed to be out of the house before anyone was awake. That was how desperate she was to avoid facing her father. So, even though she had gotten home very late, barely making the last train out of Grand Central, she had dragged herself out of bed this morning, quietly dressed, and headed out the back door. Unfortunately, despite the early hour, her mother was already up, immaculately dressed, and sitting out on the back veranda, playing a small wooden ukulele as the sun came up. This had been a recurring scene throughout Felicity's childhood, so her mother's playful strumming didn't surprise her. Instead of passing her mother, Felicity silently turned, slipped out a side door used by the maids and servants, and made the pleasant half-mile walk to Braeden's stable.

"Sure," Felicity finally answered, doing a pretty good job of hiding how little she really wanted to have the conversation.

Braeden eased his horse closer to her. Felicity was always amazed with how fluid and smooth Braeden was when he rode. He was so completely in sync with his animal that it often was hard to see where the man ended and the horse began. It was as if he was born to ride. The same was true when Braeden yachted or rowed crew or did pretty much anything else he chose to do. From the first moment he tried something, he never looked awkward or clumsy; instead, he was polished and put together, as if he had been doing it his entire life. But horses—more specifically, thoroughbreds—were his great passion. The Talbots, along with the Kensingtons, were one of the great families of Greenwich. Also, like Felicity, he still lived at home. But unlike

Felicity, he probably would for the rest of his life. What would be the point of moving? Their horse-breeding operation, started by his great-grandfather right after the Civil War, occupied most of the forty acres of the Talbot estate. Braeden, when not away at Exeter and then Yale, spent all of his time working among the dirt, mud, and manure of the family stables. They'd raised several horses good enough to compete at the highest levels, winning the Preakness twice and a Belmont Stakes during Braeden's lifetime. But the Kentucky Derby had eluded the family, their closest finish being fourth in 1941. Braeden refused to live with this shortcoming and was determined to get them into the winner's circle at Churchill Downs. Since his father's stroke two years earlier and Braeden's consequently taking over the stable, he had focused all of their horse operations in that quest. Subsequently, along with a firm, almost workman-like muscular frame from all the time he spent outdoors, supervising workouts and time trials in the search for the perfect horse to take them to victory, he had an enticingly weathered complexion from the sun, a decidedly brownish hue, and sun-lightened blondish hair and eyebrows.

"As you know," Braeden began carefully, "coming up soon are the Derby preps. I'd sure love to be standing in the winner's circle with someone who was more than my girlfriend."

Felicity closed her eyes and exhaled. "Braeden. Soon. I promise you."

"That's what I've been hearing for two months," he shot back, jumping on what he knew she'd say. "It's a bit strange to get engaged but not to tell anyone." Braeden then looked away. "I'm beginning to think you don't really want to marry me."

"No, that's not true," Felicity said, genuinely alarmed. "There just are things that I need to do before…you know…it all starts happening." She looked him straight in the eyes to convey her sincerity. Being the wife of Braeden Talbot was an honor she did not take lightly. She knew she had taken the spot that virtually every young woman in the town longed for; in many people's eyes, she had won the lottery. Even her two older sisters, Patricia and Kathryn, who had married well, were impressed that a man like Braeden Talbot was interested in their younger sister.

Braeden glowered, clearly not believing her.

Felicity reached over and took his arm. "Braeden, it's like you with the Derby. You won't be satisfied until you've won."

"That's right; I won't be. But it's not stopping me from going ahead with the wedding."

"How many times do I have to say this? The wedding won't take over your life the way it will mine. And I can't afford for my life to be taken over right now." Felicity fought to keep her exasperation in check. *Why doesn't he get it?* she wondered. She couldn't wait to become his wife. He was a Talbot, after all, and so wonderfully perfect, from a good American family with good American values. They would have a splendid life together, and it would all start with their wedding, which would be a phenomenal affair, the social event of the decade, and long remembered in this town.

And that was precisely why she didn't want anyone to know about their engagement yet.

Once it was announced, no matter how hard she tried, nothing else would matter in her life. Her mother, already dropping hints at every possible occasion, was like a cocked pistol, waiting for them to pull the engagement trigger. Once it was, and they went public with the news, the plans for the wedding would consume every moment, every conversation, every action. She wasn't ready for that. She had a more important mission to complete. Then she would dutifully become Mrs. Braeden Talbot and gleefully take the envied spot next to him at garden parties and country club dinners and Sunday socials and, God willing, in the winner's circle at Churchill Downs.

"Your father...always your father," Braeden muttered exasperatedly.

"Yes, until the election," Felicity assured him. "Then it will be just you and me for the rest of our lives." When Braeden was not mollified, she pleaded, "Don't you see what we're trying to do? It's not about you. It's not about me. It's not about him. It's about our future."

But her words seemed to go unheard. Braeden simply shook his head, as if bewildered. "You know, there are one or two other women in this town who might not be unwilling to be publicly engaged to me."

Felicity threw up her hands. She leapt off her horse and handed the reins to Braeden. "I don't have any more time for this today." Suddenly, the inevitable confrontation with her father sounded a whole lot more appealing. As she stalked away toward a small path that led down the hill to her house, she waited for Braeden to say something.

But he didn't.

Instead, she heard the rustle of horse bridles behind her, followed by the rhythmic clip-clop of hooves as Braeden retreated. *Why doesn't he understand?* she wondered as she turned to watch him slowly trudge away. Braeden was part of this same world, the one that she and her father were fighting so hard to keep safe from the forces that meant to do nothing less than destroy their very way of life. Yet Braeden had not the least bit of interest in, or appreciation for, what they were doing. How would he feel when the Communists took over, and suddenly the state told him he could no longer breed racing horses? How would he feel when he was forced to raise horses for farming? For the people! For the peasants!

As the path leveled out, with the house less than a hundred feet away, Felicity still ruminated over Braeden's failure to see the stakes of the war they were fighting. Suddenly, Viola, one of their colored maids, appeared at one of the back doors, waving her hands frantically, calling, "Miss Kensington! Miss Kensington!"

Oh, great. What now? Felicity wondered, fighting the urge to turn and run away.

"There's a phone call for you!"

Felicity sped along the two-lane road, fighting the urge to push the gas pedal all the way to the floor. She whipped past the Civil War memorial in the town square, rolled through the stop sign that marked the beginning of the small business district, and ran the red light that demarcated the other end. After speeding through another mile of undeveloped countryside, a sleepy gas station next to a small, two-story building suddenly appeared, as if cut into the thick foliage. Felicity screeched her car to a stop in the tiny parking lot of the building and jumped out. A roadside diner occupied the first floor, but a door at the far end of the building led to a stairwell that took her up to the second floor.

Felicity hurriedly climbed the creaky steps, the passageway smelling of fried food and gasoline. Nearing the top of the stairs, she heard the busy voices of three or four people. It was Monday, after all, and there was a whole weekend of television to deal with.

Felicity stepped into the open room that occupied the entire second floor. Windows dominated all four walls, giving the room a spacious, airy feel. She immediately recognized the three workers; they were regular hires who were at small desks, talking on phones. At a fourth desk, the one nearest to her, was Paul Venton, her father's right-hand man in this operation. Paul was a tall, skinny wisp with hollow features and a perpetually dour scowl, who, when given really good or great news, would at best say, after a pause, "That's not terrible." He was in his early fifties and had never married; he probably never would, as he seemed to have no interest in women at all. In fact, he was the only one of her father's friends who hadn't looked her up and down at one time or another.

Seeing Felicity, and without so much as a greeting, Paul held out a slip of paper to her. It was the list of weekend shows with actors who, according to their thorough files, were subversive. Next to each show's name was the name of the offending network and its main phone number. Paul nodded, directing her toward an empty desk with a waiting phone. Felicity shook him off; today she wasn't there to make calls.

As Felicity crossed the room, she could hear the three hires making calls again and again to express their horror at what they'd seen on their television screens that weekend. When Felicity thought about it, her previous, almost daily participation in working the phones and rousing the networks with her anger was probably what made her think she could pass the acting audition and fake her way on to *Hermie's Henhouse*. To be most effective, the networks had to be called repeatedly, requiring Felicity and the others to adopt different voices and to pretend to be different outraged citizens each time.

Felicity spotted her father, Scott Kensington, at the other end of the room and immediately slowed. He wasn't alone. Quite to Felicity's surprise, he was with Roland Graves, the head of the Connecticut Republican party. They sat in a pair of leather club chairs. Between them was a small table with coffee and Danishes. Even seated, her father, at six foot two, towered over the diminutive Roland. Besides the height difference, they were a case study in contrasts. Where her father was thin-faced with sharp, angular features and, even at fifty-two, still had dark brush-like hair, Roland barely reached five feet and was chubby-faced. Despite being only in his early forties, a band of short gray hair ringed his baldhead. Where her father was always crisp and clean-shaven, Roland had compensated for his lack of hair with a thin mustache, which, for some reason, had not gone gray like the rest of his hair. But despite having a look that was almost comical, when it came to Republican politics in the Nutmeg State, Roland Graves was the man with all the power.

Felicity had met Roland on a few occasions, the last time being a few weeks ago at a lunch in Hartford. She had accompanied her father, along with her mother, to a suddenly very important event. With the unexpected death of Senator Cummings, the race for who would succeed him in the Senate began before the corpse was even cold. By sheer luck, her father already had a scheduled lunch with Roland for the week after the senator's funeral. With Felicity's and her mother's approval, her father was going to lobby to be the party's pick for the upcoming special election to fill the suddenly vacant Senate seat. Wanting to make an impression, Scott had decided to bring his elegant wife and stunning daughter with him to the lunch.

They were meeting at the Red Room in the famed Dorshire Hotel, and from the moment the lunch began, Felicity could tell that Roland was not seriously interested in her father. He was friendly and courteous—after all, they were on the same side of the great battle against Communism—but clearly, he was not going to give her father any real consideration to be the party's pick. There were two other prospects ahead of him, and one of them, Conrad Hollins, was the clear favorite. He was the current mayor of Hartford, a friend and political ally of Roland's, and, as if it couldn't get any better, had a son who was a recent Korean War hero.

But Roland was the head of the state party, which meant he was an expert at politics, so he dutifully listened to Scott Kensington's pitch—even as his eyes constantly darted around the room to see if he might need or want to talk to anyone else in the posh eatery. Though Roland must have known some of the story—what Scott was doing was well known and well lauded in Republican circles—Scott started from the beginning.

He had been working at the State Department during the war as a liaison for the top brass at the Pentagon. While there, he met Paul Venton, who was assigned to the European Advisory Council; his focus was relations between the United States and the Soviet Union. Surrounded almost entirely by New Deal Democrats, the two men found themselves the only ones horribly alarmed by what they saw as the US government's capitulation on certain issues to the Russians at the end of the war. When the Cold War broke out, Scott and Paul both fumed even more at what they had seen, convinced that some of the people they had been working with must have been secret Soviet agents. Scott quit the government and returned to the family business, all the while staying active in various anti-Communist organizations. Paul eventually moved on to the FBI, immediately joining in on the fight against the spread of Communism into American society, with a particular emphasis on the movie business. He stayed in touch with Scott, whose important and thorough work alerted him to some of the dangerous things broadcast on television—stories about immigrants, censorship, civil rights, and more left-wing Communist propaganda being delivered right into unsuspecting American homes. At Scott's insistence, Paul brought all of this to the attention of his bosses, but they were more interested in bringing down some of the big names in Hollywood. Finally, frustrated by how little emphasis the FBI focused on the new medium of television, Paul quit. Scott immediately hired Paul, and they went into business together. Scott was the public face and the head of the patriotic venture, publishing *Fight Back*, a pamphlet derived mostly from information Paul had secreted away from the Bureau, which listed hundreds of known Communists, radicals, and subversives working in the world of television.

Roland had listened to all of it, nodding as if impressed. But when the lunch ended, even though the selection wouldn't be made for at least a month, it was pretty clear that Roland had already made his mind up which one he would support. It was on the ride home from Hartford, with the car heavy with the failure of their trip, that Felicity had gotten her idea of going undercover into the subversive world of television.

Roland sitting in the office gave Felicity hope that maybe they had all been wrong. Maybe he was going to choose her father to represent the party in the special election after all.

As Felicity approached, her father and Roland stood up and shook hands, their meeting clearly over. "You remember my beautiful daughter," her father said as Felicity joined them.

"How could I forget?" Roland answered, looking Felicity up and down in the manner to which she was accustomed.

"Nice to see you again," Felicity said, ignoring his penetrating eyes.

They engaged in a few minutes of small talk, and Roland was his usual pleasant, charming self. Felicity studied her father closely, wondering if his bright smile was the product of hearing good news or was held in place out of expediency. Finally, after Roland departed, her father's smile left with him.

"Oh...," Felicity said, seeing his heavy face and getting the answer she had been waiting for. "I thought since he was here, maybe he had come to his senses."

Paul joined them, also clearly curious about the conversation with Roland, but Scott shook his head. "He was in the area and wanted to confirm some of the details of the party fund-raiser we're throwing in a few weeks. He'll let me raise money for the party, but he doesn't seem interested in me as the candidate."

Felicity cracked a big smile. "Well, that may just change." She began to quiver with excitement. "I've just been cast in the lead role on a new series written by the writer that I'm almost positive was the one who was fronting on *Hermie's Henhouse*."

Scott and Paul stared at her blankly.

She went on, still vibrating. "A brand new show! That means lots of focus, lots of attention. It premieres this Sunday. Supposedly, he's writing the whole thing himself, but I don't believe that, not after what I saw last week." She took a step toward them, lowering her voice and smilingly perversely.

"I'll be there every step of the way, and I'll find out who he's really working with. Imagine being the one to announce that a new show, just on the air, has some blacklisted writers on staff. That would get you some attention. That would make you stand out from the others."

They still stared at her blankly.

"Well?" she asked, her frustration growing.

Her father turned and looked at Paul.

Paul shrugged. "That's not terrible."

Her father looked to her and nodded slightly, seemingly pleased. "Nicely done."

It was the look and words she needed.

...

Hogart's list of ideas sat on the table between them.

Jonny and each of his three friends stared at it as the tinny clatter from the kitchen of Veleska, a tiny Ukrainian restaurant, filled the silence. Finally, Annie Quinlan, seated in the wobbly wooden seat next to Jonny, reached out a home-manicured hand and snatched it off the scratched Formica surface. She held the paper in front of her, moving it back and forth until her near-sighted eyes brought the words into focus. Her cheeks twitched as she read, and her face creased with just the hint of age lines, exposing her as being in her early thirties. Aghast, she threw back her head, sending a ripple through the frizzy brown hair that cascaded down her back to just below the shoulder line of her floral peasant dress. "This...this is terrible."

Jonny nodded in agreement. Annie was the oldest of his gathered friends. When he first went to work in the writers room at *Hermie's Henhouse*, he assumed she was the head writer, given her age, her strong to-the-point attitude, and the fact that she seemed to run things in the room. He soon found out that was not the case when, on the second day he was there, the head writer was fired—an event that seemed to occur whenever Hermie was in a foul mood, which was often. Through a succession of head writers—Jonny gave up counting at five—it was really Annie who ran things. It was pretty clear to those willing to say it and risk their job that if Annie hadn't lacked a penis, she would have been named the head writer. But she didn't mind, at least not in public. Flying under the radar kept her out of Hermie's sights and gainfully employed—at least until a couple of months ago.

Disgusted, Annie passed Hogart's ideas to a muscular man to her right, who grabbed the list with his rough hands. Burton Stanz held it steadily in front of his face, his biceps bulging through the suit jacket that framed his white dress shirt. A bow tie was wrapped tightly around his thick neck. After a quick read, he sighed and ran his hand through the short, stiff lawn of yellow hair that was his blond crew cut. "You ain't lying, sister."

Jonny had not liked Burton when they first met. He had been hired two months after Jonny, and Burton's arrival ended Jonny's special status as the whiz kid comedy genius among the other staff writers—something Jonny would never admit he liked, but if the truth be told, he loved. Now Burton was the fair-haired boy genius, always quick with a sharp line or a great new approach to a dying sketch. Even though Burton was a full five years older than Jonny and, at the age of almost thirty, could hardly be called a "whiz kid," the term stuck. And even after other new writers were brought in, Burton remained the star. Jonny's animus toward Burton only grew and worsened by the fact that Burton didn't seem to care one way or another. And to top it all off, Burton was a World War II veteran, which only made his bond with some of the other writers, actors, and crew people on the show that much stronger. Just when it seemed there was no way the two of them could survive in that stifling closet of a writers' room without coming to blows—or without Jonny taking a swing at him—they suddenly found themselves becoming fast friends. The long hours of working together under incredible stress broke down Jonny's wall of jealousy, and they soon found they had in common a love of foreign films, the New York Giants, the work of the turn-of-the-century Russian playwrights (though they both agreed Chekov was overrated), ethnic foods, and the Living Theatre.

Burton tossed the list to the final member of their clandestine foursome. Shel Ezralow placed a single finger on the paper's typed surface, as if he might catch a disease if he touched it any more intimately, and slid it toward him. Shel had been Jonny's first friend on the show, partly because they were so close in age and partly because the other writers more or less ignored him. He was quiet, to the point of not being there, and unassuming, to the point of not seeking, and therefore not getting, the credit he deserved for his indispensable job. Though a good writer in his own right, it was Shel's job to sit at a typewriter in a dark corner of the room and sift through the crazed banter that all eight of the writers shouted at the same time, grabbing it, shaping it, and molding it into a cohesive monologue or sketch. Herding mosquitoes with a butter knife would have been an easier job, but somehow, every time they reached the end of a session and an exhausted silence descended on the room, everyone would instinctively turn to Shel, who would be calmly finishing up his typing. He would then ease the paper out of the typewriter, slowly, purposefully, deliberately turning the knob until the sheet was free. Then he'd briefly arrange the three or four sheets produced during the session, clear his throat, and read. Amazingly, what would come forth would be a clear, concise comedy piece, with the best of their shouted lines arranged in just the right order. It was a thankless job for which Shel was never thanked.

Peering down through his comically thick glasses teetering atop a tiny nose, Shel bent his skinny neck and read from Hogart's idea list. "Justice Girl saves a busload of orphans, who thank her by baking a cake. A cake? Seriously?" Shel looked to the rest of the group, joining in their incredulity.

"I think he's going after Betty Crocker to sponsor the show," Jonny offered, only half in jest.

Before anyone could respond, Mrs. Belinski, the perpetually annoyed, middle-aged woman who co-owned (with her combative husband) and operated the insignificant restaurant hidden away among the boutiques and bars just off St. Mark's Place in the East Village, plopped four plates of food on the table, without even the slightest attempt at getting the placement right. With a grunt, she headed back to the kitchen. Ritualistically, they all passed the plates until each person got what he or she had actually ordered.

Shel returned his gaze to the page, scanned it again, and then looked up at the other three. "These are the worst story ideas I've ever seen."

"You're missing the best part," Jonny said nonchalantly as he turned a ketchup bottle over and dumped its blood-red contents all over the list. "We don't have to pay any attention to what's on it!"

Annie and Burton jerked their heads back at the explosion of ketchup. Reflexively, Shel jumped to his feet, grabbed a couple of napkins, and began to carefully clean off the list.

"Leave it," Jonny said firmly.

On the walk over from Hogart's office, Jonny had been bursting with edgy energy from the stunning turn of events at the meeting, and he had mulled over how to break the incredible news to his friends. Monday lunch was a ritual with Annie, Burton, and Shel, always at the same time in the same place in this hidden corner of New York City, where they knew no network executive or producer would be caught dead. They all had met as part of the writing staff of *Hermie's Henhouse*. At that time, Jonny was the new kid, brash and full of ideas. Now, not even two years later, he was brash and full of ideas...and the only one left with a job. One by one, they had been dismissed for various reasons. Burton, an Emmy nominee in 1953 for comedy writing, was suddenly no longer funny in 1954. Shel, who had received a personal letter from Hermie, proclaiming him the glue of the writing staff, "holding the whole gang of convicts together better than any iron chain," was let go two months later for "no longer fitting in." Annie, known throughout the claustrophobically incestuous world of live-television writers for her tart, biting, and witty dialogue, suddenly found her work described as dull, hackneyed, and passé on the day they fired her.

But none of them was fooled; they all knew the truth. Before the war, Burton had been a stage manager for the Delancey Street Players, a Soho-based theatre group that specialized in performing the works of emerging playwrights, with a few established ones thrown in for good measure—Odets, Ibsen, Shaw, and, as an afterthought, a couple of Russian playwrights. That afterthought cost Burton his job on *Hermie's Henhouse*—and any other show in television. The three pieces of a German grenade he still carried deep within his left shoulder apparently didn't offset his overseeing a single matinee production of Gorky's *The Lower Depths*. Annie had worked on and written for the performances that accompanied several clothing drives for the Soviet Union during the war. Obviously, that meant she was sympathetic to the Communist cause—never mind that the Soviets were our allies at the time. Shel had actually attended a couple of Communist Party meetings. Never mind that his "political interest" came to an abrupt end when it became clear that the pretty, free-love-proclaiming party member in the tight green angora sweater he was trying to screw was only leading him on.

Because they shared an abiding friendship and he was sympathetic to their plights, Jonny had siphoned work their way, slipping some of their sketch ideas and monologue jokes into the writers' room as if they were his own. If any of their ideas made it to air, Jonny would personally slip them some cash from his weekly salary. So, the Monday lunch was started, where Jonny would divvy up his salary accordingly. No one ever skipped; they all were desperate and needed the money.

On this day, Jonny had slid through the sagging front entrance of the restaurant and past the straight-to-the-point neon sign that proclaimed rather blandly "Good Food." On the windy autumn day when Jonny had first found the restaurant, he had wandered in because one of the letters in the sign had burned out, so at that time—and for the next three months before they got around to repairing it—the restaurant seemed to offer the rather irresistible "God Food."

Seeing that Burton, Annie, and Shel were already there—seated at the same square, lopsided, scuff-covered table where they always sat—Jonny tensed his muscles, forcing himself to let go of the excitement that pulsed through every molecule of his body. As was often the case, they were the only patrons. This unwavering loyalty, however, garnered absolutely no favor from Mr. and Mrs. Belinski, who offered not even the slightest nod to Jonny as he strode past them to join his friends.

Jonny sat down, but instead of the traditional distribution of cash that always began their lunch, he informed them that there would be no money this week. But Jonny couldn't hold in his excitement any longer, and before they could protest the lack of money, he explained what had happened over the previous twelve hours—although with the understandable omission of the slap from the actress and the vomit in the toilet. By the time he got to the part about the new show he was to lead and the added detail that they were now all staff writers on it, their gaping mouths had broadened into toothy grins.

"I said leave it!" Jonny barked, as Shel ignored his first proclamation and continued to wipe off ketchup from Hogart's list of story ideas. When that didn't work, Jonny grabbed the list, crumpled it into a ball, and dropped it on the table. "Speaking as the executive producer and head writer, I am commanding all of you to ignore every word on this page!" They all grinned and nodded, Shel finally getting it, as Jonny continued. "Now, let's get to work. We've got a show to create."

"Wait a minute. Wait a minute," Burton interjected. "You're forgetting one very important fact. None of us knows how to write this kind of show. We're comedy sketch writers."

Jonny's eyebrows arched. "So?"

"So what in the hell do we know about writing superheroes?" Burton demanded.

"Yeah," Annie agreed.

"What's to know?" Jonny shot back. "We all read comic books. And we've all watched *Superman*."

"I've been to baseball games. That doesn't make me a baseball player," Burton jabbed.

Jonny was growing frustrated. "We can do it. It's a story. It's got a beginning, a middle, and an end."

"But I've only written sketches," Burton argued.

Annie nodded. "Monologue jokes, one-liners, situational stuff."

Suddenly, Shel, who had been his usual silent self since trying to clean off the list, jumped to his feet. He was almost trembling. "Are you two out of your minds?" he said, his eyes blazing at Burton and Annie. "It's a fucking *job*! He's offering us work! What more do you need to know than that?"

Two hours later, after finishing lunch and taking a walk, they'd reached Washington Square Park. The four of them had orbited one another in a chaotic swirl as they all shouted out story ideas. Shel, pen and paper in hand, sifted through the shouts, jotting them down and giving them shape. At the fountain that dominated the center of the park, Jonny, Annie, and Burton sat down on the curved concrete rim. Shel stood in front of them and read back what they had come up with: Justice Girl was the adopted daughter of a rich businessman, who went about his life of high finance completely unaware of her crime-fighting activities. By day, she attended City College, but at night, when she was supposedly studying in her room, she was actually out patrolling the streets as Justice Girl.

Before Shel could get any farther, an argument broke out between Burton and Annie about whether she should drive a car or ride a motorcycle in her guise as Justice Girl. Burton argued for the car, Annie for the motorcycle. Neither would give ground, and things started to get nasty. Jonny and Shel stood on the sidelines, watching, hoping the argument would peter out. But it didn't. Jonny wanted to jump in and stop them, but Shel was Annie's boyfriend, so Jonny waited, giving him the first opportunity. When he didn't take it, Jonny cut off the arguing duo and suggested they all move on to a new locale.

Passing through the faux Arc de Triomphe that was the main entrance to the park, they headed uptown. But the argument persisted, degenerating, as it often did, into political beliefs.

"You don't think a woman should drive a motorcycle!" Annie said, practically spitting in Burton's face.

"I never said that! But now that you mention it, yes, I prefer a woman who has the taste and decorum to drive a car!"

By the time they reached 10th Street, Jonny had had enough. He declared that along with her super strength, Justice Girl would have the ability to fly. If she could fly, why would she need a car *or* a motorcycle? The argument was now moot.

They continued up Fifth Avenue, shouting, prodding, and gesturing emphatically, each one declaring that his or her idea was the best—until a minute later, when someone's next idea was the best. When they reached Madison Square Park, in the creeping shadow of the Flat Iron building, the rich adopted father and Justice Girl's studying was long gone, having been discarded somewhere around 17th Street. Justice Girl was now a secretary at a high-performance aircraft factory, a gleaming high-tech palace full of the latest streamlined supersonic jets, where she quietly pretended to go about her mundane tasks, while secretly helping the company with their top-secret aircraft plans by day and fighting crime by night. Sadly, her career in aviation was over by the time they hit 33rd Street, as well as a brief flirtation with her working at a major metropolitan newspaper. Shel put an end to that one, pointing out that Superman did that as Clark Kent. Now, feeling dispirited and lost among the throbbing late afternoon crowd, they stopped to sit on the steps of the main post office.

Another (thankfully briefer) argument broke out over Justice Girl's costume. Annie wanted her in a skirt that hung below her knees, and Burton wanted something short, mid-thigh.

"Why don't we just put her in bikini?" Annie yelled at him.

Burton grinned. "Works for me."

Once again, Jonny jumped in, cutting them off. "We'll just keep the costume that she's already got; that'll save money." Jonny knew he could change it if he wanted, but the truth was, he kind of liked what she already wore—that, and the fact that the skirt just happened to end above the knees didn't hurt either.

Jonny's eyes drifted upward to the top of the heavy stone building. His gaze locked on the engraved words adapted from Herodotus: "Neither snow, nor rain, nor heat, nor gloom of night stays these couriers from the swift completion of their appointed rounds." Jonny said to the group, his mind racing, "That's pretty powerful stuff, kind of like a superhero oath. Maybe she could work for the…"

The decidedly negative stares of the three members of his writing staff told him what they thought of the idea that was forming in his head. Jonny didn't bother protesting.

The next ten blocks uptown got them nowhere, so they cut over to Times Square and ducked into Burton's favorite Automat. Jonny protested, wondering loudly why they weren't supporting one of the numerous mom-and-pop restaurants, instead of giving their money to one of a chain of bland, characterless, homogenized food dispensaries. His power as head writer, not to mention executive producer of the show, did not extend to culinary choices, and he was easily voted down.

In the Automat, an unexpected wave of warm nostalgia engulfed Jonny. The other three scurried off toward the bank of windows for food—but Jonny found himself frozen just inside the door. As a child, he had loved the place and remembered his father taking him there. Jonny must have been five or six when he had accompanied his father on one of his occasional trips to meet someone who wanted to sell his stamp collection. To Jonny—whose mother's cooking ranged from undercooked chicken to overcooked chicken—it was paradise. But it wasn't the food that Jonny really loved about the place; it was the view.

The Automat was across the street and about half block from the smoking Camel sign that had become a landmark of Times Square since its first appearance. If he sat at a table near the front window and leaned forward at just the right angle, he could watch the perpetually open-mouthed smoker in the sign blow his smoke rings out into street.

Jonny revealed none of this secret nostalgia as, food in hand—roast beef sandwich, glass of milk, side of potato salad—he steered the four of them into a booth near the front window. He gave a quick lean and was comforted by the sight of the sign, still where he remembered it, still blowing smoke.

Lunch went by with no mention of Justice Girl. They were hopelessly stuck, and years of experience told them that talking about it would only make things worse. So they filled the time between bites of turkey a la king and swigs of Blatz beer with gossip about friends, excitement about great art, anger at politicians, distrust of authority, and laughs at the ridiculousness of it all.

Jonny joined in none of it.

It was a job to them. To him, it was a chance, maybe the only real one he'd ever get, to be completely in control. The leverage he had was unheard of, and it would almost surely never come again. To create and produce a show that was his and his alone was incredible. But it would all disappear as quickly as it had appeared if he couldn't deliver a complete, well-thought-out, well-written pilot script in two days. A quarter of the allotted time was already gone, and they were nowhere, just a few failed plots scribbled on Shel's notepad. Jonny felt sick to his stomach as he poked aimlessly at a flap of perfectly cooked roast beef that stuck out past the crust of the moist rye bread of his sandwich. As far as he was concerned, it was the fat tongue of fate stuck out and taunting him. He knew he'd better eat something. One way or another, whether they wrote something or not, it was going to be a long night. He jabbed at his potato salad with his fork, but when he brought the yellowish-white mound to his lips, the smell of boiled potatoes mixed with whipped mayonnaise and mustard repulsed him. With a snap of his wrists, he deposited the clump back on his plate. What difference did it make? If they didn't come up with something soon, he might as well starve to death.

The others were oblivious to Jonny's pain and went about devouring their food and happily chatting, seemingly without a care in the world. Jonny was about to steer them back to the job at hand when a young woman, probably not even twenty, bumped into him. And it wasn't just a slight bump or subtle knock; it was a heavy blow to his upper arm. And painful. Annoyed by her carelessness, Jonny turned to glare at her, but she had walked away, so self-involved she wasn't even aware of what she had done. The frustration of the day, his partners' lack of concern, the fist of tension in his stomach, and the disgusting food in front of him all came together in a sudden burst of anger. Jonny leapt up from the table and chased after the shallow, thoughtless girl.

He spotted her up ahead, just sitting down with her friend, another young, pretty, and probably vacuous girl. Given the chance, he was certain that she, too, would have bumped into him and not cared that she had. Well, Jonny was going to make sure they both learned a thing or two about manners. As he approached, he noticed that they both carried large black portfolios, the kind used to carry artwork or large photographs. Pretty girls. Portfolios. Photographs. *My God, they're models*, he thought. *Of* course, *they're models. Just look at them, with their high, perfectly rouged cheekbones and thick, flowing hair.* They were obviously young girls who got by on their looks. Probably rich, too. Making others feel inadequate by appearing in newspapers and magazines as unattainable images of perfection. They didn't know a thing about living in the real world. Or what it was like to be responsible for anything, especially their actions. Well, Jonny was about to change that. After he was done with them, they'd remember to say excuse me the next time they bumped into someone, even if they thought that person was beneath them.

The girls both looked up as Jonny sternly approached their table. "Look," he began firmly. "I know in our society, because of your appearance, you are given a free ride, but that doesn't mean you have the right to bump into me without saying you're sorry. You really need to—" Jonny suddenly hesitated, his eyes flickering rapidly. Abruptly, he spun on his heels and headed back to the table.

They all loved Jonny's idea that Justice Girl worked at a fashion magazine. Burton could see the potential for quick, sharp, cutting dialogue in this high-pressure and high-stakes world, packed with outrageous characters in wonderful, witty opposition to one another. Shel loved the cohesiveness of the workplace. It was a firm, structured environment, and that, in turn, had the open-ended potential for the stories to move into different locales that were still soundly rooted in this world. Annie was initially in opposition to the idea. "Let me guess. She's a model," she intoned, her brows showing she was displeased. But after Jonny informed her that, when not fighting crime, Justice Girl would be an assistant to the editor of the magazine, *a woman*, Annie was on board.

Jonny was so pleased they liked his idea that he didn't bother boring them with why he loved it: the contrast of the shallow with the worthwhile. How could such beauty be used to perpetuate such ugliness? It was a world where callous, uncaring creatures used their gifts to bring out the bad in others—inadequacy, jealousy, self-loathing, and the rest of the menagerie of horrors they helped promote in the slick, color pages of their employers' magazines. Imagine if someone with some worth dared come into their world. They'd tear her apart—no, they were so self-consumed, they wouldn't even notice.

All Jonny cared was that they all agreed it was perfect.

Now, all thoughts of food and time disappeared as they went to work, tearing into the idea. They poked it, punched it, slapped it, shook it, tore it apart, rebuilt it, shaped it, tossed parts of it out, put parts of it back in, argued, agreed, disagreed, fought, made up, fought again, and made up again, until five hours later they found themselves just a tick after midnight, outside the ACE subway station at Columbus Circle. Annie, Burton, and Jonny stood in front of Shel as he read from the organized chaos that was his notepad.

"The magazine is," Shel began in the authoritative voice he had developed in the writers' room, "*Focus on Fashion*, a women's fashion magazine. In her public persona as the mousy Sally Smalls, she is the dutiful assistant to none other than Margaret Crawford, the legendary editor of the magazine. In this high-pressure world, Sally goes about her duties, ever the efficient servant, always ready to do the bidding of her demanding boss. But when justice calls and without the slightest hesitation, Sally sneaks away, quickly assuming her secret identity as Justice Girl, fighter of crime, champion of the weak, dedicated servant of justice. It's a tough existence, made just bearable by a ray of light and hope that shines daily in her life: Chance Crawford, Margaret's playboy son, with whom Sally is madly in love. But sadly, when Chance makes his daily visits to the office, he barely notices Sally, with her thick black-rimmed glasses and boring brown hair cut into a shapeless bob. On top of that, he runs around with every pretty girl in town and is a regular cast member of the society and scandal pages. As if living with that is not bad enough for Sally, there is one girl who holds a special place in Chance's heart, the one true love of his life, Justice Girl. Chance is hopelessly smitten with Sally's alter ego, and as tempting as it is, whenever he strides into the office, hungover from a wild night on the town chasing after some starlet or even Justice Girl, she knows she can never reveal who she really is. But Justice Girl/Sally never gives up, knowing one day, when all the criminals are caught, when the weak are forever safe, when the streets are truly safe for one and all, when justice has finally prevailed, she can then reveal her true self to him. But until that far-off day, one that she works toward and dreams of in every free moment, Justice Girl will be alone, forever making sure 'Justice is served!'"

Finished, Shel lowered his pad from his face and looked out at the other three. Silence. No one wanted to say anything. Finally, Jonny slowly nodded his head "Not bad. Not bad at all."

The others sighed, relieved, and then heartily agreed with Jonny. But it wasn't necessary. Though no one wanted to say it, they all knew the only opinion that mattered was Jonny's.

After a round of satisfied hugs, they all disappeared into the subway, Jonny shooting uptown, the other three sliding downtown.

Riding the express, Jonny allowed himself to relax against the ribbed cushion, and the thumping rhythm of the jiggling car pulled him inward. His thoughts drifted back a million years to just this morning, a mere fifteen hours ago, when he was just another fired and blacklisted writer. He was going to sit down and write something great, something grand, something announcing his arrival, with lights flashing and trumpets blaring, as one of the important literary voices in America. But instead, he was now committed to at least one season of *Justice Girl*—if not more. With this aching thought, his pleased sense of satisfaction vanished. The whole-body stiffness returned, and a swelling sense of disappointment pushed out from inside him. It was great that he was in charge of his own show—miraculous, really—but where was the piercing scalpel in all this? The uncompromising critique? The unrelenting exposure of the truth? Oh, sure, the premise they'd just come up with was solid, and they'd sure as hell think of better storylines than Hogart had suggested—no orphans cooking Betty Crocker cakes—but in the end, would it really be that different from what he'd been doing for the last two years? Insipid writing with no other goal than to simply entertain in the most banal and noncontroversial way?

As the train shot out of the darkness up onto the elevated tracks, the dim gray haze of artificial light stained the low clouds. Jonny knew there was only one way he could survive this. It was the same plan he'd tried two years previous, when he'd first started writing for *Hermie's Henhouse*, but this time he meant it. This time he would really do it.

After the rest of the jiggle uptown on the A train, the endless ride in the elevator to the fifth floor of his building, and a soft tiptoe past his sleeping father—the *Linn's Stamp News* riding up and down on his stomach—Jonny collapsed on his bed, not even having the time to finish the thought, *What a day this has*—before he was sound asleep.

A mere five hours later, before the sun had risen and seeped through the cracks in his blinds, before the tap-dance barrage from above began, before the river of clomps down the stairs, Jonny was awake, showered, and sitting upright at the small desk in a corner of his cramped room. Though he should have been exhausted, he wasn't; the desire to not let his plan fail again drove him.

Twenty-two months earlier, Jonny had nothing more on his writer's résumé than a six-show run of a black-box production of his play, *The Road to Damascus*, performed in the basement of Our Lady of the Saviour on Charles Street in the West Village. Not even a year graduated from City College, he and the horde of actors and actresses he had befriended over the four years of pretending to be interested in subjects other than the theatre had pooled their resources to stage this premiere production of his play. Using postcards, phone calls, contacts, and anything short of sexual favors—though the last was considered in a slightly more than joking way—they tried to get the critics to come see their work. It didn't work. With the exception of a slightly deaf elderly reviewer for the local free paper, the *West Village News*, and an extremely bored and scowling reviewer from the *Daily Worker*, the production went completely unnoticed. Jonny couldn't have cared less about the critics. He didn't slave and wrestle over each and every line for their validation. His work was for the people, the masses, those yearning for enlightenment. Unfortunately, they weren't interested in his work either.

The sixth and the final performance, a rainy Sunday matinee in late November, had a typical audience. Five people. Two supportive friends of cast members, a bum who wandered in just before curtain and spent the entire performance snoring, the mother of the show's stage manager, who just *loved* the show, and a mysterious man in a three-piece suit who sat slumped in the back row.

The next day, Jonny found out who the mysterious man was.

Just after midday, with Jonny seated at his work desk, trying to come up with a new play to write by taking advantage of the glorious quiet in the building between the eager morning departures and the weary evening returns, the phone rang just outside his bedroom. Jonny answered it. A curt, straight-to-the-point female voice inquired if this was the residence of one Jonny Dirby. Jonny answered in the affirmative, whereupon he was enlightened as to the occupation of the mysterious man in the three-piece suit: he was a television producer. The female voice then immediately invited Jonny, at his earliest convenience, to attend a meeting at the Regal Television Network. Jonny swiftly agreed, smiling self-assuredly as he hung up the phone. Of course they had called him in, he thought, rocking on the balls of his feet. After all, they had seen his play and naturally wanted him to adapt it for one of their live, dramatic anthology programs.

And Jonny couldn't have been happier.

Unlike most of the other playwrights that ran in his self-assured circle—certain to a person that they would very soon change the world with their masterful words—Jonny did not scoff at the world of television. Oh, sure, it was mostly a commercial medium used to tell consumers what they wanted to buy, even if they didn't need it, but it also could be an intimate medium, reaching right into the American home with a vast potential to share an idea with the whole country simultaneously. Jonny had joined the rest of America as they cried for *Marty*, laughed along with *No Time for Sergeants*, and felt the indicting sting of *Patterns*. Most importantly, when the shows were over, the lights didn't come up and the audience didn't walk out into a night of neon and traffic and forget what they had seen. No, this was work that reached right into their homes, into their very world, where they thought they were safe behind their own wall of lies. It reached right through and shook them to their very cores. There was no place they could go to escape the message.

So the next day, Jonny happily marched down to the Crestview Theatre with a freshly mimeographed copy of *The Road to Damascus* tucked inside his satchel. He met with the same producer who had attended the show—he was an oddly dressed man named Charles—and sadly discovered right away that they were not interested in his play. They were interested in talking to him about coming to work as a writer on *Hermie's Henhouse*, a silly comedy review he had seen his parents enjoy on Sunday nights. Apparently, the only part of his play that Charles liked, at least while he was still there, was a small scene where two of the characters went to the movies. Jonny had wanted to make a statement about the emptiness of the current cinema, so he had written an entire scene for the made-up insipid comedy that they were watching.

Charles loved it.

It had just the right tone, tenor, and wit for what they needed on *Hermie's Henhouse*. And they were desperate for new writers, Hermie having sacked a big chunk of the writing staff just the other day. Rather shocked by the unusual turn of events, and after some soul-searching, Jonny took the job. It was not an easy decision. Sure, the money was good, and it was nice to be able to say he was a professional, but writing dumb comedy was not the mission he was on. But he did it because, secretly, he had his own plan. Once on the inside, actually working for a network show, he figured it would be easier to get his dramatic work on the air. So he dutifully submitted *The Road to Damascus* to *American Stories*, where, much to his astonishment, it was summarily rejected. *All right*, he thought, *then I'll write something else. Something so important, so good, so powerful, they'll have to put it on the air.* That was the bargain he made with himself. By day a comedy writer, by night a writer of serious drama.

But unfortunately, it didn't work out like that. Writing for *Hermie's Henhouse* became such an all-consuming experience that any chunks of time he had carved out to get other work done were taken from much-needed sleep. After a few months, Jonny forgot the bargain, and his serious work went unwritten.

Consumed by his refusal to let history repeat itself, Jonny hefted his bulky typewriter from its storage space just inside the leg hole under his desk and up onto the worn wooden surface. He lifted the hard shell, and then, almost like greeting a long-lost friend, ran his fingers along the smooth, obsidian, metallic curves of the body until both hands came to rest over the jutting tentacles of the alphabetical keyboard. His back arched, his shoulders tensed, his fingers stiffened and pulsed; he was ready to go to work. He reached into the upper-right side drawer which, as well as being a depository for paper clips, staples, pens, pencils, old polo grounds tickets, assorted family photographs, an Atlantic City snow globe, and an impressive collection of miscellanea from twenty-five years of being alive, served as Jonny's story file. After a quick bit of fishing, Jonny pulled out four random scraps of paper. Over the last year and half, he had methodically accumulated them, each one representing a different idea for a play. The hurried sentences outlined a play about the blacklist, scrawled on a torn page from one of his father's stamp magazines, which he'd jotted down during an afternoon when he was home sick, watching the McCarthy-Army hearings. The first shred of a notion of an idea for a play about political corruption, written on the back of an *Adlai Stevenson for President* flier, came to Jonny one morning while dressing and listening to the radio, as Richard Nixon spoke about his financial situation. A stained cocktail napkin held smeared words in pen, spelling out the plot to a play about workers' rights, which came to Jonny while watching the overworked staff at the Catskills resort where his family took their disastrous one-and-only vacation since the had war ended. The last one, an idea for a play about racism, inspired by watching a newsreel of a South Carolina lynching, made him pause. It wasn't the story idea, as potent as it was, that stopped him. It was what the idea was written on—the back of an article that he had meticulously cut out of the *Daily News*: a profile of the television writer Rod Serling that had appeared just days after his teleplay "Patterns" had been shown as an episode of *Kraft Television Theatre*. Serling's brilliant drama about the high-pressure and cutthroat world of business had enraptured and enthralled Jonny, like the rest of the country. For a week after cutting out the article, Jonny had reread it daily, gleaning anything and everything he could from it and making a vow that one day, when he got the chance, he would produce work as good as Serling's.

Now, flush with the memory, he was determined that that day was today, and even more driven to create something important, Jonny flipped through the pile, searching, hoping one idea would jump out at him, demanding to be written right then and there.

But it didn't happen.

They all had their merits. The blacklist was timely and demanded to be exposed yet again for its true identity: political demagoguery. Racism was a topic that needed exploration, as was political corruption, as was workers' rights. They were all good, solid, rich ideas that Jonny knew he could really sink his teeth into. He could make them all great, but sadly, he had to pick one, if he had even a chance of actually finishing it while fulfilling his commitment to *Justice Girl*.

Exasperated, Jonny leaned back in his chair, sucked in a mouthful of frustration, and rubbed his sagging eyes. The lack of sleep finally caught up to him, and combined with the no-win situation he was facing, Jonny's mood crashed, and he slumped in his chair. He knew what he should do, and he knew what he wanted to do: he wanted to write all of them. All four. They were all great and all deserved to be brought into the world. Now. While they were still relevant. But it just wasn't possible when almost all of Jonny's time was committed to *Justice Girl* and dreaming up her silly antics.

Still hunched over, Jonny flipped through the ideas yet again. Pausing briefly on each set of scribbled notes, he forced himself to read them again, hoping for some sort of objectivity. But it was useless. Every idea seemed just as good and fresh and demanding of his attention as the first time he had written them down. Even more frustrated, Jonny tossed the entire pile atop his desk.

He was about to give up the whole thing— maybe he would just suffer through the next couple of years with only *Justice Girl* in his creative life— when suddenly Jonny shot up in his chair. His eyes darted back and forth, and he found himself almost struggling for breath. Slowly, carefully, methodically, like watching the screen of his family's television slowly brighten after turning it on, an idea coalesced in his mind. Maybe...he didn't have to choose.

Jonny burst through the door, his chest heaving. Burton, Shel, and Annie looked up at him, startled. Jonny began to pace around the spacious office that Charles, in response to his request, had secured for them. He tried fitfully to catch his breath, because in his excitement, he had been unwilling to wait for the elevator and had climbed the four flights. Initially, Jonny had figured, the big event of the day would have been the grand reveal of the new office. He had kept it a secret, only telling his fellow writers—not even ten hours ago—that the next day they should meet at this address. He was very casual about it, playing it down. But inside, he had been bursting with excitement. Finally, a workplace designed on their terms. It was a large, airy space, perched in a corner of the building, so large, bright windows dominated two of the freshly painted walls. In the middle of the room, delivered early in the morning, long before any of them arrived, were four brand-new couches, arranged in a square around a circular wooden coffee table. No longer would there be a fight to see who got to sit on the couch. Instead, they would each have their very own to sit, sprawl, curl up, or even sleep on. But most important, as far as Jonny was concerned, was that there was no ceiling fan.

Now, all of that was forgotten as Jonny finally caught his breath. "Why does she have to fight silly bank robbers and dumb kidnappers?" he began, gesturing emphatically with open palms. "The stories don't have to be stupid."

Burton, Shel, and Annie, their attention now completely removed from exploring their new digs, looked at him, confused.

Jonny stepped toward them, imploring them, "Wasn't I fired because I was standing up to an injustice? Didn't I create her to right an injustice? So, she was born of injustice. And the same should be true for the character herself. Justice Girl has to be here on Earth because of an injustice. Her whole mission is to right injustice. She has to fight it everywhere—not just by stopping the crook and the criminal but in society as a whole!" As he finished, his eyes were wide with excitement, and his whole head was nodding at the sheer rightness of it all.

No one said anything.

Annie slowly slunk onto one of the couches, Shel's jaw twitched back and forth, and Burton teetered on his heels.

"Well?" Jonny's face was still bright and hopeful with the brilliance of his idea.

"I kinda liked what we had last night," Burton finally offered as Shel and Annie's bobbing heads immediately joined him.

"That stuff was great, but this is better," Jonny insisted, his eyes slowly returning to their normal size.

"Is it?" Annie asked ingenuously.

Jonny sighed, fighting the childish urge to be overly dramatic about it. These were the times that he hated writing with a team, when he was so certain, so positive, that what he had come up with was absolutely brilliant. *It's a goddamn great idea!* he was screaming inside his head. But he knew the thought had to stay there, safely tucked away inside his skull. If he did scream, that would only make things worse. The others would collectively put up a wall he couldn't scale no matter how convincingly he argued. Instead, he had to be calm, careful, and practical.

"Yes," he began matter-of-factly. Then, very methodically, with his arms held tightly at his side, he told the story of his pained feeling the night before, his epiphany early in the morning, and finally, the plethora of story ideas of which they could now avail themselves. By the end of his tale—and he was careful to keep it calm, smooth, and to the point—they collectively nodded at the sheer practicality and rightness of it.

He had won them over. "Good," he said, hiding his considerable annoyance at having had to waste time convincing them. "Let's get to work."

...

As a general rule, Hogart despised being late, but as he slipped out of his limousine in front of the Stardust Ballroom on a largely forgotten block of 32nd Street almost at 10th Avenue, he was running ten minutes behind. Exactly as he had planned it. The last three days had been an overwhelming menagerie of meetings, memos, phone calls, conferences, and casting sessions, all pertaining to the all-important first episode of *Justice Girl* that was set to premiere in just over seventy-two hours. To the outside world, his distant, strong, in-charge leadership veneer was firmly in place. But inside, as far as he was concerned, everything—his career, his employees, the legacy and survival of the Regal Network—was riding on the success of this one show. Time was running out, and as much as he hated to waste the precious twenty-five minutes it took to make the crosstown trip from his office, he made the best of the journey, fighting the swaying limo as he balanced a dozen costume drawings on his lap, flipping through them, until settling on one he liked. In the end, it was an obvious decision: Justice Girl's skirt would be shorter, her top more low-cut, and the cape would stay—it would look good in flying shots.

To maximize his time even more, his senior secretary, Mrs. Decosta, was riding next to him on the lumpy backseat. She was reading aloud (though with little emotion) the background information of each actor cast in the five lead roles. Seeing that Hogart had finished with the costume sketches, she handed him a crinkly stack of set designs without missing so much as a syllable. As Hogart pored through them, Mrs. Decosta returned her full attention to the cast bios. Normally, each actor would have been thoroughly vetted before being cast, but with so little time, the process had been reversed. Cast first, vet second. Though definitely not the preferred way of handling things, it was not unheard of to replace actors at the last minute—sometimes just moments before going on air—and surely, if need be, they could and would do it again. Fortunately, as she came to the end of her reading, Hogart had yet to hear anything alarming. The blacklist meant nothing to him; at best, it was an extreme annoyance he complied with, which made the rest of his nearly impossible job possible. Frankly, his solidly nonpolitical makeup made it an unspoken truth that if he could put the Communist Party of America's weekly meetings on the air and pull in a solid rating with a good share, all backed by a deep-pocketed sponsor, he would do it. But that being a ludicrous notion and with myriad forces waiting to jump on even the slightest seemingly un-American notion in one of his shows, he complied with a vengeance. After all, their attacks were bad for ratings. He was already taking a huge chance with Jonny and his unseen staff of writers who, almost assuredly, were all blacklisted. But in this, he had no choice.

Not for now, anyway.

With a quick scribble of his signature, he signed off on the set sketch he liked—there really wasn't much choice, once again, because of the time frame involved, so compromises were made. *Night Eye*, a hard-hitting drama about a detective who sleeps all day and works all night, had premiered not even two months previous on the Regal Television Network, with the idea that the mid-season replacement would revive an otherwise floundering Thursday night lineup. It was a resounding failure, with audiences quickly becoming bored with seeing the main character sneak around at night in almost entirely black sets. There was some discussion of giving Rock Branniggan, the main character, some daytime cases, but in the end, it was decided—largely because after Winston Tobacco backed out, no new sponsor stepped in—to just shut the show down. Fortunately, the minimal sets had yet to be thrown out, so they would be used as the basis for the new ones that would make up the world of Justice Girl. "Get these right over to the studio," Hogart said, handing the sketches back to Mrs. Decosta before dashing out of the limo.

He knew it was highly unusual for the head of the network to attend a first read-through of a script, even if it was the first episode, but as he strode through the weathered wooden front door, he knew there was no way he could stay away. Oh, sure, he had an important conference call with his Midwest affiliates, but none of his well-rehearsed hyperbole—"I see light at the end of the tunnel," "Things are definitely trending our way," or "We're so proud to have you as part of the Regal family"—would placate their understandable concerns about plummeting ratings as effectively as the presence of a new hit show in their Sunday night lineup.

Making his way deeper inside the Stardust Ballroom, with the scent of neglect and decay accompanying his every breath, Hogart was reminded of just how awful a place this was. He gingerly walked on the faded red carpet, its gold accents worn almost to the point of extinction, and was careful not to get too close to the walls, which were covered with water stains and peeling wallpaper. Most of the molding was long gone, replaced by shadowy lines as lingering reminders of better days. Hogart had frequented this place—and others like it around town—often during the earlier part of the decade, when he had been in the programming department and was on his way up the corporate ladder at Regal.

With the public's insatiable appetite for television—comedies, dramas, game shows, news shows, talk shows, sports shows, anything that could by fed to the bottomless stomach that was the viewing audience—studio space was at a premium and always in use. For seemingly less important things like rehearsals, costume fittings, casting sessions, and read-throughs, an informal network of disjointed structures, scattered all around the island of Manhattan, were put into use. Nothing was beneath their need—old stables, abandoned firehouses, foreclosed restaurants, and in this case, a sagging ballroom. The decaying building had made the long fall from being an elegant playhouse for the rich at the turn of the century to being largely unused, except for Friday and Saturday nights when a lonely-hearts club would use it to hold dances for unattached single men and women. That is, until the Regal Television Network stepped in and rented it five days a week as its primary rehearsal space.

Of course, Hogart could not have cared less about the history of the building. If need be, he would have had them work out of a whorehouse. All that mattered was that the show got on the air, one way or another.

Hogart yanked open the door to one of the small rooms that lined the hallway just off the main ballroom. Two seamstresses, their hands busy adjusting the costumes that hung on dress mannequins and their mouths filled with pins, looked up at Hogart, seemingly annoyed by the interruption. Whether or not they knew he was the head of the network, Hogart wasn't sure. But he was sure that they and everyone else connected to this new show were well aware of how little time they had to put it all together. And there was certainly no time to stand on ceremony.

From behind one of the half-dozen racks of costumes squeezed into this far-too-small room, the costume designer of *Justice Girl* emerged. Zelda Lopez, a squat, middle-aged women of not even five feet in her oversized heels, took one look at Hogart, and the pins that were in her mouth fell to the floor. She had gotten the job just two days earlier, having been pulled off—or more precisely, ordered off—*What's My Job?*, a moderately successful game show that filled the 7:00 p.m. slot on Mondays, Wednesdays, and Fridays, to take on this new show that was being launched in an unprecedented five days. She relished the challenge, having long since grown bored with the easy job of putting together the costume for the doctor or construction worker or soldier or policeman or whoever the contestant turned out to be at the big reveal at the end of the show.

Zelda knew this new show had top priority, but seeing the head of the network standing before her was clearly not something she was expecting.

"The drawing on the top—that's the one we're going with," Hogart said, holding it up for her. Zelda barely had a moment to see which of the costume drawings she had hastily done the day before had been selected before Hogart turned on his heels and left.

It was barely twenty more feet down the hallway to the arched entrance to the ballroom. Reaching it, Hogart stopped short, careful to be out of view to anyone inside. He pitched slightly forward, listening to the voices that echoed inside the cavernous space. Hogart had made sure to hire Arnold Lamasagne, an old, massively overweight network employee, as the show's floor director. True to his track record as a strict disciplinarian—the main reason Hogart had hired him—the reading had started exactly on time. Hogart looked down at his watch. He was now seventeen minutes late.

Perfect.

Hogart burst in and raced toward the far end of the empty ballroom, where the assembled cast and crew sat around a long rectangular worktable, an open script in front of each of them. Nearby, another contingent of crew sat in folding chairs, watching the reading. As Hogart moved briskly, a man in a hurry and clearly sorry he was late, he noticed that among the second group was the head of the Affiliates Department. *So, Affiliates decided to show up for a reading,* Hogart thought, amused and quietly pleased that the buzz from this new show was enough to get one of his executives to actually show interest.

The reading came to an abrupt halt when everyone finally noticed Hogart's approach. "Sorry; sorry," Hogart huffed between hurried breaths. When he reached the one empty chair, placed dramatically at the head of the table, the entire group rose out of respect. "That's okay. Please. Sit," he said, waving them off and succeeding in hiding his pleasure at their deference. He especially was pleased to see that Jonny begrudgingly acquiesced and rose. Part of Hogart's plan had been to send Jonny a little reminder of just who really held the power. Seeing everyone who Jonny felt he had under his thumb rise at Hogart's entrance sent the message Hogart wanted to send. Jonny may have won some battles over the last couple of days, most of them because of the time pressure they were under, but in the end, Hogart was the one in charge.

Hogart slipped into the metal folding chair, with Charles to his right and Lamasagne to his left. "Please continue," he said as everyone settled in again.

"Where were we?" Jonny asked Arnold Lamasagne, not entirely hiding his annoyance at the interruption.

Arnold searched his heavily annotated script. "I believe we had just finished scene three."

Hogart shot a look at Charles.

Charles nodded that he understood. "Actually," Charles said, addressing the entire group, "why don't we start from the top?"

"We don't really have time for that," Jonny shot back reflexively.

"Well, I think it would be a good idea," Charles answered.

"That's good to know," Jonny said, "however—"

"I think it's a good idea, too," Hogart interrupted. The entire group, who had been watching the exchange like a tennis match, turned en masse and looked to Jonny.

Jonny rolled his eyes. "Very well then, from the top," he said flatly.

A collective sigh fell over them, followed by a brief rustling of scripts as everyone turned back to page one.

"*Justice Girl*, episode one," Arnold began. "Scene one: Justice Girl's Home World. A beautiful, idyllic land, hidden high above in the clouds. A tall, handsome man, Justice Girl's father and the ruler of Nadaali, the cloud kingdom, walks into view, Justice Girl at his side."

As the first of the actors spoke, Hogart settled in, pleased with how the last ten minutes had gone. He had clearly established his authority, and he was winning his battle of wills with Jonny. But his good feeling didn't last long.

In fact, barely two minutes later, Hogart knew he had a problem. A big problem.

...

Felicity pursed her lips into a tight oval and carefully applied the brick-red lipstick. Though the mirror in her handheld compact was quite small, she finished the job with great efficiency, dabbing her lips together to evenly spread the enticing hue, despite being in the middle of 33rd Street and pressed tightly into a stone alcove to avoid the strong wind whipping across Manhattan. Stepping out into the thick flow of pedestrian traffic and bracing herself for the jostling that came with each hurried step, she rushed on to the appointment.

She eyed each passerby with growing disgust. How did people actually live like this? Rushing through stinking streets and dodging cars, cabs, buses, and each other—all against the disjointed symphony of honks and shouts and the ever-present loud, numbing, vibrating hum that pulsed from the very ground itself. The notion that she would soon be back home—where her world was one of calm, of slowly sloping hills, of lazy winding roads, of rich green shrubbery—instead of here among this world of crashing angles, jutting buildings, intersecting trolley tracks, and thrusting elevated train lines was what kept her moving as she sliced her way along the sidewalk.

Her plan was about to come to fruition; the early completion of her task was made possible by the target himself. Jonny had come up to her very shortly after the read-through had ended and asked if she would meet him, in private, in a couple of hours. She immediately agreed, knowing that the low-cut blouse she had worn had served its purpose. Before the read-through, nothing more than a brief head nod had passed between them, a perfunctory acknowledgement that they were prepared to work together as professionals and put what had happened just a few days ago behind them. But from the start, Felicity had other plans. When she sat down at her spot at the rehearsal table, careful to make sure Jonny was in sight, she slipped off her sweater to reveal her low-cut top. It worked. Out of the corner of her eye, she saw Jonny give her a slight once-over before returning his gaze to his script. So, when the reading was over, and he did eventually come up to her, she did her best to act surprised and delighted. *How delicious it is*, she thought as she rushed to meet him, *that this Commie was done in by his own base inclinations.* An hour alone with him, and she knew she'd get anything and everything she wanted out of him. Then she could end this thankfully short foray into filthy Manhattan and the seedy, dirty, Jewishy world of entertainment, once and for all.

Felicity found Jonny exactly where he said he would be—sitting on a bench in the small triangular park created by the awkward intersection of the diagonal Broadway and straight Fifth Avenue. Since Jonny had not spotted her yet, she gave her breasts a final enhancing adjustment for good measure. *He is toast*, she thought, closing in.

But just before she reached him, she slowed. He wasn't alone; Jonny was in deep conversation with a woman seated next to him on the bench. Did he have a girlfriend? This perilous thought hadn't even crossed her mind. Not that it really mattered. She could still get what she wanted from him. It just might take a bit more time. Or maybe this was just some random woman who'd sat down next to him, and he was chatting with her to pass the time until she arrived.

Felicity quickly got the answer. After a polite greeting—Jonny respectfully rose from the bench—but a cool one, Jonny turned to Felicity and said, "Denise Yarnell, I'd like you to meet a good friend of mine, Alexis Du Champ." Jonny nodded in the woman's direction.

Alexis also rose, standing several inches taller than Felicity, and sternly held out her hand. By any standards, she was an imposing figure, and as they shook hands—her grip firm but the skin surprisingly soft—Felicity gave her a closer look. She was almost six feet tall, dressed in a cascading loose-fitting cotton top of the darkest black that flowed over equally dark loose-fitting black pants. In stark contrast was her glowing white skin, visible only in small doses at her hands, ankles, and tight face. And topping it all, like a cherry atop a hot fudge sundae, was a thick mop of fiery orange-red hair that flowed down to her shoulders in a manner that defied any style, past or present. If Felicity had to guess, she would have said Alexis was mid-forties, but her look was so incongruous, so unable to categorize, that she wouldn't have been surprised if she were off by a decade in either direction.

Jonny cleared his throat. "Alexis is an acting teacher. A very good one," he said, almost succeeding in hiding his discomfort.

"That's wonderful," Felicity offered, confused, but with a genuinely pleasant smile in Alexis's direction. Alexis was stone-faced.

"I thought she might be of some help to you," Jonny continued.

"Why's that?"

"Well, you seemed to have some trouble at the reading this afternoon."

Really? Felicity thought. Sure, she had stumbled over some of the words, and she surely wasn't as polished as some of the other actors were, but hadn't she just received the script only the day before? Did they expect her to have memorized it already? No one said anything about that when they slipped it to her the day before at the publicity photo shoot. "I really don't think that's necessary," she shot back. "I'll do better next time." She smiled, knowing— or at least hoping—there would be no need for a next time.

"Can I talk to you in private?" Jonny said softly to her.

"Sure."

"Excuse us," Jonny said to Alexis, who, still quite stone-faced, nodded her consent.

Jonny eased Felicity over toward a pigeon-dropping-covered statue of Horace Greeley and carefully leaned close to her. "I don't have the time to be any more polite about this. You must let her help you—"

"I just mixed up a few words," Felicity snapped, feeling highly irritated. This was not going the way it was supposed to go. "I really think you are overreacting."

"Or else they are going to fire you," Jonny finished, just inches from her face.

Both his words and his closeness startled her, and she backed up, almost tripping over the knee-high concrete wall that surrounded the statue. She lowered herself and sat on the rough, cool surface. Fired? That would be a disaster. She would have gone through what she'd already gone through for nothing. Worse, she'd have to go back home to Greenwich, face her father, and tell him she had failed.

Jonny sat down next to her. "I don't have a lot of time for this today, so here it is: they want you out. But I think you at least deserve another shot. There's not a lot of time, but if anyone can make you better fast, it's Alexis."

What a choice, Felicity thought. *Waste time learning how to act or be thrown off the show before I can corner Jonny.* "Okay," Felicity answered, without looking at him.

Jonny stood up. ""Good. Then I'll leave you to it."

How strange is this? Felicity wondered as he started to walk away. *The very person I'm trying to destroy reaches out and saves me at the very moment my failure is all but assured. When it all comes out, with Father making the big reveal at a press conference, how wonderfully delicious it will be.* On the other hand, Felicity reasoned, Jonny was a smart guy; as her father always had warned her, these subversives were a clever lot. Was she missing something? Did he actually have something up his sleeve that she wasn't aware of? Felicity found herself calling after Jonny, "Why are you doing this?"

Jonny turned and gave her a sad smile. "I don't really know. To be honest, it would have been easy to let them fire you. It's really in my best interest to pick my battles with the network. But something tells me you're the right person for the role. I don't know why I feel that way, but I do." He took another step but then turned back. "Also, I think I may owe you one." Then, with a brighter smile and wink, he continued walking, giving Alexis a confirming nod on his way out of the park.

Felicity filled her lungs and then exhaled, letting her shoulders sink. Her whole body and mood followed suit, sinking lower, and the cold of the indifferent concrete began to seep through the thin cotton of her dress. If she wanted her plan to succeed, and she did, she'd have to last a few more days. She'd have to last long enough to get another chance to pry information out of Jonny. And apparently, that meant becoming a better actress.

Steeling herself, she stood up, brushed off her dress, and marched toward the unwelcoming Alexis Du Champ. Felicity tried again to break the ice with a smile; once again, Alexis gave her nothing. *If this is the price to pay,*

Felicity thought, *so be it*. In the end, her temporary discomfort was insignificant compared to what was at stake. If it took becoming a better actress, then a better actress she would become. After all, it was her patriotic duty.

...

The light fixture hit the concrete floor and shattered into a hundred small pieces. Jonny quickly sidestepped it and hurried on. On any other day, this would have brought the studio to a dead stop, but this was show day, and a knocked-over light barely raised an eyebrow. Nor was it really noticed over the loud din of sets being finished, equipment being moved into place, and orders being shouted, along with the rest of the chaotic preparations as actors and crew, like too many rats packed into one maze, scurried in every direction of the small, cramped studio.

Stepping over several snaking camera cords and ducking under a passing mic boom, Jonny caught a glimpse of one of the many studio clocks. It was persecuting him, taunting him, its sadistic hands telling him it was 7:17 p.m., and they were on the air, *live*, in fewer than fifteen minutes.

And there was no way in hell they were going to be ready in time.

Jonny walked between a pair of hurrying lighting technicians—one with a broom and dust pan, the other with a replacement fixture—and then cut around a makeup artist, just as Arnold Lamasagne stepped in front him.

"We're still long," Arnold said, showing him the script inside his open binder. "You have to give me the cuts, now!" But as Arnold stuck the script under Jonny's nose, the three silver rings popped open, and the pages poured out and onto the floor. "Shit!" Arnold exclaimed.

"I'll get back to you on that one," Jonny answered, rushing off as Arnold struggled to bend his enormous girth and pick up the scattered script pages.

Hoping to save time, Jonny cut through a small side set that was dressed to look like a shoe store. Immediately, a young assistant set dresser, who he kind of remembered as Neil, accosted him. Neil thrust two shoes in Jonny's face. "The people at Remington Shoes sent over a pair of shoes for us to use for their commercial, *both left-footed!*" Neil said in a panic.

Remington Shoes? Jonny wondered. *Why does that name sound so familiar, and why am I being bothered with this ridiculous detail?* But Jonny knew it would take more time to tell Neil to find someone else to deal with the crisis than to just give him a solution. "Instead of having both shoes on the actor," Jonny began, "have one on his left foot and the other about to be fitted on his right foot. But tell the actor playing the shoe clerk to never actually fit the shoe. No one will ever notice." And with that, Jonny hurried off, leaving behind a nodding Neil.

Passing behind a wall of flats, another clock caught his eye, tormenting him that they were now just ten minutes to being on air. Normally, on *Hermie's Henhouse*, by this time, he would be across the street in a bar with some of the other writers, drinking away the stress of having gotten the final writing done. Or maybe, if he had a sketch on that night he was particularly proud of, he'd have found a quiet corner of the control booth or, if he could get away with it, an empty seat in the cushy viewing area set up for *Hermie's* sponsors.

Sponsors?

Even with all that was going on around him, the word danced in his head. Remington Shoes was the sponsor of *Justice Girl*. They'd sponsored the entire half hour, covering the budget in return for a mention at the top of the show, and a big, fat, two-minute commercial in the middle, between the first and second acts, neatly dividing the additional twenty-eight minutes into two fourteen-minute segments. *This would be good*, Jonny guessed, *if I cared about such things.* In seemed to make Hogart happy, which was certainly good for Jonny, as it meant Hogart would leave him alone. Or at least there was a better chance Hogart would leave him alone. Remington Shoes? Why was that name so familiar? He shook it off—no time to think about it. For the first time in his career, Jonny was a producer, so everything, from something as important as the current crisis he was in, to something as trivial as mismatched shoes, was his problem. The buck stopped here, as one of his heroes had famously said.

Technically, Charles was his co-producer, but Jonny had worked it so that Charles was out of his hair and safely stuck inside the control booth, going over the shots with the show's director, Sal Reece. Sal was an almost-ten-year veteran of television, having been around since just after war. His veteran status in this infant medium, inhabited almost exclusively by the young and new, made him decidedly cranky and stubborn, so Jonny knew whatever Charles suggested, Sal would ignore, which was just fine with Jonny.

Jonny slipped around a pair of stagehands who were hammering as fast as they could, desperately trying to replace a section of wall to one of the sets that a camera had crashed through during the dress rehearsal. He leaped over a production assistant who was down on his hands and knees, hurriedly collecting the show's props that had scattered across the floor moments before, when a harried costumer, passing with a rack of costumes, had knocked over the prop table.

Finally, he arrived at his destination.

Standing at the entrance to the studio, next to the door that led from the long hallway where their dressing rooms were located, were the four lead actors of the show. They were, much to Jonny's relief, dressed in the costumes they needed for their first scene, along with tissue paper ringing their necks to keep makeup from smearing on their collars.

Remington Shoes? Why was that name so familiar? he wondered again, returning his attention to the four actors in front of him. "You wanted to see me?" Jonny asked, responding to a message one of them had sent. In the back of his mind, he was expecting trouble with the cast. This process had been so fast, so unusual, so haphazard when compared to the usual production of a live show, and the brunt of it had fallen on the cast. He was sure there would be some eventual pushback. His eyes landed on Felicity; he was sure she must be the source of this last-minute issue, whatever it was. Since hooking her up with Alexis, Jonny had noticed an improvement in her acting—slight but definitely noticeable. If nothing else, she seemed more focused, more locked in on the job at hand. Most important, it had been enough to get Hogart off his back and stay his insistence to replace her, if only for the one show.

Felicity and two of the actors looked at each other, confused. The fourth and youngest, Thomas Hughes, turned to Jonny. "Actually, it was just me,

Jonny. I was the one who wanted to see you." Thomas's voice cracked as he looked away, not wanting to make eye contact with anyone.

"Okay," Jonny answered, masking his surprise. He was sure Denise would be in full panic right about now and threatening to quit the show, but she wasn't. Instead, it was Thomas, and maybe it did make sense. At barely twenty-three, he had the least experience, with the exception of Denise. Thomas was a ridiculously handsome young man, over six feet tall, with pronounced features and thick, dark eyebrows that perfectly matched his thick, dark hair. His cheeks still got ruddy when he got excited or out of breath, and the touch of baby fat that softened his face only made the ladies like him that much more. He had come to acting late, having spent his high school and college years enjoying the good life as a star athlete before a particularly ferocious tackle in his final bowl game had put an end to it all. Fortunately, because of his good looks, he had done some male modeling during that time. When his athletic career was clearly over, he slid pretty easily into the world of show business. And quite amazingly, for someone seemingly a bit shallow and pampered, he was a darn good actor. Up until now, he'd had a succession of small roles—ironically, often playing athletes—but this was his first major role.

Now, Thomas began searching for his words. "I...uh...I...uh..." Jonny could see just how much trouble they were all in. Thomas's usual swagger, the kind women had swooned over since he was quite young and the reason he was cast to play the editor's playboy son, was gone. Also missing was the strong, confident posture that was a product of the world always being his for the taking. Instead, he was hunched over, his shoulders bunched up and pushed against his neck. "I...uh...don't know if I can do this," he finally finished, still unwilling to make eye contact with anyone.

This is bad, Jonny thought, his stomach sinking. *Really bad. Thomas can't possibly go on. Remington Shoes? Why was that name so familiar?* There it was again. Angrily, he shook the thought out of his head. He had a real crisis right in front of him. But what to do?

"Can't do this?" the older man next to Jonny mocked. "Well, you damn well better, my boy. Or we're all in a bit of a sort." Reginald Milo was in his late sixties and a veteran of stage, screen, radio, and most recently, television. His early career achievements could fill one side of a playing card with room to spare, but the last twenty years had been a very different story. In his forties, when his prematurely gray hair had quickly turned to white, he suddenly found himself cast in a series of screwball comedies as a stuffy, upper-crust husband/father/boss. Realizing that was his meal ticket, and despite being from a decidedly working-class neighborhood in Detroit, he had transformed his whole persona to that of an English blue blood—on screen and off—complete with tails, cane, and bowler. "Surely you can find the courage. After all," he added as a hopeful punctuation, "it's only television."

Now there's seasoned confidence, Jonny thought, looking up at Reginald. *But how to instill just a dash of some of that in Thomas?* Then he lightly sniffed the air, and Jonny's face wrinkled. "Give it to me," he said flatly to Reginald.

Reginald raised a single bemused eyebrow, a move that was almost his signature. "Whatever could you mean?"

"You know."

"I most certainly do not."

Jonny pointed away from them, across the studio. "Look! Ava Gardner!" The four actors all swiftly turned in the direction of his pointing finger. As Reginald spun around, the jacket of his Savile Row, double-breasted suit fell open, and Jonny reached between Reginald's lapels and pulled out a small bottle of whiskey.

Jonny held it out for all to see.

"I'm sure I have no idea how that got there," Reginald insisted, without even a hint of how ridiculous that sounded.

"Good, then you won't mind if I take it," Jonny said.

"Oh, come now. Be a sport, Jonny," Reginald said. "This whole show has been a bit of a whirlwind."

"I'd like some, too," Thomas said, reaching out desperately.

Jonny took a step back from both of them and slipped the bottle into his pants. *One lightly sauced actor*, he thought, *is a whole lot better than two completely drunk ones.* Realizing half his cast was struggling, he quickly checked in with the other two, first turning to the woman next to Reginald. She was in her early fifties; her hair was a stylish gray highlighted by the first wisps of white. Veronica Sanders had a striking, taut face, smooth skin, and pronounced cheekbones that made it hard to look away from her. Her dramatic features had arrived early, so she always had acted older than she was. At fourteen, she easily passed for eighteen, getting her first job as a chorus girl on stage. By her early twenties, she was working steadily in silents, often wearing a bathing suit or other sexy outfit. Her voice had an enticing purr, so she easily made the transition to talkies, often playing the bad girl or wild friend of the lead. She never had a lull in her career, smoothly making the transition from starlet to ingénue to established actress to character actress to sought-after veteran. So consistent was her employment that she was able to afford homes on both coasts.

"How are you doing?" Jonny asked her, hopeful she wasn't as stressed as the men.

"Oh, I'm just fine," Veronica answered assuredly. "Old hat." Indeed, it was, Jonny knew. Live was nothing new for her. Veronica worked a lot on television, and when she wasn't on the tube, she always found work in one Broadway show or another. She clearly had her nerves under control. "Been here dozens of times," she continued, smiling at Jonny. "Nothing to worry about, nothing at all." She then turned away and, barely missing Felicity, threw up into a nearby garbage can.

Felicity jumped back, almost bumping into Jonny.

Nervously, he looked into her face. Despite the start from Veronica's sudden attack of nerves, Felicity seemed oddly composed.

"Mind and body relaxed," she offered before he could inquire.

"Good. Good," he responded, greatly relieved. Alexis really was a miracle worker.

"Mind and body relaxed," Felicity said again.

Wow, Jonny thought, *Alexis really drums the stuff into her students. As long as it works.*

"Mind and body relaxed. Mind and body relaxed. Mind and body relaxed." The rapid pace of Felicity's words revealed that she was anything but.

Uh-oh, Jonny thought. What he had interpreted as calm was actually abject terror. Seven minutes to air, and all four of his leads were a mess. Unfortunately, Jonny knew it could get worse. And it did. From the other side of the studio, Arnold began to shout, "Five minutes! Five minutes! First positions!" Suddenly, standing before Jonny were four ghosts, as all of them went white with fear. "Five minutes! First positions!" Arnold continued shouting.

Something had to be done. Something fast. What he wanted to do was grab them all by the neck and squeeze. How dare they threaten all his— *all their*—brilliant work! The script had come out fantastic, better than he could have dreamed. The writers' room had been a pure joy, a swirling, creative cauldron with him, Annie, Shel, and Burton working together in unison, pounding through draft after draft in only six days. And now, a bunch of scared actors threatened to screw up the whole thing.

He thought of yelling at them, but other than making himself feel good, it wouldn't help; it'd only force them to retreat further inside themselves. Desperate, his mind drifted back to one of his first days working at *Hermie's Henhouse*. As the new man on the writing staff, he'd had the unenviable task of being the one who had to stick with Hermie during the live broadcast. He'd had to follow Hermie around the studio as Hermie went from set to set and slipped in and out of costumes in case Hermie wanted to punch up any scenes at the last minute or needed to write material based on something that had happened on the show—like the time Jane Russell almost popped out of her dress during a sketch about the Old West. On that particular day, Montgomery Clift was the guest—a wonderful actor who had little theatre experience and no live television experience. Montgomery was dropped in to a recurring sketch of Hermie's, where he played an American Indian who always had some sort of comic interaction with the white man. As he was about to go on, dressed in his cavalry outfit, Montgomery lost it. "I can't do it! I can't do it!" he shouted over and over.

They were less than one minute from going on the air. Hermie grabbed him, looked straight into his eyes, and began to talk. It worked. Two minutes later, as Montgomery scurried off to his first position for the sketch, Hermie turned to Jonny and said, "Back in vaudeville, that's what we called the 'the big distraction.'"

Yes, that's what needs to be done, Jonny thought. *If it worked on Montgomery Clift, it sure as hell ought to work on these four.* "Okay, listen up, all four of you," Jonny said sternly, moving his gaze from face to face to face to face. "Fall in." They all looked at him blankly. "I said, *fall in!*" He punctuated his words by pointing dramatically at the floor in front of him. They quickly surrounded him in a tight huddle. Jonny turned to Thomas. "In your first scene, I want you to cut the last four lines of your monologue about your night out on the town. Got it?"

Thomas's eyes rolled back in his head as he thought for a second. "Got it," he said, suddenly focused.

Jonny turned to Veronica and Reginald. "In the second scene you guys have in Margaret's office, end the scene after the phone call. Okay?"

Veronica and Reginald squinted their eyes for a second, thinking. "Okay," they said in unison.

Finally, Jonny turned to Felicity. "After you untie Chance in the final scene, cut your entire page of dialogue except for 'Justice is served' then leave. Sound good?"

Felicity nodded quickly, taking in his words. "Sounds good."

Arnold approached them. "Five minutes! First positions!" All four actors nodded to Arnold, gave a reassuring nod to Jonny, and then turned to head off to their first positions. Jonny reached out and stopped Felicity. When she turned back to face him, Jonny snatched the ring of tissue paper from around her neck.

"Thanks," Felicity said, genuinely appreciative.

Jonny smiled. "No problem. Break a leg."

Felicity nodded her thanks.

"Or should I say, 'break a jaw,'" he added, playfully rubbing his cheek where Felicity had slapped him almost exactly a week earlier.

Felicity spit out a short, hard laugh—clearly relieved that they had finally dealt with the incident—and then turned and ran off to her first position.

Pleased, Jonny watched her disappear but then realized the other three actors all still had tissue hanging around their necks. He started to go after them, but Arnold blocked his way. "I need the final cuts, now!" Arnold said, carefully holding forward his reconstructed script binder.

Jonny pulled a pen from his pocket and quickly rifled through the script, scratching out four lines here, a half a page there, and then, with a final flourish, he ripped out an entire page, curled it up in a ball, and threw it on the floor. "Done," he said with finality.

"Control booth, I got the final cuts. Here they come," Arnold said, walking away and relaying Jonny's work as he went. Jonny watched him go and then suddenly, unbelievably, he was alone. No one said a word to him. No one bothered him. No one came to him to solve a problem. Alone. This was it. It was about to happen. Ready or not, it was about to spill out into thirty million homes across the country. Warts and all.

He looked up at the clock—one minute left, and the second hand was making its final orbit around the clock face. Terrified, Jonny slowly wandered out onto the floor. Despite being mere moments from air, everyone was still rushing in every direction, futilely trying to get control. A shudder ran through Jonny's body. They weren't ready, and they weren't going to make it. They were driving over a cliff, with him at the wheel. He turned to the row of sets lit by hot, angry lights and surrounded by vulturistic cameras that waited to absorb the whole chaotic disaster and spray it sadistically across the nation. He watched the second hand above his head clear the six and begin the sweep upward. Less than thirty seconds. Less than thirty seconds until the end of his career.

And then, as it always somehow did, everything suddenly worked out: the broken light was just done being fixed, the damaged wall was just finished being repaired, the prop table was just back to its original position, and the tissue was just removed from every one of the actors' necks. It was the only time Jonny was inclined to believe in the Divine.

Finally, with the second hand of the clock sweeping toward the twelve, Jonny collapsed against the studio wall. From his spot, looking through the spindly tentacles of the studio's permanent wiring, he could just see the glowing blue of the monitor at Arnold Lamasagne's floor director station. *I'll watch the show from here*, he thought. The grip of the heavy black curtain covering the bare concrete wall helped keep him on his feet. The thick burlap was surprisingly soft and warm, and he allowed himself a long, relieved exhale. He fished Reginald's whiskey out of his pants and took a good-sized, satisfied gulp. Whether destined to be a huge success or a dismal failure, he knew he had worked as hard as humanly possible and had done all he could. Now it was time for his work to be judged. And he felt good.

Then, he suddenly remembered where he'd heard of Remington Shoes.

...

Not even thirty miles away, within the sturdy walls of Hogart's comfortable home, things were considerably calmer. Just as it had been a week ago—*had it really only been a week?*—Hogart was seated alone at the dinner table overlooking the living room, where his two children fought their way through a game of checkers and his wife perused her catalogs. The television played largely unnoticed, as on its bluish-white screen another episode of *Square Dance Round-Up* ended. To anyone viewing from the outside world, this was just another Sunday with just another family enjoying just another quiet night at home.

Nothing was further from the truth.

Inside Hogart, a storm raged, a collision of dramatic forces no less chaotic than what was going on in that studio in the center of Manhattan— the source of all his stress. He went through it all again: the newspaper ads had been run; the radio commercials had been played; and the quick teases had been placed in the beginning, middle, and end of other Regal Network shows. All three ratings services had been hired to do analysis of how the episode was going; the sponsor had been successfully made to feel important; and even the ad agencies—a group Hogart had ignored by going around them and procuring the sponsor himself—had been successfully mollified by the offer of discount airtime for some of their other shows. Yes. Yes. He had done everything he could.

He checked his watch again, something he had been doing compulsively for the last five or six hours—all through his son's Little League game, his daughter's recital, and finally, through their Sunday dinner—and seemingly always caught by his wife, who would give him a playfully disappointed head shake.

Now, finally, after this one last gaze to his wrist, they were just seconds from going on the air. Early on, he had extinguished the urge to be in the studio, knowing that at this point, his presence would only cause trouble. He had signed off on everything, even if Jonny more or less ignored what he had to say, and any changes at this point would be minor at best. Besides, even though tomorrow he would voraciously dissect the reviews and any and all ratings data, he knew the true test of how the show was going over would be revealed right here, tonight, in his very own living room.

"You're watching the Regal Television Network," the familiar deep-voiced announcer said dramatically as the simple crown-shaped logo splashed onto the screen.

Hogart shifted in the stiff wooden chair, keenly aware of the importance of the moment. His wife gave him a quick glance before returning to her catalogs.

"Born into privilege on a distant world..." a stern, determined voice began over a black screen. It faded up to reveal the silhouetted image of a young woman against a white background. "But then falsely accused of a crime..."

Now the silhouette of a much larger man joined the woman, pointing accusingly at her.

"She is banished forever to a distant planet..."

The silhouette dejectedly departed from a crowd of disapproving silhouettes.

"Where she struggles to make herself a new home."

The silhouette of the young woman stopped, her whole figure turning toward the audience and filling the screen.

"And because she never forgets what brought her here, she fights every day for what's good and right and honest."

The full-screen, dark silhouette began to lighten, and then it was slowly replaced by the resolute figure of a strong, powerful, attractive blonde woman in boots, short skirt, low-cut top, and cape, standing forth, hands on hips, ready for any and all comers. Emblazoned across her chest were the letters "J. G." And then, with a swell of loud, triumphant music, one final intonation: "For *this* is…Justice Girl!"

Suddenly, in a display better than even Hogart could have hoped for, both of his children jumped to their feet and started cheering. "Mommy, look what's on!" his excited daughter exclaimed.

"Yes. Yes," his wife answered, also clearly happy.

Hogart had to admit that, despite still not being completely sold on Denise Yarnell as the right actress for the role, she made an impressive sight with her blonde hair and well-fitting costume that highlighted her obvious attributes. The opening credits had been filmed the day before, and this morning, Hogart, having made a rare trip into Manhattan on a Sunday, had signed off on this sequence. Jonny had first suggested that they pre-film the opening titles before going to the live broadcast for the rest of the episode, and in one of the few agreements they'd had during the hectic week, Hogart had gone along with the idea wholeheartedly. In his eyes, it was a no-brainer. It assured that they would start the show with a bang, a little something that would catch the eye of the viewer. And if the show was a success, they could reuse it over and over again, week after week. Jonny had had some crazy ideas of what exactly this sequence should be, but Hogart had fought him on it, and because the money necessary to shoot the sequence was not in the original budget and would have to be secured from a fund that Hogart controlled, he had won. So Hogart steered it in the direction he wanted, standing up to Jonny's bellicose screams of "It's such an obvious rip-off!" This had really thrown Hogart. So what if it was derivative? If it worked for another hit show, wasn't that a good thing?

The sequence went on, with another image appearing over the stunning, ready-for-action Justice Girl.

"Hidden from friend and foe alike, she goes about her day as the innocent Sally Smalls, obedient secretary, working hard at *Focus on Fashion* magazine." The image of Justice Girl was gone, replaced by a mousy woman dressed in a drab dress, with dark hair poorly cut in a short, almost impish hairstyle, and oversized horn-rimmed glasses. Even Hogart, who knew full well that this, too, was Denise—especially as he had been standing not ten feet away when the shot was made—found the contrast stunning. Whether she could act the role was still to be determined, but there was no doubt she had pulled off the look—both of them.

Next, as the music became a bit more playful, the rest of the cast appeared in single shots, tailored to the character each was playing on the show. Reginald made an elaborate bow, appropriate for the staid, standoffish, man-of-substantial-means publisher he was playing. Veronica gave the camera an icy stare before relaxing her expression just a touch, so the audience knew that, despite the fact that she was Sally Small's boss, she could also be nice, if only occasionally. And finally, Thomas gave the viewers a big "Aren't I a handsome devil?" smile, before punctuating it with a knee-weakening wink for the ladies.

But as successful as this part of the show was, Hogart had stopped watching closely. His mind had wandered. Something was wrong…something minor. Small, but still important. It took a second, but then it crystallized in his mind. It wasn't that something was wrong; it was that something was missing. A name. An important name.

Remington Shoes.

Remington Shoes was supposed to be announced at the top of the broadcast. "Remington Shoes presents" was what the hastily agreed-upon deal memo had stated would begin each broadcast, but, as Hogart was realizing, it had not happened. In his weariness and excitement at the broadcast finally beginning, he had initially missed the omission. Perhaps this was what had happened in the studio, too—either it was completely forgotten, or the audio channel wasn't open when the announcer made the introduction. One way or another, someone would have to pay on Monday. Hogart's mood soured further. Then there'd be the angry call from Yardley Tipton, the owner of Remington Shoes. He and Hogart were old army buddies, and Hogart had personally lobbied for and then negotiated the sponsorship deal. Now that was coming back to bite him on the ass. He wouldn't be able to pawn this off on some flunky in the advertising department. He'd have to take the call and the abuse personally. "Hogie, my friend, you've gone and screwed me good this time," he could hear

Tipton shouting into the phone in his Texas drawl. Hogart would have to give him a free spot on another of their shows. Or maybe—just maybe—he would catch a break, and the numbers from the broadcast would be so good that the two-minute commercial in the middle of the show would satisfy Tipton. *Yes. Yes. That might just do it*, Hogart concluded. Two minutes devoted to nothing but the greatness of Remington Shoes on a top-rated show just might make three forgotten words be forgotten.

At the end of the opening credits and as the first live scene faded up and shined brightly on the TV, Hogart focused back on the episode. And as the broadcast proceeded, Hogart began to swell with confidence that he might just survive the opening mishap without an angry phone call, maybe not even a slightly miffed one. As he watched, the corners of his mouth tugged upward in a partial grin. What was happening on the screen was nothing short of a revelation. A miracle. Hogart was, by no means, an expert on storytelling, but that was part of his success, knowing what he did not know—and, frankly, not caring what he did not know. He saw only the broad strokes, the overall.

And the overall was working perfectly. There was an ease, a confidence, a surety to what was dancing across his television screen at that moment. He had the hit he needed, the one he had prayed for—the one that just might save the whole damn network.

As the show went on, he became surer and surer of this impending salvation; he only needed to look as far as his living room for final confirmation. His two children and his wife were completely enthralled. They all squealed with delight when Justice Girl, in her public identity as Sally Smalls, was hired to be the magazine editor's secretary because, using her superpowers, she was able to type two dozen letters in a matter of seconds. They all laughed when the silly and foppish publisher, Benjamin Portis III, tried to put his foot down on Margaret Crawford's out-of-control spending, only to have her hilariously manipulate him into giving in to her yet again. The only chink in this impressive storytelling armor was when the rakish and charming Chance Crawford came to visit after another night out on the town, making Sally Small swoon, along with Hogart's wife and daughter, but it lost his son, if only for a split-second. But the first half of the show, coming to an exciting conclusion, sucked Tommy back in. Now, Hogart's wife and two children were on the edge of their seats, almost as if they were being pulled into the TV screen, as Chance Crawford was kidnapped by several hulking, sinister figures that'd been hiding in the shadows at Baron Von Fugle's fashion show, the biggest event of the year. As they pulled Chance Crawford into the darkness and the screen faded to black, even Hogart felt tension in the pit of his stomach.

His thoughts drifted to Yardley Tipton, who no doubt would be feeling the same exhilaration. The timing was exquisite, and Hogart could imagine Tipton in the cozy den of his sprawling ranch house, scotch in one hand and cigar in the other, seated in one of his overstuffed leather chairs, his big black cowboy boots resting proudly atop a cowskin ottoman, his body pitched forward, and his gaze sharply focused on his television screen. The tension of the ending would still be palpable when *bam*, the commercial would come on—two solid minutes promoting *his* company.

And Tipton new a lot of other rich people—dozens of wealthy manufacturers scattered throughout the South, who, seeing his success, would be desperate to join the parade. And Hogart just happened to have several shows in need of new sponsorship. He'd do the deals himself, once again going around the ad agencies, maybe even breaking their stranglehold on the network once and for all.

It would be a triumph.

Hogart sat back, satisfied. But just as quickly, his reverie ended. The show started right back up, with no interruption—no commercial break! Any mention of Remington Shoes, not to mention the entire two-minute commercial spot, was nowhere to be seen.

Had they gone long? Had someone cut the commercial for time? No, that was impossible. No one had that authority, except for him. And he'd certainly not given the order. But just in case, Hogart checked his watch. It was seven forty-four. The first act had ended on time. Now there was supposed to be two minutes for the ad; then back for act two at seven forty-six. But instead, it was seven forty-four, and the second act was already underway.

What the hell was going on?

Hogart leaped out of his chair and grabbed a nearby phone. He frantically dialed, trying to get hold of the control room in the studio. It wasn't easy; the show was so new that the operators at the network—really only on the job in the evening to record the incoming comments from viewers about the programming—had trouble locating the number for the direct line. While getting the answer to the very troublesome mystery consumed Hogart, he was missing the rest of the broadcast. He missed a great scene, revealing that Chance Crawford's kidnappers were actually some of the baron's workers, the same workers who had made the clothes for the very fashion show they were all attending. In desperation, they had kidnapped Chance, hoping to use him to bring attention to the abuse that the baron dished out to them. Hogart was so caught up in his own drama that he even missed the explosive cheering from his children and wife when Justice Girl burst in and saved the day—the baron himself had taken Chance from his kidnappers and was about to kill him to make it look like it was the work of his workers.

Finally, after a lot of yelling, Hogart got through.

"Control room," Charles answered softly, not wanting to interfere with the chaotic shouting in the background, which was actually Sal Reece's "calling the show," or as the crew might describe it, "being told what to do."

"What the fuck is going on!" Hogart shouted into the receiver.

"Hogart?" was all Charles could utter. "What can I help you with?"

"*What can you help me with?*" Hogart screamed back. "What can you help me with? How about, what the fuck happened to my commercial?"

"Jonny canceled it," Charles said, way too casually for Hogart's taste.

"*Canceled* it? On whose authority?"

"His own. Believe me, I fought with him, but *he's* the executive producer."

Hogart twitched; he couldn't believe what he was hearing. If he hadn't needed the conversation to continue, he would have slammed the receiver down onto the table, hoping it would explode into a dozen pieces. Instead, he exhaled sharply. "Well, on *my* authority, which I'm pretty sure trumps Jonny's, I want the commercial back in. Now."

"Can't do it."

"I don't care if it screws up the story. Do it. Now!"

"It's not that. There's no talent. Jonny sent home the actors who were supposed to do the commercial."

Realizing there was now no reason for the conversation to continue, Hogart slammed the receiver onto the table. As he had hoped, it broke into a dozen pieces. Furious, he began to punch the air. Caught up in his fury, he missed the very end of the episode, with Justice Girl turning right into the camera and saying, "Justice is served!" And then she flew away.

His two children and wife gave the episode a spontaneous round of applause—a reaction beyond anything Hogart could have hoped for. Only he wasn't listening.

All he could think of was how shitty tomorrow was going to be.

...

Felicity warily stepped out of the cab and onto the deserted sidewalk. She looked down at the address on the crumpled slip of paper in her hand; it did indeed match the building in front of her. *This must be the place*, she thought, but looking around, she couldn't help but have doubts. The building was run-down, in desperate need of new paint and basic repair. The streets were empty, except for one or two scavenging animals who rifled through various tipped-over garbage cans. And there was an eerie silence, as if anyone who did happen to live in this godforsaken part of the city was too afraid to come out.

Not exactly the place for an after-party.

She turned around to check with the cab driver, but he was already gone, speeding away down the block. Even he wanted the hell out of this part of town. Felicity checked the paper one last time; unfortunately, the address still matched the beaten building in front of her, so she headed up the crumbling front steps. The front door was an uninviting dark slab of cracked glass, but amazingly, there was a call box. The cover was smashed, the speaker hung outside its socket, and the names were faded with several missing letters. But with some deductive reasoning, Felicity found the right name. Holding out a tentative finger, and thankful she was wearing gloves, Felicity pushed the filthy button and waited.

She had absolutely no desire to be here, but after the show had ended and everyone gathered for a round of congratulatory hugging, Felicity had tried to get close to Jonny. All week long he had proved an elusive target as he ran to put out one fire and then the next, and everyone else on the show just shrugged when she asked if he was the only one writing the show. But now that the show had aired, she figured she could finally get to him. He would probably have his guard down and she could get the information she needed with some clever questioning.

But he had disappeared.

She inquired after him—subtly, of course—but no one had an answer, except to say he would certainly be at the after-party. It was finally Thomas who offered her an invitation and the address to the party. So instead of heading over to Grand Central and hopping on a train that would take her the hell out of the city, she slipped into a cab and headed downtown to the west side and an apartment near the Holland Tunnel.

She tried the grimy button again. Still nothing happened. No inquiring voice. No buzz to let her in. Maybe she'd been given the wrong address.

Then the door opened from the inside, and a man scurried out in a rumpled gray suit and shapeless gray hat. He walked straight toward Felicity.

"Excuse me?" she asked. "Do you know if—?"

But the man kept on going, seemingly not even seeing her. Quickly, Felicity snagged the filthy door—again thankful she was wearing gloves—just before it slammed shut, and she slipped inside.

The hallway was narrow and dark, and two of the three overhead fixtures were burned out. She stepped gingerly across the cracked cement floor, found the elevator, and pushed the call button. Immediately, the elevator wheezed to life, creakily descending. *Can this really be the place?* she wondered as the elevator took its time reaching the first floor.

As if in answer, Felicity watched as a cab pulled up, and Jonny jumped out. So she was in the right place. If she was lucky, maybe she could get the information from him in the elevator on the way up and then not even have to go to the party. As he bounded up the front steps, she rushed to open the dingy front door for him. Before she reached it, Jonny pulled open the unlocked front door and walked straight into the hurrying Felicity. They came together in a jumbled collision, Felicity's forehead smacking into his mouth.

Startled, they separated, Jonny rubbing his face. "You really have a thing for my jaw, Denise," he said with a smile.

Having become accustomed to being called Denise, Felicity only flinched for a split second. Then, returning to the embarrassment of the moment, she looked away. Though Jonny had made a joke about it, they'd never really talked about what had happened when she'd slapped him. "About that...I've been meaning to—"

The elevator announced its arrival with a ding. Jonny's eyes went wide. "It's working! Come on!" He grabbed Felicity's hand and pulled her toward it. They both hopped inside, and Jonny pushed the button for their floor. The crooked doors stammered shut, and the elevator began its halting ascent.

They rode in silence, both staring at the closed door in front of them. Finally, Felicity turned to him. "I thought things went really well tonight."

Still looking straight ahead, Jonny bobbed his head with a slight frown. "All things considered, not bad." Then he turned to her. "You did a good job."

"Thanks." Then, almost surprised, Felicity added, "It was fun."

"And I could see that your working with Alexis made a huge difference."

"Yes, it did." She nodded for emphasis. It was also the main reason it had been fun. Given the little time they had, Alexis had spent their few hurried sessions concentrating on basic relaxation exercises. "Relaxing, my dear, is the key to it all," she had said repeatedly as she made Felicity take deep breaths—telling her to fill her abdomen all the way to her sex—and then release them in a slow, smooth pattern. Just before going on the air, after Jonny's fortunate interference had interrupted her panic attack, she had employed Alexis's techniques, and they had worked. By achieving calm, she found herself open and ready, and most important, she listened. She heard what the other actors were saying and trying to do, and she reacted accordingly—not as herself but as Justice Girl. She would say a line, one of the actors would say one back, and she found herself reacting to it, as if the actor were really saying it to her. She found herself in a glorious tennis match, but instead of balls, they were hurling lines of dialogue at one another.

"I think the script really turned out nicely, too," Felicity added, trying to turn the conversation in the direction she wanted.

"Thank you."

"That's gotta be a lot of work, writing."

Jonny shrugged. "It's what they pay me for."

"But still..." Felicity paused, knowing she had to tread carefully here. "You ever thought about getting some help?"

Jonny raised a curious eyebrow.

Had she gone too far? Had she blown the whole thing already?

The elevator reached their floor, and the door stuttered open. Loud waves of music, laughter, and shouting hit them. Without answering her question, Jonny stepped off the elevator. Should she ask again? Or would that be pushing it, she wondered, making him suspicious? Or should she be patient, hoping he would offer her an answer in another moment or two? Felicity silently followed Jonny.

The hallway was not much better than the lobby. Fortunately, the door to the apartment was open and shooting a shaft of light, like a beacon, into the dark hallway. They both headed toward it, and the party sounds grew louder and louder with each step. Reaching the door, Jonny stepped inside, but when Felicity saw what was in front of her, she stopped cold.

Through a hazy film of cigarette smoke, she saw a tiny, cramped apartment stuffed with a wide variety of party guests. They sat, stood, and lay on chairs, couches, and tables, while drinking from bottles, cans, and cups, all the while engaging in animated conversations, arguments, and monologues. Scattered trays of picked-over food doubled as dumping areas for used napkins, spent cigarettes, and other trash. Sounds from a screeching record player mixed in with the din of the loud voices to make an almost ear-shattering concoction, and in one corner, for some reason, lights appeared to be turning on and off. Overwhelmed, and more than a bit disgusted, Felicity hung back by the door. Even if she'd wanted to enter this chaotic cesspool, she wasn't sure if there was room.

As if sensing her discomfort, Jonny stepped out of the wall of people and moved up beside her. "Fear not. I promise there is enjoyment to be found inside."

Felicity nodded in agreement but not particularly convincingly. "It's just not what I'm used to." Indeed, it wasn't; her last party had been late-afternoon cocktails at Braeden's estate to celebrate the arrival of a promising new foal. The thirty or so guests had glided easily about the back veranda, sipping drinks delivered on silver trays by a myriad of servants, as a soft, warm breeze greeted the setting sun. It was all set to the comforting sound of Brahms, performed by a small chamber orchestra.

"Then let's break it down," Jonny said optimistically. "Get the lay of the land."

"Know thy enemy?" Felicity said, joining in.

"Exactly." They both turned to look at the crowded jumble. "Basically, you've got two groups here," Jonny explained. "My friends, writers and actors, who tend to congregate around the food." He pointed toward the packed living room and the coffee table with its stripped-bare food trays. "They ask each other what they are doing, and either lie in response or hide their jealousy at the answer. Then you've got Annie's friends—that's whose apartment this is."

"Annie? What does she do for a living?" Felicity asked, hoping it might just be this easy.

"She works in a gallery. You know, the ones that are all over Soho."

Felicity didn't, but she nodded anyway.

"Her friends," Jonny continued, "tend to hang around the booze." Jonny pointed to the tiny dining area, where about fifteen people were jammed into a space not big enough for five, all surrounding a round Formica table that was littered with several dozen empty wine bottles. "They're a touch older than the first lot, artists and poets, and love to tell each other about the latest art gallery they went to in Harlem or a great Ethiopian restaurant they found in Alphabet City—not the fake Ethiopian you get in the Village, mind you, but the real deal."

Felicity nodded, taking it all in and wondering if she should be taking notes.

"Then there's a third group, really a subset of the first group." Jonny pointed past the dining area into a small, dark nook that was the kitchen, where five people—one woman and four men—were locked in an intense conversation. "I like to call them the Process Heads. They're all actors. And I mean, *actors*." His sarcasm was not subtle. "They like to talk about being in the moment, taking risks, finding their inner cores, and all the rest of the masturbatory stuff that goes into 'great' acting." Jonny threw open his hands. "So there you have it." He winked at her. "Have fun."

He stepped away, but Felicity knew this might be her last chance tonight, so she had to take a risk. She placed a hand on his shoulder, stopping him. "Jonny, you never told me if you've considered using other writers."

This time there was no doubt; Jonny raised his eyebrow again, and his look was definitely one of suspicion. She'd done it; she'd gone too far. But just as quickly, his eyebrow lowered, and he shrugged. "They pay me to write, so I write." With that, he disappeared into the party.

Felicity watched him go, feeling defeated. Despite his helpful descriptions and insightful dissection, she still found the party more than a bit intimidating. She was not used to dealing with these types of people. They were uncouth and ill-mannered. The women smoked openly, the men wore hats indoors, many men weren't even wearing a tie, and everyone shouted over all the noise. But if she could find a way to navigate these difficult and uncharted waters, she decided, maybe her situation wouldn't be hopeless. If Jonny was using other writers—blacklisted ones, according to the tip—someone else was bound to know, someone else who just might be at this party. She would ask subtly and carefully and see what she might find out. Then another thought occurred to her, and this one made the sides of her lips curl upward. Perhaps the other writers, the blacklisted ones, might themselves be at this party at this very moment.

Steeling herself, Felicity waded into the mob, heading for the living room and the pack of actors and writers. She spotted several actors from the show, including Thomas, who was talking excitedly with someone who seemed about the same age as Felicity. Here at the party, Thomas's manner was much looser than what she'd seen at rehearsals and in the studio. His gestures were bigger, his whole being more flamboyant. There was something almost feminine about him, quite a contrast to the strutting playboy he played on the show or even the cocky ex-athlete she'd seen standing around before and after rehearsals. When he saw Felicity, he greeted her with a genuine smile. She was introduced all around to the rest of the living room group, and several people congratulated her on the show, though Felicity had the distinct sense that they didn't really meant it. Her entreaties into who might be writing the show along with Jonny, asked in a subtle, off-hand way, went nowhere.

Frustrated, she moved on to the cadre of poets and artists. This went even worse. Beyond a couple of indifferent nods in her direction, no one paid her any particular notice, and when she brought up the show, none of them were even aware of it, most of them proud to proclaim that they didn't even own a television set.

Her last chance was the grouping in the kitchen.

The five Process Heads, as Jonny had called them, were locked in a fierce conversation, all talking at once, forehead veins throbbing, hands gesturing wildly, and smoke from their chain-smoked cigarettes billowing in all directions. Since no one acknowledged her approach, Felicity pretended to look through a cupboard to mask her presence as she tried to overhear their conversations. Almost immediately, things sounded promising. She kept hearing the word "Stanislavski" repeated over and over. When she listened further, she discovered he was a person; someone they greatly admired. She wasn't familiar with the name. Stanislavski? Perhaps lesser known than Marx or Engels but a writer of Communist ideology? Or maybe a Communist Party leader, perhaps the head of the local chapter they all belonged to? Ultimately, it didn't really matter; the name was Russian, so clearly, she'd hit pay dirt. They were obviously Communists; after all, who else in this day and age would talk so warmly of a Russian. Her heart began to race. Maybe they were the rumored blacklisted writers working on the show.

Needing to hang around longer, Felicity moved on to another cupboard. But as she rummaged about, leaning in the direction of the conversation as much as she could without being too obvious, her mood soured. It turned out that none of the group was a writer; they were all actors. And worse, Stanislavski wasn't even a Communist; he was an acting teacher. A dead one.

Defeated again, Felicity shut the cupboard. It was time to move on to some other possible suspects. It would be so much easier if she knew what a Communist looked like, but wasn't that ultimately the heart of the problem? *They look like you and me,* she told herself, *and they are everywhere.* Or maybe she should locate Jonny and give him another stab. Perhaps he'd had a couple of drinks by now and might be more open to probing.

But as she turned to walk away, she suddenly found herself stopping and listening again. The Process Heads had moved on to a heated discussion of character backstory, debating ferociously just how much an actor needed to know about his character's life before the action of the story took place—what the character had been doing before those tantalizing first words on page one of a script. It was more of the bullshit that Jonny had so correctly labeled it, but she found it oddly intriguing. *What exactly was Justice Girl doing before she decided to get a job at* Focus on Fashion? *Sure, there was some information in the opening credits, but it didn't say how long she had been there. Or what she did when she first arrived on Earth.* Felicity decided to stay and listen, just a little while longer. She knew she was letting herself be drawn away from the mission, but it would only be momentary. And it had the added benefit of giving Jonny more time to drink.

...

Having successfully launched Denise, Jonny walked through the party, heading for Annie's bedroom. Along the way, many of the guests, most of whom were friends, gave him congratulatory head nods. He smiled politely, wondering what this same walk would be like next week. Would he receive excited nods and slaps on the back, or would everyone look away as he passed?

As usual, a crowd stood around in Annie's bedroom, smoking, drinking, and laughing, while a pair of couples fought for space on the bed to make out. Jonny passed by them, stepping out the open window and onto the fire escape. With the noise of the party still his companion, the glittering lights of New Jersey greeted him from across the Hudson. Jonny watched the busy river traffic, as tugs pulled ships both out to sea and into the harbor. He wondered where he was on his journey. Was he just being pulled out to sea to begin a long, arduous but exciting and adventurous trip? Or was he being tugged back to the harbor to eventually be mothballed and forgotten?

Suddenly, the window behind him slammed shut, cutting him off from Annie's bedroom. Jonny jumped at the sound, not sure how to react. But when his shock subsided, he began to feel strange. The sounds of the party were gone, blocked by the thick glass and replaced by the throbbing hum of the city. More strikingly, Jonny realized that, for the first time in a week, he was alone. Oh sure, he'd had a stolen moment here or there to himself, but the show had always been with him, consuming his thoughts. But not now—he could do nothing but wait. It was hard for him to believe that, just a week earlier, he had been out of a job, but now, just seven days later, he had written and produced a half-hour of network television.

Looking back through the closed window, he watched the party in silence. The crowd in Annie's room had thinned out, perhaps in response to the heated action on the bed, and Jonny could see through her doorway into the living room. Denise seemed to be doing well, really making an effort to enjoy the party by moving from person to person. *It's good that she's being so open and social*, Jonny thought. Perhaps he had been wrong about her. She had clearly responded well to Alexis's training, and her acting had significantly improved to the point that, given how well she did in the pilot, Jonny was almost certain he wouldn't have to fight any more battles with Hogart over her. He found, much to his surprise, that he liked her. Their repartee just a few minutes ago had been fun, and he liked that she seemed to have a lot of interest in him. Usually, with women, he was the one asking all the questions, but she really seemed to want to know all about him. And it certainly didn't hurt that she was easy on the eyes—those long legs and curvy thighs that couldn't stay hidden in that ruffled dress, her striking face, and her gorgeous hair. Jonny caught himself. What the hell was he doing? The last thing he needed was to get involved with an actress on his own show. Besides, he could see from the way she carried herself that she was way out of his league. This was a well-bred woman, a product of country clubs and lawn parties and yacht races, and frankly, a bit too high-class for the world of acting, when he really thought about it. She was probably already involved with someone from her tony world, and she would end up marrying a count or a duke. And who was he? Just some poor slob writer who dated about as often as the country elected a new president.

Jonny's last female involvement of any decent length crossed the living room and moved into his view through the window. Annie—dear, dear Annie. Had they really dated for nearly two years? It was almost impossible to believe. It was really a foxhole sort of thing. They both worked so hard, and the only person who would put up with such hours was another person forced to put up with such hours. When she'd been blacklisted and subsequently fired from working on *Hermie's Henhouse*, their relationship had withered and died.

Shel moved into view, moving up next to Annie and taking her hand. Jonny smiled knowingly. When Annie was let go from the show, Shel and Burton had already been fired. They became an inseparable trio, supporting each other emotionally and financially through this very dark time. But since Burton's foxhole was filled by any number of young ladies at any one time, Annie had jumped into Shel's. They were quite happy, with Shel adopting a bit of a strut in social situations, which included, as at this very moment, his taking up pipe smoking.

The noise of the party suddenly returned, as the Process Heads had opened one of the kitchen windows, and they were now piling en masse onto the apartment's other fire escape. Jonny noticed that a new person joined them, someone he recognized as a young actor who had been making a bit of a name for himself in the Village, doing stand-up comedy. This new person produced a reefer to share. Having partaken once or twice himself, Jonny could only imagine what ridiculous depths their analysis would now reach.

But before he could give it much thought, Jonny could see a commotion in the living room, and everyone moved toward the front door. He knew what was going on, and if he needed any confirmation, he need only look out at the river, where the first hints of dawn were glinting off the mirror-smooth surface.

Morning was coming, and the first newspapers were out.

Ready to discover his fate, Jonny steeled himself and then opened the window and climbed back into the apartment. In the living room, the excited crowd surrounded the two latest arrivals to the party: Reginald, who had several papers tucked under his arm, and Veronica, who feverishly tore through the *New York Times*. Finding the page she was looking for, she folded the paper a couple of times and pressed her face close to the article. "All right, Mr. Gould, let's see what you think."

Suddenly light-headed, Jonny felt the breath leave his lungs. This was it; this was the moment. His future was about to be decided in the next few moments. The ratings were important, but to Jonny, what really counted was whether what he was trying to do with the show was working. Even if the ratings were strong, if he failed with his real objective—to be more than mindless entertainment—he doubted he could go on writing the show. His fate, as far as he was concerned, was in the hands of that most elusive figure, Jack Gould, TV critic of the *New York Times*.

Veronica dramatically cleared her throat. Then, like the *grande dame* she was, she did it again, milking the moment. Friends, the rest of the cast, and some of the other partiers started shouting at her. "All right, all right…" She took a deep breath and read, "*Justice Girl* arrives, a review by Jack Gould. Preparing this evening to watch the much-ballyhooed new entry on the Regal Television Network, this reviewer has to admit to not being very excited about another entry into the genre of wannabe Supermans. However, after viewing the first episode, I am very pleased to have been quite wrong in my dread." A collective sigh melted over the room. "Supposedly a kids' show, it is clear that the show's creators are aiming a bit higher, and for the most part, they hit their target dead on." Spontaneous clapping erupted, followed by the sound of a champagne cork popping. "This clever, quick-moving, and thought-provoking creation has much to be enjoyed by both children and adults alike. It'll make the kiddies laugh and the parents think."

Veronica read on, her voice getting louder and louder and her speech faster and faster, as she and the rest of the room grew more and more excited. Jonny spotted Burton, Annie, and Shel among the excited crowd. Happy and pleased, they offered clandestine smiles to one another. Jonny felt his knees weaken with relief and his whole body slump, and he caught himself against a wall. The rest of the review went by in a blur, but it was the last line that really stuck in his head: "I, for one, can't wait to see where this show goes from week to week." Veronica finished reading the review and then thrust a fist in the air in excitement.

Week to week. Week to week. Week to week. Over and over, the words swirled around Jonny's head. All they had achieved was one show. Thirty minutes. Eighteen hundred seconds. In less than seven days, they'd have to do it all over again.

Week to week.

Fortunately, Jonny had a lot more to say, and Justice Girl would say it for him. Without even a good-bye to anyone, Jonny headed for the door. He had a lot of writing to do.

...

There was a time, not so distant, when Jonny might have been the last to leave one of Annie's parties, when he would have huddled with the others on the fire escape and watched the sunrise over the Hudson River, contently full of hope and excitement and optimism. There was a time before he knew this was a godless world. Before he learned of the horrors of unchecked greed. Before he realized the stink of political avarice. It was a time when Jonny Dirby was still Jacob Drabinowitz, just another fourteen-year-old boy trying to win a war.

It was 1943, and he was winning. They were all winning. The mighty military strength of the United States had finally begun to turn the tide in Europe. Patton, with Jonny's older brother in tow as the chief of staff to one of his generals, had chased the Nazis out of North Africa and now had them on the run in Sicily.

As Jonny lay on damp sheets—a by-product of a particularly sticky August night—he felt like an overfilled balloon, pressure pushing him in every direction and ready to burst at any moment. He imagined great battles in his mind—valiant American soldiers battling horrific Germans and Italians, pushing them back, hill by hill, and defeating them handily. In his imagination, every American was always his brother. Whether firing a machine gun or driving a tank or even flying a bomber, it was always Mitchell Drabinowitz's courageous grimace that led the charge. Mitchell had just single-handedly cleared out a pillbox of three gargantuan Nazis when Jonny flipped his pillow to the cool side and finally drifted off toward sleep.

Despite all the chaos of fierce battle, Jonny's last thought before sleep finally claimed him was of cans. Tin cans. Hundreds and hundreds of tin cans. Did he have enough? He had to have enough. But did he?

Awake again, Jonny shot up in bed and grabbed his flashlight, which only a half-hour ago had been the British army in another nightly ritual, where he re-enacted the day's war news on a weathered map of Europe, using his toys to represent the various forces. He flicked it on and aimed it across the room. A towering mountain of metal glinted at him. Tuna cans, soup cans, oil cans, paint cans, glue cans—every tin can he had scrounged over the last few days shone brightly in the shaft of light. It was an impressive collection. He fell back on the pillow, sleep finally vanquishing him once and for all.

It was no surprise that the sound of clinking cans would fill his dreams. But when Jonny burst awake again, he still heard the unmistakable sound. What was going on? He was awake. It couldn't be a dream. Through hazy eyes, he noticed that the door to his bedroom was slightly ajar, a shaft of light from the hall spilling across his bed. Jonny reached up to a small reading light on his nightstand and turned it on.

The door was open, and a slender hand was reaching in, holding a brown paper bag. "Hello?" Jonny said, fighting to push more sleep from his mind.

The door was pushed open to reveal, in silhouette, a round, short woman with curly hair. "You're awake," Rachel Drabinowitz said, surprised.

"Uh-huh" was all Jonny could groggily manage.

"Or maybe not." Rachel was fully dressed, complete with light evening coat, as if heading out for the night. "Here's a couple more for you," she said, placing the paper bag next to Jonny's impressive collection. "I went ahead and made my lunches for next week so I could give you my tuna fish cans."

It always made Jonny laugh that she called it lunch. Rachel worked the graveyard shift at a tire factory on Staten Island. She would be eating her sandwich at six in the morning.

"Since you're up, I have something else I want to give you." Rachel crossed the room and sat on the edge of the bed. Even in the low light, Jonny could make out the two clouds of sweet freckles that dotted her plump cheeks. Her ample dark curls, which she was forever blowing away from her playful eyes, sashayed across her shoulders as she dug for something in her purse. Finally, she pulled out a four-by-six inch photograph. "Look what I found in my dresser when I was going through things for the clothing drive." She handed it to Jonny.

Wearily, he slowly turned it over, and a big smile broke out over his face. It was a black-and-white shot of Jonny, Rachel, and Mitchell, standing in front of the Trylon and Perisphere at the 1939 World's Fair. They all looked much younger, as if a dozen years had passed since the picture was taken. "Was it really only four years ago?" Jonny asked, seeing the date etched into the photo: April 30, 1939.

Rachel nodded slowly. "Yes, only four years."

The thought sent Jonny's mind reeling. Only four years. The day had been like a dream, full of wonder and hope and promise. It was opening day of the fair, and God bestowed his blessing with a spring day full of crisp sunshine to warm the body and a slight breeze to cool the brow. Mitchell had gotten hold of a map of the fair the day before, so he had meticulously planned their day, and they had wandered excitedly, the three of them in constant orbit of one another, from one nation's pavilion to the next. Britain, France, Germany, Spain, Poland, Russia—all the great nations of Europe standing next to each other. *How could there be a war?* Jonny had wondered, remembering that strange, terrifying word that kept creeping into his parents' conversations. They were all neighbors, both in Europe and here at the Fair. Neighbors didn't fight. Neighbors didn't turn on each other. Neighbors were friends.

Then there was the speech.

Just as Mitchell had planned it, they were back at the main entrance just in time for President Roosevelt's speech that officially opened the fair. But what Mitchell hadn't planned on was the crowd. The three of them, with Mitchell as the head of the plow, fought to get close enough for a good view, but it was no use. Thousands of people—many had camped out for hours—stood between them and the president. They craned their necks, trying to see, but the dais was nothing more than a speck far in the distance.

Fortunately, Mitchell was just as good at improvisation as he was at planning. "Come on!" Mitchell had ordered, and they followed him out of the crowd, back to the main concourse. "Follow me," he said, walking quickly.

They ran to keep up with him, rushing over to the RCA pavilion. Inside, it was crowded with small groups of people, all split into huddles of varying sizes. Mitchell led them over to a mother, father, and young daughter. As they approached, Jonny noticed the family seemed bathed in a blue-white glow. *Are they staring at precious gems?* he wondered. *Or perhaps being zapped by some new miracle ray?* When he stood next to the young daughter, he got his answer. The little girl and her parents were staring into a small, glowing, eight-inch square. On it, to Jonny's astonishment, was the image of President Roosevelt, giving the speech that they had just tried to see on the other side of the fair.

"It's called television," Mitchell had proudly proclaimed.

"It's like…a newsreel," Jonny said, trying to comprehend.

"No, it's very different. What you are seeing is happening now, on the other side of the park. The images are flying through the air"—he waved his hand for emphasis—"and landing inside this box so you can see it."

Jonny's mouth hung open as he watched amazed. A half mile away, President Roosevelt was speaking, and Jonny was watching him, right here, as it was happening, on a tiny blue-white screen. In awe, he turned to his brother. "There'll be no war now," Jonny said assuredly.

Mitchell looked down at him, cocking an eyebrow. "Why's that?"

"With such miracles, why would anyone want to hurt anyone else?"

Jonny wasn't certain, but he thought he saw Mitchell and the mother and father share a bemused look. Mitchell put a hand on Jonny's little shoulder. "We'll see…we'll see."

Only four years ago, Jonny thought again. *Only four years.* Now, Rachel worked in a factory, Mitchell was on the other side of the world dodging bullets, and every day when he walked through the lobby of his building, he prayed that another Gold Star had not been added to the two that already hung there.

"I had two copies made. You can keep that one," Rachel said.

"Thank you," Jonny answered, placing the photo on his nightstand. He adjusted it so he had a good view of the happy trio as he lay back down on his bed.

"I sent the other one overseas to Mitchell," Rachel said, getting up off the bed. "But God only knows when he'll get it." She paused at the bedroom door. "Now you get some sleep, and I'll see you in about eight hours."

Jonny slept fitfully, dreaming of his brother in full battle gear, throwing tin cans at the Germans. Finally, with the first light of dawn singeing the room a pale yellow, Jonny leapt out of bed. It was almost 6:00 a.m., and he had to get to it if he was going to meet Rachel on time.

He dressed quickly, finishing by slipping on his Junior Commando armband, and hurried up to the roof, where he dragged a stiff green hose across the soft tar surface to the ten-foot-by-two-foot wooden trough that was his victory garden. There were a few other similar troughs scattered across the roof, but their owners had neglected the hard work it took to grow vegetables on a rooftop in Manhattan in the summer, so all they could show for their efforts were rectangles of crumbly, dried-out, almost white dirt. Jonny had pulled a successful, if not particularly tasty, crop of tomatoes and corn from his garden two weeks earlier and then right away planted the next seeds. With slightly cloudy water, he quickly sprayed his fledgling vegetables; the first tiny bulbs were just beginning to peek out from the rich, brown soil.

Then he rushed back down the stairs to his apartment, where he heard his mother in the kitchen, and the smell of something frying filled the air. *No time for food*, he thought as he pulled out his little red wagon (now painted olive drab to resemble a B-17 bomber, complete with white star), loaded it up with his mountain of tin cans, and headed out. Leaving the apartment, he noticed he was a few minutes ahead of schedule, so he decided to take another sweep of the building.

Jonny and his little green wagon were a common sight in the hallways as he moved from floor to floor, knocking on doors to collect things for the war effort. He was thriving as a Junior Commando, the only one of his friends to have reached the rank of second lieutenant in the children's home-front army. Besides the victory garden on the roof, he'd studied up on enemy plane silhouettes, did rounds with the neighborhood civil defense warden, had taken a few trips to the Brooklyn shore to help watch for Nazi subs, and most important, had discovered the importance of a good battle plan. On Mondays, he collected newspapers (the best day for that because of the previous day's large Sunday paper). Tuesdays, it was grease and fats; Wednesday, spare clothing; Thursdays, scrap metal; and Friday, tin cans. His routine was so consistent that, in many cases, when Jonny arrived at several of the doors, the items were already waiting for him, neatly stacked in the hallway. But he also noticed that some people got the days mixed up. He might find a bundle of newspapers waiting on grease day or a pile of clothes on scrap-metal day. As the day before was a Friday, Jonny thought his neighbors' anticipation of the end of the workweek might lead to similar confusion, and when he passed the Hoffmans' door on the third floor, he saw he was right: he'd hit pay dirt. Calmly waiting for him, piled high in a soiled shopping bag, was a huge cache of tin cans. Jonny hungrily added them to his wagon.

The collection station for the Washington Heights division of the Junior Commandos was a few blocks up Broadway from Jonny's apartment building. This was the Saturday for the monthly contest, and the line was already long when Jonny approached with his overflowing wagon. From nine to ten o'clock, any boys or girls who were members of the Junior Commandos could drop off as many tin cans as they wanted, and whoever had collected the most would win a brand-new, shiny silver dollar. Even before Jonny made it inside the door of the abandoned storefront the Junior Commandos were using, it was clear from his overloaded wagon, not to mention the extra bag of cans in his hands, that he would win.

At 10:05 a.m., Jonny received his silver dollar, but there was no time to celebrate, as this was just the beginning of a long day. With his winnings safely stowed in his front pocket, Jonny turned his wagon over to a boy who lived in the building next to him, who, despite being only a corporal to Jonny's rank as a second lieutenant, required a nickel bribe to take the wagon back to Jonny's apartment. Jonny sprinted for the subway and, after a short ride downtown, emerged into the patriotic fervor that was Times Square. Red, white, and blue bunting was everywhere, hanging from awnings and lampposts. Huge billboards implored citizens to "Buy War Bonds" or "Keep Silent" or "Work Harder." Even the smoking Camel cigarette sign, a favorite of Jonny's, had joined the fight, as it featured a confident serviceman blowing smoke rings into the air. To him, this was the center of an energized country, united in one goal: winning the war.

As he walked up the street through the constant throng of servicemen, Jonny felt he was looking at the clenched fist that was going to smash the Nazi war machine. He loved being among the soldiers and wondered how many of the men he had seen on previous trips to Times Square were now overseas, valiantly fighting alongside Mitchell in Italy. As he made his way to his goal—his shirt making him a red-checkered buoy among an ocean of blue and brown—he wondered how many of these brave men would be there when the Allies finally made it into Germany. Maybe one of the men he casually passed on Broadway would be the one to put a bullet through Hitler's skull. Beaming at the thought of such heroics, Jonny made it to the Astor Theatre and the culmination of his quest. Reaching the front of the line of the metal-and-glass ticket booth, Jonny happily added the silver dollar to his pile of assorted coins and crumpled bills and slid them all across the small ledge toward the ticket-taker. "I would like two tickets to attend the premiere of *Thousands Cheer*. Here is my money so that I may buy a twenty-five dollar war bond," Jonny said, in a speech he'd rehearsed in his head at least a dozen times.

The ticket-taker sighed at the pile of money in front of her and then rather peevishly began straightening the bills and sorting the coins so that she could count them. Jonny watched, thrilled. His plan was coming to fruition. When he'd heard the announcement three months earlier—"See a real live Hollywood premiere. Two tickets are yours when you buy a twenty-five-dollar war bond!" —attending was nothing more than a pipe dream. But now, as the annoyed ticket-taker reached for two large, colorful tickets, Jonny almost wanted to cry. He had done it.

"Thank you!" he said gleefully, before turning and hurrying away. Feeling giddy, he slid the tickets in his pocket, dreaming of the moment— not that far in the future—when he would meet up with Rachel and dramatically pull them out of his pocket. Or maybe he should be nonchalant about it, he wondered as he disappeared into the subway again, as if to say "No big deal. Of course I scored us a pair of tickets—that's the kind of guy I am." He would decide later; he still had work to do.

Jonny next emerged topside near City Hall and quickly headed south to Nassau Street, a slender sliver of a road that was the beginning of the Old Dutch part of the city. This particular stretch housed dozens of street-level stamp shops, with a six-story raised arm of a building at 116 Nassau Street being the signpost of this area known as the Stamp District. It was in this building, on the fifth floor, that Jonny's parents had their stamp store.

It was a miserably cramped space, smaller than the rest of the stores that ringed the fifth floor, but his mother's father, the original owner, had chosen it because it was the first store anyone saw when stepping off the elevator. When Jonny entered, his father was at his customary spot at the crowded front counter, dealing with a customer, while Jonny's mother was at her customary spot in the tiny back office, doing the books and filling mail-order approvals. Jonny only needed his eyes to know what the customer and his father were saying. The man's dress told the whole story; even though it was August, he wore a hopelessly worn, heavy-wool top coat, along with tattered wool pants with frayed cuffs, and he carried—the biggest telltale sign of all—a hopelessly battered suitcase, held together with twine. This was a refugee from somewhere in Nazi-occupied Europe.

As Jonny drew closer and heard the disheveled man speak his soft, desperate Yiddish, it only further confirmed what he knew. A page of bright German stamps were on the counter, and from the look on the man's face, Jonny's father had just delivered the bad news. The stamps someone had sold him were not the rare variety as he had been told but an almost worthless common issue. Sadly, this scene had become a weekly occurrence. Traffickers, not satisfied with the huge sums they charged to smuggle people out of occupied areas, had started a side business, exchanging their cargo's life savings for stamps. They reasoned, correctly, that it would be much easier to smuggle stamps into America than gold coins. But what they didn't tell their desperate victims was that the stamps were essentially worthless.

Jonny had watched this scene play many times. The reactions varied, from resignation to knowing nods to anger to—as with this man—tears that quickly turned into uncontrollable sobbing. Jonny then saw his father sigh, and with a quick look at Jonny, his father jerked his head in the direction of the back room. Jonny got the message instantly; he scooted past the bereaved man and into the back office. His mother looked up, stamp tongs in hand, and greeted her son with a familiar nod.

"Here to see your work in print, no doubt," she said, sliding a stack of about fifty stapled documents across the desk to him.

"Yep," he answered as he grabbed one off the top of the stack. It was about four pages all together, and Jonny flipped through it, all the while using his body to block his mother's view of the front counter. On the pages were black-and-white images of stamps, each accompanied by textual descriptions. It had started almost two years ago as a lark, his father having little Jacob write up his weekly newsletter, which was the customary sales tool for each stamp dealer on the street. But soon, it became apparent that Jonny had a real knack for writing. Instead of describing a particular Scott number C3 24-cent Curtis Jenny Bi-Plane stamp as an "excellent example, with good centering, nice color, original gum, and no hinge," Jonny would write, "With reds and blues so vivid you can feel the wind blow against your brow, hear the engine roar, and smell the gasoline." A rather mundane example of the Scott number 69 one-dollar Trans-Mississippi Cattle in the Storm became

"So clean and crisp you can feel the cold and can see each and every snow-flake as if it were falling on your own shoulders."

Among the several dozen stamps for which Jonny had provided descriptions was one of his favorites, and he flipped to the last page to see it. A week earlier his father had purchased the collection of a soldier headed overseas; having just gotten married, the soldier had decided to sell his stamp collection so he could leave some money with his new wife. Contained within was a particularly nice copy of the 1869 24-cent Signing of the Declaration of Independence—or as Jonny described it, "So clean, so vivid, so alive that, if you lean in close enough, you can hear them arguing over the preamble."

Jonny smiled as he saw his words in print. He held out the page to show to his mother. "Did you see..." he began, but she was looking past him, her gaze zeroing in on what was happening between Jonny's father and the disheveled man in the next room, as they appeared to be concluding their business. Jonny moved to block her view again, but it was too late. Suspicious, his mother was already on her feet, heading for the front counter.

Jonny watched as she reached his father, just as the disheveled man slipped out the front door. Seeing the sad collection of stamps still sitting on the counter, she frowned. "All right, Mr. Big Shot, what did you do?"

Jonny didn't need to hear the answer; he knew what his father had done. Samuel had "suddenly realized" the stamps *were* the rare variety and paid the thankful refugee top dollar. Of course, they weren't rare, and his mother knew that. This was not the first time his father had done this and not the first time his mother had caught him.

Still, Samuel hemmed and hawed before Lena cut him off with an icy stare. Finally, he threw his arms in the air. "What do you want me to do? He looked like your uncle Morty."

"I don't care if it *was* my uncle Morty," she said dismissively. "We don't give away money." Sighing, she headed back into the office, muttering, "Mr. Big Shot thinks we're running a charity here."

The offhand comment made it clear that she really wasn't that mad. After all, the very same scene had played out almost thirty years earlier when her father had still owned the stamp shop, and it was Samuel who had come through the door, a desperate refugee with worthless stamps. Back then, instead of giving Samuel money, her father had given him a job. One year later, Samuel had fallen in love with Lena, two years later they were married, three years later they had a son, and four years later he had taken over the business.

"Next he'll be passing out bills on the street," Lena said, further proof that her bluster was all show. Truth was they could afford a little charity. The business was doing better than ever. The wartime economy was exploding, and for the first time in a long time, people had money in their pockets but very little to spend it on. Almost every luxury item was rationed, as was all nonessential travel. With nowhere to go and money to spend, many people turned to things they could do at home, especially hobbies they could do while glued to their radios, listening to news of the war. The result was that on Nassau Street, prices were up, and inventory was flying out the door—as was Jonny, with the latest edition of the weekly newsletter in his hands. On the ride back uptown with his sister, as was their Saturday tradition, Rachel would read the weekly newsletter aloud, marveling at Jonny's work.

In Battery Park, Jonny had to wait through two overcrowded ferries before making it on board and taking the quick journey out to Staten Island. Sitting inside and looking out through the stained windows, he watched the Statue of Liberty pass by. Currently, the giant green lady's job was one of saying farewell, a last sight of America for the hundreds of thousands of men who were headed overseas. Jonny dreamed of the day when she would return to her rightful job—that of a greeter, welcoming home those from abroad. Welcoming home his brother Mitchell.

Reaching the island, Jonny flowed off the ferry with the crowd. Most of them were workers, so Jonny joined them as they walked en masse toward the factory. It was a short walk, less than ten minutes, and soon he was standing before the massive red brick fortress that was the Vleets Tire Company.

In the 1880s, the Industrial Revolution finally had reached Staten Island when Stanton Vleets broke ground and built his factory. Jumping on the bandwagon that was the bicycle craze sweeping America, he quickly made

a fortune selling one of the first inflatable bicycle tires. The difference between the ride of the typical hard rubber model and the Vleets Air-O-Matic
was profound. By the turn of the century, Stanton had expanded his factory
three times. A fourth expansion, to its current corpulent size, came in the
mid-1920s, when the thirst for automotive tires kept the factory humming
six days a week.

But that was nothing compared to what was happening now.

It seemed the United States Army needed tires for everything. Tires
for bombers, tires for fighters, tires for jeeps, tires for trucks, tires for am-
phibious landing vehicles. Tires. Tires. Tires. It needed tires. The factory,
currently run by Stanton's great-grandson, the notorious Manhattan playboy Anderson Vleets, now ran around the clock, twenty-four hours a day,
in three shifts, seven days a week, producing tires. And still, there weren't
enough. If you weren't in the military or in a civilian job deemed "essential,"
you had no means of finding a new set of tires—no legal means, anyway.

As the next shift descended on the iron gate that guarded the main entrance of the factory, Jonny veered off from them and headed around to the
side. A couple of months after Rachel had taken the job, Jonny had started
meeting her after work on Saturdays. During the shift changes, because of
the heavy crowd flowing in and out, they found they had trouble finding
each other, so they started meeting around the side of the factory, at the
loading dock. Here, except for the constant roar of trucks and the spirited
curses of the cargo loaders, they could easily find one another.

Jonny took up his usual spot at a small gas pump used to gas up the
dozen or so forklifts that ran around the loading dock, moving cargo.
Oddly, the whole place was strangely quiet. The usual surging energy was
absent. About a hundred feet down the block, workers were loading a truck
with stacks of freshly made tires. But the workers were oddly silent. Jonny
watched them, curious. Where was the playful joking? Where was the
steady stream of loud curses? Where was the rumble of hurrying trucks?
Where was the dash of rushing forklifts? Where was the thunder of a factory working at full force to win a war? He looked all around, taking in the
whole eerie, silent scene.

Where was Rachel?

Jonny waited another five minutes, and finally, from the other end of the loading dock, maybe three hundred feet away, a figure moved toward him. He wasn't sure if it was Rachel, but it was definitely a worker. He could make out the pale blue jumpsuit that all the factory workers wore. As the figure got closer, Jonny could see that it was Doris, Rachel's best friend.

This made Jonny smile. He liked Doris. She was a couple years older, several inches taller, many pounds lighter, and a whole lot blonder than Rachel. Doris Zucker lived in the same building as Jonny's family, three floors below. She lived with only her mother, her father having disappeared since heading out for a pack of cigarettes in 1935. No one bothered to go looking for him, as many had noticed that he had taken a suitcase with him for the short errand.

Rachel and Doris had been best friends for as long as anyone could remember. When they hit their teenage years, they dubbed themselves the Terrible Two, led mostly by the practically parentless Doris.

Another part of Jonny's Saturday ritual, a part he enjoyed almost as much as the time he spent during the day with Rachel, came in the early evening, when he would watch Rachel and Doris get ready for their night out. Inevitably, they had dates, usually with a pair of servicemen. They always did their final primping in Rachel's room, with Jonny dutifully sitting on the edge of her bed. It was his job to zip up their dresses and help them get into their shoes or slip on their coats.

But his favorite part had started the year before, when stockings had gone the way of the dodo, all the silk in the country having been commandeered by the army for parachutes. Rachel was content to go barelegged, but not Doris. Now, every time they got ready for a night out, the final step was always Doris's stepping atop a chair so that Jonny could draw the line of a stocking seam up the back of her legs.

He loved it, especially when Doris really liked the guy she was going out with, so the skirt she had selected was on the shorter side. "Higher, higher," she would implore Jonny as he moved the eyeliner pencil up the back of her calves, to the back of her knees, and finally up the back of her thighs.

When he got high enough, sometimes seeing an enticing glimpse of her white cotton underwear, Rachel would inevitably admonish her with a sharp, "Doris! Really! Who's gonna see it all the way up there?"

Doris would then turn to her, flashing her most devilish smile, and say, "How else am I going to get my mink coat?"

Finished, the two girls would head out, a festival of giggles as they passed through the door into the hallway. As Jonny watched, just before the door shut and they disappeared from view, Rachel would give him a soft wave, and Doris would give him a hard wink and say, "See you in the scandal sheets, kiddo."

Now, as Doris crossed the loading dock and came into full view, Jonny could see that something was wrong. She had red paint all over her jumpsuit, and her joyous, flirty smile was absent. She stopped just a few feet from him. "I...I...knew you would be waiting out here."

"Where's Rachel?"

"She's...she's..." Doris began to cry, collapsing onto a bewildered Jonny.

It was only later that he learned the red paint on Doris's jumpsuit was actually blood. Rachel's blood.

Rachel was buried four days later, next to her three dead grandparents, in the Jewish graveyard in the Inwood section of Washington Heights. She would have been buried sooner, as per Jewish tradition and at the insistence of the one surviving grandparent, Clara (the only immediate family member who could be called an observant Jew), but the police wouldn't release the body for two days, due to a formal investigation. In the end, it was ruled an industrial accident. Such accidents had become an all-too-common side effect of the manic production sweeping the nation, as everyone from helmet makers to boot suppliers tried desperately to keep up with demand. It was simply a case of being in the wrong place at the wrong time, the police surmised in their final report, though in much more clinical language. Rachel had been one of a dozen girls, each operating her own tread-making machine. It was their job to pop the finished tires out from the heavy metal molds after the rough, jagged tread teeth were pressed onto the unformed tires under severe pressure and heat. As Rachel went about her work, popping a tire out every fifteen minutes, a crack had opened, unbeknownst to her, in one of the molds.

Finally, just minutes before she would have finished the latest tire, the mold exploded. Shards of thick, ragged lead went in every direction, injuring several other girls as they dove for cover behind their own tread-making machines. A large piece tore into Rachel's left shoulder, practically tearing her arm off. She bled to death five minutes later, in Doris's arms.

This being an accepted, albeit sad, part of the war effort, there was a strong outpouring of genuine sympathy. Mayor LaGuardia sent a telegram, the borough presidents of both Staten Island and Manhattan called Jonny's parents, and over a hundred people, most of them residents of their building, attended the funeral.

Jonny stood between his parents as the rabbi, once again at the insistence of Clara, began the service. As Jonny blinked in the bright afternoon sun, with Rachel's dead body in an oak casket not six feet away, he struggled to remember the last four days. They had been a blur of relatives, food, and mourning. His mother had been practically catatonic; Jonny was unsure if he'd heard her utter a single word since finding out about Rachel, and his father had become almost robotic in his handling of all the arrangements. Jonny was numb, except at night, when he would cry until falling asleep. Then, as he awoke, the pain would flood back, followed, thankfully, by the quick return of the numbness. He wished Mitchell were here with them. Jonny missed him terribly. He was too old to think Mitchell could somehow bring her back to life—he knew being picked to be Superman in all the street games didn't mean Mitchell actually was Superman—but his brother's presence would have made a huge difference—if nothing else, for the sake of his parents. Seeing Mitchell in the flesh, instead of worrying about a stray bullet from a random rifle tearing into him, would have made a world of difference. Word was sent through the army, but no one could say exactly when it would get to him.

The rabbi moved on to reading from a prayer book, and a pair of photographers, one from the *Times*, the other from the *Daily News*, snapped a couple of shots. They'd been standing respectfully off to the side since everyone arrived, seeming rather bored, as there really wasn't much to shoot. Occasionally, they'd fire off a couple of shots and then sling their cameras back over their shoulders and reassume their bored stances.

An outburst of soft crying yanked Jonny's gaze away and over to Doris, who stood about fifteen feet away, toward the back of the crowd. Her face was pale, her eyes bloodshot and puffy, as she tried to stem the flow of tears. But she failed miserably. She'd been in and out of their apartment over the last few days, part of the steady stream of condolence-offerers, only able to stay for short, painful visits before having to retreat to her own apartment.

Suddenly, a rapid volley of camera shutters went off. Jonny whipped his gaze away from Doris. Had something happened? Had he missed something? Had someone fallen into the open hole dug into the ground? But when his eyes landed on the photographers, he saw that they had turned away and were photographing in the opposite direction. Jonny mimicked the neck twisting of the crowd as they all craned to see what was so important. Hurrying toward them was a pack of dark-suited men, led majestically by a raven-haired young man who strode confidently toward them. As he drew closer, Jonny recognized the jutting jaw; the piercing, ne'er-do-well eyes; the stylish, slicked-back haircut; the double-breasted silk pinstripe.

It was Anderson Vleets.

As the realization swept through the crowd, everyone began to murmur. Even the rabbi paused in the service. Anderson, his pack slowing behind him, walked up to Jonny and his mother and father. He took Lena's hand in his and looked sincerely into her eyes. "I'm sorry. I hope I am not disturbing you. But I had to come. I had to convey my deepest condolences on this senseless tragedy." At that point, the photographers dropped any attempt at decorum and rushed over, standing well within the pack of mourners as they snapped away.

Lena, still unable to speak, merely nodded her thanks. Anderson moved on to Jonny's father, repeating his condolences. Jonny watched him, but when Anderson then crouched down to look Jonny in the eye, Jonny looked past him, at Doris.

She was no longer crying.

The tears were gone. Her eyes, though still swollen, were in a squinted, tight, lock on Anderson. It made Jonny think of only one word.

Hate.

For some reason, Doris hated Anderson Vleets.

Jonny nodded to whatever it was Anderson had said to him. The service continued, with Anderson taking a spot next to Jonny and his parents and joining in their mourning. The two photographers snapped away.

Jonny looked back to Doris, but she was gone; a pile of crumpled Kleenex on the green grass marked where she had stood. He looked all around, finally spotting her halfway across the graveyard, heading for the road. Why was she leaving? Why did she glare at Anderson like that—like he was the worst man in the world? Sure, he was a notorious playboy, but Jonny had never heard his sister or Doris say a bad word about him. In fact, they had never mentioned his name at all.

Jonny slowly backed away and moved through the crowd. He caught up to Doris just before she reached the roadway. "Doris!" he yelled, but she didn't stop. "Doris, where are you going?"

She finally turned around, her face a crimson mask. "He shouldn't be here," she said through gritted teeth.

"Who? Anderson?"

"Yes."

"Why?"

Doris's eyes flittered all around. Jonny could have sworn she was checking to see if anyone was watching them but decided that was ridiculous.

Finally, Doris stepped closer to him. "Because he's the reason she's dead."

Jonny knew, even as a young boy, that happenstance had made it possible for Lena's older brother, Saul Buntz, to become the first member of the Buntz family to attend college and thus become the lawyer who would handle their wrongful death suit against Anderson Vleets. As Jonny had heard many times, when Saul returned from serving overseas in World War I, his declaration that he no longer desired to work in the family's stamp store was met with extreme resistance. His father, Julius, had struggled to keep the business going with Saul in Uncle Sam's service, and with Saul home, he desperately needed Saul's help in running the business. The fact that Saul had no interest in stamps was irrelevant, as far as Julius was concerned. He couldn't afford to hire someone, and though Lena was now old enough to work in Saul's place, it was not considered acceptable for a young woman, even with her father present, to work inside the all-male stamp world that was 116 Nassau Street. Despite numerous arguments, Julius did not relent, and under a cloud of seething tension, Saul went back to work in the stamp store, dutifully riding the subway downtown to the store every morning with Julius.

Then, on May 18, everything changed.

Over two hundred miles away, William Robey, a casual stamp enthusiast, went into a post office in Washington, DC, and purchased a sheet of one hundred 24 cent air mail stamps that depicted a beautiful engraving of a blue Curtiss Jenny biplane flying within a bright red border. When Robey got home, he was shocked to find that the airplanes were all upside down on the stamps. This meant that during the printing process, during one of the two trips through the press to create the bi-colored stamps, the sheet had been placed between the printing plates upside down. Knowing that he had something unusual and potentially valuable, Robey contacted a dealer he knew. From there the tale of the amazing discovery and the $12,000 for which Robey sold the sheet exploded and quickly spilled from the stamp world into newspapers nationwide. The great stamp craze of 1918 was on.

Business exploded on Nassau Street, with the area flooded by new collectors, old collectors, those wanting an appraisal for the old stamp album left by a dead relative, and even the just plain curious. Two years later, when the trend picked up even more with the good economic times, Julius realized he could afford to hire someone to work in the store, and Saul entered City College in the spring term of 1920. While Saul excelled, his replacement did not, but in the two years since his return from overseas, the country had changed; women were now allowed to vote, so when Julius brought Lena in to work with him at 116 Nassau Street, it hardly raised an eyebrow.

Saul passed the bar in 1928 and worked at a large law firm in Manhattan for ten years, but as the only Jew, the firm always passed him over for promotion, and he knew he had zero chance of ever making partner. He left in 1938 and went out on his own, setting up an office on the Grand Concourse in the Bronx. His practice, as Jonny had heard his parents discuss, was successful and stable, if unremarkable, as he handled estates, immigration, property, and only the occasional lawsuit. But he was family, so he was the one to whom they turned.

Crouched in the hallway, hidden behind an oak credenza, Jonny listened closely to what was playing out in the living room. Normally, he would have been able to see as well, but because they were only in the sixth day of sitting shiva, a dark sheet covered the mirror that would have allowed him a good view. But moving to a better spot was too risky, because Jonny's parents had banished him to his room, as they did on all serious occasions.

His parents were retelling Rachel's whole saga to Saul. Things had moved very quickly after Doris had come clean to Jonny and then to his mother and father about what she knew about the accident. The only reason Rachel had been working on that particular set of machines, with molds that everyone knew were old and faulty, was that the factory was also supplying tires directly to the black market. With the factory producing around the clock, they were easily making their quota of tires for their government contract. Doris had learned from a shift foreman she dated that Anderson, at the suggestion of some of his less-than-honest friends from the world of New York nightlife, had come up with the idea of making a few extra tires to "go out the back door," as it was commonly called. Since all the machines with brand new molds were hard at work for the government, older, out-of-date, and in some cases, damaged molds were put to use for his side business. The graveyard shift was chosen as the best time—the fewer prying eyes, the better—and that is how Rachel came to be working those machines on that night.

The story had confused Jonny. *Why would Anderson Vleets need more money? And why would he go about getting it in that way? Wasn't everyone all in this together—fighting evil, defeating the Nazis and the Japanese? And how did this help the war effort? Didn't the army need all the tires it could get?* But Jonny's parents didn't seem confused, so Saul pressed them for answers. Samuel just shrugged angrily. "Some men are just greedy." Money. He did it for money? This astonished Jonny. *A man with all of Anderson's wealth cared more about money than winning the war!*

Saul stood up and began to pace, saying nothing. He merely walked back and forth, occasionally muttering something unintelligible to himself. Finally, he turned back to Samuel and Lena. "How serious is this Doris? Does she really want to go the distance to see justice done?"

"Yes," Lena said firmly. "You'll see when she gets here in a few minutes."

From his hiding place, Jonny nodded in agreement. Saul would see what Jonny had seen when Doris had first told him the truth—the anger, the determination, the outright hate that Doris had for Anderson Vleets. She had almost trembled when she recounted what she knew was the real cause of the accident, and now an unmitigated need to somehow make things right consumed her.

"But what do you think?" Saul persisted. "Do you think she has what it takes to see this through? She is about to have her whole life turned upside down."

Lena thought for a moment. "She and Rachel are...were best friends since they were little girls. Always together, those two. Morning, noon, and night. When Rachel had a problem with some girls from bad families, Doris stepped in and set them straight. When Doris was alone on holidays because her father was gone and her mother had to work, Rachel always made sure she was with us." Lena stopped for a moment, thinking. "They weren't best friends; they were sisters."

Saul nodded, absorbing Lena's tale. "This could work," he concluded.

Yes. Yes! Jonny thought. They were going to do something about it. They were going to get the man who, just as if he had put a bullet between her eyes, had killed his sister.

But Jonny's heart sank when his father interjected, "Of course it could work...for you." Samuel had been listening closely, evaluating without jumping in. Now, he was ready to join the conversation. "No matter what the outcome, you come out okay. You get attention. You get work. What do we get? More heartache."

"Sam!" Lena said angrily.

"Is what I said not true?" He looked directly at Lena's brother. "Saul, unlike you, I do not wish for more attention. With attention comes problems."

Lena shook her head. "Always the peasant."

Jonny didn't fully understand the comment, but it seemed whenever Lena and Samuel had a disagreement—a major one—that phrase always came from his mother's mouth. He'd asked Mitchell about it once, and Mitchell had answered that it had to do with Dad's growing up in the countryside and Mom being from the big city.

"Lena, is that really necessary?" Samuel said, with more than a tinge of disappointment that she had resorted to *that* again.

"Sam," Saul said, jumping in before Lena could respond. "I am fully aware of the attention this would bring to you, too. The last thing I want to do is make things worse, but you called me because you are in pain. You feel the need to hold someone responsible for what was done to your daughter. And I am the one who can make that happen." Stepping in front of Samuel, Saul spoke slowly, letting his words sink in. "But I can only do it if you let me."

Let him! Let him! Jonny was screaming in his head, fighting the urge to run out into the room and yell it out loud.

Samuel said nothing. Suddenly, there was a knock at the door. Doris had arrived. Samuel was still silent. Lena's lips parted, but Saul cut her off with a slash of his hand through the air. "He must make up his own mind," Saul said, "or there is no point to doing this. It will only work if we're all on board."

Doris knocked again.

Finally, Samuel sighed. "Okay, we will give it a try."

Lena and Jonny exhaled in relief. Samuel clasped his hands together, almost as if he were praying he had made the right choice.

From the moment Doris entered the apartment, Jonny knew there was a problem. Doris's vanity was a well-known fact within the Drabinowitz household. Rachel often joked that Doris would comb her hair fifty times just to take out the garbage at 2:00 a.m. And Jonny had seen it firsthand when he had helped the girls get ready for their nights out. Doris was always the last one ready, with Rachel almost having to push her out the door to keep her from looking herself over in the mirror one more time.

But now as she stood in front of his uncle Saul and his mother and father, dark circles ringed her eyes, her dress hung in wrinkles, and her hair clearly had not seen a brush in two days. *Maybe she's really struggling with the grief,* Jonny thought. He wanted to believe it, but in his heart, he knew something else must be at play.

"Doris, this is the lawyer we told you about," Lena said, standing to greet her.

Saul took Doris's hand. "Very pleased to meet you," he said. If her appearance threw him, he didn't show it.

"Nicc to meet you," Doris answered flatly.

Saul and Doris stood uncomfortably for a long moment, almost as if sizing each other up. "Please, sit down, " Saul finally said, ushering her over to the nicest chair in the room, a soft easy chair that Samuel was quickly climbing out of. Doris sat. Saul grabbed a wooden chair from the dining room table, placed it in front of Doris, and sat in it. He looked her square in the face. "Okay, Doris," he began, with a friendly but serious tone, "I need to hear everything you know, in your own words."

Doris's eyes found the carpet. "That's...um...something I wanted to talk to all of you about." Her voice started to quiver. "I'm not so sure about what I told you. Maybe I got things wrong."

Saul pulled his head back, knowingly. Lena and Sam exchanged a confused glance. Instantly, Lena was on her feet, moving toward Doris. "Tell him, Doris. Tell him what you told us about my Rachel having to work bad machines, making tires for the black market."

Doris sighed while rocking her body, struggling, maybe a bit too much, to make her next statement. "You know it was late at night. We were all tired. Maybe I saw something; maybe I didn't."

Lena's arms flapped in the air. "But what about the foreman? The man you dated who told you what was really going on?"

More sighing and rocking. "I might have heard him wrong. It was late. I was tired." Doris ran through all her excuses again before adding a final new one. "I think we were drinking…"

"Well, thank you for your time," Saul said, standing up. He held out his hand for Doris, who, a bit bewildered, took it. Saul helped her to her feet and escorted her to the door. "Best of luck to you," he said, pulling open the door.

Doris stepped out, but then she stopped and looked back. "I really wish I could help," she said, not entirely unconvincingly. Then she left.

Saul looked at Lena and Samuel, turning his hands over as if to say, "What ya gonna do?"

Samuel answered the unasked question. "Well, that's that," he said, not hiding slight relief.

"What happened?" Lena wondered aloud.

"I'll tell you what happened," Saul said, replacing the chair and then grabbing his hat from the dining table. "I've seen it a million times before. One of two things." He put his hat on. "Either she got scared, or she got money."

"Scared? That girl? Never," Lena said with her own hand-slash of the air for finality.

"Then she got money." With that, Saul was gone.

Over the next few weeks, things slowly returned to their routine. Every day, Jonny's parents got up, dressed, and went to work in the store. Every day Jonny got up, dressed, and did his work to support the war. After all, weren't they just the same as all the other families who had lost loved ones to the war? But the others at least had the luxury of knowing that with every day, the people who were responsible for killing their sons, daughter, uncles, aunts, nieces, nephews, grandsons, and granddaughters were one day closer to their demise. Not so for the Drabinowitzes. Anderson Vleets was out there, enjoying his life, and unless Doris changed her mind, he would go unpunished. Hitler, Tojo, Mussolini—they would meet their fates. But not Anderson Vleets. Though Jonny still was just as committed to winning the war as he went about his business as a Junior Commando—collecting for various drives, tending his victory garden, and following the troop move ments on his map—he carried inside him a secret dream that Doris would soon change her mind, and they would go after Anderson Vleets. Maybe, Jonny thought, he could convince her to help, but he never saw her. Now that Rachel was gone, Doris never went above the second floor.

Eventually, to the outside world, things seemed to return to normal for Jonny's family. But nothing could have been further from the truth. The three of them said virtually nothing to each other; it was as if they had all suddenly gone mute. They were silent in the morning. They were silent in the afternoon. They were silent through dinner. They were silent afterward in the living room. Even when the radio announced good news about the war—things were going well in Italy; the Nazis were on the run—no one said a thing.

The most visible change was in their nightly routine. Normally, after work, they would sit together; Samuel would read his stamp magazine, Lena would do her newspaper crossword, and Jonny would do his homework. Now, on some nights, Samuel would announce to Lena that there was no crossword. Though Lena never questioned it, it seemed odd to Jonny. Before Rachel died, he couldn't remember a single night when there had been no crossword in the paper. After several weeks of the strange, occasional lack of a crossword puzzle by the *New York Times*, it happened again on the night before Jonny collected old newspapers for a paper drive. The next day, as Jonny dragged his wagon around the building from door to door, he encountered a stack that held the previous night's paper. He tore through it, searching—and found a crossword puzzle on the lower right corner of page twenty-three. But his surprise was short-lived; his eyes moved up the page, and he realized what was happening. The crossword was on the bottom of one of the newspaper's society pages, and there on the top of the page, smiling for all the world to see, was Anderson Vleets, escorting a young starlet to a charity ball for Russian War Relief. Jonny ripped through several other issues of the *New York Times*, and sure enough, over the last few weeks he discovered at least a half-dozen other smiling pictures of Anderson on the same page as the crossword puzzle. It became clear in a snap: Jonny's father had been going through the paper in advance and hiding it from Lena. And as Jonny's anger boiled, he realized it was a good thing he hadn't seen the photos either. Rachel was dead, millions of men were in harm's way, and all the while, Anderson played.

That night, under the guise of wanting to collect cooking grease for the fat drive the next day, Jonny headed down to Doris's apartment.

She answered quickly after the first knock. Her big smile faded at the sight of him. "Oh…I was expecting someone else."

Jonny could see that she was. She was dolled up, ready for a night on the town, and looking much better than the last time he had seen her, several weeks ago in his apartment when her memory had suddenly gone fuzzy. "Can I come in?" he asked assertively.

She looked at him blankly for a moment and then nodded. "Yes. Of course."

She moved aside; Jonny slipped by her. He hadn't been in her apartment for some time, and seeing it again reminded him of why Doris and Rachel always had gotten dressed for their nights out in his family's place. Doris's apartment was a small, dingy space: just one bedroom, with a slight indent off the living room for a dining area, which had served as Doris's bedroom since she was about four, and a tiny kitchen. All of the windows looked straight through a small alley to the building across the way, so barely a touch of light seeped in. Doris's mother worked—*when* she worked—at a succession of bars on the other side of Broadway, on 181st, so over the years, the décor had become dominated by giveaways from the various liquor and cigarette salesmen: Lucky Strike ashtrays, Schaefer Beer lamps, Canadian Club serving trays, and Pall Mall trash cans.

"How have your mom and dad been?" Doris asked, closing the door behind Jonny.

"They're okay, I guess. They don't say much. They miss her. I miss her."

"I miss her too, Jonny," Doris said, taking his hand.

"That's why I came to talk to you." Jonny took a deep breath and proceeded carefully. "I was wondering if your memory might have…improved."

Doris dropped his hand. "I really need to finish getting ready." She began to move around the room, grabbing her gloves, her coat, her purse.

"'Cause Uncle Saul said if it did, then maybe we could still do something. There's still time," Jonny said, moving after her, "and my mother and father are still interested." He was determined to use anything he could to sway her, even if he wasn't sure it was true.

"I really have to go," was all Doris said in response. She looked into a mirror near the front door and gave herself the customary final look-over. Her dress was still not zipped, and she reached back to try to reach it. As she fumbled, Jonny moved up from behind and zipped it for her. "Thank you," she said with a weak smile. Then she began to cry, softly at first but then forcefully and with a painful urgency. "You don't know how much I want to go after Anderson, but I can't. I just can't," she said between sobs. "You have your uncle Saul and your mother and father. And your brother and the rest of your family. I have nothing. Nothing. I'm alone. I can't go through it alone. I just can't. I'm sorry."

Jonny watched her, realizing his mother had been wrong about Doris: she was scared. Desperately, horribly scared. And worse, she was going through it alone. Jonny hugged her, and Doris hugged back, clasping him desperately in her shaking arms. They stood together for a long moment, two people in agony, painfully missing the person they shared.

Finally, Doris broke away. "I really do have to go." She looked at herself in the mirror and frowned. She was a puffy, red-faced mess. She quickly pulled out her compact and worked as fast as possible. "Could you grab my coat? It's in the closet."

"Sure." Jonny opened the closet and reached inside for the coat.

Doris finished her work with the compact and then peered closely in the mirror. Resigned, she wrinkled her nose and let out a long sigh, "Well, this is one way to find out if he really loves me." She pulled out her lipstick, puckered her lips, and carefully applied the bright red lipstick to her lips with her right hand, as she shook her left arm in Jonny's direction. "Just slip it on," she said. But nothing happened. "Come on; I'm in a hurry." But still he didn't respond. Finally, finished with the lipstick, she turned around.

Jonny stood behind her, holding her coat—her brand-new mink coat. The expression on Doris's face only lasted a split-second, but Jonny saw it, and it was unmistakable. Caught. But then she waved her hand dismissively. "Oh, that silly old, ratty thing," she said. "That was a gift from an admirer."

Jonny nodded but didn't believe it for a second. He wasn't stupid; he could see it was an extraordinarily fine and expensive coat.

Doris turned her back to him. "I don't even think it's real," she insisted. "Come now; I'm in a hurry."

Jonny placed the coat over Doris's shoulders, and she reached back and slid her arms into it. She turned around and gave Jonny a quick kiss on the cheek. "Stop by again, soon."

The first thing to go was his "Americans will always fight for freedom" poster, depicting soldiers from the American Revolution juxtaposed with modern soldiers, which he had carefully and painstakingly peeled off the wooden wall that surrounded a construction site. Now, he tore it from his wall, ripped it to shreds, and threw it in the garbage. As far as he was concerned, the war was over. The Germans had won. The Japanese had won. The Italians had won. Anderson Vleets had won. Jonny continued his surrender by tearing down the rest of the US Army and US Navy posters that decorated his walls. Next, he shredded his map of Europe, along with the "Keep America Strong" guidebook he received in school. Next, his Junior Commando armband went into the trash, along with his lieutenant's bars and his meritorious action citation. He gathered it all, including a bag of tin cans he had collected for this week's drive, marched into the hallway, and tossed it all down the garbage chute. As a final coup de grâce, he grabbed several piles of newspapers someone had placed in the hall for him and threw them into the garbage chute too.

He stepped back into his war-free room, basking in the cleanliness and order of surrender. But his work wasn't done. Sticking out from a novel titled *Baseball Heroes* were two colorful cardboard tickets. Immediately, Jonny knew what they were. They were the tickets he had gotten for buying the twenty-five-dollar war bond so that he and Rachel could go the premiere of *Thousands Cheer*. Tickets that he had gotten on *that day*. He grasped them in his hands, ready to rip them to shreds. *What a perfect final act of defeat,* he thought as his grip tightened. But then, his mind wandered, dreaming of the event and the way it was supposed to have happened.

He and Rachel were going to get all dressed up in their Saturday-night best and attend. They would stroll down the red carpet together, mingling in and around all the celebrities. *"Look, there's Judy Garland, and over there, that's Gene Kelly."* Yes, they would be there with all the big Hollywood celebrities. And the famous of New York would attend, too—the mayor, the chief of police, the borough president, lots of Broadway stars, the cream of Gotham society. This last bit of fantasy made Jonny pause. Yes, it was true— the cream of Gotham society would be there. The theatre would be packed to the rafters with the glittering somebodies from the society pages, especially those who never missed a chance to be seen. Especially somebody like Anderson Vleets.

Jonny loosened his grip on the tickets. He would need them. Perhaps the war wasn't lost quite yet. Perhaps it could still be won.

The next day, for only the third time in his life, Jonny dared to venture east of Broadway on 181st Street on his own. The first time was on a dare from some friends, where he had to return with a flier from one of the numerous movie theatres that dotted the busy thoroughfare. The second time was to a candy shop that was rumored, even though it was 1938, to still be selling packs of 1933 Goudey baseball cards. And the third time was today.

It wasn't that this was a bad part of town; a person didn't cross Broadway and then suddenly descend into hell. And it wasn't so much different from *his* side of Broadway. It was just that everywhere you went, there was more. The stores were a little more crowded. The theaters were a little more packed. The people, especially the farther east you got from Broadway, were a little more rowdy, a little more rambunctious. And there were other more subtle differences. The diners would serve cheap greasy food, just like the ones on his side of town, except that east of Broadway, there very likely would be a guy sitting in a corner booth who might kick your butt if he was in a bad mood. The front of the candy store on the other side of Broadway would be just like the front of Jonny's candy store, except there would always be two or three guys hanging around, keeping an eye on things. If you wanted to place a bet on a ball game or a horse race, the old woman running the newsstand on his side of Broadway would give you a blank look back. On the other side, the young guy at the newsstand would happily take your bet and ask if you wanted to play the daily number, too. And east of Broadway, you could find things that weren't available on the west side of the street. You just had to know where to look.

And Jonny did.

Nervously passing the entrance to the Montrone Theatre, Jonny pressed on, moving farther east of Broadway than he ever had before. It was just after noon, and the sidewalks were packed with people seeking lunch. He then turned onto Audubon Avenue and walked about twenty feet before cutting down an alleyway that ran behind the shops on 181st. His feet crunched on the unpaved gravel, and Jonny walked until he saw a sign—"Zannis Laundry. Deliveries only"—plastered on the rickety wooden rear door of a shop. Steeling himself, Jonny knocked.

A moment later, a tough-looking kid in his early twenties, with brash suspenders holding up his baggy pants, opened the door. He squinted at Jonny. "Whaddya want?"

"I…uh…I…" Jonny couldn't get the words out.

"Good-bye."

"I want to see Frankie," Jonny said hurriedly, stopping the door from slamming shut.

"What for?"

"I want to ask him a question."

"Well, he don't like questions, and neither do I." The door started to close again, but Jonny grabbed it again. The tough kid snarled, "Whaddya doing, kid? Scram!" But Jonny wouldn't let go of the door.

Finally, from inside, another pair of hands appeared and pushed the door open. "What's going on, here?" asked another tough of about the same age.

The first tough stiffened, as if he'd been caught—the second one clearly out ranked him. "He wants to see Frank."

"Oh, yeah?" the second tough said, looking suspiciously at Jonny. But then he smiled. "I know you."

Jonny's brow furrowed; then there was sudden recognition. "Eddie?"

"Yep," Eddie Kubinski answered, nodding. Though he was the same age as the first tough, he was dressed better, wearing a sport coat over an open-collar shirt. "This is Mitchell Drabinowitz's kid brother," Eddie said to the first kid. "He's all right."

The first kid stepped aside, letting Jonny enter. Though Eddie was just as imposing a figure as the first tough, seeing him actually calmed Jonny a bit. They weren't exactly friends; they just knew a lot of the same people. They had even traded some baseball cards a few years back. Eddie was a huge Yankees fan, and Jonny loved the Giants, so they made some trades that were good for both of them—although as much as Eddie had tried, and he had made several very tempting offers, Jonny wouldn't part with his 1939 Playball card of Joe DiMaggio. Jonny hated the Yankees, but like every kid in New York, he sure loved "Joe D."

Eddie led Jonny into the large storage area of the laundry. Stacks of cleaning supplies were piled precariously high. Passing by them, Jonny instantly saw why they were stacked almost to the ceiling. Even though this really was a functioning laundry, the supplies created a wall to hide what was really in the storage space. Stretching before Jonny was pile after pile of almost-impossible-to-get rationed goods, awaiting sale on the black market: crates of coffee and sugar, stacks of gas-ration books and nylons, a butcher's cooler filled with butter and steaks, even a couple dozen brand-new rubber car tires.

Sitting in the middle of it all, at a metal desk flanked by several more toughs, was Frankie Zannis. Frankie had become a legend in the neighborhood by the time he was twelve, achieving the distinction of being the person about whom every kid's parents warned, "Keep that up, and you'll end up like Frankie Zannis." It was the refrain around the neighborhood for things as trivial as coming home late or as serious as getting into a fight. What parents didn't realize was that, even though most kids were terrified of Frankie, they all would have gladly traded places and become Frankie, if only for an afternoon. His participation in the educational system ended around his tenth birthday. The truant officers gave up on chasing after him, and his merchant-marine father was gone most of the time, so Frankie was on his own. He was soon hanging around with a bunch of low-level gangsters, running errands for them, bringing them coffee—anything so he could stay in their midst and learn.

And learn he did.

By the time he was fourteen, he was the kid you went to for M-80s and cherry bombs. By fifteen, he had branched out to French postcards and booze for underage kids. By seventeen, he could get you reefer, if that was what you were into. But when the war began, Frankie went big time. For someone in the procurement business, what could be better than a sudden demand—and with it, a strong mark-up—for previously easy-to-obtain household items? So Frankie and his gang set up shop in the back of his uncle's laundry, kicking him a few bucks for the use, and turned it into the place people went to get what they needed, if they had no other way to get it. Even Jonny's parents knew about Frankie; in fact, that was how Jonny first found out about the place—he'd overheard a debate about whether to buy additional gas-ration booklets from Frankie for a trip they wanted to take to Mississippi to see Mitchell in basic training. But before they made their decision on whether to cross this ethical boundary, Mitchell's letters about the anti-Semitism he was encountering in the Deep South put an end to the whole idea.

"He's got something he wants to ask ya," Eddie said, pushing Jonny in front of Frankie and his desk.

"Oh, yeah?" Frankie asked, cracking a crooked smile. Amused by the sight of a little kid, Frankie stood up, showing off a brand-new suit. "What can I do for you?"

Jonny felt his palms moisten and his heart race. Here he was, in front of Frankie Zannis, with a chance to get what he needed, but he couldn't get the words out. "I…uh…I…Frankie…uh …"

"It's 'Frank' these days," Frankie corrected him, still smiling.

"Well, I was…ah…" The words still eluded him. Jonny forced himself to calm down. He thought about everything that had happened over the last couple of months. Rachel's death. Doris's betrayal. His parents' anguish. And most of all, the need for vengeance against Anderson Vleets. Jonny swallowed loudly. "Frank, I want to buy a gun." Everyone in the room burst out laughing. Everyone except Jonny. As they were still cracking up at his expense, Jonny dug through his pockets and pulled out an envelope. "I have a twenty-five-dollar war bond," he said, pulling out the red-white-and-blue slip of paper and showing it to them. "I'm hoping that's enough."

The laughter slowly subsided as they realized he wasn't kidding. Frankie, in particular, lost his smile; his whole posture drooped. "Get him out of here," he ordered as he collapsed back into his chair.

Seconds later, they tossed Jonny back into the alley, and slammed the door to the laundry behind him. He thought about knocking again—after all, getting a gun was the key to his entire plan—but thought better of it. Defeated, he turned and walked away. His mind raced, thinking of where else he might be able to find a weapon. There was Mr. Donatelli, the super who lived in the basement, who Jonny had once seen brandishing a small pistol when there was a blackout.

Footsteps approaching from behind made Jonny turn around quickly. Eddie came running up and slid to a stop right in front of Jonny. Without saying a word, Eddie opened his coat and showed Jonny a small, snub-nosed revolver hidden inside. Jonny's eyes went wide. Handing over the war bond, he reached for the pistol.

Eddie took the war bond but then asked, "Do you still have that '39 DiMaggio Playball card?" Eddie stepped back, making it clear that the card had to be part of any deal.

Jonny nodded.

A week later, on the morning of the premiere, Jonny awoke just after 7:00 a.m., much later than he had planned. His sleep had been fitful, with wild dreams of Anderson Vleets drowning in tin cans, run over by car-less tires, and being suffocated with a fur coat. But as he climbed out of bed, Jonny knew he was arising into a world where Anderson was still very much alive. At least, for now.

Dressing quickly, he slipped the gun into his pants pocket. It was a tight fit, with the outline of the gun more visible than he liked. He'd deal with that as soon as he got out of the house, which he had to do as soon as possible, or he might run in to one of his parents. He'd almost made it to the front door when his mother called to him from the kitchen, "Jacob?"

Now she decides to talk? Jonny wondered. *For weeks nothing, then suddenly, she picks today to start again. Just keep going, open the door and leave.* He gripped the doorknob. *Who cares if she'll be mad at you? In twelve hours, it'll be the last thing on her mind.* But instead, he loosened his grip. "Yes?" he said defeatedly.

"Where are you going?"

"I'm meeting Dewey and Larry. We're gonna spend the day at the 151st pool," he lied, careful to pick two friends who didn't live in his building.

"That's nice." Lena emerged from the kitchen, carrying a brown paper bag. "I made lunch for you." She handed it to Jonny. Her mood, for some reason, was a bit lighter. She actually had a slightly pleasant look to her. Did she know what he was about to do? Could she sense that Jonny was going to get the vengeance they all deserved? "There's a little something extra in there for you that I think you'll like," she said warmly.

Clutching the door, Jonny turned away from her. "We might go to Larry's house afterward, so I might be late."

"Your dinner will be waiting."

Through it all, she is still a good mother, Jonny thought, *a wonderful mother who deserves some measure of peace.* Now even more driven to bring her this sweet taste of justice, Jonny left.

He was about to toss away the brown paper bag as he left the building when he realized it might be of use. Slipping into an alley, he pulled out the wax-paper-covered tuna sandwich and a slick red apple and dropped them on the ground. Then he put the gun in the bag and shoved the whole thing back into his pants.

As he walked out onto the sidewalk, his pants pocket was now an amorphous bulge, free of the telltale outline of a small, snub-nose revolver.

Jonny rode the subway all day, taking it as far as Coney Island to the south and the Bronx to the north. As the boroughs of New York City whizzed by, he went over his plan again and again. His seat at the theatre was in the top balcony; his twenty-five-dollar war bond was the cheapest available and therefore came with the cheapest seats. Anderson's presence was sure to cause almost as much commotion as the film's stars, so even from that extreme height, Jonny knew he wouldn't have any trouble spotting Anderson far below. From the gossip columns Rachel had always excitedly read to him, he knew Anderson would be seated in one of the boxes that lined either side of the theatre. Jonny would get a firm fix on him, wait for the lights to go out, and then as the opening newsreel started, he would carefully make his way down to the mezzanine level and follow the small hallway that led to the boxes. He'd wait outside the box for the film to begin and when it did, using the rousing explosion of noise from the expected ovation as a cover, he'd slip in next to Anderson and fire. Unlike John Wilkes Booth, whom Jonny realized, in some twisted way, he should thank for the plan, Jonny would not jump down onto the stage and scream, "Death to war profiteers!" Instead, he would calmly drop the gun and wait to be arrested.

At 6:00 p.m., Jonny finally ended his orbit of New York City and climbed the stairs up into Times Square. It was a quick walk over to the Astor, where above the marquee hung an enormous sixty-foot poster for *Thousands Cheer* and the war bond drive. Even though it would be at least another hour before the first celebrities arrived, there was already a thick crowd lining both sides of the red carpet that stretched from the street to the gigantic bronze doors that were the theatre's entrance. The door was open, with a few early arrivals straggling up the red carpet, completely ignored by the gathered fans and press. Jonny wanted to leave as little as possible to chance, so he had decided to go into the theatre early.

But now, for the first time, just fifty feet from the beckoning entrance to the theatre, with his goal clearly achievable, he hesitated. Was he really going to do this? Take another person's life? Commit an act he had been taught his whole life was wrong? What if things went badly and he was caught before he achieved his goal? His parents would suffer the shame of his arrest without the satisfaction of Anderson's demise. Or worse—what if he shot the wrong person or hit an innocent bystander? *No. No. No!* he finally told himself. *No hesitating.* His plan was well thought out, his quest just. He took the sight of the swirling crowds of servicemen all around him as further vindication of his cause. Hadn't they all been taught that killing was wrong? Didn't they all learn "Thou shall not kill" in Sunday school? Yet the sole reason they were covered in either brown or blue wool on a hot night in New York City was because they had been trained to kill.

There was such a thing as a justified killing.

The matter closed, the mission clear, Jonny marched toward the entrance to the theatre. He handed over the ticket and kept going.

"Whoa! Whoa! Where do you think you're going?" the ticket taker asked, his usher uniform comical compared to that of the real soldiers.

"To my seat."

"Where're your parents?"

"They're not here."

"Then you're not seeing the movie." The ticket-taker pointed to a sign on the wall that read "No unaccompanied minors." Not waiting for Jonny's response, he grabbed him by the shirt and moved him back toward the entrance.

"But...but..."

"And don't try sneaking in here, pretending someone else is your parent. I'll remember you," the ticket-taker added for finality before returning to his post.

Jonny stood his ground. *This is not part of the plan.*

"Go!" the ticket-taker shooed him, punctuating his words with a swipe of his hand.

Jonny turned and wandered back down the red carpet to the street, where the crowd of rabid fans sucked him in. In a daze, he stood at their edge, contemplating his next move.

Is this a sign? he wondered. *Should I just turn and walk away?* He could jump on the subway, head uptown, dump the gun in a sewer drain, and be home in time for a late dinner. Or was this merely a test? An obstacle to overcome? He thought of Mitchell overseas, somewhere in Sicily with Patton. If they attacked a hill and it failed, they didn't just turn around, give up, and head home for a late dinner. They found another way to achieve their objective and attacked again. The mission had to be completed.

As Jonny considered his options and searched for a new plan, the first of the celebrities started arriving. They climbed out of sleek, night-black limos that stopped one at a time at the head of the red carpet. With each arrival, the crowd squealed in delight, surging and rocking and threatening to burst through the velvet ropes that held them back.

Yes! Of course! In that crowd, Jonny realized, no one would notice if he pulled out a gun and fired. It could work. Jonny waded into the crowd, pushing toward the front so he could get a clear shot of anyone on the red carpet. But some of the stars of the movie had arrived—Kathryn Grayson and Mickey Rooney—and the rabid fans closed ranks, all trying to get a better look at their idols. Jonny couldn't move an inch, and when Mary Astor stepped onto the red carpet, the crowd came together so tightly, it pushed Jonny out, right back to where he had started.

This was not going to work.

He spotted a pack of photographers very close to the curb who had their own cordoned-off section. They'd be too busy taking rapid, flash-popping pictures of each celebrity climbing out of the limousines to notice the fourteen-year-old boy who slipped into their section. There was only a handful of them, Jonny reasoned, so it would be easy to slide through their jostling bodies, reach the front of the rope, and quickly fire some shots at the right moment. As a bonus, he realized the dark flash of metal, which would be him drawing his gun, would be lost in the barrage of white blasts that the photographers around him would be unleashing.

Jonny waited, his heart racing as one limo after the next drove up and dropped off movie stars in a heavy hail of screams and camera flashes. The start time for the film was closing in but still no Anderson. *What if he doesn't come?* Jonny fretted. What if he'd decided to stay home and enjoy the night in private with any one of a dozen starlets who would be thrilled to be chased around the marble floors of his Fifth Avenue penthouse? But then, Jonny spotted him in the back of a long limousine, two cars back.

This was it! Anderson was here.

But could he do it? All the dreaming, all the planning, all the practicing was coming down to this one singular moment in time. With his heart threatening to burst through his skin, Jonny eased the paper bag out of his pocket and held it close to his body. He slid his hand in, feeling the cool, hard metal. But as his fingers gripped the gun, he felt—to his extreme shock—something else, something he'd missed when he'd tossed out the sandwich and apple. It had a coarse texture with sharp corners. It was very thin and bent easily when he slid his fingers across it. Jonny fished it from the bag. He instantly recognized the small blue envelope covered with postmarks and censor stamps. It was a piece of victory mail from overseas—from Mitchell. Jonny tore it open, knowing his brother's angry, fury-filled words about Rachel's death would spur him on even further, giving him greater strength and sharpening his aim.

As the car in front of Anderson's dropped off its passengers—an older pair of stars that Jonny sort of recognized—he began to read.

Dear Jacob,

I hope this letter finds you, Mom, Dad, and Rachel well.

Jonny's head jerked back. When Mitchell wrote this letter, he didn't know yet. It was from a time Jonny almost couldn't remember—a time when they both still had a sister.

You may not know this, but in her last letter, Rachel included a wonderful photo of us, taken on the opening day of the World's Fair. I don't know how well you remember it, but I have very fond memories of that day. We walked around for hours, and we all saw television for the first time. You were quite taken by it. You said something at that time that I laughed at. But now, with all I've seen, I feel it was the truth, or at least it should be. We do live in an age of miracles, and there should be no war. We should spend our days, enthralled with our achievements, not plotting to kill each other. People like you, who are willing to express crazy, naïve ideas, even when others laugh at them, are what we need. They are the fools, and you are the wise one. Jacob, you have a very bright future ahead of you, as I pray the world does, once this nightmare comes to an end.

I dream every day of the day I will be home again with you and Mom and Dad and Rachel.

Love,

Mitchell

As Jonny lowered the letter from his eyes, Anderson passed not three feet away from him. But Jonny didn't notice. He turned around and fought his way out of the pack of crazed photographers and away from the premiere.

He tossed the gun into a storm drain and hurried home. Once inside his room, he began to write.

And not about stamps.

Episode Two

JUSTICE GIRL

"GUILTY, UNTIL PROVEN INNOCENT"

April 3, 1955

"Great show last night!" Mr. Donatelli, the building superintendent, yelled to Jonny while sweeping the building's front steps.

"Thanks," Jonny hurriedly said back, as he shot past him and headed away.

As he sped down the sidewalk, Jonny could see Mr. Donatelli turn to a couple of other residents and confer with them, no doubt discussing that Jonny had had a show premier on "the television" the night before. Though his parents had said very little about his show, Jonny discovered, as he left his apartment, that everyone in the building was quite aware of it, which could have come only from his parents. This was their way of saying they were proud of him.

Dodging the thick morning traffic, Jonny slipped across Broadway and headed toward Benny's All Nighter, a diner Jonny frequented as often as he could get away with avoiding his mother's cooking. His plan was to suck down a quick breakfast and then hurry on to the writers' room. There was much to do. But, actually, he needed coffee more than food. A lot of coffee.

He'd settled on the idea for this week's show around 4:30 a.m., finally falling asleep at 5:00 a.m., but his fantasy of sleeping in until 10:00 a.m. had been thwarted by a steady stream of phone calls that had started just after 8:00 a.m. Charles had called four times, saying that Hogart demanded to see Jonny right away. Jonny ignored the first three calls, but on the fourth, finally agreed to see Hogart at 11:00 a.m., in Hogart's office, but he might be a little late. More entertainingly, there had been two calls from Jonny's agent.

His agent.

Though Jonny hadn't bothered to call his agent when he'd had his initial meeting with Hogart, satisfied that he and Mitchell could handle everything, Jonny did try to reach him after things started to roll toward the first episode. Jonny thought, at the very least, as a courtesy, he should let his agent know what was happening.

The agent had not returned the call.

That is, until this morning. Jonny ignored both calls, telling his mother to tell his agent he would call back later, if he had time.

Though it was after 9:00 a.m. when Jonny entered the diner, he found it crowded, and most disappointing, his favorite booth—farthest from the door under the front windows—was occupied.

"What's wrong, Jonny?" Benny asked, reading the disappointment on Jonny's face as he hurried toward him from the other side of the front counter.

"Oh, nothing. There's just someone in the booth I—"

"You want your usual table?" Benny offered as he slipped around the cash register. Not waiting for an answer, he marched his large girth toward the booth in the rear. Before Jonny could get another word out, Benny had shooed away the two patrons and quickly cleared the table. "Here you are," Benny said to Jonny. "Your usual table."

"Thanks," Jonny said a bit shyly, having never before heard it referred to as his table. He slipped into the last booth, his gaze facing forward toward the front door.

"Great show last night!" Benny said as he wiped down the table with a rag that lived permanently in the apron wrapped like a sausage skin around his huge stomach.

"Thank you."

Benny moved away, and immediately Larraine, a pretty, young waitress with curly brown hair and a curvy figure that even her shapeless, off-white uniform couldn't ruin, took his place and handed Jonny a menu. "Great show last night," she said brightly.

Jonny almost jumped up in the booth. He'd tried for months to make conversation with Larraine, and she had spurned him at every turn. "Thanks," he managed to get out.

"You never told me you were a writer," she said with a playful smile.

Yes, he had, about a dozen times. "Yep." Jonny shrugged.

"Well, I think that's really great." She gave him a wink and then walked away.

Jonny watched her go, enjoying the sashay of her shapely hips before he lifted the menu to his eyes. He laughed to himself and shook his head, enjoying the unexpected attention. He eyed the menu, more out of reflex than anything—after all, he always ordered the same thing: eggs, bacon, hash browns, orange juice, and coffee.

Standing before him was Marty Nussbaum, his agent. "How are ya, kid?" Marty asked, even though he was maybe—*maybe*—two years older than Jonny. Not waiting for an answer or an invitation, Marty slipped into the booth across from Jonny.

"I'm fine," Jonny said, a bit leery.

"Fine! We'll you oughta be better than fine. Good thing I tracked you down."

"And how are you, Marty?" Jonny asked, resignedly. Jonny hadn't actually laid eyes on Marty in almost a year, and he could see very little had changed. Marty still wore his trademark porkpie hat, even indoors, and tailored black suit with a piercing red tie. Jonny had signed with him right after getting hired on *Hermie's Henhouse* at the behest of the show. The William Morris Agency had put the show together as a package deal and, besides handling Hermie himself, they represented almost the entire producing and writing team. With no leverage, Jonny had gone along with the request and was given Marty as his agent. After a couple of initial meetings, one before Jonny signed and the other when he signed, Marty had largely ignored Jonny. Jonny figured out very quickly that Marty was content to sit back and let the commissions roll in from Jonny's weekly paycheck.

"Who cares about me? Let's talk about you," Marty said, narrowing his dark, aggressive eyes and locking in on Jonny.

"Okay, let's." Jonny tilted his head back. "Did you read my script?"

Marty was thrown for only the briefest of seconds. "Which one would that be?"

"'The Road to Damascus.' I sent it to you about a year ago." Indeed, he had sent it to Marty after *American Stories* had rejected it in the hopes that Marty would submit it to one of the other anthology shows on another network. Jonny never heard back—not even a single word. "It's a drama, perfect for *Kraft* or *Studio One*," Jonny offered, as a further reminder.

"Loved it! But I want to read it again. It's right on the top of my desk. I was just about to get to it," Marty answered, without a hint of embarrassment. "But let's not talk about three-day-old bread. Let's talk about the future. Let's talk about an ice cream sundae with a cherry on top."

Oh yeah, Jonny thought, remembering that Marty was one of those agents who thought part of his job was to talk like he was in a Clifford Odetts play. "Isn't that what I was?" Jonny asked matter-of-factly. "'The Road to Damascus' could be my future." *And why not?* Jonny thought. He was going to be busy with *Justice Girl* for some time, and as much as he was happy with the important issues he planned to work into the stories, why not make a push for one of his other projects?

Marty shook his head. "Kiddie shows are hot right now. Let's ride that train all the way to the station. I see possibilities."

Jonny bit his lip. "One kiddie show at a time is enough for me, thank you."

Marty exhaled in mock disgust. "Well, excuse me for wanting to help feather your nest. If you're not interested in what I'm selling, I'll take my pushcart uptown. Someone up there probably wouldn't mind making some money."

Larraine was back, order pad in her hand. Jonny indicated her with a jerk of his head and sighed. "Look, I'm already running late, and I really need to get my day started."

Marty jumped up out of the booth. "Got ya, kid. Call me at my office, and let's set up a meeting, tout suite, 'kay?"

"'Kay," Jonny shot back with a quick finger point, his mockery completely missed by Marty. "And read my script."

"Will do, Jonny. It's right on the top of my desk. But kid, you're a rocket headed to the moon. Don't let the clouds get in your way." Marty then turned and hurried out of the diner.

Watching him go, Jonny and Larraine exchanged a bemused chuckle.

...

Tired of pacing in his office, Hogart headed for the elevator in a fury. It was after 11:00 a.m., and Jonny was over an hour late. As he descended alone to the lobby, Hogart was so angry, he actually punched the air. This morning should have been a triumph. He had done it; he had gotten a full half-hour pilot episode of *Justice Girl* on the air in less than a week. Though he had missed much of the content, it was clear that it had been a resounding success. From the excited response of his own family, gushing reviews in the morning papers, spontaneous applause of the network staff when he arrived, and the exceptional first glimpse of the ratings, one thing was for sure: *Justice Girl* was well on its way to being the hit show and just possibly the network-saving colossus he'd envisioned.

But Jonny's removal of any mention of the sponsor had ruined the possibility of even a split second of satisfaction on Hogart's part. As expected, when Hogart entered his office, even though it was not yet 8:00 a.m., Tipton had already called three times. The bright pink message slips sat threateningly atop his polished oak desk. Hogart eyed them warily for a second before brushing them aside. It was a huge problem but one he would ultimately be able to manage.

Jonny, however, was another problem altogether.

Not sure he could control his anger, Hogart had Charles call Jonny, requesting that Jonny be in his office by 10:00 a.m. Hearing that it took four phone calls to get confirmation only made Hogart angrier.

For the next three hours-plus, Hogart paced, ignoring a bevy of congratulatory phone calls and two more from Yardley Tipton. Finally, with his desk clock's two hands telling him it was eleven, Hogart could stand it no longer. If Jonny wouldn't come to him, he would go to Jonny.

The ride downward in the claustrophobic elevator only furthered his rage. When the operator opened the heavy metal doors, Hogart burst out and rushed as fast as his stiffened leg allowed across the polished marble floor toward the exit. But as he closed in on the revolving door, he suddenly stopped. Jonny had just entered and was casually sauntering toward him.

Over an hour late, and he looks like he's out for a Sunday stroll. Hogart tightened his jaw. "Nice of you to finally arrive," he seethed.

"Oh, yeah, sorry about that. I wanted to get started on next week's—"

"Don't you ever pull a stunt like that again!" Hogart raged as he shoved a finger in Jonny's face. "Canceling a sponsor without getting approval from anyone at the network!"

If Jonny was surprised by the outburst, he didn't show it. He just took a slight step back and gave a mild smile. "I seem to recall that I am not only the writer but also the executive producer of the show. I believe that gives me the right to determine who the sponsor is."

Hogart raised his finger again but then stopped. Firing a producer— or anyone, for that matter—was something Hogart always looked forward to doing. He'd said the next words he planned to say on so many other occasions that he could say them in his sleep. But now, his mouth just hung open. Nothing came out of his frozen, parted lips as he remembered he wasn't in his usual position with Jonny. In every other case, when dealing with difficult producers, Hogart had a signed contract that made them practically chattel. But things had moved so quickly with this show, there was no such contract. In fact, the contract that went out last week to Jonny's brother, which was packed with the hidden subsets and clauses that Hogart relished, had been sent back the very next day, covered with rewrites, redactions, and outright removals. The guy was sharp, Hogart had admitted to himself. Jonny's brother had caught every legal game they had tried to maneuver, removed them all, and even inserted a few of his own.

When Jonny saw that Hogart was lost for the moment, he continued. "Of course, if this arrangement isn't to your liking, I could always take the show to someplace…more accommodating."

160

Hogart felt deflated. He hated the fact that he did not have the upper hand. "Very well then," he said. "I'll find a new sponsor."

Jonny nodded. "And this time, be sure to run it by me before you make the deal."

Hogart's head snapped in disbelief. "I will do no such thing. I am the head of this network, and I will not—"

This time Jonny thrust an angry finger forward. "How can we have a character who is fighting injustice on a show that is about defeating injustice, and yet have it sponsored by a company that perpetuates injustice?" Jonny didn't wait for an answer. "The Remington Shoe Company is a despicable practitioner of segregation. And I'm sure I don't have to remind you what happened during the war."

He didn't. Hogart, as well as most of the rest of the country, was well aware that the Remington Shoe factory in Beaumont, Texas, had been the scene of one of the worst race riots of the Second World War. After switching over to the production of boots, demand was so strong and labor so scarce, that the factory had no choice but to hire black workers for its graveyard shift. Almost from the outset, the situation was tense, and after the accusation that a black worker had whistled at a white woman who worked in the front office—which later turned out to be false—the situation turned violent. The following evening, as the night shift ended, a pack of angry white workers waited for the black workers to get off work. As soon as they exited the factory gates, the bat-wielding mob attacked them. Defenseless and with no help from the factory security guards who stood off to the side doing nothing, the black workers could only run. In the end, over fifty suffered injuries and thirteen died. A final inquest by the factory and local police determined that the black workers were at fault because they'd engaged in provocative activities. What exactly these "provocative activities" were, the inquest failed to mention.

"The Remington Shoe Company will never sponsor a show that has my name on it," Jonny said, ending with one final jab of his finger. "Is there anything else you wanted to talk about?"

Hogart sighed heavily and shook his head. "No."

"Good." Jonny turned for the door. "Now, if you'll excuse me, I have an episode to write."

As Hogart watched Jonny depart, the full weight and seriousness of the problem descended on him. Obviously, he knew Jonny was a writer, and that meant he carried with him the usual pretensions of making art. Hogart could easily deal with that problem by allowing the "artist" a certain amount of control, or at least the appearance of control. But this was something much, much more dangerous. And potentially fatal.

In Hogart's mind, Jonny was inflicted with the worst possible malady: he was obsessed with doing good. To Hogart, having been on his own since fifteen, sometimes sleeping in train cars and dreaming of the luxury of a bread line, such pretension seemed downright disgusting. He'd seen one hundred men willing to tear each other to pieces for a single day's work on a road project or willing to slit a child's throat for an apple. He knew what the world really was. But Jonny knew nothing of that and had the curse of thinking he could actually make the world a better place. Worse, he thought he could do it through a TV show. *This* TV show. The show Hogart needed to succeed on his own terms, not Jonny's.

As he rode back up in the elevator, Hogart began planning his next move, mentally scanning his ample Rolodex for just whom he would need.

...

The cup of coffee hit the ground just inches from her feet, soaking through her shoes, but there was no time for Felicity to wipe them off. Jonny had unexpectedly exited the building that housed the main offices of the Regal Television Network, bursting out onto the sidewalk just moments after he'd walked in. From across the street, Felicity had been watching the offices since nine in the morning, hoping that she would be lucky enough to run into him. She had gotten her wish, as Jonny suddenly had appeared and strolled inside. Preparing herself for an indeterminate wait, she had bought the cup of coffee to keep her company. But then, Jonny had suddenly reappeared. Now seemingly invigorated, his nonchalance had vanished, and he was moving with a sense of purpose as he hurried down the sidewalk. Ignoring her soggy feet, Felicity went after him but stayed several feet behind, keeping pace from across the street. Then, without warning, Jonny hailed a cab and sped away. "Shit!" Felicity said, flinching at her uncharacteristic utterance. Waving frantically, she flagged down her own cab and reached for the crusty door handle—but then paused. Peering through the window, she could see the backseat was filthy, torn, and stained. A quick glance to the front seat offered no comfort. She was about to send the cab on its way and try for another one but realized that Jonny was getting farther and farther away. Pulling her coat sleeve down over her hand, she grabbed the door handle, opened the door, and slipped inside. Pitched forward so that as little of her body as possible would touch the seat, she pointed through the windshield and said, without a touch of irony, "Follow that taxi!"

The cabbie rolled his heavy, bloodshot eyes. "Very funny, lady," he said, releasing more than a whiff of cheap alcohol.

"I mean it."

"Seriously?"

"Yes!"

"Okay!" As the cab streaked off, Felicity slammed against the backseat. When she tried to lean forward, she found she was stuck to the back of the seat. Grimacing and not really wanting to know what exactly she was stuck on, Felicity ripped herself free.

Even though she was exhausted, she willed the cab to catch up with Jonny's. Last night she'd been so caught up in the conversation in the kitchen and then on the fire escape that she hadn't trudged back wearily to her hotel room until after 5:00 a.m., and then she was awakened at 8:00 a.m. by a screaming phone call from her furious father. Scott Kensington had started the day, as he often did, with an early round at the club, and a couple of the members had remarked that the star of a new show on television that their kids were going crazy over bore a striking resemblance to his daughter. Fortunately, due in large part to Felicity's having used the stage name of Denise Yarnell, they dropped the matter after a couple of playful digs. But Felicity's father was in no joking mood as he yelled at her that having a daughter publicly mixing in the Commie world of television was the exact opposite of what he needed. She had better make her rather outlandish plan work, he warned, or get the hell out of there before she was exposed and did fatal damage to his already weak chance of getting the party nomination. He then hung up on her.

As much as she wanted to be angry at her father, she knew he was right. What was she doing, wasting precious time listening to a bunch of self-indulgent and narcissistic actors talk about taking risks and character spines and backstories? Backstories? Seriously? The history of a stupid character that didn't even really exist? How could she have let herself get caught up in such nonsense? She needed to focus on discovering the truth behind the show, not the character.

Even the tears welling up in her eyes at the memory of father's lambasting were a waste of time. She shook her head determinedly and peered through the front window, searching the sea of cars for Jonny's cab.

"There it is!" Felicity yelled, jamming her finger forward.

The cabbie sped up, and Felicity slammed into the backseat again. By the time she had recovered, her taxi had caught up to Jonny's. With the streets overrun with bright yellow cabs, it was easy for them to follow without being noticed. They wound their way across town until they reached Broadway, and then they headed south. When Jonny's cab slowed and pulled over in front of Gimbels, Felicity thought she had failed once again. He was heading into the studio, and she would have to wait before picking up the chase again. But then, instead of going inside, he crossed to the other side of Broadway, heading for an ornate office building. Her spirits rose, and Felicity quickly paid her cabbie and hurriedly climbed out. With no time to wait for a green light, she sprinted across the street, dodging a horn-honking bus and a speeding delivery truck.

Felicity waited for Jonny to disappear inside the building so he wouldn't spot her, and then she raced up to the front window and peered inside. The marble lobby wasn't much different from the one at the network offices, except it was smaller and quite a bit less elegant. This was clearly a building emphasizing work, not presentation. She saw Jonny step inside an elevator.

As soon as the elevator doors closed, Felicity streaked across the slick marble floor, her hard soles making a hell of a racket, and arrived at the elevator bank just in time to see the bronze indicator hand stop at the fifth floor.

When she reached the fifth floor, Felicity carefully poked her head out of the elevator. The hallway was clear, so she stepped off. Felicity crept along, reading the hand-painted signs on the frosted glass sections of the doors. The first three stood guard in front of multi-named law firms. Next she passed by a doctor's office and then a dentist's office. She wasn't sure what exactly she was looking for, but she knew it wouldn't be as simple as "Communist Writers Room." She passed two more dental offices and an import/export business before finding the door she was searching for. "Focus on Fashion" stood out in brand-new gold-leaf letters on the last door of the long hallway. Chuckling quietly, she carefully leaned against the frosted window and listened. The muffled voices were hard to distinguish, but what they were talking about was not.

Amid shouting and arguing, she heard, several times, the words "Justice Girl."

Felicity's pulse quickened. This was it! This was the place. Her instinct had been right; Jonny was working with others. And they had to be Communists. After all, why would he lie and claim he wrote the show himself? Felicity took a deep breath and exhaled, proudly. She had done it! She had made the discovery that she so desperately needed. But now, what to do? Should she stake out the lobby and wait to see Jonny exit, along with the seditious writers? Should she come back after business hours and break into their office to discover their names? Should she run to the nearest phone and call her dad so he could pass the information on to his contacts at the FBI?

Approaching footsteps startled Felicity, and she quickly jerked her head back, hoping to make it appear as if she had been studying the name on the door. With an exaggerated sigh that would have made Alexis cringe, she backed away from the door and headed down the hall, passing an approaching food deliveryman in a stained apron and creased paper hat. The deliveryman, carrying a stuffed brown paper bag, reached the door to "Focus on Fashion" and knocked. As she hurried away, Felicity could hear the door open.

"Denise?" an uncertain but familiar voice called after her.

Keep going! Keep going, she thought, but her legs didn't hear, and she slowly turned around.

"It *is* you!" Jonny called out as he paid and took the bag of sandwiches.

Caught, Felicity sheepishly headed back toward Jonny.

"What are you doing here?" Jonny asked.

Though the question was innocent, Felicity could tell there was unease on Jonny's part. She had to be careful; if he got too suspicious, he might fire the writers before she and her father had a chance to take advantage of the discovery. "I…well…I was heading into the studio for a meeting with Zelda," she said convincingly, because it was partially true—she did have a meeting with Zelda, just not for another couple of hours—"and I saw you head into this building. I didn't get a chance to say good-bye to you last night and wanted to thank you for, you know, helping me out at the party."

"Oh…no problem," Jonny answered, genuinely pleased.

He bought it, Felicity thought.

Suddenly, from inside the room, a familiar woman joined them. She slid up next to Jonny and said, almost trembling with excitement, "What if we discover that the crime she was falsely accused of on her home world happened when she was trying to right a great wrong? So she had been fighting for justice, even before she came to Earth!"

"I like it," Jonny answered, his eyes widening excitedly as he thought through what she had just said.

"Oh, hello," the woman said, finally noticing Felicity.

"Hi," Felicity answered, realizing this was Annie, the woman whose apartment had hosted the party the night before.

"I…ah…think you did a real nice job last night," Annie said.

"Thank you."

Annie grabbed the paper bag from Jonny and slipped back inside the room.

"I should be going," Felicity said. "You know how Zelda is." She turned, but Jonny reached out and stopped her.

He stepped close and lowered his voice. "If you could do me a favor and keep what you saw here quiet," Jonny said sincerely. "For…uh…budgetary reasons I promised the network I wouldn't use a writing staff."

What a pathetic liar, Felicity thought. *You just want to give work to your Commie friends so they can shove their Commie beliefs in the show.* She smiled convincingly. "Of course."

"Thanks. I guess I'll see you at the read-through on Thursday?"

Felicity nodded. "Until then." Suppressing the urge to scream with excitement at completing her mission, she calmly walked away. The door slammed shut behind her, and she quickened her pace. A name! She had a name. Annie. And searching her memory from the party, she remembered her full name: Annie Quinlan. Jonny was fronting for Annie Quinlan. She'd check the name as soon as she got home, but she was certain that Annie was on the list. Why else would Jonny want to keep it quiet?

Felicity looked back at the office door. *Enjoy your day writing together*, she gleefully thought, *because it just might be your last.* So they were working on Justice Girl's backstory. *Figures*, she thought. They were just as indulgent and narcissistic as the fellow subversives she had spent time with in the kitchen. What a waste of time. Although, the idea that Annie had suggested at the doorway was kind of reminiscent of one Felicity had had just last night, before falling asleep. It would be kind of interesting if Justice Girl had herself experienced something of what she was fighting against. It would give her character, as Alexis would say, a solid, grounded motivation. They were definitely heading in the right direction. Felicity also had another thought—an interesting idea for Justice Girl's relationship to her parents—that probably would fit in quite nicely with what the writers were considering.

Felicity walked back and knocked on the door to their office. What was the harm in making a few suggestions? And maybe she could use the additional contact to glean more information. This time, a short, bespectacled man answered the door. Felicity thought she also recognized him from the party, but she wasn't positive.

"Oh, hi," Shel said, clearly recognizing her.

"Her parents, who both love her very much, might be a bit too caught up in their own worlds to notice what Justice Girl is doing! They love her, but their neglect might lead to the trouble she gets herself into!" Felicity said excitedly.

Shel blinked rapidly several times, genuinely impressed. "You wanna come in?"

"Yes. Yes. Much better," Felicity said truthfully to Zelda. To be absolutely certain, she turned around and looked into the full-length mirror that dominated one of the walls of the costume room. The sight gave her further confirmation. The wig looked a thousand times better, and more important, it fit snugly to her head. During some of the flying sequences the night before, Felicity had been petrified that her wig was going to fly off. After the show finished and she was removing her makeup, a disgusted Zelda burst into her dressing room, picked up the wig, and threw it out the tiny window down to Fifth Avenue below. "Tomorrow afternoon, we give you new hair!" she announced with a stern flourish.

Finished with the fitting, Felicity left the costume room and headed for the main entrance to the studio. Once there, with the muffled noise and energy of New York seeping through the thin glass, she paused and looked back. This would be her final glimpse of this Sodom and Gomorrah, and she was glad to be rid of it. She'd only gone to the fitting because, at the end of her meeting with the writers, Jonny had announced that he had to dash across the street for a moment and that, because she was going there herself, they should walk together. Still not wanting to arouse suspicion, she had agreed. As they walked, they continued the discussion of the Justice Girl character. Felicity still found it strange to refer to Justice Girl as if she were a real person, but she also had to admit there was some enjoyment in it. She really liked what they had all come up with together. The Process Heads and Alexis would all be pleased. They were well on their way to developing a detailed and grounded spine for the character, as well as a backstory that answered all questions as to her motivations and desires. But most important, during Felicity's three hours in the writers' office, by listening carefully and asking subtle questions, she was able to come away with the full names of all three of the secret writers. Now, all that remained was to get home and check her father's files.

Felicity stepped out onto the sidewalk and walked almost directly into Jonny, Shel, Annie, and Burton, who were huddled by a newsstand, clearly waiting for her. Right away, she was sure she knew what had happened. She had pushed it too far, and they had caught on to her. She wasn't sure what she'd done to give herself away—maybe in the heat of one of their story riffs she had let something incriminating slip, or maybe they had been on to her all along and were now going to do something about it. Whatever it was, the sight in front of her made it clear that in some way, somehow, she had screwed up.

"Hello," Felicity said warily, wondering if she should turn and run in the opposite direction.

"We've got something for you," Jonny said flatly as he stepped out of the pack. As he reached inside his coat, Felicity actually flinched, fearing the worst. But when he removed his hand, he was holding a manila envelope. "We finished a first draft of the next episode," Jonny said, holding it out for her, "and we'd love for you to read it."

There they were—all three names, burning her eyes with their obvious malevolence, printed for all the world to see in her father's seminal issue of "Fight Back." She stood by a lamp in her father's study, wanting to be absolutely sure. Felicity again flipped between the pages of the twenty-page pamphlet. The names she'd acquired in the writers' room merely hours ago were definitely there. All three of them. Sheldon Ezralow, Burton Walker, and Annie Quinlan.

She'd done it.

She'd found absolute proof that a show on the Regal Television Network was using blacklisted writers. But that was an understatement. What she'd found was beyond anything she could have hoped for. She'd hit the mother lode. An entire show written almost entirely by blacklisted writers. Three of them on one show! Going public with this would be a huge story, sure to garner enormous attention for her father and, most important, vault him to the lead for the Republican spot in the special election. She couldn't wait to tell him, but unfortunately, she hadn't made it home until after 8:00 p.m., and her parents were over at the Hendersons' at a cocktail party. They were very close to the Hendersons, so they would stay well into the night, gossiping about the guests who had already departed. She would surprise him with the great news at breakfast.

Felicity turned off the lamp, but as she went to replace the copy of "Fight Back" to its normal place on the small bookshelf behind her father's desk, she felt compelled to look at the names yet again. Something was bothering her. Turning the lamp back on, she flipped open the pamphlet. Yes, the names were there, and the spellings were the same as she had written down. But the difference in their listings from most of the other six hundred actors, writers, and directors named was the minimal amount of information on their subversive activities. For Sheldon, it read, "Dated girl who was known Communist." For Burton: "Was involved in production of Russian play." And for Annie—the strangest of the three: "Known to have many actor friends." Sure, they were a seamy lot, and of course, they were subversive, but surely they had done more than that to end up on the list.

Maybe she should get a little more information about them before turning their names over to her father. Just to be sure. After all, it would be a disaster for him if he went public and it turned out that one or more of the names didn't really belong on the list. Maybe even fatal to his political ambitions. Not that she thought for a moment that he could have made a mistake. If there were a screw-up, it would have been some of the people working for him. After all, not everyone was capable of working at the high level her father demanded.

She noticed a packet on her father's desk, ready for shipment to Washington. She'd seen these packets dozens of times; they used them to send information back and forth between his organization and sympathetic members of the FBI. *Perfect*, Felicity thought as she dug out several copies of the forms her father used when he wanted information on someone he thought might be subversive. She quickly filled out three, one each in the name of Burton Walker, Sheldon Ezralow, and Annie Quinlan. After carefully unsealing the packet, she slipped them inside. Unfortunately, it would take a week or two to get an answer, but then she would be absolutely certain.

In the meantime, she had better stay on the show. *Yes, that is definitely the way to go*, she thought. That way, she might gather even more information. She headed upstairs to her room; she had a script to re-read and to make notes on it, as Alexis had suggested at their first meeting as a way to help organize her thoughts about the character. On the train ride home, she had devoured the new script and loved it. They had incorporated a lot of her ideas, and seeing them in print made her think of some new ones that she was eager to share with them.

Ultimately, it was too bad she had to wait to break the big news to her father. After all, time was of the essence. But on the other hand, playing Justice Girl one or two more times might not be so bad. It might just be tolerable.

...

So this is the famous Oak Room, Jonny thought as he sat at a table, craning his neck in all directions, taking in the overwhelmingly tasteless and gaudy display of wealth. But as his wait dragged on, he found himself begrudgingly admiring the beauty of the famous restaurant situated on the first floor of the Plaza Hotel. After all, though it was created as a playground for the rich, good, decent, hard-working immigrant workers had built it. And their craftsmanship deserved recognition.

Jonny checked his watch again—it was ten minutes past one, and his lunch companion was late. With each sweep of the second hand, Jonny was becoming more and more annoyed. He had work to do, lots of it. He had just come from the first read-through of this week's script, and though it had gone well, there were still a lot of changes he wanted to make. Mostly small stuff. Polishes. But important, nonetheless.

Then there was the issue of whom he was waiting for. Hogart had called him up this morning, out of the blue, saying that he would not be at the first read-through but that he thought they should have lunch. Jonny had agreed, figuring that if Hogart were going to try to fire him or try some other power play, he wouldn't do it in person. A bigger mystery was when Jonny, the first to arrive, discovered four place settings instead of the two he was expecting. After confirming with the snooty maître d' that this was indeed the right table, Jonny sat down, wondering who would be joining him and Hogart for lunch.

Finally, at 1:35 p.m., over half an hour late, Jonny got his answer, as Hogart strutted across the restaurant with a man and woman in tow. Jonny recognized them right away. The man was Mike Langston, a reporter for the *New York Times* Sunday magazine, and the woman was Kitty Hughes, the head of publicity for the network. All three slipped into the open seats at the table, surrounding Jonny.

"Sorry we're late," Hogart said, shaking Jonny's hand with one hand, while unfolding his napkin and placing it in his lap with the other. "Shall we get right to it?"

Jonny nodded. "Sure, okay."

"You're probably wondering why I asked to have lunch with you."

"That would be a safe bet."

"Because I felt bad about what happened the other day." Hogart looked Jonny right in the eye. "Not just because we disagreed, because you were right. It is your show."

"Thanks," Jonny said. Hogart's directness knocked some of the cynicism out of Jonny's tone.

"And I think it's time that we let the world know." Hogart nodded at Kitty Hughes and introduced her.

Jonny pretended not to know her, though she was a legend within the world of New York television and not just because she was the only female with any real power at one of the four networks. It was because she was damn good. As the head of the publicity department, she was ferocious in promoting a show on the Regal Network, willing to hound a style editor with phone calls and telegrams and even making a personal appearance in someone's office, if necessary, to get a feature written about one of their stars. Her hair was pulled back in a tight bun, like a lot of other women in their forties, though in her case, it was more from indifference than anything else, and her clothes were nice, though a bit on the frumpy side. She had a plain face with even features that usually were in a concerned scowl, as she was sure there was a deadline for a newspaper somewhere that she was about to miss. As always, she had her famous three-ring notebook with her. The disheveled volume was on the table in front of her with what looked like hundreds of notes sticking out from the pages.

"I've instructed Kitty to build a complete campaign around you and your work," Hogart said. "You're going to be the centerpiece of the show's promotion."

Kitty nodded in agreement with Hogart. "By the time I'm done, when they hear the title *Justice Girl*, the first thing that will come to mind is... you," Kitty said, punctuating her sentence with a finger pointed right at Jonny's head.

Jonny's eyes twitched. This was unexpected. Build a publicity campaign around him? He'd seen them many times for actors and even a few directors. But a writer? Never. "Why?" he finally asked.

"Because it's a great story," Hogart offered, as if it should be obvious. "Comedy writer scribbles out a quick sketch that turns into a TV sensation—"

"It's a story people will want to hear," Kitty added.

"But you know I'm not the only one...responsible," Jonny said, his gaze locked on Hogart. "And some of the others who are, may not be...well served by being in the public eye."

"That's why we're building the campaign entirely around you," Hogart offered, hoping to allay Jonny's fears.

Jonny shook his head. "It's not fair for me to take all the credit."

Hogart calmly clasped his hands. "So, then no one gets it?"

Jonny shrugged. "I guess so."

"Why should you be penalized for someone else's mistakes?" Hogart retorted matter-of-factly.

Mistakes! They had chosen to exercise their constitutional rights, only to be unjustly stripped of their livelihood, and Hogart called it mistakes! These were good, hard-working writers whose lives had been turned upside down because of the cowardice and expediency of others—like the opportunistic jackass who was sitting in front of him right now. Jonny felt the urge to scream at Hogart or, at the very least, to simply storm out and join up with his dear friends at their favorite Ukrainian restaurant.

But instead, Jonny said nothing.

He certainly didn't agree with anything Hogart had said, not for a moment, but it just didn't seem to make sense to cause a scene. The show was on the air, and Jonny was getting to do what he wanted to do. And he'd made his thoughts quite clear to Hogart the other day—and at a loud volume. Now, Jonny pointed at Mike Langston, asking. "What's he doing here?"

"He's here because the deadline for the *Times* Sunday magazine is 5:00 p.m. today," Kitty said plainly.

"And Mike has kindly offered to write a profile of you for the issue," Hogart added.

Offered? Jonny thought. *Sure, after being bribed.* Mike Langston had a reputation for being easily bought. A twenty-year institution at the *New York Times*, Langston had the weathered look and faraway stare of having heard and seen it all. Twice. Jonny wondered how many "exclusives" Hogart had offered to get him to write the profile so quickly. And judging from Langston's swollen and veiny nose, probably a few cases of Crown Royal, too.

A silence descended on the table, and an unexpected game plan had been laid before Jonny. Now was his chance to leave, to make a grand exit with his moral authority intact. But instead, he sat motionless and slowly nodded his consent.

As if a starting gun had been fired, Kitty whipped open her notebook, and Mike pulled out a pad and a pen.

"Here, fill this out," Kitty said, shoving a piece of paper in front of Jonny.

"What is this?"

"I need your sizes."

"Single or married?" Mike asked.

"Single."

"Woman-loving carousing playboy, or hopelessly romantic boy next door?"

"Excuse me?"

"What do you want the angle of your profile to be?" Mike persisted.

"I thought it was about me as a writer."

"We'll get to that."

"Your sizes. I need your sizes," Kitty implored.

"Sizes of what?"

"Your clothes. Waist? Length? Inseam?"

Jonny looked confused. "What for?"

"Your new wardrobe."

"Why do I need a new wardrobe?"

Kitty rolled her eyes. "For the photo shoots."

"Which do you favor? Blondes or brunettes?" Mike interjected.

"What photo shoots? Blondes or brunettes? What?"

And so it went for the next thirty minutes as Kitty and Mike peppered Jonny with questions. At one point, when one of Kitty's assistants appeared next to Jonny with a measuring tape—Jonny didn't have a clue what his sizes were; he'd not had a tailored suit since his bar mitzvah—he looked to Hogart to stop this insanity.

But Hogart was long gone, leaving Jonny alone with the two barracudas. The perplexing lunch lasted another fifteen minutes before Jonny made a hasty retreat back to the safety of the writers' room. The first read-through had been earlier in the day, so now they were rewriting and polishing. But Jonny found it hard to concentrate; his mind tried to grasp what had just happened but also, more importantly, what Hogart was up to.

The question kept swirling around Jonny's head as the week continued. What was Hogart up to? No one made it to Hogart's position without going to war a few times, and he certainly didn't reach the top of the pyramid by giving in. Why had he folded so quickly, and why was he now trying to build up Jonny, praise his ability, and make him a star?

What was Hogart up to? What was Hogart up to? What was Hogart up to?

The question nipped at him, even when he had other far more important things to worry about. It was in his head when he learned his director was sick, so the usual snappy day of stage blocking turned into a sloppy slog, going far into the night. It kept him company, even when the director finally felt better, and the camera blocking was moving along at a good pace—although the process almost ground to a halt when the technical director and one of the cameramen came down with the very same flu. It finally became so burdensome that, even after a lackluster dress rehearsal the day before going on the air, Jonny went all the way out to Coney Island to see his brother during the dinner break, even though he knew he wouldn't make it back to the studio without being a half-hour late.

It was a Saturday, a playfully warm afternoon, and the boardwalk was overrun with people taking advantage of the unexpected preview of the summer weather to come. Though Jonny hadn't spoken to his brother at all during the week, he knew exactly where to find him. It was one of Mitchell's daughter's birthdays, and that meant the traditional family picnic on one of the tables that made up the dividing line between the boardwalk and the sand. Every time, Mitchell made sure they got the same table, not because he was superstitious, but because it was the one directly across from the entrance to Astroland. With the ebb and flow of the day being between rides and lunch, and rides and cake, and rides and snacks, Mitchell knew this made for the most efficient use of time. When Jonny walked up, Mitchell was the only one at the table. He was carefully arranging the small plates needed for the cake before his daughter Darla returned to blow out the candles. He worked methodically, as he always did, making sure each plate was placed exactly the same distance from the others. *He sure seems like his old self,* Jonny thought as he watched his brother go about the mundane task as if the future of the Free World depended on it. Jonny hadn't had time to really think about it, but if he added in Mitchell's stellar performance the other day in Hogart's office, it sure seemed as if Mitchell had gotten things under control and was moving on.

"I knew exactly where I would find you," Jonny said brightly, genuinely happy to see his brother.

Still focused on the job at hand, Mitchell didn't look up. "Only because we were lucky," he answered, letting his frustration show.

Jonny laughed. "Let me guess. You had to do the walk?"

Mitchell finally looked up and nodded. "Of course."

"The walk," as Jonny and Mitchell called it, was their mother's perennial need to parade her war-hero son around the neighborhood at any chance she could get. Even though Washington Heights was completely out of their way, when driving from Midtown to Coney Island, their mother still insisted that this outing—and any family outing, for that matter—begin at their place. So as was the custom, Mitchell had arrived with his family in his brand-new Buick, hoping to scoop up his parents and head right out to Coney Island, only to discover that his mother needed something from the corner store, and would he escort her there? Thus began "the walk," with his mother slowing or stopping in front of every building along the way, making sure the assembled stoop-sitters saw who was with her.

As comical as all this was, Jonny also knew that the need to revel in Mitchell's greatness filled a much deeper need in his mother. After Rachel's tragic death, his mother hadn't snapped out of her walking coma until Mitchell's return from the war. Seeing him alive, returned from overseas in one piece, she slowly began to return to the world of the living. Further dissipating her fog was the increased stature her well-decorated son gave her in the neighborhood, sometimes displayed in blatant congratulations or other times more subtlety, such as receiving a better cut of meat at the butcher's for no additional cost. Knowing this, despite some frustration at the occasional bad timing, Mitchell was more than happy to indulge in her little game whenever he came for a visit.

"Aren't you needed somewhere else?" Mitchell asked, suddenly remembering that this should be a very busy day for Jonny.

"We're on dinner break."

Mitchell nodded. "Ah…I know you're very fond of Darla, but that is still very nice of you to schlep all the way out here."

"I am very fond of her, but that's not the only reason I'm here."

"I figured. Let's hear it."

Jonny quickly went through what had transpired between him and Hogart over lunch at the Oak Room. He also threw in additional details about what Kitty and Michael had said. Mitchell asked a few questions and then paused to think everything through.

Finally, after two agonizing minutes, he pursed his lips and blew. "Well," he began, "you're right to be suspicious of Hogart's motives. From what I saw at our meeting in his office and what he tried to cram into the contract, it's clear we're dealing with a highly unethical person." He exhaled loudly again. "On the other hand, there is a point where everyone, no matter how underhanded, realizes he has to deal with someone to get what he wants. I'm not saying this is the answer, but it might be possible that Hogart so desperately needs this show that he truly wants to make things work with you. And making you happy might go a long way to achieving that."

Incredulous, Jonny shook his head. "So he smothers me with kind words and offers to promote me in newspapers and magazines?"

Mitchell laughed. "Strange as it may seem to you, there are some people who would appreciate that." When Jonny smirked, Mitchell responded with a lazy grin. "You know, the world wouldn't end if you allowed yourself to enjoy the success."

"Uncle Jacob!" a young girl's voice shouted. Jonny and Mitchell turned to see Darla running toward them with happily surprised six-year-old eyes. When she reached Jonny, Darla dropped her doll and jumped up into his arms. She covered him with kisses as Jonny swung her in the air.

"You're getting so big!" Jonny shouted over and over. "Soon you will be able to lift me!" After a couple more swoops through the air, Jonny put her down, and she rushed to take her spot at the head of the table in front of the cake that bore her name.

Mitchell grabbed Darla's dropped doll, looked it over quickly, and then shoved it into Jonny's hands with a laugh. "You guys sure don't waste any time."

"What's this?" Jonny asked, looking at the doll.

Mitchell shrugged. "Mom must have bought it for her. Remind me to add a cut of the toy money into the next draft of your contract."

Jonny turned the doll over in his hands a couple more times before realizing what Mitchell meant. Though it clearly had been made with cheap, hurried construction—it had sloppy seams and rough cloth—there was no mistaking what the doll was supposed to be: Justice Girl. Jonny turned to Mitchell, shocked. "We haven't made any toys yet."

It didn't take long to track down where the doll had come from. Lena had bought it for Darla when they had snuck off to get some Nathan's hot dogs (even though they had several picnic baskets full off food). Near the stand, where the hungry patrons waited in the consistently long line, stood an old, disheveled man with the familiar weariness of a refugee from Europe. Placed atop his creaky pushcart was a large wooden clapboard covered with cloth dolls for sale. About half of them were Justice Girl.

"I kept be asked, so I make them myself," the old man said nervously after Jonny quizzed him about where the dolls had come from. The old man then produced a copy of *TV Guide* with a cover that featured a photo of Justice Girl under the headline "Television's Newest Sensation."

"I learn how from this," the old man offered brightly.

"Oh, my." was all Jonny could manage.

...

The opening credits of *Justice Girl* popped onto all four of the televisions, and everyone applauded loudly, just as Hogart had planned it. He stood by himself in the back of the studio's packed VIP viewing booth, overseeing the crowd of about thirty people that he carefully had handpicked. There were children from crew members, secretaries with their husbands, and executives with their wives—Personnel, Affiliates, Programming, Advertising were all there; Legal was the only one not to show up—all chosen because Hogart felt they would make an appreciative and excited audience. As the opening credits ended and the first scene of the latest episode came on, the crowd applauded again at the first sight of Justice Girl in her Sally Smalls disguise, sitting at her desk in the workroom of *Focus on Fashion*. But despite this enthusiastic reception, Hogart was stone-faced, unable to enjoy his plan's coming to fruition.

The target of his scheme, the reason he had stacked the deck in the viewing booth, was not there.

Clinton Fortis, the network's chairman of the board, was the main force behind the drive to take the deal and sell the network. Though there were seven members on the board, including Hogart, it was Clinton who held the most sway. As Clinton voted, so voted the board—or at least a majority of the members. With the board meeting to decide whether to take the deal just a couple of weeks away, Hogart knew he had to do something to sway Clinton; otherwise, all his hard work, all his ambitious plans, would die with the sale and eventual dismantling of the network. Fortunately, he had a fledgling hit on his hands and wanted to make damn sure Clinton knew about it. But despite being the chairman of the board, Clinton paid little attention to the network—with the exception of the yearly balance sheet—as it was just one of about a dozen boards on which he served.

To Hogart's good fortune, after he had Mrs. Decosta ring up Clinton's office in the Chrysler building, and he discovered Clinton was in town, Hogart issued an invitation for Clinton to come down on Sunday and watch the show live, in person, from the VIP viewing booth inside the studio. Clinton was also encouraged to bring anyone he wanted, and Hogart secretly hoped he would bring his two grandchildren, which he doted over. Days passed after the initial invite, with no response. Finally, with Sunday just two days away, Hogart bypassed Mrs. Decosta and called Clinton directly, with the hope of personally getting his attention. It did, sort off. Clinton's secretary had requested that a single seat be held in his name for that Sunday's broadcast. It wasn't everything Hogart had hoped for, but he was ecstatic that Clinton would at least be there. He made sure the center seat in the front row—the one that showed what the viewers around the country were seeing—was taped off for him.

Unfortunately, a minute into the episode—with the crowd roaring with laughter as Chance Crawford made his comical entrance, hungover from a wild night out on the town—the seat was still empty, a giant X of masking tape still standing guard. *He'll be here*, Hogart thought repeatedly. *He'll be here. He has to be. He has to see this.*

Suddenly, an usher appeared, heading toward the front row of seats. Hogart jumped with alarm as the usher ripped the masking tape off of the seat held for Clinton, crushed the tape into a ball, and walked away. Hogart quickly intercepted him. "What are you doing?" he quietly hissed.

"I just got word from downstairs," the usher said, terrified to be talking to Hogart. "Someone's on the way up for the seat."

"Oh, I see," Hogart said, backing off. "Okay, good." Hogart retreated to his spot in the rear of the viewing booth, his eyes aimed firmly at the empty chair in the front row. He hoped it would be soon—the plot of the episode already had begun: A rival magazine had somehow gotten hold of an inside scoop about *Focus on Fashion*, and accusations were flying all around the office as to who had leaked the vital information. No one was safe from the growing inquisition.

Someone tapped Hogart on the shoulder. He turned around to see Danny, a well-scrubbed production assistant in his late twenties. "Sir, as you requested, here is the final draft of this week's script."

"Thank you," Hogart said hungrily, as he began to rifle through it. Stopping on page nineteen, his eyes whipped through the text until he found what he was looking for. "Son of a bitch..." he said, as much disgusted as resigned. He handed the script back to Danny and, without another word, hurried out of the VIP viewing booth. He was furious that he had to leave the excited audience, especially with Clinton on his way up, but he had no choice. As important as it was for Clinton to see how much of a hit the show was, ultimately, the bottom line was what counted the most.

As he stepped down onto the studio floor, amid the swirling chaos of moving cameras, sliding booms, and dashing actors, he spotted Jonny calmly watching it all. Seeing him sitting there, seemingly without a care in the world and completely in control, made Hogart seethe. Yes, he had come to lunch, and yes, he had done the interview, plus a couple more, but by the end of that first day of peace, things had gone sour. And all over a single word: gas.

Hogart fought the urge to go over to Jonny and punch him right in the face. *I'm the head of the network, damn it, and this is the kind of pissant bullshit I have to deal with?* But as much as it would be almost orgasmic to feel Jonny's jaw shatter under a direct hit from his closed fist, ultimately, laying him out flat on his ass would only cause more problems. A scene like that played out in front of cast and crew and within sight of the VIP viewing booth would be a complete disaster. And given Jonny's arrogant temperament, pathetically disguised as artistic, there was always the chance he would do something insane, like shut the whole thing down mid-show. Obviously, it would mean the end of Jonny's career in television, but Hogart knew Jonny was not beyond a stunt like that.

The only bright spot was that what Jonny had done was not entirely unexpected, and Hogart was prepared for it. They had battled all week over a new sponsor. The show was a hit, so there was a wide variety of companies interested, as well as a plethora of ad agencies offering up their own clients. But somehow, Jonny found a problem with each one—this one won't hire blacks, that one won't hire Jews, and on and on it went. Finally, Hogart found Consolidated Oil and Gas, a small company out of North Dakota that was looking to expand to the East Coast. Because most of their business was in the upper Midwest, little was known about them, which was perfect as far as Hogart was concerned. Try as he might, Jonny couldn't find a problem with them, and they were signed as the sole sponsor for the first season of *Justice Girl.*

Then the problems began.

Mel Fielding, the president of Consolidated Oil and Gas, was not particularly a fan of television, and the decision to sponsor the show was largely the work of his son, Trent. After the signed deal, Mel read the script for the next episode, the first one that would feature a short spot at the beginning, a two-minute commercial in the middle, and short spot at the end, all about Consolidated Oil and Gas. Within minutes of finishing it, he was on the phone, screaming at Hogart. Unbeknownst to Hogart, near the end of the episode, after Justice Girl has once again rescued Chance from the clutches of a villain, he turns to her and says, "Thanks. I don't remember anything after I was gassed." Mel Fielding made it quite clear he was not going to sponsor a show that in any way inferred anything bad about gas, whether it was the type he sold or something else. Hogart completely agreed and said he would get it changed.

Jonny did not agree. "It has to be 'gas.' It has to be a resource that is exploited and taken from the third world." Jonny refused to make the change. So from Thursday evening on, they had spent the next three days bickering endlessly over the one word. Hogart sent memo after memo with solid suggestions for a replacement for the offending word—"before I was knocked out," "before I was slipped a Mickey," "before I had my lights turned off"— but Jonny summarily dismissed each one. As Jonny made plainly clear, in memo and in person, when Hogart confronted him after the camera run-through, "gassed" was the only word that worked.

Worse—and this was the part Hogart hated the most and that was the hardest for him to take—was that there was nothing Hogart could do about it, short of canceling the broadcast, and that would be a complete disaster, maybe even destroy the show forever. With little else to go on, Hogart appealed to Jonny to make the change as a personal favor to him. Jonny said he would think about it. But Hogart knew that, in the end, if Jonny wanted the word in the script, the word would stay in the script. Jonny was the one with the power.

For now. Until Hogart wrested control from Jonny, which would come soon enough.

Fortunately, Hogart had prepared for what he had just discovered—the word was still in the script.

As the first act neared the end, Hogart headed for the control booth to institute his back-up plan. Stepping down onto the studio floor, Hogart moved through the silent ballet that was live television. As the actors locked in and focused, intensely performing their scene, all around them, just outside the frame of what was visible on television, dozens of technicians rushed about. They were moving cameras, pulling cables, repositioning lights, swinging boom arms, helping actors change in and out of costumes, touching up makeup, and performing a dozen other key tasks—to the demands of the script. Benjamin Portis III proclaimed that under no circumstances would he allow the employees of his magazine to attend his party in the Hamptons. So when the next scene showed them all showing up at his beach house, the cameras, mics, and lights were moved and in place and the actors changed into their best beach clothes before the thirty-second, prefilmed transition shots of ocean waves and birds came to an end. All in complete silence.

The first act ended, and Hogart passed a small kitchen set where the commercial for Consolidated Oil and Gas was just beginning. A pretty spokeswoman dressed as an average housewife began to prattle on about how natural gas was making lives better. Hogart paused to watch for a short moment. As the commercial ended and the second and final act of the episode began, Hogart quietly slipped into the back of the tiny control booth.

As usual—and this was a key part of Hogart's plan—it was a state of pure chaos. Facing a wall of four small television sets, each showing what the individual cameras filming the episode saw at that exact moment, was the director, Sal Reece, along with his assistant director, board operator, sound technician, and several other key crew members. All of them were seated in a row behind a control board that was covered with lights and switches. A fifth television, larger than all the rest, showed what the broadcast looked like to the viewing audience across the country. The image constantly cut between what was seen by one of the four cameras filming the episode—close-up of Margaret Crawford, close-up of Benjamin Portis III, wide shot of both of them, dolly move as they hurried toward the door to Margaret's office. Sal called for each cut and action, shouting into his headset, directing the four cameramen in the studio and the board operator seated next to him.

Hogart crept along the back wall, moving stealthily toward the sound technician, Schmitty, a skinny, sallow-faced reed of a man who was wearing headphones and was busy manipulating the buttons on the board in front of him. As Hogart moved up within several feet of him, Schmitty turned, and his saggy eyes briefly widened at the sight of Hogart. Hogart gave him a quick nod, and Schmitty answered it with a nod of his own. Then Hogart carefully retreated to the back of the booth, where he leaned against the wall...and waited.

Charles, seated next to Sal, turned around, saw Hogart, and gave him an "Isn't it going great?" smile. *Yes, it is*, Hogart said with his own tight smile. Charles turned back around, and Hogart's tight smile vanished. *It may be going well now, but not for long*, he thought.

On the large television in the booth, the image cut to a completely different set. Chance was being untied by Justice Girl. Watching closely, Hogart swallowed. *Here we go*. Relieved, Chance opened his mouth to speak to her, but when his lips moved, no sound came out of his mouth. He said the line with the offending word "gas," but unless viewers could lip-read, they would not have known.

"Sound, what the hell is going on?" Sal yelled, as a panic swept through booth.

In a panic, Schmitty pushed a series of buttons, and when nothing happened, he pounded on the board with his fist. Suddenly, the sound from the scene reappeared in the booth. "Sorry, sorry. Must be a short," Schmitty said, seeming harried.

"It's back; that's all that counts," Sal said, returning his attention to the job at hand. Everyone else followed suit, and when things were back to their usual level of chaos, Schmitty turned and gave Hogart a nod. Hogart returned it and then slipped out of the booth.

Hogart liked to have at least one inside man on every show who was known only to him. Schmitty hadn't been hard to recruit, just a few veiled hints of what Hogart might do for him somewhere down the line. That was one of the things that Hogart loved most about entertainment. Everyone wanted to be something more, and even the lowly sound technician dreamed of one day being the director.

Making his way back to the VIP viewing booth, Hogart wished his problem with the chairman of the board could be as easy to fix as this had been. The episode was ending as he stepped into the booth, and the audience was applauding loudly, which then morphed into a standing ovation, with parents joining their children in enthusiastic approval. As he moved through the exiting crowd, he was besieged with congratulations, with Programming and Advertising being particularly effusive in their praise for him and the show. Hogart took it all with a painted-on smile, while fighting upstream, heading for the seat where he knew Clinton had been sitting. But when he finally reached the seat, it was empty.

Son of a bitch, Hogart thought. *I must have missed him.* He immediately turned to search for Clinton in the departing throng as a young man walked up to him. He appeared to be in his early twenties and was wearing a crisp, conservative business suit. "Mr. Daniels?" the young man asked.

Hogart studied the man. "Yes?"

"Mr. Fortis regrets not being able to make it. I am one of his assistants; he sent me instead."

Hogart nodded, hiding his disappointment. "I understand. Did you like it?"

"It was terrific. Very entertaining."

"Will you please let Mr. Fortis know how much you liked it?" Hogart asked hopefully.

The young man gave a slight bow of his head. "Of course," he answered, in an officious tone that said he would if Mr. Fortis bothered to ask, and then he walked away.

Hogart watched him leave. "Son of a bitch," Hogart spat out.

Episode Three

JUSTICE GIRL

"FASHION OF THE BORDER"

April 10, 1955

"**G**reat show last night!" Benny said proudly as Jonny strolled into the diner just after ten o'clock Monday Morning. "Thanks," Jonny answered as he walked past, heading for his booth in the back. As he crossed the restaurant, several of the patrons did a double take or leaned over to say something to the person next to them, clearly recognizing Jonny. Just before he reached the booth, Larraine removed a "reserved" sign and placed a fresh cup of coffee on the table.

"Thanks, Larraine."

"No, thank *you*. Great show last night," she finished with a wink and stepped away. A moment later, she ceremoniously delivered Jonny's breakfast, with steam rising off the freshly cooked eggs, bacon, and hash browns. He was about to dig in when Marty suddenly appeared in front of him.

"How ya doin', kid?" Marty asked, sliding into the booth across from Jonny. As always, he was wearing his black suit, red tie, and porkpie hat.

"Did you read my script?" Jonny asked sharply.

"It's right on the top of my pile. You never called for an appointment, so I'm bringing the meeting to you."

Jonny put down his fork on the table and glowered at Marty. "Marty, I gotta ask you. For almost a year I can't get my calls returned, and now, I can't get rid of you."

Marty looked at him as if astonished. "Of course not. It's a numbers game, kid, and right now your numbers are headed for Pluto."

"So now you're just interested in me because you see dollar signs?"

"Welcome to the world, kid. Ain't she a hoot?" Marty pulled out a couple of pieces of paper and proceeded to unfold them. "I've been tickling the dial, and the offers have been coming in like rain in April."

Larraine returned. "Can I get you anything, Jonny?"

"I'm good."

Larraine turned to leave, but Marty reached out and grabbed her apron, stopping her. "Honey, I'll have the same thing he's having, but ix-nay on the ashbrown-hays, 'kay?"

Larraine turned back around, but she fixed her gaze on Jonny, ignoring Marty. Jonny thought, *This is really the last thing I want to deal with right now.* He was still annoyed with the "sound problem" from last night, and he had yet to settle on the story for this week's episode. He had planned to work on it last night, but his afternoon interview was moved to the evening, which meant he had to push back the interview that already had been planned for after the show. Doing back-to-back interviews had wiped him out. It was exhausting, trying to come up with clever responses to inane question after inane question—"What's it like to be the hot new writer?" "Any special gal in your life?"—all while trying to steer the conversation to a real discussion of the craft of writing. So, talking to Marty about yet another stupid topic was not really what Jonny was in the mood for, especially when he was already behind on this week's script. He was about to tell Marty to leave (he had a perfectly good excuse in that Marty still had not read "The Road to Damascus" as he had promised), but then, for some reason, he found himself nodding his okay to Larraine. *What would it hurt to just listen?*

Larraine took Marty's order and moved away.

Marty smoothed out the top sheet of paper. "Okay, let's start with—"

"Take off your hat."

"Excuse me?"

"If you want to stay, take off your hat."

"Whatever floats your boat, kid." Marty slipped off his hat and placed it on the cushion next to him. "All right, let's start with CBS. They've been looking to get into the kid's market and…"

...

Felicity sat back down in the chair. Instead of accomplishment or even pride, what she felt was relief. Deep, deep relief. She had done it. She had gotten up in front of the twenty-odd students in Alexis's acting class—a tough, chain-smoking bunch with deep, searing, judgmental eyes—and done a monologue. As she sat in the lone chair that occupied the small raised platform at the far end of the concrete basement that was home to the class, the room came slowly back into focus. It was tiny, with very little light, and the scent of curry from the Indian restaurant above them permeated everything. Having watched several others go before her, she sat emotionless, awaiting the critique.

Alexis sat in the front row of the small riser of seats that took up most of the space in the room. She was surrounded by a surly gang of her students—Felicity had already figured out that the closer Alexis let you sit to her, the better an actor she thought you were. When not performing a monologue, Felicity's seat was in the back row. Alexis finished making notes on a piece of paper and then tilted her head back, almost to the point of peering over her cheeks, and looked appraisingly at Felicity. "Okay," she said, "you choose a monologue from *Golden Boy*?"

Felicity nodded enthusiastically. "Yes." Then she steeled herself; after having watched Alexis critique other students' work, she knew what to expect—and it wouldn't be as easy as acknowledging the name of the play.

"Wonderful play," Alexis said. "Cliffie Odetts was a dear friend."

Felicity nodded again. She had loved reading it and had torn through it in less than two days, even reading it in her dressing room when she had a few spare moments. The idea of reading it in the first place had come up the previous week, during one of her private tutorials, when Alexis suggested she examine a different text than the *Justice Girl* scripts and practice breaking it down, as if she were going to play one of the roles herself. They'd gone to a bookstore together, and *Golden Boy* was one of the only plays, short of the classics, that Felicity had heard of before. Mostly what she'd heard had been in derogatory terms, derided as another one of those Jewishy socialist plays. Nonetheless, she had chosen it and, much to her surprise, had loved it.

It didn't seem very socialist to her, anyway. Besides, hadn't Odetts given vital information to HUAC? She seemed to remember watching him testify to the House Committee on Un-American Activities in a newsreel. So in the end, he had turned out to be a loyal American.

"Tell me…what is the play about?" Alexis asked straightforwardly.

"Well…" Felicity began, her eyes rolling upward as she nervously edged forward in her seat, thinking. "It's about this guy, Joe, who's a boxer but who also plays the violin really well. He can't decide what he wants to do more, and he's also in love with this girl. In the end, he doesn't want to box anymore, and he runs away with the girl." Finished, Felicity sat back, relieved. "Oh, and then they die in a car crash."

Alexis nodded, taking it all in and seemingly agreeing. But then, without a perceptible stop, she began shaking her head. "That sounds like a nice play. I'd probably go see it, but it's not *Golden Boy*."

Felicity felt the air go out of her lungs. She wanted to slink down into the chair, but she knew that would only make things worse. As Alexis stood up and moved toward her, Felicity began to regret her decision to attend Alexis's class, let alone do a monologue. The whole ridiculous idea had been born from her excitement after the live broadcast of the second episode. After they had gone off the air, Felicity was so alive, so pulsing with energy, the thought of slinking back to her hotel room or slumping into a seat on the train back to Greenwich was inconceivable. She briefly considered calling up Braeden to see if he wanted to come to the city or, if that wasn't possible, if he wanted to take a midnight horseback ride. But that idea died when she realized that either event would end with Braeden's pestering her again about going public with their engagement. So instead, she was one of the first to arrive at the after-party at Annie's. With no need to investigate the attendees—the list of suspected names was already on its way to Washington for further verification—Felicity had positioned herself in the kitchen, awaiting the Process Heads.

She was with them until dawn.

The idea of her attending Alexis's class came up early in the boisterous conversation, and by the time the sun had poked through the tiny window above the sink, she had decided to not only attend but to do a full monologue.

Now, she stared up at Alexis's imposing image. She projected a stern, focused, and completely different persona than the helpful, supportive acting coach she had been in their private tutorials. Suddenly, Felicity regretted even getting out of bed this morning.

Alexis took a cursory look at her notes and then looked at Felicity. "Are you a virgin?" she inquired plainly, as if asking for directions.

Felicity stared in stunned silence before managing to say, "Excuse me?"

"It's an easy question. Are you a virgin? Have you had sex?"

"What does that have to with acting?"

"Everything—when you're doing a play about whores."

Whores? What whores? Felicity wondered.

"Joe's a whore." Alexis told her. "His trainer, Moody, is a whore; his promoters, Roxy and Eddie—whores. Everyone in the story is doing what he or she is doing for money. They are all whores. And Lorna is the biggest whore of them all. She literally sleeps with Joe for money."

"But they end up together at the end," Felicity said, finding, to her surprise, that she wanted to defend her interpretation of the play. "True love prevails."

Alexis exploded with laughter. Her students followed suit, the most favored ones laughing a bit too loudly. "Is that what you think? It's about love? Lorna wants love?"

Felicity nodded.

Alexis shook her head. "No, it's not love; it's lust. Lorna's not in love with Joe; she's in lust. She wants to fuck Joe."

Felicity found herself wildly blinking at the unexpectedly coarse language.

"And Joe wants to fuck her," Alexis said, moving around the room. "There's no love. There's nothing real, there's nothing permanent. It ends with them dying in a horrific car crash. And even if they didn't die, how long would it have lasted?" Alexis paced faster. "How many nights before the passion would have died and the booze would have run out? Then where would they have been? Two broke whores in the middle of nowhere."

Felicity wished she were in the middle of nowhere. She wished she were anywhere but here. "Yes," she said strongly.

Alexis turned and looked at her. "Yes, what?"

"Yes, I've had sex." She was more or less telling the truth. She forced herself to sit up in the chair but was unwilling to make eye contact with anyone in the room.

Alexis offered a faint smile. "Okay. It's a start," She moved closer to Felicity, saying, "That's at least one thing you have in common with Lorna. Now, we can't become entirely the characters we play, but we can at least try to get as close as humanly possible." Alexis pointed at Felicity's shoes. "What are you wearing?"

Felicity self-consciously slid her feet under the chair. "Christian Dior," she said quietly.

"Do you think someone who as recently as a year ago was nine weeks behind on her rent and was now the mistress of a washed-up fight trainer could afford shoes like that?

Felicity's face fell. "No."

"And your dress," Alexis said, pacing again. "Someone of Lorna's breeding wouldn't even be allowed in the store where you bought that."

As uncomfortable as this was making Felicity, she knew Alexis was right. "She probably wouldn't have hair like this either," she offered, wanting to get ahead of the stinging assault.

"Exactly," Alexis agreed. "Your trip to the salon probably cost more than someone like Lorna made in a week."

More like a month, Felicity thought.

Alexis stopped in front of her and pointed right at Felicity's head. "To be the character, you have to feel them from your long hairs"—Alexis trailed her hand down to Felicity's crotch—"to your short hairs. And everywhere in between." Alexis then broke down the entire story with Felicity as it related to Lorna and, more specifically, how she might have performed the monologue. Felicity listened intently, and the more she heard, the more she agreed with Alexis. Felicity had missed the entire true meaning of the play and, in that failing, had completely missed the mark in her portrayal of Lorna. They moved on to a discussion of the specific scene that preceded the monologue, with Alexis coaxing her toward more eye-opening discoveries. "Now I need you to think of something from your own life, where you felt the same level of desperation, of confusion."

Felicity searched her memory and found the one she needed. She shifted uncomfortably, not wanting to share it, but Alexis kept her gaze locked on her. "Well," Felicity began, "there was the time I—"

"No," Alexis interrupted. "Don't tell me. Just think about it."

"Okay," Felicity said, relieved. She closed her eyes and, to herself, relived the entire frightening nightmare.

"Good," Alexis said calmly, after a few minutes. "Now do the monologue again."

"Right now?"

"Yes. Go." Alexis slowly sank back into her seat in the front row as Felicity warily rose from hers.

This is going to be a disaster, Felicity thought, as she finally summoned the courage and began. But as the words began to flow from her, she felt anything but fear. Suddenly, each line, each word, had a new meaning as Lorna came to life as a real, breathing person. Instead of just repeating words on a page, Felicity thought of her own first stirrings of true love—or what she thought was true love. The wanting, the confusion, the need, and finally, the disastrous ending. Armed with this, along with Alexis's analysis as she went along, she found an undiscovered universe within the text: hidden meanings, sadness, vulnerability, bravado, even some joking sarcasm. Finished, she stood proudly on the stage, although drained.

The students, along with a pleased Alexis, gave her a spontaneous round of applause. But as Felicity basked in it, her mood suddenly darkened as she thought about the two episodes of *Justice Girl* that had already aired. Even if her reason for being on the show had nothing to do with being a good actress, she certainly didn't want to make a fool of herself. With what she had just learned—that she had to live and feel like the character and that she had to do a thorough textural analysis—she wondered if her performances had been a complete joke.

They had to have been. But if that were true, why hadn't Alexis said anything in their private tutorials. During those scattered hours, fitfully dispersed over the previous two weeks, Alexis had been supportive and help-ful, not piercing and cutting, not complaining about Felicity's clothing, and not tearing the script apart, only to rebuild it in a way to help Felicity with her portrayal. Then it hit Felicity why: in the case of the coaching sessions for the show, Alexis was in Felicity's world, helping her to just get by. That was the job Jonny had hired her to do. But here, Felicity was in Alexis's world, and the rules were different. Since she had dared to venture in, at her own insistence, more was expected of her. A lot more.

Her thoughts began to wander to the script for this week's episode. She hadn't received it yet, so she had no idea what her character would be called upon to do. But when she did, she would make damn sure she was properly prepared this time. There was nothing she could do about the last two epi-sodes, but at least now, she knew what to do to make sure she didn't fail again.

...

From the moment Jonny walked into the writers' room, he knew he was in trouble. The first clue: it was eleven in the morning, and they were all there. Burton, Annie, and Shel, all in place, all on their respective couches, seemingly ready to go to work. This had never happened—not when they wrote on *Hermie's Henhouse* and certainly not in the last two weeks they had been writing *Justice Girl*. Shel was never on time, Annie was even worse, and Burton, who was often early, always began the day with his face buried in the racing form.

But today, Jonny was greeted by six eyes, all staring right at him. First, he thought it might be because he was late—breakfast had gone almost an hour and a half, as it took Marty that long to finish pitching all the kiddie shows the other networks were interested in developing with Jonny. But that didn't really make any sense. How would they know to be on time because Jonny was late…before Jonny was late?

After they exchanged greetings—Jonny greeted them warmly, but their responses were cold and perfunctory—he was about to inquire why they were being distant, when he spotted the second clue: three well-worn copies of the *New York Times Magazine* on the cluttered center table, one in front of each of them. Jonny shook his head knowingly. So, the profile was pissing them off. He thought about explaining to them how he had resisted, but that just seemed a waste of time. Besides, what got him through that interview, and all the rest, was the realization that it was good for the show. And what was good for the show, in the end, was good for all of them. Hoping he might be able to stave off the inevitable confrontation, Jonny chose to ignore the clues and threw his coat onto his couch, plopped down next to it, stretched his arms, and then fished under some empty soda cans until he found a single piece of white paper with typing on it.

"*Justice Girl*, episode three," he began. "This week, I thought we'd all decide together." He tapped his finger on the typed paper for emphasis. "Which one of these episode ideas shall we choose?" No one said anything. "Come on—the page is blank, awaiting our brilliance."

"*Our* brilliance?" Annie said. "I thought you wrote the show on your own."

Jonny sunk into the couch. *Here we go*, he thought. "All right, let's get it all out in the open."

Instantly, Burton, Annie, and Shel grabbed their copies of the *New York Times Magazine*, flipped to the article on Jonny, and all at once began reading sections of it aloud.

"Working alone is so satisfying."

"It's not really hard; the ideas just come to me."

"I tried working with others, but it was so unproductive."

"Whoa, whoa, whoa!" Jonny said, waving his arms.

But they went on. "It's nice not having to fight over every story idea."

"It's easier to concentrate without the clatter of others."

"Shakespeare worked alone."

"Stop!" Jonny finally yelled. When they did, he took a deep breath and said, "Thank you. Number one, not one word attributed to me in that article came out of my mouth. Number two, even if I had said it, who cares? Any press is good for the show. And what's good for the show, in the end, is good for all of us."

"So you admit you said some of these things?" Shel said, peering over his glasses.

"No, I'm saying you should be appreciative of the article, regardless."

"But we're not even mentioned," Burton snapped.

"Now, how in the world could I mention you?" Jonny shot back. "Do I have to remind all of you that you're blacklisted?"

They all looked up at him, a little stunned to hear him actually articulate the thought. And had they detected a touch of insult in his tone?

"Look, I'm on your side," Jonny said plainly.

"That's what we used to think," Annie retorted.

Jonny fought to keep his exasperation in check. "On the old show, I got you some money. On this one, I hired you. What more could I possibly do?"

Shel jumped to his feet. "You could have refused to do the article altogether!"

Jonny leapt up to stand next to Shel. "Then no one would have gotten credit for creating her!"

Shel shrugged. "That's better than a bunch of lies."

Jonny shook his head. "Why should I be penalized for someone else's mistakes?"

Burton, Annie, and Shel all gasped. Had he really just said that?

Their reaction immediately let Jonny know he had screwed up, big time. "Look, I'm sorry." He exhaled slowly. "I thought I was doing what was best for the show."

"Best for the show or best for you?" Annie demanded.

"I'll be honest. Call me naïve. I kind of thought they were the same thing," Jonny said genuinely. "But that goes for all of us. We are all the show. We are all *Justice Girl*." His words settled over them like a comfortable blanket. The tension eased a bit, and Jonny sat down, followed by Shel. Everyone took a collective breath. "Now can we please get to work? We have a show to write."

One by one, they all nodded, and work resumed. In a matter of minutes, a plot was chosen from Jonny's list, and they went at it. They made good progress, but something was definitely missing.

They finished for the day around 9:00 p.m., and after a round of cool but respectful "good nights," they all headed for home. An hour later, Jonny found himself unusually spent as he slipped into bed. It was hard enough fighting the war to write a good script without getting into skirmishes with those who were supposed to be on his side. But he quickly decided there was no point in wasting any more energy thinking about it; he needed his sleep. Tomorrow he had to be up at five o'clock for a photo shoot, followed by two interviews, and then off to a full day in the writers' room. *Ugh, the writers' room*, was his last thought before finally drifting off to a fitful sleep.

...

The three young art directors jumped back from their design tables when Hogart casually walked in on them. Hogart was not surprised; after all, it wasn't every day that the head of the network strolled into their workspace on the sixth floor. But this wasn't every day.

The board meeting was less than a week away, and Hogart's attempts to reach Clinton since his no-show at the broadcast the previous weekend had gone nowhere. His calls were ignored, his letters went unanswered, and even his telegram didn't get a response. It was quite clear to Hogart that the only shot he would have in changing Clinton's mind would come at the meeting itself. He vowed to be prepared.

"Can I see what you've got?" Hogart asked no one in particular.

"Yes, of course," one of the startled art directors answered, as all three nodded and then began scurrying around the crowded workspace, gathering items.

They were scheduled to make their presentation to him the next day, but Hogart had found he couldn't wait any longer. After a few chaotic moments, three large three-foot-by-three-foot cardboard presentation boards were set up on three hastily assembled easels. Hogart stepped back toward the door to examine them.

They were all dramatic black-bar graphs designed to show the amazing growth of the viewing audience of *Justice Girl* from the first week to the second. The first graph was the show's ratings; *Justice Girl* had jumped from an impressive premiere rating of 22.3 to a stellar 26.8 in the second week. That was an increase of almost four million viewers.

The second chart was the audience share, the percentage of all televisions that were tuned to the show. The premiere of *Justice Girl* had pulled in a thirty-nine share, meaning almost 40 percent of the televisions in use at that time were watching the show. The second episode had pulled in a sixty-three share; well over half of all televisions in use while the show aired were tuned to *Justice Girl*!

The third chart, and the most important to Hogart, was the average ratings for the entire network. In *Justice Girl*'s first week on the air, the average had ticked up about three-tenths of a point, a subtle rise but a rise nonetheless. But in the second week, the up-tick had been 1.9, almost two entire rating points! This was a staggering week-to-week jump for an entire network's ratings. As Hogart had hoped, *Justice Girl*'s success was lifting the entire network's schedule.

Seeing the numerical evidence of *Justice Girl*'s success laid before him in bold black and white, Hogart allowed himself a thin smile. Most enticing was the blank spot left on each presentation board next to the second week's ratings, where the rating numbers for the third week would be installed after this weekend's episode aired. That final shaft added to each graph, sure to be taller than the two to its left, would make each chart a jutting cityscape of *Justice Girl*'s and the network's undeniable growth and success.

But Hogart was not a man to miss anything, and something wasn't right. He could feel it. He took another step back and stared at the presentation, narrowing his eyes in search of the answer. A thick moment passed, with Hogart locked on the three boards, and the three art directors locked on Hogart. Then his head suddenly snapped back. He chortled at the sheer obviousness of it. "Bigger," he said flatly to himself, pleased. He turned to the three art directors who were still watching him, wide-eyed. "I want the charts to be bigger. Twice the size. Huge." He threw his arms open for emphasis. "I need to really knock him out," Hogart added, not concerned that no one else had any idea whom he was talking about.

The three art directors answered with enthusiastic nods.

Hogart nodded rapidly, more and more convinced. Yes. Yes, this was just what was needed. Clinton Fortis was a tough, stern, difficult man who moved through life, sure that his was the right path. But he also was a smart man, a man who lived for the good deal and, to his very core, despised losing out on one. Oh sure, the common sense of turning down the offer from Worthington Camera and Instrument would be presented matter-of-factly in the slick, well-produced annual report booklet given to all in attendance. But seeing the growing success of the network laid out in a large, unignorable fashion on a gargantuan scale would do the trick. Clinton wouldn't have any choice; he'd be forced to vote no. Keeping the network alive was undeniably the best deal.

"When can I see them?" Hogart asked, barely able to control his excitement, buoyant with the knowledge that he had solved his problem.

Before they could answer, Mrs. Decosta slipped into the room holding a manila envelope. "This just came for you, from the *Journal American*," she said, a bit winded.

"Just a moment," Hogart answered with a raised finger and then turned back to the three art directors.

But Mrs. Decosta took a step closer to Hogart and held out the envelope for him. "It came via courier; it's from *our friend*."

Five minutes later, Hogart was back in his office, the door locked, and the contents of the manila envelope in front of him on his desk. It was a simple, single piece of white 8½-by-11 typing paper, and it sent shivers down Hogart's spine. During his days in the advertising department of the network, he had made contacts at all the newspapers around town. Even though he had jumped over to programming years ago, he had made a point of keeping up the contacts, and from time to time, it had paid off.

This was one of those times.

On the surface, it wasn't much—just a single-page mock-up of a half-page ad that was to run in the Sunday television supplement of the *Journal American*. But what it said was undeniable, and what it could mean was devastating. It was an ad for this week's episode of the *Percy Williams Show* on ABC, a show that aired every Sunday night at 7:30 p.m.

The exact same time and day as *Justice Girl*.

The *Percy Williams Show* had been a minor hit for ABC since going on the air the previous fall, with Percy's wholesome good looks and decidedly non-rock and roll singing appealing to a wide audience. A few weeks into the season, it had won its time slot, a position it went on to hold for the next twenty-eight weeks...until the premiere episode of *Justice Girl*. With *Justice Girl* trouncing it in the ratings for two weeks in a row, Hogart had expected ABC to do something but nothing this dramatic or this soon. In large block letters, the ad screamed, "The *Percy Williams Show*—tonight with special guest star Bette Davis!" They were bringing in a major Hollywood movie star to try to slow *Justice Girl*'s climb.

And what terrified Hogart was that it just might work.

Even if it was just a short blip—after all, they couldn't afford to pay a big star every week—if *Justice Girl*'s ratings leveled off—or worse, fell—because of Davis's undeniable appeal, it would destroy Hogart's entire presentation to the board. Hogart felt his entire body slump, followed by a flash of queasiness. He sank back in his chair, his face a tight grimace. What could he possibly do in the face of true Hollywood star power?

...

Finally, something I'm looking forward to, Jonny thought as he bounded up the steps, leaving behind the stale subterranean air of the Columbus Circle subway station. The overhead sun warmed him against the morning chill, further buoying his mood. He hurried the one block to a café right across from the southwest entrance to the park and saw the reporter waiting for him, already seated at one of the outdoor tables. Jonny further quickened his pace; he was really looking forward to this interview.

The last three days had been a Coney Island of fluff-piece interviews, silly photo shoots, avoiding Marty, ignoring Hogart, and arguing with Charles. But most exhausting were the writers' meetings. After a couple more articles came out about Jonny, including a cover story on *Justice Girl* in *TV People* that featured a full-page picture of him, things had gone from bad to horrible. The irony was, in terms of their work, he and the other writers were making fantastic progress on the episode, and it was coming together faster and better than either of the previous two, by a long shot.

But they were all miserable.

Gone was the gyrating cloud of craziness. Four gears spinning in each and every direction: shouting out lines, arguing over take-out, creating crazy stories that led to crazy impressions, all followed by the sudden locking together of all four gears as a great idea was stumbled upon, worked over, discarded, reclaimed, worked over again, solved, and finally proclaimed brilliant. Then back slaps, congratulations, yelling, until it again descended into more shouting out lines, more arguing over take-out, more creating crazy stories that led to more crazy impressions until the next great idea was stumbled upon. Instead, in its place, was a tense, methodical process fraught with terse exchanges and a whole lot of silence between focused but drab discussion.

They just worked.

And as the days wore on, nothing changed. The situation didn't get worse—they were all polite with each other—but it didn't get better. It just stayed the same.

After a while, seeing that it was getting him nowhere, Jonny stopped trying to lighten the mood. If they wanted to act like petulant children, so be it. He hadn't done anything wrong. He was a professional. If he could handle a manipulative power-hungry boss like Hogart, he could certainly handle their immaturity. And why shouldn't he get a little attention for himself? *When people look at great buildings, they remember the name of the architect, not the guy who put the plaster of paris on the wall or put the bricks in place. I'm the architect of this; they're merely the workmen.*

He needed a break from it all.

And an hour talking about writing—and only writing—was just what he wanted.

He looks just like his picture, Jonny thought as he closed in on Sidney Landau, recognizing his soft face, pencil-thin moustache, and dark, greased hair from the byline photo that dutifully accompanied his column in *Radio and TV Monthly*.

"Hello," Jonny said brightly, standing over the diminutive reporter and shaking his hand with genuine excitement. Sidney Landau was famous for his thorough, in-depth interviews with writers, and after Jonny's enduring the endless stream of stupid questions and silly profiles from the previous reporters (despite his best efforts to steer conversations to more substantial topics), he now was ready to talk seriously about his craft. It didn't hurt that Sidney's column was read very closely by producers who were interested in the more serious work being done on television. If his agent wouldn't push him in the direction he wanted to go, then maybe Jonny needed to do it himself.

Sidney returned the handshake, and after the greetings were completed, Jonny sat down across from him. He quickly ordered and then sat back, ready. It was time to get down to business. Sidney already had a pad of paper in front of him, so when he reached into the pocket of his overcoat, which hung against the back of his chair, Jonny expected him to pull out a pencil or pen.

Instead, he produced a newspaper.

"Normally, I'm not in the business of mentioning what other journalists write, but I wouldn't be a good reporter if I didn't get your comments on something that was written just this morning," Sidney said, as he matter-of-factly opened his copy of the *Daily Mirror*.

When Sidney finished reading the column to Jonny, Jonny abruptly ended the interview and excused himself. Infuriated, he jumped on the subway and headed downtown, packed in with the rest of the riders, seemingly all of whom were holding a copy of this morning's *Daily Mirror*. Jonny was convinced they, too, were reading what he had just seen.

After some snooping and cajoling, he finally found out where Hogart was and, leading with his own copy of the libelous article, Jonny charged down the concrete hallway of the warehouse. Stopping at one of the doorways that led to the loft in the converted space, Jonny pushed open the door.

Hogart was huddled with Charles in a corner of the vast photographic studio, where assistants were cleaning up equipment from a shot that had just ended. He looked up as Jonny marched straight at them. "You missed the cast. They've already—"

"Did you see Winchell's column this morning?" Jonny asked, practically yelling.

"Of course," Hogart said calmly.

"Well, aren't you furious?"

"Not at all."

Incredulous, Jonny lifted his folded newspaper and, through venomous lips, began to read. "It has not gone unnoticed by this humble typer of rambling missives that the hottest thing tickling its way across our televisional transom is a fine lass from a borough even farther away than Queens. The little ones love her for her spunk, but it's the ones out of school who are really taking note, especially those who do the razor dance on their face each morning. They sure like that short skirt, and it's a lot cheaper than plunking down five hard-earned bucks in one of those girly joints just off Times Square, even if that is the more appropriate place to see that much leg." Jonny lowered the paper and glared at Hogart. "He's saying all our hard work is nothing more than a cheap striptease! Doesn't that make you mad?"

"No."

Jonny fought not to explode. "How is that *possible*?"

"Because I told him to write it."

Jonny looked at him, stunned. "You?"

"Yes."

For the first time, Jonny turned to Charles, who reinforced Hogart with a slow, knowing nod. Turning back to Hogart, Jonny shook his head incredulously. "You told him to write *that*?"

Hogart nodded confidently. "Yes. Word for word."

It had long been rumored that Hogart had done a big favor for Walter Winchell a few years back, when a young actress felt Walter had been a bit too aggressive in his advances during an interview at his apartment, which had been conveniently scheduled when his wife and children were out of town. In return for giving her a couple of guest spots on a couple of different shows, Hogart had been able to get her to drop the charges. After that,

Winchell, a man not known for throwing around a lot of praise, on occasion became quite complimentary of things associated with the Regal Television Network. In this moment, Jonny realized the rumor was completely true.

As an assistant walked up and handed a folder to Hogart, Jonny started to shake, trembling in disbelief. "Why would you want him to make a mockery of the show? Why would you want him to print something like that?"

"So we can respond with this," Hogart answered. He held open the folder and showed the contents to Jonny like a proud papa. It was a crisp eight-by-ten black-and-white photo that showed Felicity as Justice Girl, in full costume, her long right leg raised on a small platform. Against her bare leg and thigh, Felicity held a ruler that clearly showed that the bottom of her skirt came almost all the way to her knee, stopping just an inch short. Standing a respectful distance away from her were a rabbi, a minister, and a priest, all watching closely and nodding in approval.

"You've got to be kidding," Jonny answered, almost laughing, sure that he was being put on.

"Not in the least."

Jonny grabbed the photo out of the folder and took a closer look. He stared at it, as if trying to understand. Finally, he shook his head in disbelief. "You really think this will make people ignore what Winchell said about our show?"

"Oh, I couldn't care less about that. It was just the groundwork so everyone would look at the photo." Proudly, Hogart snatched the photo out of Jonny's hand and carefully placed it back in the folder. "Because of Winchell's column, every paper in the country will run it. Parents will be reassured that what their kids are watching is wholesome, but with a bit of a wink, they'll also be reminded why so many of them like watching. New fans will tune in because the show is obviously good clean fun...or because they want to check out some seriously sexy legs."

"Wholesome, though," Charles added.

Hogart raised an authoritative finger. "Exactly."

"But it's just a gimmick, it's fake, it's a lie," Jonny pleaded. "We're better than this. We've created something that's good enough to stand on its own." Just then, an assistant went by pushing a rack of costumes. As Jonny stepped aside to let her pass, he recognized the Justice Girl costume hanging next to those of a rabbi, minister, and priest. Jonny pointed at the swaying costumes. "This sort of thing isn't necessary."

The conversation was annoying Hogart. "Not that this is anything you need to know, but there are some people out there who aren't so happy that our baby is doing so well. If they had their way, she'd be smothered in her crib. Well, I won't let that happen. There's too much at stake."

"But this? How can this possibly be good for the show?" Jonny pleaded.

Hogart waved him off with his hand. "Sponsors and what comes out of the actors' mouths fall under your purview; this does not. So, I suggest you turn around and get back to work. You have a show that goes on the air in three days. And it better be a good one."

Jonny slapped the folder with the photo. "Well, according to you, it doesn't really matter how good it is."

Hogart ignored the barb and kept his gaze locked on Jonny.

Jonny seethed, but he knew there was no point in arguing any further. This was one battle he was not going to win. He took Hogart's advice and sulked away, not sure whether to go back to the writers' room or jump off the Brooklyn Bridge. Either promised to feel about the same.

...

Light mist. Heavy foliage. Scratchy branches. The jungle. With a look of trepidation, Felicity, as Sally Smalls, pushed her way through the almost impassable growth. "How much farther to the village, Chance?" she asked carefully.

Viola, who was walking behind Felicity and carrying a script, answered in her best imitation of Thomas's voice. "Oh, it's just a little bit farther."

"That's what you said a little bit farther back," Felicity snapped.

Viola flipped to the next page of the script and affected a fairly decent simulation of Reginald's stuffy British accent. "My dear girl, remind me to never accept a dare from you again."

"Oh, Benjamin," Viola said now, with the nasally, arrogant, northeastern accent of Margaret Crawford, as played by Veronica Sanders. "You know not even free highballs at 21 could have kept you away."

Felicity turned around to face Viola with apologetic terror on her face, her presence very much that of the timid Sally Smalls. "Sorry to interrupt, but I think I hear something—and I don't think it's good." Then, suddenly, Felicity's fear vanished, along with her timidity, and her entire body slumped. She kicked the ground in frustration. "Ugh," she said, defeated.

Viola looked at her quizzically. "But Miss Felicity, you got all the words right," she said encouragingly as she closed the script.

"I know, I know," Felicity said. She and Viola stepped out of the dense foliage and away from their makeshift Amazon jungle made from a collection of potted plants, trees, and shrubs. Quite amazingly, despite the looming image of the back of Felicity's house, with its stuck-out tongue of a red brick pool, Felicity had managed to turn a small section of her backyard into a surprisingly successful reproduction of the deepest and darkest jungles of South America.

Felicity turned back to Viola and hung her head. "But darn it. No. No. No! It's not right. It doesn't feel right. I'm just saying words. I'm not *being* them." Frustrated, Felicity ran her hands through her wet hair and then snapped her wrist to get rid of the moisture. "Yuck," she said, but then she paused, rubbing her wet fingers together. She began to rub her face with the moisture. "It's the jungle! I'm not feeling the words because I'm not feeling the jungle. I have to feel the jungle to feel the words." She stuck her hands out matter-of-factly. "I'm gonna do it again, but this time without saying any words. I have to let the jungle inside me." She tapped her chest for emphasis. "Feel it in here. And I don't want you to say anything either. I just want you to make animal noises."

"Miss Felicity?" Viola asked, confused.

"Animal noises, like in the jungle. Lions, tigers, birds—that sort of thing, okay?"

Still confused, Viola nodded. "Okay."

"Good." Felicity kicked the ground with determination. "I'm just gonna feel the jungle. I'm just gonna listen."

Moments later, Felicity crouched at the entrance to her fake jungle. "Okay, start the rain," she said to Jorge, their gardener, who stood atop a ladder with a garden hose. Jorge nodded and pulled the trigger on the spout, releasing a shower of water. Felicity entered.

It was a tight fit, but she forced herself forward and pushed through the cramped foliage. *I'm in the jungle; it's wet; it's hot*, she thought, opening herself to all that was around her. *I don't want to be here. I'm a city girl. Even though I have superpowers, this is uncomfortable, and I'm worried about the others who are with me.*

Felicity came out of her creeping-forward crouch and stopped. She grimaced. It still wasn't working. "Viola—lions and tigers!"

"Yes, Miss Felicity."

She returned to her crouch and moved forward. "I'm in the jungle; it's hot," she said, now talking out loud. "I'm uncomfortable; I'm miserable."

"*Rrrrrr!*" Viola roared.

Felicity's eyes went wide at the sound. "And I'm scared by the thought of all the wild beasts that surround me on all sides."

"*RRRRRRRR!*" Viola roared, louder this time.

"I'm so scared, I jump at the smallest sound." Felicity jumped, as if being startled. The sleeve of her blouse caught for a second on a branch. Suddenly, Felicity's eyes widened with an idea. "My clothes—they are being shredded by the dangerous foliage." Felicity grabbed her sleeve and tore it. "Yes. Yes, it's a true house of horrors I'm trapped in, ripping my clothes to shreds." Felicity grabbed more of her blouse and tore it in several places, creating huge rips on the sleeves and neck and sides.

"RRRRRRR! Ca-caaaah! EEEEE-WWWWoopppp!" Viola yelled.

"I'm surrounded! My only chance to survive is to get low and stay hidden." Felicity fell to the ground, crawling. "Mud is everywhere, but I have to fight through it if I want even the slightest chance to survive." Inching along the ground, Felicity scooped up some mud and smeared it on her torn clothing. "It gets everywhere—on my clothes, on my body, even on my face." Felicity smeared the mud across her face. "But I fight forward because I have to survive. And I can survive because I can feel the horror all around me."

Felicity began to smile excitedly. "The jungle. I feel it. For the first time I really feel it. In my bones, in my body, in my mind, in my heart." Reaching the end of the fake jungle, Felicity climbed back to her feet. "And I will survive!" she exclaimed, as she burst out of the tight foliage into the real world of her backyard…and the sight of both her horrified parents staring at her.

The excitement of her success quickly faded as reality returned. The shock on her parents' faces suddenly made her feel practically naked, and she self-consciously wrapped her arms around herself.

"What exactly are you doing?" her father asked, disgusted at the sight of his daughter with mud on her face and body and covered in torn clothing.

Should I tell them the plot of this week's episode? About how this scene is key to the story? Felicity wondered. *Should I explain how I am trying to make the situation real to me? To have some actual experience to draw upon to bring meaning to the words? How can I act like I'm walking through the jungle, scared, if I've never walked through the jungle, scared?*

She opened her mouth, but her parents' deep scorn kept the words from coming out. Her father was in a suit, and her mother wore her tennis outfit. Clearly, they had been in the middle of their busy day when they somehow got word of what she was doing and raced home to confront her. Hearing about what she was attempting to do or that it had actually worked was not what they wanted to hear. They would only tear into her for playing such childish games, and her father would lambaste her for losing focus on the job at hand: battling Communism.

That's it! she thought brightly. She could give him the names; that's what she could do! Yes, just tell her father about her amazing discovery—an entire show written by blacklisted writers! So what if the final verification hadn't come back from DC yet? Just tell him, and he'd be so happy that he'd forget about what she was doing.

But again, when she opened her mouth, nothing came out. The small, nagging fear was still there—what if the list was wrong? Even though it couldn't possibly be, what if it was, just in this one, rare instance? Would it be fair to drag Shel, Annie, Burton, or even Jonny through the mud for no reason? Also, if she gave up the names now, she wouldn't get a chance to do the show on Sunday night. And she really liked this week's script.

But she had to tell them something. They weren't just simply going to turn around and walk away. If only she really were Justice Girl, she could simply fly the hell out of there. But since she wasn't quite that good at the role yet, she had to think of something else. What could she say so that the sight of their youngest daughter in torn clothes, dirty and dripping wet, in front of a fake jungle would be instantly forgotten?

Then it hit her. She smiled and took a step toward them. "Braeden and me—we're engaged."

...

Hogart stared at the long rows of workers, all with a pad and pen and telephone in front of them on small wooden desks. "And I'll be able to see the results as they come in, right?" he asked the project manager, a very nervous Martin Twindle, who stood next to him.

"Absolutely," Martin answered with a jerky nod. He clearly was not used to dealing directly with the head of a network.

"Good." Hogart and Martin then exited the room and stepped out into the busy hallway of the Trendex Corporation. "If you'll excuse me," Hogart said, walking away without waiting for a response. Hogart headed for the small private office that he had requested as part of the special deal between the company and the network. Trendex was in the business of monitoring television viewership and creating the ratings used to establish which shows were the most popular and—most important—which ones could charge the most for advertising time. Of the several companies that did what Trendex did—Nielsen, ABS, Pulse—they were the only one that could turn around the information in the time Hogart needed it. Trendex specialized in having a team of workers make calls to viewers around the country while a show was actually on the air. They would then ask the person who answered the phone what the family was watching at that very moment, and if Justice Girl was the answer, they would then follow up with a series of short questions—size of household, ages of viewers, weekly income. All of the information would be recorded rapidly before the caller hung up, and then the worker would quickly move on to another call. The other ratings companies used a myriad of other techniques—an in-house measuring device, diaries, follow-up interviews, all of which required additional time to get results, which Hogart did not have. Even Trendex generally waited several days to release its information, but Hogart had paid extra, so additional callers and number-crunchers were put on the job. He'd be able to watch the numbers as they came in, as the show was actually on the air live, and then he'd have the preliminary numbers broken down, processed, and collated by the end of the evening. If all went well, by midnight, he'd leave with a briefcase full of organized viewing data.

Walking the sterile hallway, Hogart checked his watch. It was six o'clock, an hour and a half until *Justice Girl* went on the air. Once again, his impatience had gotten the best of him, and he had arrived very early. But unlike his unscheduled visit to his art directors, this time it was borne of excitement, not fear. The "wholesome" photo of Justice Girl had made a bigger splash than he could have dreamed. As expected, nearly every paper in the country had run the photo, but it was *where* they ran it that really put things over the top. The *San Francisco Chronicle* placed it inside the front cover of its television supplement, covering the full page. The *Dallas Morning News* placed it above the fold of the front page of its TV section, in the spot normally reserved for the lead article, and the *Daily Mirror* put it on the cover of its weekly television guide, even going as far as to colorize it. And Hogart's favorite, the coup de grâce, as far as he was concerned, the *New York Times* placed it directly next to the suddenly puny and insignificant text-only ad for the *Percy Williams Show*, with special guest star, Bette Davis. Oh sure, the name Bette Davis had plenty of sizzle and snap, but it was nothing compared to the animal pull of a sexy photo of a couple of gorgeous gams.

Hogart couldn't wait to see the numbers. He knew that, by the end of the evening, he would have just what he needed to go into the board meeting, locked and loaded and ready for bear.

As Hogart stepped into his makeshift office, Mrs. Decosta looked up at him from the one desk in the bare room. She started to clear away the paperwork she had been working on, but Hogart waved her off and grabbed the phone. After the disaster during the first episode, he'd had a direct line to the control room installed. Charles answered after only one ring. "How is everything going?" Hogart asked sharply.

"Fine. Dress went great," Charles answered. "Everyone's back from break. We're ready to go."

"Any...problems?" Hogart asked.

"Nope." Charles knew exactly what Hogart was getting at. "Jonny's behaving himself, and there were no last-minute changes to the script."

"Good." Hogart hung up. Mrs. Decosta, eyeing him as he stood silently, awaited his command. Hogart was nervous but pleased. The script for this week was blissfully free of anything controversial. Oh, sure, it was the usual pretentious allegory—this week it was civil rights and Jim Crow, but it was hidden wonderfully within a solid adventure story that had all the characters traipsing through the Amazon.

He flexed his hands and checked his watch again—6:05 p.m. He had well over an hour to kill. "Anything come in while I was with the project manager?"

Mrs. Decosta slid a couple dozen slips of paper across the desk. "You had a few phone calls," she said flatly.

Even on a Sunday, he thought. *Well, that's what I get for having my business calls forwarded.* He reached for them, knowing that if he worked fast, he could get through them before the broadcast. But then he paused, thinking, *What's the point?* If things didn't go well tonight, what difference did those calls make anyway? There wouldn't be a network to whom the affiliates could complain, or ad agencies lobby, or producers and agents to sell their clients.

Tingling with nervous energy, he turned to Mrs. Decosta. "I have to run something by the project manager. I may not be back until just before we go on the air." Mrs. Decosta, as always, nodded her understanding, and Hogart left.

But once in the hallway, instead of heading back to the room where the call center was set up, Hogart hurried toward the elevator. Passing through the lobby, he was amused to see all of his top executives sitting and waiting. Programming, Affiliates, Advertising, Personnel, and now even Legal were all there and rose en masse when they saw Hogart. *So the rats have decided maybe the boat isn't sinking after all.*

But Hogart ignored them, and when the elevator came, he disappeared inside. The thought of something nearby that he had passed on the cab ride over to the Trendex offices excited him a hell of a lot more than standing around with those buffoons.

It was a dark, dingy, damp place, stinking of sweat and blood, but as Hogart trundled down the rickety flight of stairs that took him well below street level and into the boxing gym, he beamed. Hogart became excited as he looked around and saw the smattering of boxing hopefuls working out in the ring, on a speed bag, on a heavy bag, or tossing a medicine ball. Despite the decrepit nature of the place, it was—to Hogart's extreme amusement—for members only. However, after sliding the slack-faced attendant at the entrance a quick twenty, Hogart gained instant approval with full benefits. Knowing time was short, he quickly changed in the locker room into a sweatshirt and sweatpants. The locker boy, no more than twelve, hurriedly helped Hogart lace on his boxing gloves. The kid was practically in a panic and doing a very sloppy job. "Whoa, slow down. You're doing it all wrong," Hogart said, stopping him.

"Sorry, I'm almost off, and I want to get home in time for *Justice Girl.*"

Hogart gave him a five-dollar tip and re-entered the gym to discover that one of the heavy bags was unoccupied.

He felt the first punch all the way up to his shoulder as his gloved hand made contact with the hard mushiness of the bag. He'd boxed a lot back in the thirties, in workers camps all around the country, once he discovered it was a great way to make some extra dough. Win or lose, they paid you something. Sometimes he took a beating, and sometimes he gave one.

Hogart landed more punches, chasing the bag as it began to swing on its overhead chain. As he followed it, jabbing and throwing combinations, he began to bob and weave as if avoiding punches thrown at him. For fifteen minutes, in spite of his gimpy leg, he danced around the bag, landing blow after blow. The pain of each impact was an officious reminder of the battle his life had been and everything that he had gone through to get to this moment. Growing up the oldest of seven on a cattle ranch in Bakersfield, California, meant that his family had made just enough money to be broke. The family lost the ranch after the herd had to be slaughtered, due to an outbreak of hoof-and-mouth disease. That forced Hogart to go it alone, because he was sixteen by then, and there was no room for him at his uncle's farm in Oklahoma, where the family had moved. He became a vagabond, riding the rails, picking fruit, working in oil fields, moving from one work project to the next—until after Pearl Harbor, when the army offered him his first permanent home in almost eight years. But after the army, the real battle had begun, as he fought his way to the top of the network.

Covered in sweat, his chest heaving, he finally stopped, but only because he had to. He took a short shower and quickly dressed. Though he'd gone into the gym seeking distraction, he found himself oddly invigorated and ran up the creaky steps to the sidewalk. The sun had set while he was in the gym, and the crisp night air felt good against his warm skin. He hurried the three blocks back to the Trendex Corporation, and at exactly 7:20 p.m., he stepped off the elevator on the floor where the phone bank was located. *Ten minutes to air. Perfect.* He felt loose. Relaxed. Focused and ready. The data would start coming in soon, and as it did, he would begin to plan the perfect strategy for convincing the board to turn down the deal to sell the network. And damn it, it would work. As far as he was concerned, the Regal Television Network was going to be around for many years to come.

Hogart yanked open the door to the room where the phone bank was located—and stopped dead in his tracks. It was empty. The desks sat unoccupied, the phones idly on their cradles, the pens and pads motionless. What the hell was going on? They were ten minutes to air; they couldn't all be on break.

He searched desperately around the office, but it was after hours, and the place was deserted. He hurried to his temporary office and whipped open the door. It, too, was deserted; Mrs. Decosta was nowhere in sight. He walked the hallways, sticking his head into office after office, searching for someone, searching for anyone. Finally, he heard the elevator ding, and he rushed toward it. He arrived just as a frantic Mrs. Decosta stepped off.

"Oh, thank God," she said, seeing Hogart.

"What the hell is going on?" Hogart asked desperately.

"I've been looking all over for you!" Mrs. Decosta answered. *"Justice Girl* was canceled for the night."

...

It was on this night that Jonny realized just how small his world—and the world in general—was becoming. A hydrogen bomb going off 5,000 miles away in Kirkuk, Russia, had preempted his show for the evening. It was only a test in a remote region of the Soviet Union, but given the size of the bomb—150 megatons—the news division decided to go on the air with a special report. *Justice Girl* would have to wait until the following Sunday to defeat bad guys.

Even more surprising, with this unexpected free time, Jonny found himself in the backseat of a black limo with Charles, making the short crosstown trip to the New Yorker Hotel. With the preemption coming less than an hour before going on the air, just as the heart-throbbing intensity was beginning to build, everyone in the studio had shared a collective anti-climax. One by one, cast and crew alike had sauntered out of the building, caught up in a strange and unexpected purgatory. There was neither the rush of success nor the disappointment of failure. Just the odd sensation of displacement, of not belonging, as if waiting for something to happen that they knew wouldn't happen—at least, not for another week.

Charles had run into Jonny outside the control booth and suggested, rather mildly, that they go grab a drink. Jonny had of course turned him down. Charles asked again, this time throwing in that he was going to a party, which did nothing to further Jonny's interest, but then Charles said the magic words: "Kraft Television Theatre." The party was in honor of the seventh anniversary of the *Kraft Television Theatre*'s being on the air, and it would be packed with actors, directors, and—most important to Jonny—writers from the show's entire run. Maybe, just maybe, *he* would be there—Rod Serling. After all, it was on *Kraft* that "Patterns" had been performed four months earlier, instantly making Serling a star.

That alone was not quite enough to get Jonny to go, but with no desire to go to Annie's party—tension between Jonny and the other three writers having not abated in the least—and having no work to do, Jonny found himself, much to his surprise, saying yes. He quickly dressed in one of the suits the network had supplied for him. If pressed, he'd have admitted that, too, was a slight incentive, as the three garment bags, sent over from Brooks Brothers, had hung unopened in a closet in the writers' room. Jonny chose the teal-blue sharkskin suit with matching string tie, which, as he slipped inside the limo, got an approving nod from Charles. "Very nice," Charles said, handing Jonny a freshly poured glass of scotch.

Jonny took the drink as he settled back into the crunchy black leather. The door was closed, and off they went.

Charles held up his glass to Jonny. "To *Justice Girl*."

Jonny met Charles's glass with his own. "To *Justice Girl*," Jonny sheepishly responded, still taking in the unfamiliar plush surroundings as they clinked glasses.

Charles finished his glass in one gulp and smiled almost orgasmically. "Nothing quite like twenty-five-year-old Chivas."

Jonny eyed Charles and took a sip of his drink, running the liquid across his tongue before letting it slide down his throat. Nothing happened. He took a larger, almost mouth-filling swig. Still nothing. Much as he wanted Charles's experience, it tasted just like every other shot of scotch he'd ever had. Except it had cost a hell of a lot more. The thought made him sad. All around him he saw wasted money. The car, the driver, the booze, the expensive crystal glasses, Charles's suit, even his own—wasted money that could have been used for something much more worthy than their own selfish pleasures. He began to shift uneasily. What was he doing here? In the back-seat of a five-thousand-dollar limo, wearing a hundred-dollar suit, drinking from a fifty-dollar bottle of scotch, riding next to a complete idiot. Even if he didn't have to work on the script for next week's episode, he could be home starting something else, something important. Yes, that's what he should be doing. He had to get the hell out of here, now. He turned to Charles, who was finishing yet another drink, eliciting the same euphoric reaction. Determined, Jonny opened his mouth, but before he could speak, Charles said excitedly, "Here we are!" The limo had pulled up in front of the New Yorker and stopped. Without waiting for his driver to open the door, Charles stepped out, and Jonny hurried after him. But when he stepped onto the sidewalk, planning to bid Charles an unexpected good-bye, Charles was already gone, having disappeared inside the swanky hotel.

Jonny thought about just leaving and then later apologizing profusely about the emergency that had suddenly come up, but as much as he didn't particularly care for Charles, that seemed excessively rude. So Jonny raced after him, hurrying through the crowded lobby, trying to catch up to him. He finally succeeded, just inside the spacious ballroom.

Almost immediately, Jonny forgot about trying to excuse himself from the party. The ballroom was packed with hundreds of guests, almost all of them, astonishingly, in costume. "Wha-what is? Why are they in costume?" Jonny asked.

"They're dressed as the characters they played on Kraft," Charles answered, as if it were the most natural thing in the world. "Brilliant promotional idea, if you ask me. Well, there's a dry martini with my name on it. Want anything?"

"Ah, no," Jonny said, so taken with the spectacle, he could barely get the words out.

"Very well. I shall return." Charles stepped away, heading for one of the numerous bars that lined the edges of the large room.

Jonny watched as, almost immediately, Charles was swallowed up by the thick throng. All around Jonny, the costume-clad crowd swirled. He suddenly felt as if he were in some strange library where a spell had been cast, bringing all the characters from its dusty books to life. Huckleberry Finn conversed with Zeus and Athena, while Hamlet and Tom Joad plucked hors d'oeuvres from a passing waiter. Two Confederate soldiers shared a laugh with a Union counterpart, and in a corner, George Washington and the Mad Hatter posed for a photograph.

Charles was back, stepping between a very drunk Romeo and Juliet, as he carried two drinks. He handed one to Jonny. "Just in case you lied," he said with smile.

Jonny took it, feeling in need of a drink at this point. "Thank you." He then noticed the woman who had come back from the bar with Charles. She was older, probably mid-forties, and very noticeably not dressed in a costume. She had a reserved, confident, business-like air. Jonny nodded in her direction. "Hello."

She nodded back, with a hint of a skeptical smile.

Charles finished his martini. "My, how rude of me." Then, after quickly grabbing another drink from a passing waiter, he introduced Jonny to Blanche Gaines.

Blanche Gaines? Jonny thought. *The Blanche Gaines?* He knew her well, if only from what he had read in the TV press. She was an agent but not just any agent; she was the one responsible for discovering Rod Serling.

Blanche looked Jonny up and down with a droll pout. "So, you're the young genius of *Justice Girl.*"

Jonny really didn't like the way that sounded. He certainly didn't mind the show's being a hit, but he could have done without the condescension. Besides, there was a lot more to him. "I've written a lot of other things," he offered back in defense.

Blanche nodded and flashed a skeptical smile. "More stuff for the diaper set?"

What is it with this lady? Jonny wondered, resisting the urge to yell at her—or worse. But he settled for a quick glower that only he was aware of. "No, very different material. More appropriate for shows like *Studio One* or *Kraft,*" he said with a swipe of his arm to emphasize that his work would fit in perfectly with the swirl all around them. He may have wanted to punch her, but this was *Blanche Gaines,* and if he could get in with her, then he would have an agent who could and would push him into the rarified world he wanted to be in.

But all he got in response from her was a series of mildly interested nods. "Perhaps you'd like to read some of it?" Jonny asked, taking the tiny morsel and running with it.

Blanche gave him another looking over. "Perhaps at some point, when you make the skirts long enough."

Now Jonny really wanted to punch her.

Blanche eyed the thin watch on her wrist. "Now, if you two will excuse me, Rod awaits."

"Rod? As in Serling? Is he here?" Jonny asked excitedly and then blushed over his almost girlish squealing.

"No. He awaits at home, where I have to take a call from him. He's in California." Blanche gave Jonny and Charles a final smile and walked away.

Jonny's entire body sank, and his chin found his chest. "Well, that was a complete disaster."

"Why's that?" Charles asked, sipping his drink with an amused smile.

"Because she has no interest in looking at any of my work."

"My boy," Charles began, pausing to finish his drink, "I've known Blanche for many, many years. If she weren't interested in seeing your work, she would have told you. A 'perhaps' from her means she's definitely interested."

Jonny's whole body rose. "Really?"

"Yes. Maybe not now, but somewhere down the line."

Jonny beamed, a new man.

Charles gave him a lazy smile. "I'm guessing you're pretty happy you decided to come to this party after all."

"Perhaps," Jonny said playfully, playing down his excitement. But inside, he was dancing. Blanche Gaines, interested in his work! Blanche Gaines, who could take his career where he wanted it to go! Could this night get any *better*?

Something poked Jonny in the ass. Startled, he turned around to see the back of a woman dressed, as best as he could tell, as Little Bo Peep, and she had just stabbed him with her shepherd's staff. "Excuse me?" Jonny said.

The woman turned around, genuinely surprised. "I am so sorry," she said. Then, looking past Jonny, her eyes went wide with recollection. "Charles!"

Charles's face brightened. "Deborah, my dear! How are you?" She and Charles embraced. Then Charles motioned toward Jonny. "Jonny, I'd like you to meet Deborah Tyler."

They greeted each other, though to Jonny, no introduction was necessary. As loath as he was to admit it, he knew exactly who she was. Jonny had first spotted Deborah Tyler two years earlier in the background of an episode of *Western Showcase*, where she had played a saloon girl, complete with feathers in her hair, corset dress, and garters over black hose. She had one line: "You forgot your hat," which, fortunately for Jonny, was enough to get her name in the credits. After that, he kept an eager eye out for her, and to his pleasant surprise, because of her ample figure and considerable good looks, he started seeing her everywhere. She had played a fast-talking secretary in several episodes of *District Attorney*, a gun-toting bad girl in Republic Pictures' *Streets of Crime*, and most recently, in a B-movie titled *The Beast from Way Under*, which was her biggest role to date. In it, she had played the sole female crew member on a pleasure yacht that had the distinct bad luck to become adrift in the Atlantic Ocean at the same time it was under attack from a vicious two-legged sea creature that developed an understandable crush on the swimsuit-clad Deborah. It was a horrible, ridiculous movie.

And Jonny saw it four times.

The final time, he trekked all the way out to Queens to see it in the last theatre in New York that was still showing it in 3-D.

With the introductions over, Jonny stared at her, tongue-tied. Despite her silly, frilly blue costume and ridiculous curly blonde wig stuffed under her virginal bonnet, she was stunning.

She, in turn, gave him a bored looking-over, running her eyes up and down his sharp suit. "I'm guessing either executive, producer, or over-compensating writer."

What am I? A chicken hanging in a store window, Jonny thought, stinging from the second appraisal he had received in the last five minutes.

"Wrong on all three," Charles interjected. "This is the rarest of the rare—a writer with talent. Deborah, meet Jonny Dirby, the creator of *Justice Girl*."

Her bored expression vanished, if only for a second, as her head jerked back, astonished. Then the sleepy, bored gaze returned. "Ah, yes. Good show, but I should have had a chance to audition for it."

"Well, there weren't really any auditions. It kind of just happened. The whole thing," Jonny offered, wanting to appease her.

Deborah sighed. "Such as the legend goes. You boys are everywhere these days. Can't seem to get away from the hottest show on television, not even here."

"Maybe you weren't meant to get away from it," Johnny retorted playfully.

Deborah raised a bemused eyebrow and held out her hand. "Nice to meet you." Jonny took it, and they shook hands. She turned to Charles. "Nice to see you again, Charles." And she was gone.

Charles hit Jonny on the arm, playfully. "Son of a bitch, you do have a pulse. You were flirting with her."

"What?" Jonny asked, trying to act astonished. "I was not doing any—" Then he through his hands in the air. "Well, she didn't like me anyway."

Charles laughed. "How can someone who writes so well be so stupid?" Charles carefully pointed across the room. "She liked you quite a lot."

Jonny followed the aim of Charles's finger to where Deborah was now standing with a group of toga-clad Romans, except she kept sneaking a peek back toward Jonny.

Charles winked at Jonny. "Something tells me you haven't seen the last of her tonight."

...

Among the numerous reasons that Hogart loved his wife, besides her charming looks, gentle wit, affectionate parenting, and tight stewardship of their home life was her rare ability to get dressed quickly. Unlike every other woman he had ever known, when they went out on the town, she was able to transform herself into a head-turning object of extreme beauty in a remarkably short time. This praiseworthy talent was never more on display than earlier, when Hogart called home, explaining to Trudy that he was suddenly free for the evening—the show had been unexpectedly preempted—and did she want to go to a museum opening with him. An hour and a half later, she was standing on the front steps of the Museum of Natural History in an elegant gown, with gloves on, hair up, and a mink stole across her enticing shoulders. Hogart arrived moments later, pleased at the visage before him, and after a warm kiss, they joined the stream of New York society heading inside.

Despite all of the objects in the second-floor dinosaur gallery being quite dead, the room was quite alive with the sound of big-band music mixed with the clatter of glasses and the throbbing murmur of a dozen conversations. The museum had just completed its restoration of the largest and most complete Tyrannosaurus Rex skeleton and was throwing a party to celebrate and thank its most loyal patrons. And of course, hit them up for even more money so they could dig up and restore even more old bones. The guest of honor occupied the center of the room, forever frozen in an eerie attack pose, as if about to pounce on one of the thirty or forty small tables set up for the event that ringed him.

Upon entering the cavernous gallery, Trudy stopped Hogart and gave him another kiss. "I'm going to go get a drink, and then I'll kill some time, pretending to be interested in one of the dioramas, while you go take care of the real reason we're here," she said with a wink.

Hogart's heart swelled even more as he watched her depart. She wasn't fooled. She knew how rarely, if ever, Hogart went to these types of events. Ever the pragmatist herself, she knew Hogart had to have a real reason for being here.

And he did.

With the preemption of *Justice Girl* having completely screwed up his plans for the board meeting, and his dream of giving the single greatest presentation on viewer trending having just gone down the toilet, it took Hogart about ten minutes to put together Plan B. And the centerpiece of that plan was currently standing alone at a table, nursing a scotch and soda beneath a pouncing saber-toothed tiger.

Before approaching this solitary man, Hogart flagged down a waiter. "See that rather short man over by the tiger?" The waiter nodded. "About a minute after I join him, I want you to bring over a bottle of wine"—Hogart pulled out a small envelope and handed it to the waiter—"with this envelope attached." Hogart then handed him a ten-dollar bill. "Sound good?"

"Yes, sir," the waiter said with a nod and then moved away.

Hogart took a deep breath, shook his body to force himself into casualness, and then marched straight toward Sylvester Nickles.

Sylvester Nickles was one of three children of the late financial baron Kenneth Nickles. When Kenneth had died, he left his empire to all three of his children, equally. Though they rarely spoke, the three siblings amicably split everything up, with Sylvester, as he wanted it, taking all of the altruistic positions on dozens of museum and gallery boards. Somehow, in all of the slicing and dicing of the numerous companies and acquisitions and subsidiaries, he also landed on the board of the Regal Television Network as one of its seven members. Chairman Fortis, along with his own vote, had the votes of three other board members, including Sylvester Nickles, to take the deal to sell the network and thus bring about its extinction. Hogart had two other votes, as well as his own, in favor of turning it down and letting Regal live. Now that he could not use the impressive trend-line presentation, his only hope was to find another way to turn one of the four yes votes into a no. If he couldn't appeal to the mind, with the right person, he might be able to appeal to the heart. It was a long shot, but at this point, it was the only shot he had.

"Well, hello," Sylvester said when Hogart joined him at the table.

"Hello to you," Hogart answered brightly. Sylvester was a tiny man who wore out-of-date suits with high collars, always highlighted by a bright ascot, and Hogart genuinely liked him. In the dreary world of corporate boardrooms, Sylvester was a breath of fresh air, if for no other reason than

...

gave Alexis one final deep hug and then stepped back and took
's big leathery hand. Despite his strong grip and the closeness of his
dy, she couldn't keep her eyes off her acting teacher. She stared at
true amazement. "I just have to say it again," Felicity said, beaming.
re truly incredible."

ank you, darling," Alexis answered with a slight nod. "Bye now."
at, she slipped back behind the wool blanket that hung over the
y of her makeshift dressing room.

ll excited, Felicity, with Braeden in tow, headed down the hallway. As
ere the only ones dressed in evening clothes more appropriate for a
Avenue dinner party than off-off-off-off Broadway theatre, everyone
assed gave them a not-so-subtle double take. They passed back through
iniscule theatre space, where they had been two of the just eleven peo-
tching Alexis perform her one-woman show as Amelia Earhart. The
nt after Arnold had knocked on Felicity's dressing room door and told
at *Justice Girl* had been preempted for the evening, Felicity grabbed
en—he was already ensconced in the VIP booth—and jumped into
and made it to the converted loft space in Soho mere minutes before
how began. She was devastated to have not gone on that night as Justice
after all, it could have been her last chance to perform the role, as the
irmation of the blacklisted names was due back from the FBI any day
. And if they did come back confirmed, as far as she was concerned, even
as much as she was learning and growing, that would be the end of her
ng career. But getting to see Alexis in the final performance of her show
an almost passable consolation prize. Almost.

Stepping out onto the sidewalk, Felicity spun with excitement. "Wasn't
amazing!" she exclaimed to Braeden and any of the passersby who were
earshot.

"Uh-huh," Braeden answered, still yawning the sleep out of his body. He
bbed his sore neck; it hurt from his constant head bobbing as he fought to
y awake during the play. He finally lost the battle and slept through the

---

his complete lack of interest in all matters financial. Whenever an issue got
too contentious or Hogart needed to be somewhere else, he could always
count on Sylvester to second his motion to adjourn the meeting. But along
with this lack of interest came an extreme dislike of rocking the boat, and
thus, when any real issue was being decided, he always voted with the dominant figure in the room, Chairman Fortis. However, as a lover of the arts—
or more importantly, a lover of the attention that came with being a lover of
the arts—there was nothing he liked more than being at the forefront of a
hot new discovery, even if it was something as passé and mundane as a banal
television show.

"Where's Gwen?" Hogart asked, pretending to care.

"She didn't come tonight."

"Pity. Trudy was looking forward to seeing her." In fact, Gwen was the
only reason he had brought Trudy, so the two women could talk, at a spot
preferably away from the men, while Hogart worked on Sylvester.

"Mahjong. Tonight's her mahjong night. If you ever want more time to
yourself, introduce your wife to mahjong."

"I'll keep that in mind."

"Aren't I seeing you on Tuesday?" Though not interested in business,
Sylvester was nonetheless very aware of the significance of the vote they
were about to take.

"That's what I was hoping to talk to you about." But before Hogart could
say anything more, a waiter walked up, carrying a bottle of wine.

"From someone who wishes to congratulate you on your recent success,"
the waiter said and then handed the bottle to Hogart.

Hogart removed the taped-on envelope and craned his neck, searching
the crowd. "I'm guessing it's from someone at an ad agency."

Sylvester joined Hogart in scanning the party. "Is it Joe Sullivan from
Young and Rubicam? I thought I saw him on the way in."

Hogart ripped open the envelope. "Nope, it's from Danny Brighton,
from Dexter, Tyler, and Thomson."

Sylvester nodded knowingly. "Of course it's not Joe Sullivan. There's
boxing at the Garden tonight." Sylvester went back to his drink.

Even though Sylvester didn't inquire, Hogart read the card out loud. "Congrats to you and the new girl on the block. May she fly for a hundred years!" He lowered the card and flashed his best pleased smile. "Isn't that thoughtful." But Sylvester was completely disinterested; his attention was on flagging down a passing waiter for another drink. "It's been like this ever since *Justice Girl* went on the air," Hogart said, giving an over-the-top sigh, as if bored by all the success. Sylvester nodded in agreement but wasn't really listening; he was more concerned with stirring his new scotch and soda. Even if it became obvious, Hogart knew he had to go further. "I'm sure you've noticed how popular *Justice*—"

"Another gentleman wishes to congratulate you on all your success," the waiter interrupted; he was back with another bottle of wine.

As Hogart took the bottle, he gave the waiter a quick conspiratorial smile. "Thank you," he said and then quickly opened the card. "Compliments of Young and Rubicon."

"I knew I'd seen Joe Sullivan on the way in." Sylvester searched the room again, but then slowly, his gaze fell on Hogart and the two bottles of wine. "You're quite the popular guy, aren't you?" he said, finally noticing.

"Yes, it's been that way for the last couple of weeks," Hogart said, as if he hadn't said it before.

"Interesting. All because of that new show, huh?"

Hogart had his opening. "Yep. *Justice Girl* is, as we like to say, a runaway train. She's the hottest thing around." He paused and then proceeded carefully. "It'd be a real shame to derail her."

Sylvester nodded, thinking through Hogart's words. Hogart knew this could be his only chance. He leaned in close, earnestly describing how great *Justice Girl* was doing, how it was beginning to bring along all the other shows on Sunday night, which in turn was going to boost the entire week and, ultimately, the entire season. He was really laying it on thick, and Sylvester was lapping it up. Then, in the midst of it all, at just the right time, the waiter was back again with yet another bottle from yet another admirer. Hogart gave him another conspiratorial smile, and then turned back to Sylvester. It was time to go in for the kill.

"You know what the best part is? I feel like something important," Hogart said. "Somethi ing people." He indicated the three gifts for emp Sylvester's direction. "And you're part of it too."

"Oh, I think that's overstating things a bit, self-consciously.

Hogart shook his head. "There'd be no ballet wit be no symphony without the donors, and there'd b board of directors to guide it. It must make you feel

Hogart watched closely for Sylvester's reaction.

After a moment, Sylvester nodded. "It does."

"I can imagine so. *Justice Girl*—the hit of the yea able to tell people you had a big hand in it."

Sylvester smiled at the thought.

"And just think, if the vote goes the right way on T to talk about it for years to come." Hogart stood up sti chest out proudly. "*Justice Girl*—I made that happen."

Sylvester watched him, eyes wide, eating it up.

Twenty minutes later, with one of the three gift parted, with a smiling Sylvester happily calling after H Tuesday!"

Hogart retrieved Trudy from in front of a display of rus eggs and headed for the exit. Passing his co-conspirato him another ten, along with a twenty.

"Thank you, sir, but that's not necessary," the waiter sa

"Yes, it is," a very happy Hogart said. "Those last two bo idea."

"That might be true, but they weren't my doing." The across the room to two different tables, where two tight cluste gregated. Ad executives. The waiter leaned in close to Hogar were sent by admirers."

Practically skipping, Hogart left the party with Trudy, joyo just as the speeches were beginning.

last twenty minutes, jolting awake to the sound of applause and the sight of Felicity giving Alexis a standing ovation.

"She was so locked in," Felicity continued. "So present, so in the moment. That wasn't Alexis up there; that was Amelia Earhart."

"Uh-huh," Braeden said again, not really listening, as he moved to the curb and hailed a cab. Almost immediately, one pulled over, and Braeden opened the back door for Felicity.

But she was still moving away, up the block, her eyes afire as she continued to recall what she had seen. "She was so on, so real. How do you get that good? How do you get that *good*?"

"Uh, Felicity!" Braeden called after her.

"How do you get that good?" she said, not hearing him and still moving away. The crowd was thickening now—people leaving shows, rushing to dinner, heading to gallery openings. Felicity studied their faces. They were excited, thrilled, imbued by some unseen rhythm that pulsed up through the ground and into everything. Felicity felt it shoot through her body, multiplied a hundred times over by what she had just seen Alexis do on stage.

"Felicity!"

She stopped and turned back. "What?"

"If we hurry, we might still make it to two or three of the places we were supposed to look at tonight."

Felicity slumped, her excitement ebbing. She slowly sauntered back toward him. "Do we really have to? I'm not really in the mood."

"Yes. Now that we're going to be married, I'd like to get the arrangements locked in as soon as possible."

Now that we're going to be married. Now that we're going to be married. Felicity had been hearing that a lot in the last few days. It had become Braeden's reason for everything. *Now that we're going to be married, I should drive you to the train station. Now that we're going to be married, I should go with you and see you do your show. Now that we're going to be married, we should go out afterward.* "And here I thought you had come in to the city with me because you wanted to see me on the show," Felicity said, more than a little annoyed.

"Of course I did. But we also have an engagement party to plan."

"You're worse than my mother," Felicity said as she joined him next to the cab, her irritation boiling over. Her statement was an exaggeration. Her mother was ten times worse. As expected, from the moment Felicity had gone public with the engagement, her mother had spoken of little else. This very morning over breakfast—on show day, no less—instead of having the opportunity to go over her lines again, her mother had taken up her time by beginning the guest list. Felicity swore it would be the last time she'd go home the night before they went on the air.

Not that Braeden had been that much better. On the train ride in, instead of asking about the episode or how the rehearsals had gone, all he wanted to talk about was the engagement party. Felicity's parents were taking care of the wedding, but Braeden's were throwing the engagement party. Despite the family passion being the breeding of thoroughbreds, Braeden's parents had a decidedly cosmopolitan edge, spending more than half of their weekends in Manhattan, attending a never-ending circuit of cocktail parties. Since the wedding was going to be in Greenwich, they had decided the engagement party should be in Manhattan. Braeden had made reservations at four of the prospective locations for after Felicity's show.

"I'll tell you what," Braeden said, seeing Felicity truly was not in the mood. "How about we skip looking at places for our engagement party and just go to Dickie Slocum's? We can't skip that; we have to at least make an appearance."

Felicity sighed. Not what she was in the mood for either, but better. Felicity nodded her agreement.

Riding up in the gilded elevator to Dickie Slocum's Fifth Avenue apartment, Felicity fixed her hair and adjusted her dress, checking herself in one of the gold-trimmed mirrors. The elevator doors opened, and the soft patter of quiet conversation and piano music floated at them. Braeden was about to take a step out of the elevator and into the apartment when Felicity stopped him. "Just as a little reminder, please, I don't want anybody to know that I'm doing the...you know...show," she said quietly to him.

Braden laughed. "Don't worry, Felicity. I'd be the last one to tell anybody about that."

Felicity flinched. She really didn't appreciate the comment. True, her residence in this strange world of acting was only temporary, but it was hard work and deserved a little respect. After finally going public with their engagement, Felicity had realized she had to tell Braeden about her little secret. She wasn't sure how he would take it. Would he be proud? Would he be curious? Would he be angry? Would he be disgusted?

It turned out to be none of the above. "You? You did what?" he had replied, more in disbelief than anything else, as if astonished that Felicity had the wherewithal to do something like that.

"There they are!" Dickie Slocum belted in his nasal Cape Cod accent as soon as he spotted Felicity and Braeden. Along with his wife, Helen, he hurried over to them.

"I understand congratulations are in order," Helen said to both of them. "I've always thought summer weddings were the best."

"That's what we're shooting for, aren't we, dear?" Braeden said, turning to Felicity, as did Dickie and Helen.

Felicity was suddenly silent and a bit overwhelmed. Over their shoulders, she could see that Dickie and Helen's spacious apartment was so crowded that she could barely make out Central Park through the huge penthouse windows. She and Braeden were supposed to be stopping by for drinks with a few friends, but this was a full-on party, jammed with the best of Greenwich society, all decked out in tuxedos and gowns. She was not prepared for this at all. "Yes," she finally mumbled. "If you'll excuse me, I need to powder my nose."

To Felicity's relief, the bathroom door had a lock on it, and after engaging it, she collapsed on the toilet. It was one thing for her family and Braeden's family to talk about the wedding, but everyone else? In public? At a party? She just wasn't ready to hear the words "engaged" roll off other people's tongues. Even if they were friends of hers, it was just too much. Too real.

Then her whole face scrunched, her eyes batted, and her mouth parted just a touch in a confused pout. *Why is it too much?* she wondered. She loved

Braeden. She couldn't wait to marry him. They belonged together. It was a fact, and she knew it the first time she'd ever seen him. They'd begun seeing each other after her third year of Wellesley, after three years of dating stupid boys, all of whom lost interest in Felicity as soon as they discovered how consumed she was with her causes. To them and to her bewildered classmates, her causes became known as Felicity's "fixations." Why was there so much Russian literature in the school library? Why didn't they take a closer look at each teacher's background? How dare they allow that liberal to speak on campus! It would only take a few weeks and, one by one, each boy would lose interest, and the short relationship would come to a lazy end. Felicity didn't care; it left her more time to focus on what was most important, and at the end of each school year, she'd return home single, with a full summer of being at her father's side, helping him every step of the way as he fought for all that was good and right.

Then she met Braeden.

Of course she knew him, as did every woman in Old Greenwich. After all, he was a Talbot, and a single one at that. When he started to show interest in her, Felicity initially rebuffed his advances, convinced that despite his being a bit older, he was just another stupid boy who would take time away from what was important. No, she didn't want to go to the summer regatta with him. No, she didn't want to go to Nancy Hastings's coming out. No, she didn't want to be his date for the Spooners' annual clambake. Finally, after some pressure from her mother and tired of the jealous glares from just about every other available college-age woman in town, she agreed to go to the Hendersons' Fourth of July party with him. She figured he'd see that she was not like the other girls—those just looking for a husband so they could sit back, have a family, and live life happily ever after, convinced of the absolute permanence of their circumstances. He'd see that she was different. One date and that would be that.

She was very wrong.

Unlike the other boys who were happy to disappear into the monotony of their family's businesses or find some other way to pass the time before inheriting their fortunes, Braeden was passionate about what he did, just like

Felicity. His family's horse stable and raising championship thoroughbreds consumed his entire being. Even though he didn't share Felicity's particular passion, politics, he never got upset when she couldn't see him for days at a time because she had other, more important things to do. Their relationship flourished, made stronger in Felicity's eyes because he didn't pressure her to get engaged. They just went along, committed to each other, while equally committed to their other passions.

Then Braeden's father died, and everything changed.

Braeden still cared greatly for his horses, but now he wanted to get married. And as soon as possible. Felicity wanted to be angry about the sudden change, but she understood. Braeden was the oldest male heir and felt the pressure to carry on the family legacy, and she couldn't blame him. Wasn't it really the same thing she was doing—protecting what was theirs?

Felicity stood up off the toilet seat, everything becoming clear in her mind. Yes, there was no doubt about it. She and Braeden were meant to be together. Any apprehension she was feeling obviously was caused by her highly unusual undertaking. Once she got through with her undercover work, once the subversives were exposed and her father's political career was in full swing, things would feel normal again. And they would have an amazing wedding.

As Felicity expected, the minute she rejoined the party, she was besieged. The Tattertons, the Welches, the Rimmers, the Fowlers, the Smiths, the Ruggleses—whom Felicity thought were abroad—and even the Elwells, who were notorious for never coming in to the city, all congratulated her as she moved about the party, looking for Braeden. Fortunately, she couldn't find him, so she had a ready-made excuse to quickly move on after enduring an endless stream of repeated questions—"Have you set the day?" "Who's gonna be your maid of honor?" "Where are you going to have it?"—mixed with inane attempts at humor: "So, you finally got him to pop the question." "He's gonna make an honest woman of you, after all." "No one will be able to call you an old maid anymore." Finally, after a quick orbit of the room and still no Braeden, she'd had enough and moved out to the balcony. It was really more of a patio, running almost the entire length of the building and giving a spectacular view of Central Park and the rest of Manhattan beyond. Farther down, she spotted a cluster of people talking, but Braeden was not one of them.

As she approached the railing, the exciting hum of the city thankfully replaced the mindless chatter of the party. Felicity exhaled, and took in a big breath of the cool night air. She and Braeden were going to be fine, but right now, she didn't want to think about engagement parties or picking the day or guest lists. What she wanted to think about was Alexis. With the throbbing lights of Manhattan egging her on, her thoughts drifted back to the transcendent performance she'd seen not even an hour ago. *God, to be that good,* Felicity thought, *to be that free, that open in front of an audience.* Alexis had been so confident, so clear in her performance, so clear in her objectives. For the ninety minutes they had sat in that closet of a theatre, Alexis really was Amelia Earhart.

Could I be that good? Felicity wondered, knowing it was a slightly dangerous question; after all, this was just a transitory experience for her. *But could I?* she wondered again.

Then, perhaps the most dangerous thought of all entered her mind: *I think I'd like to be.*

"Felicity?"

Felicity turned around to see Braeden standing behind her. "There you are," she said. "Where have you been?"

Braeden pointed to the small group standing farther down the patio. "Right there. Didn't you see me?"

"No. I didn't notice."

Braeden shrugged. "Oh well. You want to go back in?" He pointed toward the door that led off the patio and back into the crowded party.

Felicity didn't mean to, but the question made her flinch.

"That was subtle," Braeden said with a smile. "All right, I get it. You don't want to be here." A bit exasperated, he threw open his hands. "So where do you want to go?"

To Felicity's delight, when they arrived at Annie's apartment, the Process Heads were in deep discussion. Even more exciting, they all knew Alexis.

After Felicity shared the life-changing experience she had just gone through watching Alexis act, they regaled her with tales of other great performances by Alexis. Ophelia, Lady Macbeth, Miss Julie, Hedda Gabler—Alexis had played them all.

While Felicity grew even more astonished over the accomplishments of her acting teacher, Braeden sat patiently on the couch, spending most of his time talking to Thomas. Despite having grown up in the decidedly urban environment of Baltimore, Maryland, Thomas seemed quite interested in hearing all about Braeden's work in breeding horses—especially any stories that involved hot, sweaty manual labor.

...

Jonny slipped into the backseat of the limo and slammed the door shut. Fuming, he then gave it a good kick with his heel.

Charles, already seated and already pouring a glass of his prized scotch, exploded with laughter. "Old friend, you're hardly the first guy to screw it up with a hot number who was ready to go."

This did nothing to mollify Jonny, and he kicked the door a couple more times. Charles poured another glass and handed it to Jonny. "Here."

Jonny downed it in one gulp.

Amazingly, it did the trick, and Jonny settled in against the backseat, satisfied merely to punch the air in frustration.

"A couple years back, I had a real shot at Barbara Stanwyck," Charles said, his eyes beginning to gloss over with the memory. "We were just about out the door when I decide I needed one more for the road. So while I'm downing my Johnnie Walker, who walks in? Robert Wagner. End of story."

Jonny's anger returned. "Yeah, but you didn't lose her because you still live with your parents."

Charles nodded knowingly. "You got me there, buddy."

The driver rolled down the window between the front and back seats. "Where to, sir?"

Charles looked at Jonny with inquiring eyes.

"Oh, the nearest subway station will be fine," Jonny said, leaving his anger behind for the moment.

"Nonsense. I'll take you home."

"Oh, okay. Thanks. Washington Heights—169th Street and Fort Washington."

The driver nodded, and the limo pulled away from the New Yorker.

As the long car made its way to the West Side Highway and headed uptown, Jonny settled in for the ride, his mind replaying the colossal disaster that was the last hour. Things had been going so well. The interesting encounter with Blanche Gaines. The even more interesting encounter with Deborah Tyler. And most important, as Charles had predicted, Jonny had not seen the last of the young starlet.

A half-hour or so after first meeting, Deborah had ended up near the bar in a long conversation with a very tall Huck Finn and an appropriately squat Falstaff. Jonny returned to the bar repeatedly until Deborah noticed him. They danced together for a few hours, occasionally parting to dance with others, but always returning to one another when the song was over. With each reunion, their bodies grew closer and closer together.

Finally, at the end of the night, Jonny and Deborah were the last pair on the dance floor, their bodies pressed together, swaying to the music. A couple, dressed like Abraham Lincoln and Mary Todd approached them. They were friends of Deborah's, and she was staying with them while in town from the West Coast. They wanted to leave and were checking in with her.

She told them she would go home with them, but when they stepped away to get their coats, she began to hem and haw, complaining about the lumpy couch she would have to sleep on and their baby, who would keep them up all night. She went on and on about how unpleasant it was going to be. Jonny listened, knowing exactly what she was really getting at. The door was wide open; all he had to do was step through with an offer of alternative lodging, and yet Jonny did nothing.

Because the sad reality was, he had nothing to offer.

He was twenty-five years old yet had no place of his own to propose as a seemingly innocent destination. Obviously, he couldn't take her back to his

his complete lack of interest in all matters financial. Whenever an issue got too contentious or Hogart needed to be somewhere else, he could always count on Sylvester to second his motion to adjourn the meeting. But along with this lack of interest came an extreme dislike of rocking the boat, and thus, when any real issue was being decided, he always voted with the dominant figure in the room, Chairman Fortis. However, as a lover of the arts— or more importantly, a lover of the attention that came with being a lover of the arts—there was nothing he liked more than being at the forefront of a hot new discovery, even if it was something as passé and mundane as a banal television show.

"Where's Gwen?" Hogart asked, pretending to care.

"She didn't come tonight."

"Pity. Trudy was looking forward to seeing her." In fact, Gwen was the only reason he had brought Trudy, so the two women could talk, at a spot preferably away from the men, while Hogart worked on Sylvester.

"Mahjong. Tonight's her mahjong night. If you ever want more time to yourself, introduce your wife to mahjong."

"I'll keep that in mind."

"Aren't I seeing you on Tuesday?" Though not interested in business, Sylvester was nonetheless very aware of the significance of the vote they were about to take.

"That's what I was hoping to talk to you about." But before Hogart could say anything more, a waiter walked up, carrying a bottle of wine.

"From someone who wishes to congratulate you on your recent success," the waiter said and then handed the bottle to Hogart.

Hogart removed the taped-on envelope and craned his neck, searching the crowd. "I'm guessing it's from someone at an ad agency."

Sylvester joined Hogart in scanning the party. "Is it Joe Sullivan from Young and Rubicam? I thought I saw him on the way in."

Hogart ripped open the envelope. "Nope, it's from Danny Brighton, from Dexter, Tyler, and Thomson."

Sylvester nodded knowingly. "Of course it's not Joe Sullivan. There's boxing at the Garden tonight." Sylvester went back to his drink.

Even though Sylvester didn't inquire, Hogart read the card out loud. "Congrats to you and the new girl on the block. May she fly for a hundred years!" He lowered the card and flashed his best pleased smile. "Isn't that thoughtful." But Sylvester was completely disinterested; his attention was on flagging down a passing waiter for another drink. "It's been like this ever since *Justice Girl* went on the air," Hogart said, giving an over-the-top sigh, as if bored by all the success. Sylvester nodded in agreement but wasn't really listening; he was more concerned with stirring his new scotch and soda. Even if it became obvious, Hogart knew he had to go further. "I'm sure you've noticed how popular *Justice—*"

"Another gentleman wishes to congratulate you on all your success," the waiter interrupted; he was back with another bottle of wine.

As Hogart took the bottle, he gave the waiter a quick conspiratorial smile. "Thank you," he said and then quickly opened the card. "Compliments of Young and Rubicon."

"I knew I'd seen Joe Sullivan on the way in." Sylvester searched the room again, but then slowly, his gaze fell on Hogart and the two bottles of wine. "You're quite the popular guy, aren't you?" he said, finally noticing.

"Yes, it's been that way for the last couple of weeks," Hogart said, as if he hadn't said it before.

"Interesting. All because of that new show, huh?"

Hogart had his opening. "Yep. *Justice Girl* is, as we like to say, a runaway train. She's the hottest thing around." He paused and then proceeded carefully. "It'd be a real shame to derail her."

Sylvester nodded, thinking through Hogart's words. Hogart knew this could be his only chance. He leaned in close, earnestly describing how great *Justice Girl* was doing, how it was beginning to bring along all the other shows on Sunday night, which in turn was going to boost the entire week and, ultimately, the entire season. He was really laying it on thick, and Sylvester was lapping it up. Then, in the midst of it all, at just the right time, the waiter was back again with yet another bottle from yet another admirer. Hogart gave him another conspiratorial smile, and then turned back to Sylvester. It was time to go in for the kill.

"You know what the best part is? I feel like I'm part of something big, something important," Hogart said. "Something that's really impressing people." He indicated the three gifts for emphasis. Then he nodded in Sylvester's direction. "And you're part of it too."

"Oh, I think that's overstating things a bit," Sylvester said, shifting self-consciously.

Hogart shook his head. "There'd be no ballet without the patrons, there'd be no symphony without the donors, and there'd be no network without a board of directors to guide it. It must make you feel proud."

Hogart watched closely for Sylvester's reaction.

After a moment, Sylvester nodded. "It does."

"I can imagine so. *Justice Girl*—the hit of the year. It must be fun to be able to tell people you had a big hand in it."

Sylvester smiled at the thought.

"And just think, if the vote goes the right way on Tuesday, you'll be able to talk about it for years to come." Hogart stood up straight and thrust his chest out proudly. "*Justice Girl*—I made that happen."

Sylvester watched him, eyes wide, eating it up.

Twenty minutes later, with one of the three gift bottles empty, they parted, with a smiling Sylvester happily calling after Hogart. "I'll see you Tuesday!"

Hogart retrieved Trudy from in front of a display of hatching stegosaurus eggs and headed for the exit. Passing his co-conspirator, Hogart slipped him another ten, along with a twenty.

"Thank you, sir, but that's not necessary," the waiter said with a bow.

"Yes, it is," a very happy Hogart said. "Those last two bottles were a great idea."

"That might be true, but they weren't my doing." The waiter pointed across the room to two different tables, where two tight clusters of men congregated. Ad executives. The waiter leaned in close to Hogart. "They really were sent by admirers."

Practically skipping, Hogart left the party with Trudy, joyously escaping just as the speeches were beginning.

...

Felicity gave Alexis one final deep hug and then stepped back and took Braeden's big leathery hand. Despite his strong grip and the closeness of his thick body, she couldn't keep her eyes off her acting teacher. She stared at her with true amazement. "I just have to say it again," Felicity said, beaming. "You were truly incredible."

"Thank you, darling," Alexis answered with a slight nod. "Bye now." With that, she slipped back behind the wool blanket that hung over the doorway of her makeshift dressing room.

Still excited, Felicity, with Braeden in tow, headed down the hallway. As they were the only ones dressed in evening clothes more appropriate for a Fifth Avenue dinner party than off-off-off-off Broadway theatre, everyone they passed gave them a not-so-subtle double take. They passed back through the miniscule theatre space, where they had been two of the just eleven people watching Alexis perform her one-woman show as Amelia Earhart. The moment after Arnold had knocked on Felicity's dressing room door and told her that *Justice Girl* had been preempted for the evening, Felicity grabbed Braeden—he was already ensconced in the VIP booth—and jumped into a cab and made it to the converted loft space in Soho mere minutes before the show began. She was devastated to have not gone on that night as Justice Girl; after all, it could have been her last chance to perform the role, as the confirmation of the blacklisted names was due back from the FBI any day now. And if they did come back confirmed, as far as she was concerned, even with as much as she was learning and growing, that would be the end of her acting career. But getting to see Alexis in the final performance of her show was an almost passable consolation prize. Almost.

Stepping out onto the sidewalk, Felicity spun with excitement. "Wasn't she amazing!" she exclaimed to Braeden and any of the passersby who were in earshot.

"Uh-huh," Braeden answered, still yawning the sleep out of his body. He rubbed his sore neck; it hurt from his constant head bobbing as he fought to stay awake during the play. He finally lost the battle and slept through the last twenty minutes, jolting awake to the sound of applause and the sight of Felicity giving Alexis a standing ovation.

"She was so locked in," Felicity continued. "So present, so in the moment. That wasn't Alexis up there; that was Amelia Earhart."

"Uh-huh," Braeden said again, not really listening, as he moved to the curb and hailed a cab. Almost immediately, one pulled over, and Braeden opened the back door for Felicity.

But she was still moving away, up the block, her eyes afire as she continued to recall what she had seen. "She was so on, so real. How do you get that good? How do you get that *good*?"

"Uh, Felicity!" Braeden called after her.

"How do you get that good?" she said, not hearing him and still moving away. The crowd was thickening now—people leaving shows, rushing to dinner, heading to gallery openings. Felicity studied their faces. They were excited, thrilled, imbued by some unseen rhythm that pulsed up through the ground and into everything. Felicity felt it shoot through her body, multiplied a hundred times over by what she had just seen Alexis do on stage.

"Felicity!"

She stopped and turned back. "What?"

"If we hurry, we might still make it to two or three of the places we were supposed to look at tonight."

Felicity slumped, her excitement ebbing. She slowly sauntered back toward him. "Do we really have to? I'm not really in the mood."

"Yes. Now that we're going to be married, I'd like to get the arrangements locked in as soon as possible."

Now that we're going to be married. Now that we're going to be married. Felicity had been hearing that a lot in the last few days. It had become Braeden's reason for everything. *Now that we're going to be married, I should drive you to the train station. Now that we're going to be married, I should go with you and see you do your show. Now that we're going to be married, we should go out afterward.* "And here I thought you had come in to the city with me because you wanted to see me on the show," Felicity said, more than a little annoyed.

"Of course I did. But we also have an engagement party to plan."

"You're worse than my mother," Felicity said as she joined him next to the cab, her irritation boiling over. Her statement was an exaggeration. Her mother was ten times worse. As expected, from the moment Felicity had gone public with the engagement, her mother had spoken of little else. This very morning over breakfast—on show day, no less—instead of having the opportunity to go over her lines again, her mother had taken up her time by beginning the guest list. Felicity swore it would be the last time she'd go home the night before they went on the air.

Not that Braeden had been that much better. On the train ride in, instead of asking about the episode or how the rehearsals had gone, all he wanted to talk about was the engagement party. Felicity's parents were taking care of the wedding, but Braeden's were throwing the engagement party. Despite the family passion being the breeding of thoroughbreds, Braeden's parents had a decidedly cosmopolitan edge, spending more than half of their weekends in Manhattan, attending a never-ending circuit of cocktail parties. Since the wedding was going to be in Greenwich, they had decided the engagement party should be in Manhattan. Braeden had made reservations at four of the prospective locations for after Felicity's show.

"I'll tell you what," Braeden said, seeing Felicity truly was not in the mood. "How about we skip looking at places for our engagement party and just go to Dickie Slocum's? We can't skip that; we have to at least make an appearance."

Felicity sighed. Not what she was in the mood for either, but better. Felicity nodded her agreement.

Riding up in the gilded elevator to Dickie Slocum's Fifth Avenue apartment, Felicity fixed her hair and adjusted her dress, checking herself in one of the gold-trimmed mirrors. The elevator doors opened, and the soft patter of quiet conversation and piano music floated at them. Braeden was about to take a step out of the elevator and into the apartment when Felicity stopped him. "Just as a little reminder, please, I don't want anybody to know that I'm doing the...you know...show," she said quietly to him.

Braden laughed. "Don't worry, Felicity. I'd be the last one to tell anybody about that."

Felicity flinched. She really didn't appreciate the comment. True, her residence in this strange world of acting was only temporary, but it was hard work and deserved a little respect. After finally going public with their engagement, Felicity had realized she had to tell Braeden about her little secret. She wasn't sure how he would take it. Would he be proud? Would he be curious? Would he be angry? Would he be disgusted?

It turned out to be none of the above. "You? You did what?" he had replied, more in disbelief than anything else, as if astonished that Felicity had the wherewithal to do something like that.

"There they are!" Dickie Slocum belted in his nasal Cape Cod accent as soon as he spotted Felicity and Braeden. Along with his wife, Helen, he hurried over to them.

"I understand congratulations are in order," Helen said to both of them. "I've always thought summer weddings were the best."

"That's what we're shooting for, aren't we, dear?" Braeden said, turning to Felicity, as did Dickie and Helen.

Felicity was suddenly silent and a bit overwhelmed. Over their shoulders, she could see that Dickie and Helen's spacious apartment was so crowded that she could barely make out Central Park through the huge penthouse windows. She and Braeden were supposed to be stopping by for drinks with a few friends, but this was a full-on party, jammed with the best of Greenwich society, all decked out in tuxedos and gowns. She was not prepared for this at all. "Yes," she finally mumbled. "If you'll excuse me, I need to powder my nose."

To Felicity's relief, the bathroom door had a lock on it, and after engaging it, she collapsed on the toilet. It was one thing for her family and Braeden's family to talk about the wedding, but everyone else? In public? At a party? She just wasn't ready to hear the words "engaged" roll off other people's tongues. Even if they were friends of hers, it was just too much. Too real.

Then her whole face scrunched, her eyes batted, and her mouth parted just a touch in a confused pout. *Why is it too much?* she wondered. She loved

Braeden. She couldn't wait to marry him. They belonged together. It was a fact, and she knew it the first time she'd ever seen him. They'd begun seeing each other after her third year of Wellesley, after three years of dating stupid boys, all of whom lost interest in Felicity as soon as they discovered how consumed she was with her causes. To them and to her bewildered classmates, her causes became known as Felicity's "fixations." Why was there so much Russian literature in the school library? Why didn't they take a closer look at each teacher's background? How dare they allow that liberal to speak on campus! It would only take a few weeks and, one by one, each boy would lose interest, and the short relationship would come to a lazy end. Felicity didn't care; it left her more time to focus on what was most important, and at the end of each school year, she'd return home single, with a full summer of being at her father's side, helping him every step of the way as he fought for all that was good and right.

Then she met Braeden.

Of course she knew him, as did every woman in Old Greenwich. After all, he was a Talbot, and a single one at that. When he started to show interest in her, Felicity initially rebuffed his advances, convinced that despite his being a bit older, he was just another stupid boy who would take time away from what was important. No, she didn't want to go to the summer regatta with him. No, she didn't want to go to Nancy Hastings's coming out. No, she didn't want to be his date for the Spooners' annual clambake. Finally, after some pressure from her mother and tired of the jealous glares from just about every other available college-age woman in town, she agreed to go to the Hendersons' Fourth of July party with him. She figured he'd see that she was not like the other girls—those just looking for a husband so they could sit back, have a family, and live life happily ever after, convinced of the absolute permanence of their circumstances. He'd see that she was different. One date and that would be that.

She was very wrong.

Unlike the other boys who were happy to disappear into the monotony of their family's businesses or find some other way to pass the time before inheriting their fortunes, Braeden was passionate about what he did, just like

Felicity. His family's horse stable and raising championship thoroughbreds consumed his entire being. Even though he didn't share Felicity's particular passion, politics, he never got upset when she couldn't see him for days at a time because she had other, more important things to do. Their relationship flourished, made stronger in Felicity's eyes because he didn't pressure her to get engaged. They just went along, committed to each other, while equally committed to their other passions.

Then Braeden's father died, and everything changed.

Braeden still cared greatly for his horses, but now he wanted to get married. And as soon as possible. Felicity wanted to be angry about the sudden change, but she understood. Braeden was the oldest male heir and felt the pressure to carry on the family legacy, and she couldn't blame him. Wasn't it really the same thing she was doing—protecting what was theirs?

Felicity stood up off the toilet seat, everything becoming clear in her mind. Yes, there was no doubt about it. She and Braeden were meant to be together. Any apprehension she was feeling obviously was caused by her highly unusual undertaking. Once she got through with her undercover work, once the subversives were exposed and her father's political career was in full swing, things would feel normal again. And they would have an amazing wedding.

As Felicity expected, the minute she rejoined the party, she was besieged. The Tattertons, the Welches, the Rimmers, the Fowlers, the Smiths, the Ruggleses—whom Felicity thought were abroad—and even the Elwells, who were notorious for never coming in to the city, all congratulated her as she moved about the party, looking for Braeden. Fortunately, she couldn't find him, so she had a ready-made excuse to quickly move on after enduring an endless stream of repeated questions—"Have you set the day?" "Who's gonna be your maid of honor?" "Where are you going to have it?"—mixed with inane attempts at humor: "So, you finally got him to pop the question." "He's gonna make an honest woman of you, after all." "No one will be able to call you an old maid anymore." Finally, after a quick orbit of the room and still no Braeden, she'd had enough and moved out to the balcony. It was really more of a patio, running almost the entire length of the building and giving a spectacular view of Central Park and the rest of Manhattan beyond. Farther down, she spotted a cluster of people talking, but Braeden was not one of them.

As she approached the railing, the exciting hum of the city thankfully replaced the mindless chatter of the party. Felicity exhaled, and took in a big breath of the cool night air. She and Braeden were going to be fine, but right now, she didn't want to think about engagement parties or picking the day or guest lists. What she wanted to think about was Alexis. With the throbbing lights of Manhattan egging her on, her thoughts drifted back to the transcendent performance she'd seen not even an hour ago. *God, to be that good,* Felicity thought, *to be that free, that open in front of an audience.* Alexis had been so confident, so clear in her performance, so clear in her objectives. For the ninety minutes they had sat in that closet of a theatre, Alexis really was Amelia Earhart.

Could I be that good? Felicity wondered, knowing it was a slightly dangerous question; after all, this was just a transitory experience for her. *But could I?* she wondered again.

Then, perhaps the most dangerous thought of all entered her mind: *I think I'd like to be.*

"Felicity?"

Felicity turned around to see Braeden standing behind her. "There you are," she said. "Where have you been?"

Braeden pointed to the small group standing farther down the patio. "Right there. Didn't you see me?"

"No. I didn't notice."

Braeden shrugged. "Oh well. You want to go back in?" He pointed toward the door that led off the patio and back into the crowded party.

Felicity didn't mean to, but the question made her flinch.

"That was subtle," Braeden said with a smile. "All right, I get it. You don't want to be here." A bit exasperated, he threw open his hands. "So where do you want to go?"

To Felicity's delight, when they arrived at Annie's apartment, the Process Heads were in deep discussion. Even more exciting, they all knew Alexis.

After Felicity shared the life-changing experience she had just gone through watching Alexis act, they regaled her with tales of other great performances by Alexis. Ophelia, Lady Macbeth, Miss Julie, Hedda Gabler—Alexis had played them all.

While Felicity grew even more astonished over the accomplishments of her acting teacher, Braeden sat patiently on the couch, spending most of his time talking to Thomas. Despite having grown up in the decidedly urban environment of Baltimore, Maryland, Thomas seemed quite interested in hearing all about Braeden's work in breeding horses—especially any stories that involved hot, sweaty manual labor.

...

Jonny slipped into the backseat of the limo and slammed the door shut. Fuming, he then gave it a good kick with his heel.

Charles, already seated and already pouring a glass of his prized scotch, exploded with laughter. "Old friend, you're hardly the first guy to screw it up with a hot number who was ready to go."

This did nothing to mollify Jonny, and he kicked the door a couple more times. Charles poured another glass and handed it to Jonny. "Here."

Jonny downed it in one gulp.

Amazingly, it did the trick, and Jonny settled in against the backseat, satisfied merely to punch the air in frustration.

"A couple years back, I had a real shot at Barbara Stanwyck," Charles said, his eyes beginning to gloss over with the memory. "We were just about out the door when I decide I needed one more for the road. So while I'm downing my Johnnie Walker, who walks in? Robert Wagner. End of story."

Jonny's anger returned. "Yeah, but you didn't lose her because you still live with your parents."

Charles nodded knowingly. "You got me there, buddy."

The driver rolled down the window between the front and back seats. "Where to, sir?"

Charles looked at Jonny with inquiring eyes.

"Oh, the nearest subway station will be fine," Jonny said, leaving his anger behind for the moment.

"Nonsense. I'll take you home."

"Oh, okay. Thanks. Washington Heights—169th Street and Fort Washington."

The driver nodded, and the limo pulled away from the New Yorker.

As the long car made its way to the West Side Highway and headed uptown, Jonny settled in for the ride, his mind replaying the colossal disaster that was the last hour. Things had been going so well. The interesting encounter with Blanche Gaines. The even more interesting encounter with Deborah Tyler. And most important, as Charles had predicted, Jonny had not seen the last of the young starlet.

A half-hour or so after first meeting, Deborah had ended up near the bar in a long conversation with a very tall Huck Finn and an appropriately squat Falstaff. Jonny returned to the bar repeatedly until Deborah noticed him. They danced together for a few hours, occasionally parting to dance with others, but always returning to one another when the song was over. With each reunion, their bodies grew closer and closer together.

Finally, at the end of the night, Jonny and Deborah were the last pair on the dance floor, their bodies pressed together, swaying to the music. A couple, dressed like Abraham Lincoln and Mary Todd approached them. They were friends of Deborah's, and she was staying with them while in town from the West Coast. They wanted to leave and were checking in with her.

She told them she would go home with them, but when they stepped away to get their coats, she began to hem and haw, complaining about the lumpy couch she would have to sleep on and their baby, who would keep them up all night. She went on and on about how unpleasant it was going to be. Jonny listened, knowing exactly what she was really getting at. The door was wide open; all he had to do was step through with an offer of alternative lodging, and yet Jonny did nothing.

Because the sad reality was, he had nothing to offer.

He was twenty-five years old yet had no place of his own to propose as a seemingly innocent destination. Obviously, he couldn't take her back to his parents' place in Washington Heights, and he certainly wasn't crass enough to suggest a hotel. His mind raced, searching for something, anything. But before he came up with an answer, her friends had returned, coats in hand, ready to leave. With a lingering kiss on his cheek, Deborah departed, clearly disappointed.

Suddenly the limo started to slow, which blissfully pulled Jonny from the unpleasant memory as they eased toward a corner to make a right turn off the Westside Highway.

"No. Go another two blocks before turning. It's a one-way street. It's faster," Charles said, leaning forward so the driver could hear his voice through the partition.

Jonny turned to Charles, shocked. "How do you know which way the streets go around here?"

"Because I spent the first seven years of my life at 191st and Broadway."

"Right across from Belinski's?"

"All skate! Ladies only. Sadie Hawkins pairs!" Charles said, emulating the amplified voice of a skating rink announcer.

"Son of a bitch!" Jonny's jaw dropped, but then he crooked his head, confused. "How does a guy from the Heights—"

"End up wearing custom-tailored suits and appreciating sixty-year-old scotch?" Charles finished, obviously used to this line of inquiry. "It's easy, when your father hits it big and isn't satisfied just moving you out of the Heights, so he sends you to prep school and then Yale to get the Heights out of you. It worked, for the most part, except I do still love a good blintz."

The limo turned off 168th Street onto Fort Washington Avenue and, after crossing 169th Street, pulled to the curb in front of Jonny's building.

"Well..." Jonny said. "I have to say, I have not had many evenings like this."

"You keep writing like you've been writing, and it's just the start, my friend."

Jonny sighed. "I also have to say—and I really didn't think I would be saying this—I enjoyed myself."

"Likewise."

They shook hands, each with a friendly smile, and Jonny opened the door and stepped out.

Almost immediately, from the shadows next to the small stack of stairs that led to his building's entrance, a woman in an overcoat appeared. "Jonny?" she called hopefully.

Jonny turned, recognizing her immediately. "Lucille?"

"It looks like your enjoyment of the evening may not be over," Charles said playfully from inside the car.

"No. It's my sister-in-law," Jonny said to him before turning back to Lucille. As she approached, he could see that her face was drawn and pale, and poking out from the bottom of her overcoat was what looked like a long nightgown. "What are you doing here? What's wrong?"

"It's Mitchell. He's barricaded himself in our bedroom again," she said, her voice strained from too much crying.

Jonny's mouth parted and his eyes widened as a horrible realization washed over him. "Oh, my God! The Russian bomb!" he said, becoming mad at himself for not thinking of it earlier.

Lucille nodded. "I'm so sorry to bother you like this. I couldn't tell your parents. Your mother—you know how she feels. When you weren't home, I decided to wait. I didn't know what else to do." Lucille started to cry uncontrollably. "I'm so sorry. I'm so sorry."

Jonny grabbed her. "No. No. You did the right thing. Where's your car?"

"I took the train."

"Let's grab a cab."

"Nonsense," Charles interjected. "I'll give you a lift."

Jonny and Lucille turned to see Charles out of his limo, standing on the sidewalk, clearly within earshot. The rear door was open, and Charles offered them the backseat with a sweep of his arm. "It sounds like you need to get there right away."

Mitchell and Lucille lived in one of the new condo high-rises that were popping up around the northern edges of Greenwich Village, built in response to the demand of the surging upper-middle class, thanks to the GI Bill. It took Charles's driver fewer than fifteen minutes to get them there.

They stepped out of the car, and Jonny looked across the plaza that surrounded the bottom of the building. He saw a doorman on duty through the huge glass windows of the lobby. "Good," he said, indicating the doorman. "After the last time Mitchell did this, I'd like to have someone with me."

Lucille turned around, her face afire. "No! Please, no. I don't want anyone in the building to know. Please?"

Jonny nodded, understanding. Reluctantly, he turned to Charles. "Can I ask—"

"Of course; of course," Charles said.

Together, the three of them did their best to look nonchalant as they walked into the lobby. The suspicious doorman lost all interest in them once he spotted Lucille's familiar face. He returned to his newspaper. After a quick ride in the elevator, they stepped out on the thirty-first floor. Charles hung back as they approached a door just down the hall.

With Jonny in the lead, they carefully stepped into the apartment. Everything looked normal—the beautiful, stylish, living room with its tasteful, spare, modern furniture looked as clean and well placed as ever.

"This way...," Lucille said heavily.

Jonny nodded knowingly. "The children?"

"I left them with my sister."

"Good." Jonny crept over to a closet, opened it, and pulled out a baseball bat.

"You won't need that," Lucille said, alarmed. "After the last time, I made him get rid of all his military stuff. Especially the guns."

Jonny nodded. "Still, if you don't mind, he is a lot bigger than Charles and me."

Lucille dropped her protest, and with Charles, Jonny moved out of the living room and down a small hallway. They passed two bedrooms and a bathroom before stopping in front of the door to the master bedroom.

"What do you want me to do?" Charles asked, a bit nervous.

"Nothing, I hope. Just be there, in case." Jonny tried the doorknob, but it didn't move. The door was locked. He knocked, softly at first. Then again, a bit louder. Still no answer. "Mitchell, it's me. Open up."

"Jonny?" Mitchell replied. His voice sounded a bit weary. "What are youuuu doing heeeere?"

"I came to see how you're doing."

"You caaaame all the wayyy to Gern-namy to see howwww I'm doing?" It was clear Mitchell was intoxicated.

"Yes. No." Jonny cleared his thoughts. "Lucille came and got me and—"

"You brought Lucille with youuuu, all wayyyy to Gern-namy?"

"The war's over, Mitchell," Jonny said strongly.

"I know that!" Mitchell shot back angrily, seemingly suddenly sober. "It ended a few months ago."

Jonny took a deep breath. "No, Mitchell, it ended ten years ago."

"How could it end ten years ago? It just ended a few months ago."

"Mitchell the war's over. It ended ten years ago. You're no longer in Germany."

"Bullshit. You're just saying that because you want me to come out. You want me to surrender. Well, I won't do it! I won't do it!

"Mitchell, calm down!" Jonny said, tugging on the doorknob once again.

"I won't go to prison! I won't go to prison!" Mitchell repeated, getting more and more wound up.

"No one's going to take you to prison," Jonny offered soothingly. "Go to the window. Look out the window."

"Why? So someone can shoot me?"

"No, so you can see that you're no longer in Germany," Jonny answered matter-of-factly. "Go to the window." He heard the sounds of movement from the other side of the door. "Are you at the window?"

"Maybe."

"Look down and across Eighth Street. Do you see the Chock Full o' Nuts? That's where you and I have gotten coffee a million times. Remember? We did it just a few weeks ago, before we jumped on the subway to go up and see Mom and Dad. Next to it is the ice cream place. We took your two children, Darla and Tim, to it just last week. I don't remember the name, it's…it's…"

"Hertzel's."

"Yes. Hertzel's." Jonny smiled. "Think, Mitchell—there's no Hertzel's in Germany. Next to it is the laundry. The place that keeps screwing up your shirts, but you still go to it, and…"

There was noise at the door. Jonny and Charles stepped back. It slowly swung open, finally revealing a completely disheveled Mitchell in his undershirt and pajama pants. He teetered on his feet, half-drunk and half-exhausted. His shoulders slumped, and his face drooped. He collapsed onto Jonny. Jonny caught him, and with Charles's help, he managed to move him over and on to the bed.

Jonny cleared away the liquor bottles so Mitchell could lie down, but Mitchell grabbed him and began to sob. "I don't want to go to prison. I don't want to go to prison. I didn't mean to do it. I didn't know. I really didn't know."

Despite the good five inches and fifty pounds Mitchell had on Jonny, Jonny managed to get his arms around Mitchell and hold him tight. "I know. I know. Everyone believes you, and no one blames you. No one blames you. Even General Darcy forgave you." This seemed to mollify Mitchell, and Jonny eased him back on the bed until he was lying flat with his head resting on a pillow. In a moment, he was asleep.

Jonny turned to see that Lucille had joined them; she stood warily in the doorway. "He'll be okay now," he said to her. "Just let him sleep. I don't know how much of this he'll remember in the morning, but he will have one hell of a headache."

A half hour later, leaving behind a thankful Lucille, they were at the Carnegie Deli with a knish and half-order of latkes in front of Jonny, a full order of blintzes in front of Charles.

"You realize you have to tell me what that was all about," Charles said.

Jonny nodded, resigned. "I trust you will keep this all in confidence."

"Of course."

Jonny quickly breezed through the backstory. His brother, Mitchell, had been in the army, serving under General Bennington Darcy. By the end of the war, he was Darcy's chief of staff. In post-war Berlin, General Darcy was in charge of the American sector of the divided city, which meant Jonny's brother could do almost anything he wanted. And for whomever he wanted to do it.

Jonny took a bite of flakey knish and washed it down with a gulp of cream soda. "The funny thing is," Jonny said, "is that it all happened because of shoes. General Darcy was always very particular about his shoes. They always had to be spit-shined, with crisp new laces, and most important, the heels could not have even the slightest bit of wear. The tiniest amount drove the general crazy. Mitchell had started out as Bennington's personal officer, so even though it was well below his current rank, Mitchell continued to be in charge of the general's shoes. Given the fact that, after the war, Berlin was in ruins and the streets were strewn with jagged rubble, Mitchell spent a good amount of time ferrying Bennington's shoes to and from the cobbler he'd found not far from their headquarters. In short time, Mitchell got to know the old German man, and he liked him, even looked forward to their encounters.

"One day when he went to drop off one pair of the general's shoes and pick up another, he found the old German man crying. Naturally, Mitchell inquired what was wrong, and the old man said that he was sad because his son had been denied a pass to get into the Russian sector, where his son's fiancé lived. They'd planned to be married a year earlier, but before they could, his son was drafted and sent off to fight on the western front. Mitchell could see the old man's pain and looked into the matter. He found out that the old man did indeed have a son who had served in the Vermacht, the regular German army, and because it was almost exclusively the SS that was being prosecuted for war crimes, Mitchell decided to help. Mitchell met the son and arranged for a pass so he could get into the Russian sector. The son thanked him profusely and crossed over to see his fiancé.

"The next day, Mitchell went to see the old man, but he wasn't there. Just gone—poof! He went back for several days in a row, and each time the knot in his stomach grew as he realized what had happened. Mitchell had been conned. Sure enough, about a month later, when things started to deteriorate with the Russians, and a spy was caught in the American sector, he came clean with the whole story under interrogation. The old German man had been a Russian operative, and the son was actually the former head of the Nazi nuclear program. They wanted to smuggle him over to the Russian sector so he could then be sent back to the Soviet Union."

Charles's face went white. "To work on the bomb."

Jonny nodded. "Who says producers aren't smart." Jonny took a drink of water before continuing. "Naturally, Mitchell's boss was furious. But instead of disciplining Mitchell, he gave him yet another medal. Darcy didn't become a general without understanding politics. Nothing good would come from letting the story go public, so the whole thing was swept under the rug. That was the end of it, as far as General Darcy was concerned.

"However, it wasn't that easy for Mitchell. He was responsible for the top German nuclear scientist ending up in the Soviet Union. He returned home a hero, which he was, but the thought of what he had done ate away at him. Soon, stories started appearing in the newspaper, on the radio, and eventually even on television about the Soviet nuclear program. Most of it was about how fast they seemed to be moving in catching up with the West, after it was thought they were way behind."

Jonny ran a hand through his hair and sighed. "It was small incidents at first—drinking a little too much at a family event, a violent fight with Lucille, a little more drinking, a strange fall, a little more drinking, throwing something through one of their windows. A lot more drinking. Then finally, the barricading. It took a while to put together what was really happening, because he kept denying anything was wrong. Every time the Soviet nuclear program was in the news, he was hitting the bottle. The bigger the event...well, you saw."

Charles's eyes went wide. "The preemption tonight, the special report..."

"Exactly."

Charles nodded, all of it coming together in his head. "Wow."

"I've begged him to get some help. Tonight was one of the worst ones. Maybe this time he'll listen."

"Wow."

"Yep." Jonny took another bite, chewing slowly before he said, "And, as I asked before, you will keep this under your hat?"

"Of course," Charles answered, throwing in a reassuring nod for good measure.

Episode Four

JUSTICE GIRL

"TIRED OF FASHION"

April 17, 1955

They were all assembled, waiting, three on one side of the conference table, four on the other. It was just past 10:00 a.m., so the blistering sun, still low on the horizon, blasted through the large bay window and engulfed the entire boardroom in bright white light. Hogart fidgeted with his stack of notes. Because he didn't have the three weeks' worth of ratings data he had planned on sharing with the board, he decided to scrap the oversized presentation, worried that seeing it displayed on such a large scale would only heighten how little he really had to work with. Instead, he had managed to cobble together a purely oral presentation of somewhat convincing trending information from the first two weeks of Justice Girl. And along with his possible persuasion of Sylvester Nickles, he hoped it would be enough to carry him across the finish line. As the rest of the board members wandered in, he made eye contact with Sylvester. Sylvester had flashed him a warm smile, but Hogart wasn't sure if it was a smile that said "I'm with you" or "I wish I could be, but I'm not."

Five more minutes passed, but still the seat at the head of the table remained empty. Not that anyone was surprised. Clinton Fortis was always late to these meetings. In fact, it was from him that Hogart had learned the trick of always being the last person to arrive at any important appointment.

Finally, at almost ten thirty, Clinton burst into the room. "Sorry I'm late," he said, although his insincerity was clear. He moved past everyone, heading for his spot at the head of the table. Clinton was a man who always moved fast, despite being well into his seventies, and seemingly brought along a gust of wind with him—or at times, a tornado—as he moved. He always stood perfectly erect, giving him the illusion of being taller than his height, which was average. Atop his head was a thick mop of white hair that had been his trademark since losing his natural dark blond color in his late thirties. This early change, along with a pinched, focused face of few wrinkles, gave him the impression of being timeless, as if he had been born at a vague elderly age and remained so the rest of his life. Reaching the head of the table, he remained on his feet and turned to the only non-board member in the room, Mrs. Decosta. "Let's begin."

Directly across from Hogart, Mrs. Decosta officiously opened a folder on the table in front of her. "With six out of the seven members present, according to the by-laws of incorporation, we may now open this meeting of the board of directors of the Regal Television Network," she said perfunctorily.

Hogart prepped his papers and swallowed hard. *This is it; time to give the pitch of my life.* "I have some things I'd like to say," Hogart said, pushing his chair back to stand up.

Clinton shot out his arm, stopping him. "No need," he said commandingly. "We all know why we're here. I say we get on with it and vote."

"But—"

"I second the motion," Karl Melzner said. Melzner and the similarly dressed executive-type next to him were on the board to represent Goliath Pictures, who owned a partial stake in the network. Hogart hated them both personally, and he had a special disdain for the studio they were empowered to speak for. Selling Goliath a stake in the network, even though infusing Regal with some much-needed cash, had been nothing but trouble since the moment the sale was closed. Despite their promises not to interfere with the network's operations, that's exactly what they did, crowding Hogart's in-box with memo after memo—all of which he happily ignored.

"But I have some very impressive data I want to share," Hogart said, trying again.

Clinton ignored him and turned to Mrs. Decosta. "If you wouldn't mind…"

Mrs. Decosta nodded and began searching her paperwork. Hogart slumped back in his chair. He wouldn't even get a chance to attempt his pitch.

He sighed; it was all going to come down to how successful his talk with Sylvester Nickles had been. Hogart looked over at him, hoping to glean something—anything—but Sylvester's gaze was locked in and focused on Clinton.

Finding what she was looking for, Mrs. Decosta pulled a slip of paper out of her file. "The matter before the board is whether to accept the offer to sell the Regal Television Network to Worthington Camera and Instruments." She pulled another piece of paper from her file; it was a large oversized envelope. "I have here a proxy from Clarence Regal." She ripped open the envelope and pulled out the small proxy sheet. "Clarence Regal votes no," she said with little emotion and then made a notation on her notepad.

This was not a surprise to Hogart or anyone else in the room. Though it had been years since Clarence Regal had attended a board meeting, his views on the sale were well known. He was against it.

"The vote stands at 1-0, in favor of turning down the deal," Mrs. Decosta stated to the room.

Despite Clinton being physically closest to Mrs. Decosta, he always voted last. So, all eyes turned to Hogart. "I wish I'd had the chance to tell all of you about the good things that are happening to the network these days," he said, summarizing what would have been his pitch. "I implore all of you who are for taking this deal to turn it down. You won't regret it. I vote no."

"Mr. Daniels votes no." Mrs. Decosta made a notation on her pad, recording the vote. "The vote currently stands at 2-0 in favor of turning down the deal."

The attention shifted to Karl Melzner and his partner, who were seated next to Hogart. The two men turned to one another and quietly conferred. Hogart rolled his eyes. This drove him crazy. Every meeting, it was the same thing; they would hold up the proceedings by conferring with each other before speaking. Why, Hogart always wondered, did they do that when they were under strict orders from their bosses at Goliath Pictures and were told how to vote on every issue in front of the board before they left California to come East for the meetings?

As per their custom, they broke from their huddle. "We both vote yes," Melzner said brightly, as if it were a decision they had just come to.

"Mr. Melzner and Mr. Ramsey both vote yes," Mrs. Decosta said. "The vote now stands at 2-2."

Across from them, on the other side of the table, Mrs. Alva Wagner suddenly straightened. "I guess that means it's my turn," she said with a dash of excitement. She was well into her sixties and had more than a touch of the spinster about her, with her outdated frumpy clothing and unflattering haircut, topped by an almost prissy manner from the last century. She had inherited the seat on the board when her husband had died several years earlier. Nelson Wagner had started with Clarence Regal as his business partner almost thirty years earlier, when Regal set up his first lab in the Bronx. Even when her husband was still alive, Alva had a bit of a crush on Hogart, having been taken in by the brash, up-and-coming executive. After Nelson's death, the crush only intensified, something Hogart used to his advantage at every opportunity. He was always sure to shower her with attention and praise whenever he saw her, just as he had when he saw her just about an hour earlier when she arrived for the meeting.

"I vote no," Alva said, flashing Hogart a warm smile. Hogart returned it appreciatively.

"Mrs. Wagner votes no," Mrs. Decosta said flatly, recording the vote on her notepad. "The vote now stands at 3-2 in favor of turning down the deal."

Well, here it is, Hogart thought, as his smile faded, and his eyes, along with everyone else's, landed on Sylvester. Just one more measly no vote, a simple pursing of the lips while exhaling, and the network lives. Or a tart yes, tying the vote at 3-3, with only Clinton left to put the final nail in the coffin.

Strange for his usually gregarious self, Sylvester hung his head, his eyes staring at his lap. Obviously, the seriousness of the decision was weighing heavily on him. Hogart stared at him, imploring him to say no. Ten years of his life were on the line, ten years of planning, scheming, and fighting to get to where he was, and now it all came down to one vote in the hands of a foppish rich kid who had never worked a day in his life.

Seconds turned into a minute, and amazingly, no one said anything. Finally, Sylvester straightened up and looked forward, focusing on nothing.

Hogart caught his eyes for a second, but Sylvester quickly turned away. "Oh, shit," Hogart said quietly to himself.

"I vote yes," Sylvester said, relieved to have gotten the words out.

"Mr. Nickles votes yes. The vote stands at 3-3," Mrs. Decosta said as she recorded the tally on her notepad.

The entire room slumped; it was over. Hogart began to gather his things. There was nothing in the by-laws that said he had to be there to watch the knife go in.

"So it all comes down to me," Clinton said, as if this hadn't been the plan all along.

The bastard, Hogart thought as he climbed out of his chair and headed for the door. This was a game to Clinton, just another board he sat on. Just another annual meeting he had to attend. What difference did it make if the network ceased to exist? Just one more open day in his schedule to play golf.

"I vote no," Clinton said, almost matter-of-factly.

Stunned, Hogart stopped at the door and turned back around. Clinton was smiling in his direction.

"Mr. Fortis votes no," Mrs. Decosta said, not hiding her pleasure at the unexpected turn of events. Happily surprised, she held up her notepad. "By a final vote of 4-3, the deal to sell the network to Worthington Camera and Instruments is turned down."

A surge of energy rippled through the room. Even those who had voted for taking the deal suddenly seemed pleased that it had been rejected. As if addressing the unasked question that was on everyone's mind, Clinton looked around the room. "It just seems wrong that an entire network would suddenly go off the air." He took a deep, satisfied breath. "Besides, my grandchildren would never forgive me if they ever found out I was the one who pulled the plug on *Justice Girl*."

The meeting was quickly adjourned, and the board members, for once oddly in agreement, headed out. Clinton moved up next to Hogart, and the two men shook hands. "Don't make me regret this," Clinton said forcefully.

"You won't."

Clinton looked him over closely. "For some reason, I believe you." He considered Hogart for another short moment. "This coming Monday, do you have any plans for lunch?"

"No," Hogart answered quickly. Even if he did, he didn't anymore.

"Good. Be at my office at noon. I'd like to hear some of your other plans for the network." Clinton walked away, leaving behind an overwhelmed and overjoyed Hogart.

...

They were almost all the way home before Jonny saw the first real indication that his mother had enjoyed their trip to the Polo Grounds. Relief washed over him, because not only had he wanted to treat his parents to a well-deserved special day but also because he had hoped it would lessen the blow that was to come in just a few minutes.

It was opening day of the 1955 baseball season, and Jonny's beloved New York Giants were the reigning world champions. Ever since they'd won the World Series the previous fall, Jonny had planned on being on hand at the Polo Grounds on opening day, when the assembled team, lined up in military precision on the first-base chalk line, would host a raucous crowd as the championship banner was raised atop the outfield flag pole. Jonny knew his love affair with the Giants was a rare holdover from the time before he learned the true nature of the world, but even though he was unable to shake this childish infatuation, he was fraught with agonizing bouts of hypocrisy. After all, didn't it ultimately represent a member of the upper class, the owner of the team, making scads of money off the hard work of the lower class, the players? Weren't the players often treated as little more than chattel? Wasn't the game another example of a spectacle to distract people from the real problems in society—poverty, racism, nuclear warfare?

Despite all this, Jonny found himself fighting through his qualms. And because he loved the game so much, he chose to view it as an example of how a community could work together, in this case as a team, and also as a rare place in society with actual signs of integration, even if it was only a handful of black players on the almost entirely white team.

Jonny's plan to attend had been decidedly placed on the back burner over the last few weeks, as the demands of *Justice Girl* had taken over every inch of his life. But with the sudden last-minute cancellation of the previous week's episode, Jonny, rather shockingly, found himself with some time on his hands. There was no episode to write, no read-through to supervise, no rehearsal to oversee, and most astonishingly, no meetings to attend until this coming Saturday, when everyone would reconvene for a run-through of the episode before putting it on the air, live, the following day. Realizing that, except for a few more interviews, he was completely free, his scheme to attend returned, and with his unexpected idleness serving as the finest fertilizer, it began to grow and grow. His father was easy to convince to go with him—he'd instilled his love of baseball in Jonny at a young age. His brother Mitchell would have been easy to convince as well, if he had not finally agreed to take some much-needed time off and relax at a resort upstate. But getting his mother to go took some serious work. "What do I know from baseball?" was her oft-repeated dismissive refrain. Jonny finally convinced her by saying that if she wasn't enjoying herself, they could leave at any time.

But Jonny wasn't satisfied with just his parents' attendance.

He wanted to take them to the game in style and show them a world they had only seen in the movies or the society pages. As Mitchell had said, would it be the end of the world if he enjoyed some of his success? Jonny purchased box seats right behind home plate, through a ticket agency, and Charles generously offered first-class transportation. Enjoying their new friendship, Jonny had agreed to do a joint interview at Charles's request for *Broadcast* magazine, a trade publication that put the emphasis on the producers of television and radio, instead of on the writers, actors, and directors. Despite the supposed slant of the article, the writer was delighted with Jonny's attendance, and Jonny made a point of showering Charles with effusive praise. After the interview, a delighted Charles made the offer to Jonny over a leisurely lunch—that he could use Charles's limousine and chauffeur to take his parents to the game. It was no bother, he assured Jonny, after

Jonny had reflexively turned down the offer. Hermie was away doing several nights of his nightclub act down in Miami, so Charles had scheduled a spa day for himself and wouldn't need the car.

An hour before the game, Jonny scooped up his parents in front of their building and made the short crosstown trip to the Polo Grounds. His father seemed delighted as they nestled three across on the spacious backseat, but his mother was silent, offering only the occasional nod in Jonny's direction. The game flew by amid the pomp and circumstance of a marching band, a flag raising, loud cheers, and—as the day grew later and darker, with clouds replacing the early sunshine—the disappointed murmur of a Giants' defeat.

Annoyed by the Giants' failure to win on this auspicious day, Jonny searched for and found some solace in the fact that, though his mother had said very little during the game—not cheering like the rest of the crowd—at least she had not asked to leave early. But the true measure of what the experience meant to her came when they turned off Broadway onto 169th Street, heading toward their building.

"Pull over!" Lena unexpectedly declared. "I need a few things."

Surprised, Jonny echoed the command into a phone that connected him with the driver. The driver immediately complied, and they slipped to the curb right in front of Lansky's Butcher Shop. Not waiting for the chauffeur to open the door, Lena immediately climbed out and headed into the small store. Jonny and his father exchanged a knowing glance. Sure, it was possible that Lena actually needed something at Lansky's, but that wasn't the real reason why she had stopped. Lansky's was the center of the neighborhood for the housewives of the southern section of Washington Heights. Every day, including today, a steady stream of women shuffled in and out of the store with their purchases, stopping to chat with one another in an ever-expanding and contracting group that often flowed out onto the sidewalk. Information was gathered and discussed; gossip was offered and released. If people wanted the entire neighborhood to know a daughter just gave birth to a beautiful baby boy or a son just got a well-deserved promotion at work, this is where they went to make sure the word got out. No topic was off limits; one's voice merely had to be modified to fit the subject matter at hand.

A son's engagement was declared in a loud, boisterous announcement, and the ripe gossip of so-and-so's daughter's husband cheating was delivered in a low monotone, with eyes constantly on the lookout for the mother of that daughter.

As expected, the murmuring began as soon as Lena stepped out of the limousine, and it only intensified once she entered the store. The group on the sidewalk hurriedly spoke to one another, shooting glances back and forth between Lena in the store and the imposing dark black automobile. The crowd parted as Lena exited, wrapped roast in hand, and headed back to the waiting car. This time Lena waited for the chauffeur to open the door for her, and before stepping back into the car, she turned to the gathering of ladies. "My son take me to opening day at the Giants. We sit right behind home base."

As they rode the remaining few blocks to their building, Jonny grinned from ear to ear. His mother had enjoyed herself; she was proud of him. For the first time in his life, his mother had wanted to parade Jonny in front of the neighborhood. For the first time in his life, he was the object of "the walk."

If there was any remaining doubt, it was shattered when they climbed out of the limousine and headed into their building. Passing Mrs. Schulman, a neighbor from the floor below them, his mother proudly boasted, "My son take me to the game today! Opening day! The Giants win!" Because they most certainly had not, Jonny and his father exchanged an amused glance. "Mel Ott hit a triple," she added with a flourish to the building manager, Mr. Donatelli. Another amused smile between father and son; Mel Ott had retired from the Giants almost ten years earlier. By the time they stepped out of the elevator on their floor, Jonny and his father now were openly laughing. His mother was regaling anyone within earshot about the day. "Hank Greenberg homered," she told a delivery man. Never mind that he played in the American League and had never set foot in the Polo Grounds.

But as they stepped back into the apartment, the laughing broke off, and Jonny's smile faded. With trepidation, he followed his parents into the living room. As fun as the day had been, now it was time to get serious. Oblivious to what was to come, his father slumped into his chair, grabbed a stamp magazine, and began to read. His mother wandered into the kitchen and began to prepare dinner. Jonny held his ground, firmly planted in the center of the room. "Mom, can you come out here for a second?" he asked, innocently.

She did, tying the back of her apron as she reentered the living room. She stopped and looked up at him, curiously. His father paused from his reading and peered over the top of his magazine. Jonny had dreaded this moment since realizing just a few days earlier that it had to be done. And the best way to do it was to just come right out and say it.

"Mom...Dad...it's time for me to move out," Jonny said flatly, making it clear that the decision was already made. His words hung heavily in the air. Neither of his parents moved. Finally, his father nodded a few times, as if considering Jonny's words, and then, more or less accepting them, he returned to his magazine.

His mother eyed him quietly, almost with a touch of suspicion. "So, where will you live then?"

"I'm renting a place in Manhattan, in Midtown," Jonny said, knowing he was raising the stakes further by letting them know he had already proceeded without their first knowing. After the disaster on Sunday night at the Kraft party, he had awoken on Monday, and besides planning the outing to the Polo Grounds, he'd begun searching for an apartment. He found one that very afternoon. and by the next morning, he already had the keys. It was a modest two-bedroom on the twenty-third floor of a decidedly average building on Seventh Avenue just north of Fifty-Fourth Street. If he looked one way, he could see a thin slice of Central Park; the other way, he caught a glimpse of Times Square. More important, it was far enough uptown from the studio—about a mile—to make it feel like he was getting away from his work when he journeyed home after a long day, yet not too far as to take up too much of his precious down time.

"Very well then," his mother said, also nodding in acceptance. She turned and went back into the kitchen.

Suddenly, he was very alone in the apartment. With the only sound the crinkle of his father's magazine and the clatter from the kitchen, Jonny slowly sauntered off toward his bedroom. His old bedroom.

He quickly threw a few items in a small suitcase, purposely taking very little, as all he had purchased in the way of furniture for the new place was a mattress and box spring. Taking in his room for one last, long look, he wondered how long it would be until his parents turned it into a guest room, or a sewing room, or even just a storage space. He found himself overcome with nostalgia. After all, except for a few weeks here or there on vacation or away at camp, this was the only room he had ever known. Maybe he should take a few other items with him—a few of the posters or maybe some of his books. What about a few of his records? *No, no, no,* he finally thought. The whole point of this was to let go of the past. He had concluded that it was wrong to be twenty-four and still living at home, so it was certainly a mistake to pack up that home and reconstitute it somewhere else. It was time to move on, to begin a new life—as an adult. From now on, this would no longer be his room. Oh, sure, he would see it again, but always as a guest, never as the true inhabitant.

Filled with certainty and clutching the small suitcase, Jonny marched out into the hallway...and almost right into his mother.

"Tell me. Your brother—how is he doing?" Lena asked.

Finally, some truth, Jonny thought. As he had always suspected, his extended residence in the apartment, never spoken about or commented on by either party, was really a truce in the never-ending battle to cope with Rachel's meaningless death. Mitchell's return from the war as a hero had pulled his mother out of her depression, giving her something to live for. It wasn't that Jonny wasn't loved; it was that Mitchell had always been the star, and seeing him return an even bigger star allowed Lena to believe in the optimism she had once worn so easily. But Mitchell's recent decline, something Jonny had thought was safely hidden from his mother, had clearly not gone unnoticed. The final link to that time when the family was whole was about to move out for good, and in order to keep from being pulled back into that dark, black chasm, possibly forever, Lena needed to know that her talisman was safe.

"He'll be fine," Jonny said, trying his best to believe it himself.

They were the words she needed to hear, and the relief washed over his mother like a cool shower on a scorching August day. Her whole body relaxed, and she reached out and hugged Jonny. "You enjoy your new place."

"I will," Jonny said, relieved himself.

"But be sure to come visit us at least once a week."

...

Felicity was in her inviting bed, leaning back against several soft pillows, with the covers pulled up almost to her neck. Braeden stood next to her, fully clothed, looking down at her with concern. Felicity shook her head, clearly perturbed. "I still don't understand why you had to say anything," she said sharply.

"Felicity," Braeden began, "now that we're going to be married, I couldn't stand by and say nothing."

"So you had to tell them I was the actress playing Justice Girl!"

"Yes," Braeden answered, as if it were the most obvious fact in the world. "And you know what? It worked. Once they realized who you were and that we are going to be married, they stopped making the inappropriate comments. The things they said about you—"

"You should have kept your mouth shut."

"No. I shouldn't have. You know, it's not a lot of fun hearing a bunch of guys say things like they want to lift up the skirt of your future wife and fuck her over the desk of some magazine her character works at."

"Braeden!" Felicity said, taken aback by the language.

"See, it's not fun. Is it?"

"You're a man. You should have been able to take it. Now the cat's out of the bag. Did you see? It got picked up in the local paper."

Braeden nodded his head wearily. "I know. I know."

"Soon, everyone will know," Felicity said, alarmed.

Braeden suddenly saw how much it hurt Felicity. He sighed. "I'm sorry. I'm sorry."

Felicity took a deep breath herself. "It's all right. I suppose it had to come out at some point."

"And it's not like you're going to be playing the character for that much longer, anyway," Braeden said helpfully.

"Right. That, too," Felicity said, trying to sound eager for it all to be over.

"And then you won't feel inclined to stay out till all hours at seamy parties in the West Village and catch colds," Braeden concluded, while cupping the side of Felicity's face with his soothing hand.

Felicity looked over at a clock that was next to her bed. "My God, Braeden, it's almost noon. You'd better be going."

Braeden sat down on the edge of the bed. "I was thinking of not going, of staying here with you. One of my stable hands can handle everything."

Felicity shifted, alarmed. "You can't do that. It's a derby prep."

"But Pimlico is a long way away, and now that we're going to be married, I don't feel right leaving you behind when you're sick."

"Relax. It's not that far. You'll be back by tomorrow night, right?"

"By 6:00 p.m.," Braeden said brightly.

"Perfect. Now go! Go!"

"You're sure?" Braeden asked, climbing off the bed.

"Yes."

"Okay." He leaned down, kissed her, and eyed her with sympathy. Softly, he touched her head, as if soothing a sick two-year-old. "Feel better."

"I will."

With a smile, he left.

Felicity grumbled. Braeden had just made her life a hell of a lot more complicated. For almost four weeks, she had been able to keep her true identity a secret from everyone except her mother and father. She'd been able to avoid interviews, having convinced the network that the more the audience invested in the character, not the actress, the better it would be in the long run, and to further this along, she should only be photographed in costume. Everything was working perfectly, until Braeden had to screw it all up in one brief moment of attempted chivalry.

Further lowering her mood, just as Braeden's footsteps faded away, she heard new ones that grew louder and louder as they moved up the stairs. Felicity's mother and father were coming. Felicity pulled open the drawer of her nightstand, where there was a bowl with water and a sponge. Braeden had been easy to fool, but her parents were going to take a bit more work.

Using the sponge, she dabbed her forehead, her face, and the pillow all around her head. She dropped the sponge back into the bowl, shutting the drawer just seconds before her parents entered. Glistening, she turned to eye them as they moved toward her. They were both dressed to travel—her father in his immense herringbone overcoat and her mother with a wrap across her shoulders and purse and gloves in hand.

"Well, we're ready to go," her father said stiffly, glaring at her.

Though he was largely motionless, Felicity could feel his rage. As the word had spread around Greenwich of the identity of the actress playing Justice Girl, her father had become furious. Her sickness had saved her from receiving his full wrath.

"I'm really...sorry...I can't make it. I really...wanted to...be there for... you," Felicity said, struggling with the words because of her weakened condition.

"That's all right," her mother said reassuringly. "You just concentrate on getting better. We'll say hi to everyone for you."

"Thank you."

Her father slashed at the air with a furious swipe. "It's the biggest event of the political year, and you can't be there with us. It's bad enough that your plan has backfired, and now you won't even be there!"

"Scott!" her mother gasped.

Felicity twisted in the bed. She was well aware of what was at stake for her father. This was Roland Graves's yearly backyard barbeque. There, all the way on the other side of the state in Stonington, among the big mansions and big wealth, they would discuss how the country was still suffering from the Roosevelt and Truman administrations. They were happy with what Eisenhower had done so far but weren't so crazy about his raising taxes, and there were still so many more Communists to root out of the State Department.

But most important, as everyone devoured chicken and steak and corn and beans, there would be subtle and not-so-subtle lobbying for who would finally get the party's nod for the upcoming special election. Felicity knew she should be there. But something else was tugging on her. And its pull was much stronger.

"Maybe it's just as well," her father said, his shoulders slumping. "Conrad Hollins is sure to be there with his war-hero son." He looked down at Felicity, his anger now growing. "With the way news of your...acting career is spreading, having you there would only make things worse. Some of the other guests are bound to know. You were supposed to come with us to help my chances, not hurt them."

"Scott!" her mother interjected again.

Felicity felt for her father; he had every reason to be angry. Once again, she felt the urge to just tell him. Just tell him about the names. Why keep waiting for more proof? So what if the information was scant? With her secret identity out there, spreading like wildfire around the upper crust of the state, this was the perfect time for him to heroically step forward with some astounding information. Felicity forced herself to straighten up a bit and opened her mouth, but no words came out. *But then again*, she thought, *what if they weren't confirmed? Wouldn't releasing the names and then having it all backfire just be worse for him? Just stick to the plan.* Felicity let out several rough coughs.

"The girl's sick. Enough. She needs rest." Her mother bent down and kissed Felicity on the forehead. "We'll be back tomorrow night. Remember, Viola canceled her day off. She'll be here if you need anything."

"That's not really necessary."

"Shh. Sleep," her mother said and then turned toward the door.

Her father stood for a moment, not sure what to do. "Well, there is one bit of good out of all this, I suppose. I'm sure they won't want us to do the fund-raiser anymore..." He sighed, defeated. "Feel better," he finally said and followed Felicity's mother.

After they'd left her room, Felicity sat up in bed and listened closely. She heard them clomp down the stairs, where they had a brief conversation with Viola. She heard the front door close, and soon after, she heard their car rumble down the driveway. Felicity threw off the bed covers and jumped out of bed, fully dressed. Peering out the window, she watched as the Cadillac reached the end of the driveway, turned onto the street, and drove out of sight. She checked the clock on her nightstand; it was almost 1:00 p.m., and she was running late. Quickly, she reached under the bed and pulled out a fully packed travel bag. She slung it over her shoulder and headed out of the room. She could still make it, but she knew she had one final obstacle to pass.

Viola.

Reaching the bottom of the stairs, she carefully hid her bag under a small end table. "Viola!" Felicity called out.

"In here, Miss Kensington," Viola answered.

Felicity found her by the front door, putting on her coat and scarf. She, too, had a small travel bag.

"Viola," Felicity said, "I'm feeling much better now. You don't have to miss your day off. I'll be fine."

"I know, Miss Kensington," she said, not meeting Felicity's eyes.

Felicity watched her curiously. "You do?"

Viola finally turned around and looked at her. "Honey, I've been with this family since you were nine years old. Did you really think you could get one past me?"

Felicity frowned. "I guess I'm not as good an actor as I think I am."

"Especially when you leave a fully packed bag under your bed." Viola smiled at her. "You have a good time with whatever it is your doing. I'll be back tomorrow afternoon." Viola opened the door and left.

Ten minutes later, Felicity pulled out of the driveway in her mother's Ford. Reaching the parkway, she drove for another twenty minutes until her exit was in sight. But as she slowed so she could make the turn that would put her on the narrow two-lane road that wound its way to Waterbury and her final destination, she found herself confused again. Had it really come to this? Had she really faked an illness so she could skip a political event that would have helped her father, at a moment when he really could have used some help, and instead was heading across the state to make a personal appearance as Justice Girl? Worse, another actress had already been hired for the job when Felicity got wind of the personal appearance a few hours before the canceled show. At first, she was mildly irritated that someone else was going to play Justice Girl, even if it was just at the opening of a supermarket, but she let it go when Charles, the person behind the booking, explained that it had to be done because Felicity needed to be in rehearsal. And it really wasn't the sort of thing that the lead actress in a hit show was called upon to do. There were dozens and dozens of models and actresses more than capable of filling in for such a lowly duty.

But when the episode was canceled and the show put on a tiny hiatus because of the recycled script, Felicity found her irritation returning as she realized she was now available to make the appearance herself. She knew there was a conflict with the barbecue, but the thought of someone else playing Justice Girl—her character—was too much for her to take. Yes, it was only a supermarket opening, but it was also the very first time Justice Girl was going to appear in person. When the irritation metastasized into full-blown annoyance, she went to Charles and demanded that she be allowed to make the appearance. Though surprised, he readily agreed.

Replaying all of this in her mind and returning to what had driven her the most—the first public appearance of Justice Girl—Felicity eased the car onto the off ramp. In the end, there was just no way she could stay away.

As she headed away from the parkway, cruising along the road that would take her to Waterbury, signs of civilization suddenly became scant—just the occasional gas station or roadside stand selling home crafts. The traffic was light, so Felicity lost herself in the impressive scenery. With winter a fading memory, the leaves were starting to bud on the branches, returning the foliage to the thick green blanket she always loved. It made her feel secure; as a little girl when she'd traveled with her family all around Connecticut, packed in the rear of the family car with her three sisters, she used to peer out the back window and see the quilt of foliage above her, protecting her, keeping her safe, and surrounding her on both sides with carpetbag hills.

A couple hours later, closing in on Waterbury, the heavy stamp of civilization returned as clusters of buildings sprouted up all around. Felicity eased into a gas station and pulled to a stop around the side, next to the restrooms.

After a quick change in the filthy ladies room—she managed to remove her clothes and slip on the Justice Girl outfit without touching the germ-infested bathroom—Felicity was back on the road, completing the last of the drive. She entered Waterbury about five minutes later and followed her directions to the market, which was located at the other end of town. Despite the plethora of stoplights, traffic continued to move quickly until, in the shadow of the city's Civil War memorial, everything came to an unexpected and sudden standstill. Desperate, Felicity craned her neck, searching for the cause. Up ahead, she saw flashing police lights. *Great. An accident*, she thought. *I am going to be so late. I am screwed.* Crawling along with the rest of the traffic, she crept closer and closer to the police car with the flashing lights. But when she passed it, she couldn't find an accident scene. There was no car crash, no banged-up vehicle on the side of the road, no ambulance screeching as it approached. Instead, two officers were out of their patrol car, trying their best to direct the heavy flow of traffic. Leaning forward and peering through the windshield, Felicity could make out a huge crowd—it looked like hundreds of people—waiting in front of the market under a huge sign that read "Welcome, Justice Girl." *Holy shit!* she thought, as she jammed on the brakes so as not to hit the car in front of her. *That's why there's no accident scene! This crowd is for me! For Justice Girl!*

It took another ten minutes for Felicity to make it to the market, and as per the information she had been given, she pulled around the back. She carefully slipped her wig back on, having removed it minutes earlier when she realized some of the children in the cars around her were beginning to do double takes. She stepped out of her car, gave her costume a final adjustment by pulling her boots up and her dress down and shaking the cape loose. Flexing her hands within her gloves, she reached out and knocked on the rear door.

The door opened quickly, and once inside, a stock boy escorted her through the storage area and into the empty market and led her to the manager, Felton Erickson. He was in his mid-fifties, with the stooped shoulders of a man who had been at one job too long. He was sweating so profusely that his constant dabbing with a handkerchief had turned his comb-over into a crazed swirl. "Thank God you're here," Felton said, breaking from a huddle of stressed employees and practically hugging Felicity. Felicity didn't have to ask why he was so relieved; from the moment she stepped inside the market, she could hear the loud din of the wild crowd outside. They were making so much noise and cheering so loudly, that if she closed her eyes, she would have sworn she was at a Harvard-Yale football game. "Let's get you right out there," Felton continued, moving Felicity toward the front entrance of the market. Nearing the glass doors, she could see the crowd outside assembled behind a thin rope partition that ran the entire length of the front of the market. There were hundreds of screaming kids with their seemingly equally excited parents.

"Hold on," Felicity said, stopping. "What am I supposed to do once I get out there?"

Felton pulled out his handkerchief again and began to rapidly pat his dripping forehead. "Didn't you read the script?"

"What script?"

Felton looked like he was about to pass out. "The script that I submitted to the booking agent."

Felicity's face was a blank stare. Charles hadn't mentioned a script.

"Okay. Okay," Felton said, forcing air into his lungs. "Just go out there, wave to the crowd, and when the two bad guys approach you, kick the one on your left in the chest, and then punch the other one in the face. They'll know what to do. Okay?" Not waiting for an answer, he pushed her toward the door again.

"Hold on." Felicity stopped again. "Why am I beating up these two guys?"

Felton looked at her confused. "What do you mean, why?"

"Why am I beating them up?" Felicity repeated plainly.

"Because they're bad guys."

"What did they do?"

"Excuse me?"

"You said they're bad guys. What did they do?"

Felton shook his head, confused. "What do you mean, what did they do? They're *bad guys*. That's all you need to know."

"But I'm Justice Girl. I don't go around beating people up for no reason. I only use my powers for good," Felicity said earnestly.

The door to the outside suddenly flew open and a harried employee stepped in. "You better get out there soon; they're going crazy," he said, spotting Felicity.

"You heard him. Get going," Felton said, pushing her toward the open door.

Felicity caught herself in the frame. "Look, you said there was a script. What happened in it? Surely, there must have been some detail. Maybe some backstory. What crime did they commit just before running into me?"

Felton looked at her, stunned. "Are you insane?"

"There she is!" a young voice yelled from outside.

"Yeah, it's her! It's Justice Girl!" another prepubescent child screamed. Instantly, the crowd went crazy, yelling and cheering, "Justice Girl! Justice Girl! Justice Girl!"

Overwhelmed, Felicity stared at them in shock. *This is nuts!*

"Get out there!" Felton said, as the screams grew louder and louder. "I beg you. Get out there!"

But before Felicity could take a step, even if she had wanted to, some of the children pushed through the rope line and ran straight for her. Like a bursting damn, the rest of the crowd followed suit, and in a flash, hundreds of screaming children rushed for her.

"Holy shit!" Felicity exclaimed as she turned and ran, rushing deeper into the store. The crazed throng of children flew through the front door, pouring into the market. Running as fast as she could, Felicity sprinted to the rear. The children followed and, like rushing floodwater, streamed down each aisle toward her. Pressed against a freezer section, Felicity looked all around. She was trapped, and screaming children were approaching from all directions. She looked for Felton or any of the other store employees, but they were nowhere to be found. Finally, next to her, she spotted a small plastic-sheet-covered entranceway that led into the storage area in the back of the store.

Felicity dashed through it and found herself momentarily alone among the boxes and crates of unopened products. But her solitude was short-lived as the kids streamed through the opening and into the back. Fortunately, because the opening was so small, only a trickle could get through at a time, and Felicity had a chance to get a head start. But as she ran around the storage area, she quickly found she had nowhere to go. More and more of the children poured into the storage area. They moved en masse toward Felicity. She was cornered.

Suddenly, on the other side of the large storage room, a rear door to the outside opened, and Jonny appeared in it, bathed in the golden light of escape. "Denise, this way!" he yelled over the screams of the children.

Felicity saw him, but there was a sea of crazed children blocking her exit. They surrounded her on all sides, moving straight at her, their ranks swelling by the second. Soon, it would be impossible for her to make it across the storage area to Jonny. With no other choice, Felicity took a deep breath and stepped forward, directly into the path of the rushing onslaught. "I am Justice Girl, and I say *stop!*" she commanded.

Amazingly, it worked; the entire group froze in its tracks. Even the screaming stopped, as they gazed at their hero standing before them in the flesh.

"Much better," she continued. "Now, boys and girls, I need you to split into two groups, leaving a path for me in the middle.

With awe on their faces, they followed her command and a slender path opened up, leading across the storage area to Jonny and the open door to freedom.

"Very good," Felicity said calmly, and then she made her way out into the crowd and along the path. *My God, this is working. They're actually listening to me!* She passed smoothly between the divided children; many of the girls wearing homemade Justice Girl costumes. Seeing this, Felicity shook her head in amazement. Other children reached out and touched her costume as she walked by. Slowly, Felicity made her way across the storage room, the children filling in behind her and following.

Finally, she was almost to Jonny, who stood anxiously by the rear door, seemingly beckoning her to hurry up. He relaxed when she reached him, and he stepped aside to let her pass. But instead of walking out, much to his shock, Felicity turned around and addressed the pack of children.

"Remember," she began dramatically, "to the guy who takes advantage of the innocent, you cannot hide." She clenched her jaw and stared forward for emphasis. "To the man who profits from others' suffering, you cannot hide." She pointed right at them. "To the person who falsely accuses, you cannot hide." She jabbed at them with a closed fist. "To the citizen who denies others their rights, you cannot hide!" She swept her arm through the air, took a long pause, and then finally said, "And remember, all of you, I am Justice Girl, and—"

Before she could get the rest of the words out, the children finished them for her. *"Justice is served!"* they all said in unison, which once again whipped them into a frenzy. The screaming returned—"Justice Girl! Justice Girl! Justice Girl!"—and the pack surged forward, right at Felicity and Jonny.

"Oh shit!" they both said, practically at the same moment. Jonny grabbed Felicity, yanked her through the door and onto the loading dock, and slammed the door shut behind them.

"You had to give a speech?" Jonny said incredulously.

"It wasn't me. It was Justice Girl. She had to give a speech."

Jonny rolled his eyes. "Well, ask her if she'll help me move this garbage bin to block the door."

Together, Jonny and Felicity quickly rolled the bin in front of the door, preventing the kids from getting out.

"What are you doing here?" Felicity asked, now that they were safe for the moment.

"A simple thank-you would suffice," Jonny shot back.

"Thank you," she said sincerely. "Now, what are you doing here?"

"Well, I don't really know," Jonny said, shrugging. "I was gonna do some writing, and then it suddenly occurred to me that this was the first time anyone was going to see Justice Girl in person. The next thing I knew, I was on a train to Waterbury." Jonny shrugged again. "I guess there was just no way I could stay away."

Felicity nodded knowingly.

Loud banging made them both jump as the children began pushing against the door, shoving it against the garbage bin.

"My car is over there," Felicity said, pointing. "Do you mind driving? I'm a little overwhelmed."

"Sure."

She tossed him the keys as they both raced over to her car and jumped in. Jonny turned over the motor and dropped it into gear, just as the children burst through the rear door and onto the loading dock.

With the pack of screaming kids in hot pursuit, Felicity and Jonny sped away. He ran two red lights as they got the hell out of Waterbury, not slowing to the speed limit until they were safely out of the city limits.

Seeing the return of the protective canopy of green in the fading sun, Felicity finally relaxed. "What have you unleashed, Jonny Dirby?" she asked, sighing.

Jonny thought for a moment and then sighed himself. "No one wants to admit it, but we all dream of writing something so popular that everyone likes it. And then it really happens and..." He paused, seemingly searching for the words in the rhythmic thump-thump-thump of passing cars. "Well, it's all very different from what I thought it would be."

They were approaching the same gas station Felicity had used on the way to Waterbury, and she asked Jonny to stop there. While she changed out of her costume, Jonny ran next door to the diner and ordered a couple of sandwiches. Forty-five minutes later, the sun was gone and their sandwiches were nothing more than empty wrappers tossed in the backseat. The first drizzle of a coming storm tapped on the windshield as Felicity dozed off.

She slowly awoke as they crossed into Greenwich, with the rain now coming down in sheets that buffeted the car like a car wash. Jonny pulled off the parkway and began driving down a small road. Felicity shot up in her seat, suddenly very awake. "Where are you going?" she asked, a bit alarmed.

"The sign back on the parkway," Jonny said, pointing behind himself, "said this was the turn for the train station."

"Oh...right," Felicity said, sliding back down into her seat. *Of course, the train station,* she thought. *I'll drop him off and then head home. He can wait in the station until the train comes to take him back into the city. If it ever comes in this weather...*She looked at him closely, studying the side of his face. *A subversive, right here in the car with me. Is he ranting? Is he scream-ing? Is he outlining his plots to overthrow the government? No, he's driving me home in a storm after rescuing me from three hundred screaming brats. And how do I thank him? I let him sit in a freezing cold train station, waiting for a train that will probably not come until tomorrow morning.* Was he really that dangerous? He looked harmless enough. Same haircut as most of the men she knew. Same peering eyes that always found their way to her chest. *Maybe I should invite him to stay over. It's not like he'd walk in the door and there'd be a sign that read "We fight Communists!" He'd be out long before Mom and Dad get back.*

Convinced, Felicity sat up again and turned to Jonny. "Say, do you want to stay over at my place tonight?" she asked sincerely. "We've got plenty of room."

"Oh, no. No, no, that's not necessary," Jonny said, waving off the idea with a swipe of his hand.

The station came into sight. Heavy rain lashed against the defiant stone structure. "But you don't know how long you'll have to wait," Felicity said, almost insulted that she had to ask a second time.

"Don't worry about it. I'm sure there'll be a train by in a little bit."

Felicity grumbled and then sat back in the seat. *If he wants to be a mar-tyr, so be it.*

They were about to pull into the station when a policeman, wearing a rain slicker and carrying a lantern, appeared and stopped them. Jonny cracked his window, and the policeman stuck his head into view. "No more trains tonight," he said through chattering teeth. "Power's out. Should be up and running by morning."

Jonny thanked him and rolled the window up. He turned to Felicity. "How's that for dramatic irony?"

Jonny drove very slowly up the drive to Felicity's house. The power also was out in her part of town, so all he could see was the tunnel of skinny birch trees that lined the narrow driveway. Finally, the driveway expanded, and they pulled up in front of her house. It was pitch black, but the headlights splattered the gargantuan structure with light.

Jonny whistled, impressed. "You weren't kidding about having plenty of room."

Once parked, they sprinted through the rain to the safety of the front door portico. Fumbling with the keys for a moment in the darkness, Felicity finally managed to get the door open. "Stay here for a second," she said to Jonny. She crept hands first into the darkness. It only took a moment, and she found what she was looking for in a nearby credenza. Flicking the flashlight on, she turned around and aimed it in Jonny's direction.

He was standing in the doorway, holding a stuffed off-gray oversized envelope. Felicity recognized it immediately—it was the kind used to shuttle information back and forth between her father and his like-minded contacts in Washington. "Where did you get that?" Felicity asked, charging toward him.

"Right here, on the floor," he said. "It must have fallen inside when you opened the door."

Felicity snatched it swiftly out of his grasp.

Jonny held up his hands, as if caught. "Okay. Sorry. If I'd known it would be such a big deal, I would have left it on the ground."

Felicity took a deep breath. "Sorry. It belongs to my father. He takes his work very seriously."

"Apparently he's not the only one," Jonny said, shaking his head, still recovering from her sudden mood change.

"Let me put this in his office, and I'll be right back." Shining the flashlight ahead of her, Felicity left Jonny standing in the dark as she moved out of the entranceway and into her father's study. She turned the envelope over in her hands, realizing the government courier must have left it at the front door when he discovered nobody was home. She'd have to mention this to her father. What if the storm had somehow opened the envelope and Jonny had peered inside? Or if the envelope had become so wet that it fell apart when Jonny picked it up, spilling the papers all over the porch for him to see?

Or what if Jonny had just simply decided to open it? Felicity exhaled sharply at the dark thoughts. A horrible disaster had been narrowly avoided.

She made her way to her father's desk and was about to drop the envelope on top of a pile of his work when she paused. Maybe this envelope held the information she'd been waiting for, the absolute confirmation about Jonny's writing staff and their subversive activities. But instead of being excited, Felicity found herself sinking, the thought giving her no happiness. Two weeks ago, all she wanted in life was to be sure that they were Communists so she could expose them and kick-start her father's political career. But now, if it did turn out they were truly subversive, that meant it was all over. No more live television. No more acting classes. No more *Justice Girl*.

But then she caught herself.

No. No. No. She was doing a job; that was all. She didn't care about acting and backstory and character spine. She cared about America. Now, praying that they turned out to be the reddest of the red, Felicity tore open the envelope. She quickly rifled through the various documents until she found what she was looking for. Reading through the response to her "additional information request," her face fell. There was nothing new on the form; it was merely a reiteration of what was already printed in her father's pamphlet. Sheldon Ezralow: "Dated girl who was known Communist." Burton Walker: "Was involved in production of Russian play." Annie Quinlan: "Known to have many actor friends." *That was it? That's all they did, and yet they were blacklisted*, Felicity thought. But then her face tightened and she pushed the disappointment away. She had to be careful; that's how they worked. They seduced you into thinking they were just regular, innocent folks. But they weren't, and if that's all they did, then that's all they did. If her father and the great people he worked with felt it was enough to put them on the list, then it was enough.

A splash of light startled her. She looked up, reflexively holding the form behind her back. Johnny was standing in the doorway with a flashlight in his hand. "You okay?" Jonny asked, concerned.

"Yeah, fine."

"Good, I was worried since you were gone for so long." He held up the flashlight. "You left the drawer open. I found this one inside."

"Oh, good," Felicity said brightly, trying not to act caught. "Give me a second, and I'll be right there."

Jonny nodded and disappeared back into the darkness of the rest of the house. Felicity precisely laid the form on the center of her father's desk, right where he couldn't miss it. She regarded it for a moment, smoothing it out for good measure with her palm, and then turned to leave. But after taking only a single step, she turned back and grabbed the form. After all she'd been through, she didn't want her father finding the names on his own. It was too impersonal, too distant. With one final look at the offending names, she dropped the paper into the trash can next to her father's desk. She would tell him herself; that's what she'd do.

She found Jonny waiting just outside the office, and leading with their two flashlights, they moved back into the entranceway and then on into the expansive living room. Felicity could tell Jonny was a little taken aback, as he slowed and wiped his flashlight beam around the room, trying to take it all in. The room was so large that only bits and pieces of it were revealed; the hint of paintings on the wall, faint faces that were marble busts, the outlines of imposing furniture, but try as he might, most of the details were lost in the shadows.

"I assure you it's not haunted," Felicity joked, playing off Jonny's seeming reticence to move farther into dark room.

Jonny laughed. "Sorry, it's just a bit overwhelming."

Felicity led him toward a brick fireplace, complete with swords and rifles above the hearth that a couch and loveseat surrounded. After several candles were lit, Jonny collapsed onto the loveseat and Felicity onto the couch.

In the quiet yellow of the flickering light, they both finally relaxed. Felicity slid her shoes off and pulled her legs up under her. Taking the cue, Jonny also removed his shoes but kept his socked feet firmly planted on the soft carpet.

"Say, how about a drink?" Felicity asked.

"I'd love one, but let me get it," Jonny answered as he jumped to his feet. He quickly sauntered over to an ornate waist-high liquor cabinet, the top covered with at least a dozen bottles of the finest alcohol. "What would you like?"

"Anything, as long as its alcoholic."

"I hear ya, sister." Jonny eyed a particularly expensive-looking bottle of Gibson vodka and unscrewed the cap.

"The glasses should be underneath in the cabinet," Felicity offered. "There should be several to choose from; if not, try one of the—"

"Relax, my dear, I've been driving since I was sixteen," Jonny said playfully. "Besides, we've got a cabinet just like this back home."

Felicity laughed. "Oh, I seriously doubt that. That one was a gift to Grandpapa from President McKinley."

Jonny pulled out two sipping glasses. He filled one practically to the rim; the other, he filled about a quarter of the way. Stepping back, he offered the smaller glass to Felicity.

"What am I? Twelve?" she asked as she eyed the slim pour.

"My sincerest apologies." Jonny poured some of his drink into hers, until each glass was a little more than half full.

"Much better," Felicity said, smiling.

"To *Justice Girl*," Jonny said, holding out his glass.

Felicity sighed. "If you say so."

They clinked glasses, and Jonny dropped back on the loveseat. They both took a big, much needed mouthful. Felicity sighed again, but this time the exhale consumed her entire body as the liquor did its job.

Still intrigued by the shell of darkness around him, Jonny whipped his light over the room again. "I gotta say, this sure is some place. Hats off to Mr. Darnell."

Felicity opened her mouth to correct him, but then caught herself. *That's right; he thinks my last name is Darnell.*

"It really is beautiful," Jonny said as his gaze finished sweeping the room and landed on Felicity.

"Thank you."

"What does he do? Your father? You know, for a living."

"Oh, you know…business."

Jonny raised his eyebrows and laughed. "Actually no, I don't. Business in my world is a stand or a shop. What does he—?"

"Where do you live, Jonny?" Felicity interrupted.

Jonny laughed. "In that most rarified world known as Washington Heights," he answered in a mock northeastern accent. "In a place about the same size as yours, Miss Darnell…only ours is divided into about thirty different apartments."

There it is again, the false name. He's being honest about who he is, and I'm lying. It irked her. She was supposed to be the one exposing subversives, yet she was the one doing the lying. Unnecessary lying. What harm could it do if he knew her real name? For some reason, it was important for her to be honest with him—at least, as honest as she could be without blowing the whole thing.

"Look, there's something you should know," Felicity began carefully. "My real name's not Darnell. It's Kensington. Felicity Kensington."

Jonny laughed. "Are you trying to tell me you have a secret identity?"

Felicity laughed too. "Well, yes, in a way, I guess I am."

"Then, naturally, you'll have to tell me the difference between your two identities."

Felicity thought for a long moment. "Well, Felicity loves Connecticut, the slow and steady and calm life. Denise has never seen a world more exciting than Manhattan, and she craves it with every ounce of her being. Felicity wants to get married and raise a family with a strong and caring man. Denise wants to act every great role at least ten times. Felicity loves her father. Denise is beginning to question some of the things he does."

"Wow," Jonny said, genuinely affected by her words.

Felicity looked away, horrified. What was this world of acting doing to her? Whether she was Felicity or Denise, she was still a Kensington. Kensingtons didn't talk about their feelings in public. And certainly not to a mere acquaintance. *Acquaintance? How about almost total stranger?* Yet, as disappointed as she was in herself, she found she wanted to say more. She took another long drink, letting the vodka ease down her throat and into her stomach, allowing it to give her the courage to keep talking. She found Alexis's words suddenly playing in her head. *If you're going to do something dramatic and unexpected, commit. Make a firm choice.*

Felicity turned and looked right at Jonny. "Remember what you said earlier about all this not turning out the way you thought it would?" Felicity whipped her hand through the air. "This used to be the place I felt the best, the safest—this was home. But not anymore. These last four weeks...I've never had so much fun, been so happy. I've never felt more that I was where I should be, where I..."

"Belonged?" Jonny said.

Felicity looked at him, amazed. "Yes."

Jonny's head suddenly twitched, and he looked at her as if seeing her for the first time. He threw his hands up. "Of course! My God, how did I not see it?"

"See what?" Felicity asked, confused.

"Your résumé. It was all made up, right?" Jonny said triumphantly.

Uneasiness flickered across Felicity's face but was gone in a fraction of a second, replaced by defiance. "What are you talking about?"

"You're new to all of this," he said, ignoring her question as he put it all together. "Television? Performing? Acting? All of it!"

Felicity sighed heavily and looked away, embarrassed. "Well...yes."

Jonny leaned forward, eyeing her closely. "And I would have to say...this is your first acting job?"

Felicity nodded.

Jonny smiled, pleased with himself. "So you're just getting it."

"Getting it?"

Jonny jumped to his feet. "I've seen it happen before, lots of times. Everyone always denies it. *Oh, it won't happen to me.* Then the next thing you know, it has happened."

Felicity was completely confused. "What has?"

Jonny slid onto the couch next to her. "The dream, the bug, the passion."

Felicity shook her head, still not getting it.

Jonny grabbed her upper arms. "The absolute need to be in front of an audience." Jonny said, almost pleading. "It's the most screwed up thing ever. You knowingly submit yourself to a miserable, horrible life filled with nothing but failure and rejection, and yet to get you to leave it, they'd have to pull you away, kicking and screaming." When he finished, his face was barely a foot from hers. "It's completely messed up."

As his words sank in, Felicity shifted, suddenly realizing just how close he was to her on the couch—so close, she could smell the last whiffs of his aftershave mixed with vodka and the hint of honey glaze from their ham sandwiches.

"Sorry," Jonny said, realizing it also. He slid a few inches away from her.

"It's okay. It's okay," she said reassuringly.

But it didn't work. He shifted uncomfortably as the storm intensified and, as if commenting on what was happening between them, let loose several flashes of lightning, followed by the angry rumble of thunder. Jonny very self-consciously looked at her drink and then at his. "Hey, we're both dry. How about another drink?" he suggested, clearly hoping for a reason to stand up. But Felicity found she didn't want him to move. There was something exciting, almost thrilling about being this close to him. This close to the enemy. Alone. In her house. With no one around to save her. Yet she wasn't afraid. Not in the least. She felt in control. She knew the truth of who was really behind the writing on the show.

She knew his secret.

Instead of handing him her glass, Felicity placed it calmly on the coffee table and leaned back on the arm of the couch. She pulled her legs out from under her and laid them across Jonny's lap.

"I'm not thirsty either," Jonny said, smiling. He put his glass on the coffee table and in a flash was on top of her. Her first thought as their lips came together was how much lighter he was then Braeden. Braeden was a thick bull of a man whose sheer weight always pinned Felicity down when they would kiss on the haystacks of his stable or on the swing on his back porch. Jonny was a skinny matchstick who practically floated atop her. Through locked lips, she almost smiled when she felt his hands on her body. That was one thing he and Braeden both had in common—quick hands. She felt Jonny's probing move from her back, to her sides, and head for her front. *Once again, just like Braeden.* But unlike Braeden, whom she would inevitably push off at this point, she found herself letting Jonny continue and, even more astonishingly, slowly moving her own hands over his torso. She grasped him, pulling him closer, as his hands found her breasts, and he began to feel them through her blouse. Amazingly, she didn't want him to stop. She wished her blouse would dissolve along with her bra so she could feel his soft writer's hands on the excited flesh of her tits. Fortunately, it became clear that the longer she allowed him to touch her breasts, the more aggressive he became. Soon, he would have her top open, followed closely by her bra.

But instead, his hand began to move downward, across her stomach toward her crotch. *Yes. Yes,* Felicity thought, the sensation exciting her. Again, Alexis was in her head, extolling her to focus her feelings, to strip everything away, and get to the essence of what was happening, to get to what she wanted. Her pulse raced, her breathing quickened, her chest heaved, because… because…because…she wanted to fuck him.

His hand slid across her crotch, briefly pressing down on the soft material and sending a shot up her spine, before continuing downward. He smoothly slipped under her dress, and for the second time in her life, a man's hand made its way up her thigh toward her sex. His touch was easy, delicate, as comforting as it was exciting, as he drew closer and closer to her. She could feel his fingers just inches away. She couldn't wait for him to touch her, further arousing her, and then they would be together. His middle finger reached her, briefly touching her swollen lips, and then slipped inside her.

Felicity suddenly pushed Jonny off her and sat up.

"Oh, my God; I am so sorry," Jonny said, alarmed, as he backed away from Felicity. "I didn't realize you were a virgin."

Felicity swallowed hard. Lightning flashed. Thunder clapped. The house shook. "I'm not a virgin," she finally said, ready to unload a burden, and then both Felicity and Denise started to cry.

...

The gas mask smashed against the wall before crashing to the carpeted floor of her bedroom in a pile of broken glass and cracked rubber. Felicity then ripped the heavy uniform from her body, haphazardly tearing off chunks of fabric and buttons, as she rid herself of the scratchy material. Stepping out of the accumulated pile of fabric at her feet, she furiously kicked the crumpled heap across the room, where it flew into a lamp, knocking it noisily to the ground.

"You okay in there, Miss Kensington?" came Viola's concerned voice through the shut door.

"No!" Felicity removed her two oversized army boots and threw them across the room for punctuation.

"I'm coming in."

"No, you're not!"

Viola pushed open the door, her face momentarily betraying her shock at the scene of destruction in front of her before it returned to its usual placid blankness. "Excuse me for saying this, Miss Kensington, but this is not the way for a girl of fifteen to act."

"It is, if she's been through what I've been through," Felicity said, before collapsing on the bed and beating the cover with a flurry of punches and kicks more befitting a girl half her age. "This was supposed to be my big day, my coming out. Instead, it's been the worst day of my life!" She returned to taking out her anger on the bedspread.

"I heard it was a lovely affair," Viola said, doing her best to sound positive. She went around the room, cleaning up the mess of Felicity's tantrum.

"Sure, for some girls. They got to wear cute little sailor outfits, or even snappy officer uniforms." Felicity shook her head. "But not me." Now overcome with anger, she struggled to go on. "I got stuck with...I got stuck with...with...*that!*" She exploded in tears, collapsing on the bed yet again, as years of frustration poured forth.

Since the summer of 1906, once a year, the Greenwich Country Club held an annual charity fashion show. Originally held to raise money to help the victims of the earthquake in San Francisco, the event continued on, year after year, in support of myriad causes. It was always held at the end of the summer and had grown to become the big event of the social season. And because the models for the show consisted entirely of the fifteen-year-old daughters of the best families in town, it had become an unofficial coming-out party for the young girls of Greenwich society.

Year after year, Felicity had sat in one of the wooden folding chairs lining the runway that had been set up in the main dining room at the country club, as the girls paraded up and down in the latest dresses from New York. An auction was held, and the fathers of the young girls all tried to outdo each other, bidding crazy amounts of money for their daughters; all of it going to whatever charity the event was sponsoring that year.

Ever since it had been Felicity's sister Kathryn's turn six years earlier, Felicity had spent hours and hours dreaming of this day. She had watched as her mother and Kathryn made trip after trip into Manhattan to find just the right dress. In the end, they did, and Kathryn dazzled the crowd in a gown by Dior. She was sold for the highest amount. Three years ago, it was her sister Patricia who turned heads in a dress by Givenchy, and she also sold for the highest amount. And today, it was to be Felicity's turn.

The event was held, as always, on the last Sunday of August at 3:00 p.m., in the main dining hall. But other than that, everything about the 1944 Greenwich Country Club's charity fashion show was different. This was, after all—as Felicity was tired of hearing—a nation at war. Gone were the elegant silk draperies that lined the walls. They had been replaced by garish—at least in Felicity's opinion—red, white, and blue bunting. Because of the shortage of virtually everything, it had been decided that the customary preshow reception would be canceled altogether. The final insult was the decision that, in support of the wartime need for austerity, they would reuse the gowns from the previous year. *The war, the stupid war,* Felicity found herself saying over and over again. Her dream day was turning into a horrible Christmas morning of opening one disappointing present after another.

Her dream of scouring every square inch of Manhattan with her mother for the perfect dress was gone. Her dream of finding the perfect shoes to go with it—from Paris, of course—was dead. Even enjoying her first grown-up reception at the county club was on the trash heap. The war; the stupid war.

The only bright spot had been her tracking down and securing the best dress from last year's event. Julie Langdon's mother and Felicity's mother were the best of friends, so the deal was made quickly, before any of the other mothers tried to get the dress. It was a Chanel, and Felicity felt that, with the right shoes, possibly borrowed from one of her sisters, and the right hat, she just might be able to make the outfit her own. And maybe, just maybe, with the right alterations—after all, *cutting* fabric would not hurt the war effort—she might just be able to turn the whole thing into a brand new outfit.

But as soon as she had all that figured out, the event organizer decided that, not only would this year's charity event be turned into a bond drive but that the girls, in honor of the courageous fighting men, would all wear military uniforms in the show. No sophisticated dresses, no fashionable hats, no high heels. Instead, it would be drab, shapeless army uniforms. The war; the stupid war!

Mr. Fontaine, an unmarried bachelor, was the coordinator at the country club—whenever one of her parents spoke of him, it seemed to elicit some sort of knowing giggle from the other—and he ran the event every year. He had the girls pull numbers out of a hat to see which one of the donated uniforms each would wear. Felicity's number got her an aging, dirty, smelly World War I brown wool doughboy uniform, complete with a musty gas mask. Horrified, Felicity begged Mr. Fontaine to let her switch with another girl. He agreed, but Felicity could not find one willing to trade with her. During the rehearsals, Mr. Fontaine came up with the idea that Felicity should wear the gas mask when she first stepped on the runway and then dramatically take it off. Felicity loved the idea, practicing over and over again in her bedroom, pulling off the mask and then throwing back her head, so her hair would spill out and over her shoulders. Even in her horrible uniform, that would get her attention. Maybe she could still be the star of the event. Maybe, just like her two sisters, she someone would buy her for the highest price.

As it turned out, she was the star of the event…but for the wrong reason. As planned, Felicity stepped out onto the runway with her face hidden behind the insect-eyed black rubber gas mask. But when the moment came for her to pull it off, revealing her perfectly curled and expertly styled hair, the straps at the back were tangled, and the mask wouldn't budge. Felicity spent her entire walk up and down the runway, struggling unsuccessfully to remove the mask, with the attached carbon canister swinging back and forth in front of her like a crazed pendulum. She hurried off the runway, leaving behind a thunderous chorus of laughs. *The war; the stupid war.*

"I looked like a bug wrapped in a blanket!" Felicity exclaimed to Viola, still kicking and screaming on the bed. "I've never been so humiliated in my life."

When Viola had finished cleaning up the damage from Felicity's fit, she went to the closet and carefully removed an elegant evening gown. She meticulously placed the dress across the back of the chair at Felicity's vanity. "You'll be wanting to get dressed now, Miss Kensington. You'll have to leave in the next half hour for the dinner."

"I'm not going."

Viola stifled a laugh and then nodded in her direction. "Very well. I'll let Mrs. Kensington know."

"You do that."

Viola left the room, but Felicity remained sprawled on her bed. Of course she wasn't going. Not a snowball's chance in hell. Adding insult to injury, the evening part of the event, the formal dinner where fathers escorted their daughters to the club, also had been ruined. Felicity's father was still in Washington at some high-level conference with the Russians. He wouldn't be able to take her, and she would have to be escorted by her mother. Sure, there would be other girls in the company of their mothers because their fathers were scattered somewhere across the globe because of the stupid war, but none of them had been the laughingstock of the fashion show. No, she would just stay safely holed up in her room until tomorrow morning. That sounded awfully appealing to her. Maybe she'd stay hidden away all day tomorrow, too. Heck, why not until the end of the week? Or the month? Or the year? How about until the end of the stupid war? Yes. That was it. She would stay inside her room until the war was over and everything returned to normal.

Moments later, or so it seemed, Felicity was roused from a light sleep by the sound of a car crunching its way up the pebbled front drive. She pulled herself off the bed to look out the window, just as the car came to a stop in front of the house. A soldier exited from the backseat and then opened the front passenger door for Felicity's father, who stepped out and hurried into the house. *He's here! He didn't forget!* He'd found a way to make it back in time and escort her to the dinner. Her heart was beating fast, and her face felt flushed. Felicity quickly dressed—within minutes, she had her evening dress and shoes on, her hair combed and fixed, and her makeup touched up and ready. With her purse placed precisely on her right arm, just past the inside of her elbow, she stood by her four-poster bed, ready for her father's knock. She knew it would come any second, and after she had commanded him to come in, he would enter and see her composed and ready, a grown woman of fifteen, ready for her entrée into adult society. He would take her arm, lead her down the stairs into the waiting car, and they would be whisked off to the wonderland that the night would surely be.

As the minutes passed, Felicity fidgeted but held her ground. Her feet were really beginning to hurt, but she refused to sit on the bed for fear she would wrinkle her dress. Where was her father? Where was the knock that would begin this special night? Felicity snuck first one and then the other foot out of her shoes and flexed them. Then it occurred to her that she had made a huge mistake. He was waiting for her! He was perched at the bottom of their grand staircase, waiting for her to make a grand entrance by coming down to greet him, one step at a time.

Yes, that was it, Felicity realized. She hurried from her room and rushed over to the top of the stairs. She gave herself one last quick look over in the hall mirror and then, one careful step at a time, she began the journey down the winding carpeted staircase to her father below…except when the bottom of the staircase finally came into view, no one was there waiting. She hurried down the rest of the stairs, and as she stepped off the last stair and onto the hard tile floor of the entranceway, she heard his voice—and it was loud. Felicity peered into the large living room where her mother and father were standing near the bar.

"What was I supposed to do? Say no?" Scott said forcefully. He had a half-empty glass of brandy in his hand and gestured with it as he went on. "He's the Soviet foreign minister, and when the secretary of war tells you that you have to play host to him, you have to play host to him!" He finished the glass and quickly poured himself another. "You think I want him here?" Scott went on. "It's bad enough I have to sit through the conference and watch as they give the godless Commies an equal place in the post-war world. We're winning this damn thing for them, and then we're going to give them half the spoils. Goddamn Rosen*feld*!"

Felicity winced. She could tell just how angry her father was. Whenever he had reached his boiling point, he would start referring to President Roosevelt as President Rosen*feld*, a reference to his being a secret Jew.

But Scott's ranting against the Commies and the president only made Felicity's mother more nervous, and she paced around the room. "I just really wish you had given me a little more warning," Martha said.

"I thought I did. I had a telegram sent, but personal communications are lowest priority, and I guess I beat it here." Scott moved toward her. "Look, he'll just be here for ten, fifteen minutes, and then he'll head on to New York, and we'll follow an hour or so after. That should give you plenty of time to pack."

"Pack!" Felicity found herself saying loudly. "Where are you two going *tonight*?"

Scott and Martha turned in Felicity's direction. "After the Soviet foreign minister departs, we're heading into the city," her father said nonchalantly. "There's a Russian war relief rally we need to attend." He glanced at her offhandedly, and Felicity straightened up, waiting for him to compliment her gown. But he didn't. Instead, Scott turned away and took another sip from his drink.

Martha offered a feeble smile. "I know you won't mind my going with him. Viola told me you wanted to skip the dinner at the club," Martha said, and then she added, "You look very nice."

"Thank you," Felicity answered. She looked hopefully in her father's direction, but again his focus was elsewhere, pouring another drink. She stifled her disappointment. "Yes. That's right. I don't want to go to the dinner. Have fun in New York." Her mother gave Felicity a kiss on the check, and Felicity found tears welling up in her eyes. She turned to run up the stairs, but Viola was on her way down, carrying her parents' suitcases. With seemingly nowhere else to go, Felicity bolted out the front door as her cheeks began to moisten with fresh tears. Her father's driver was enjoying a smoke as he leaned against the hood of his car, and he looked up at her as she ran out onto the front porch.

She could feel the driver's eyes on her. No longer caring about her dress or her shoes or her hat, she ran toward the side of the house and darted behind the clumps of bushes that surrounded it. As she pushed her way through that small space between the bushes and the house itself, her dress caught on branches and leaves, but Felicity kept going. Ten years ago, her mother had added a second solarium on to the house for her committee meetings. The extension had created a small nook where the old section ended and the new one began. Felicity considered it her secret place, and she used it whenever she wanted to be alone in her own private world, away from everyone in the house. She would sit for hours, peering out through the bushes, watching the comings and goings of the house—her father heading off to work, her mother greeting fellow committee members as they arrived for meetings, her oldest sister with her boyfriend, and her middle sister running off with a gaggle of her friends. She could see the whole world go by, all from the safety of her little nook. Now, as Felicity collapsed onto the slightly wet soil, she cared not the slightest that her dress was hopelessly ruined. Forget about hiding out in her room; this was where she would spend the rest of the war. Safe in her nook, watching the world, without the world's knowing it was being watched.

Suddenly, she saw her father's driver drop his cigarette, crush it into the ground, and move quickly. Felicity tensed, sure he was coming to look for her and would expose her secret hiding place. But instead, the driver leaped behind the wheel of her father's car and drove away, parking several hundred feet down the driveway. A moment later, another large staff car drove up. A soldier in a strange brown uniform hopped out from the front seat and opened the rear door behind him. A short, gaunt man in an ill-fitting dark suit stepped out. Almost perfunctorily, he took in his surroundings before marching up the front stairs and into Felicity's house.

Russians! These were Russians!

Felicity had seen pictures of them in newspapers and magazines and newsreels but never before in person. They weren't that strange, though they definitely looked a bit different. She watched as two other Russian soldiers got out of the car and joined the soldier who had opened the door for his superior. Felicity shifted her position for a better look. She realized it wasn't that they looked different; it was that they acted different. Their mannerisms, their body language, their very being was so different from what she was used to. They were brusque, angular in their movements, harsh, and, Felicity thought, as if they were on the ready for something bad to happen. But it wasn't as if they were humorless; quite the contrary, they were almost comical as they messed with each other, knocking off hats from heads, slapping away cigarettes from mouths. They just seemed a bit on guard. Perhaps she'd feel that way if she came from a country that had come within an eyelash of being conquered by the Nazis, or if she was visiting a foreign land five thousand miles from home.

The three Russians suddenly marched off toward a thicket of birch trees about a hundred yards away, and Felicity saw that they'd spotted the swing that hung from a high branch. They soon were taking turns swinging back and forth. Felicity again moved to get a better view of their play, though staying safely hidden behind the shrubs. They took turns standing on the swing so they could use their whole bodies to make them swing higher and higher. Soon, they were swinging wildly, all the while laughing and cursing, as at each end of their swooping arcs, they were almost parallel to the ground. Then two of the soldiers got on at the same time, trying to swing even higher. But it was an awkward fit, each soldier working against the other, and they swung chaotically in all directions. Finally, completely out of control, both soldiers fell off the swing, landing hard in a puddle of mud. Laughing, both soldiers climbed to their feet, brushing mud from their uniforms. As all three Russians headed back to their car, Felicity moved farther back into the safety of her nook. When they reached the car, one of the two who had fallen spotted something and pointed right at Felicity.

Oh, my God! I've been seen!

The two dirty Russians walked straight for her. Felicity pushed up against her house, desperately attempting to keep herself hidden. But it clearly was not working, as the Russians closed in on her. She was going to be caught!

But then, when they were just three feet away, just on the other side of the shrubs from where she crouched against the house, they didn't stop. They kept walking, finally stopping about fifteen feet away at a faucet attached to the outside wall of the solarium. Felicity relaxed as the two soldiers turned on the water and began to wash the mud from their hands.

Being this near to them, Felicity could see even more clearly just how different they were. Though they continued the playing around and joking, their faces were hard, their gazes focused as they muttered to each other in Russian. Intrigued and wanting to see more, Felicity carefully eased herself forward until she was fewer than ten feet from them.

They both had broad shoulders and thick chests that easily filled their strange uniforms. The blond-haired soldier, a tad taller than the other one, was finished cleaning his hands and moved aside so the one with thinning dark hair could get at the faucet. When the dark-haired soldier stuck his hands under the flowing water, he briefly washed his hands, and then he grabbed his left hand with his right hand and pulled. His left hand easily separated from his left arm, popping out of his uniform sleeve like a cork from a bottle of wine, revealing that it was made of wood.

"Oh!" Felicity gasped, shocked as she realized there must be a stump hidden up his sleeve. Her hands quickly clasped her mouth, but it was too late. Her exclamation had already betrayed her.

The two Russians began a loud conversation in jabbing, curt Russian as the dark-haired soldier tried to quickly reattach his wooden hand. Felicity froze, unable to move a single part of her body. She could only pray that they might just turn and walk away. But her prayers went unanswered as the blond Russian, a mischievous smile lighting his otherwise grim face, stepped toward Felicity. The closer he got to her, the more excitedly the dark-haired soldier shouted at him in Russian. Finally, when the blond soldier was just a feet away from Felicity and clearly eyeing her through the thick shrubbery, the dark-haired soldier yelled one last time in Russian and then hurried away.

Felicity was now alone with the blond Russian, who moved from side to side, trying to get a better look at her through the foliage. "Come now, Little," he finally said in broken, guttural English. "I no mean harm."

But Felicity was not about to go anywhere. She scurried back into her nook and clutched the wall.

The Russian laughed. "Okay, Little. I back up. Then you come out. Okay?" Not waiting for an answer, he moved about twenty feet away from the shrubbery. But Felicity stayed in her nook. "Come now," he coaxed. "You cannot stay there all night."

Oh, yeah? Felicity thought. *Watch me!*

"You will catch cold."

Fat chance; it's boiling out here. In fact, it's more comfortable here in the bushes than in the house.

"Or maybe is too hot in there. You need to be cooled down?" The Russian moved toward the faucet, attached a coiled hose, and turned it on. He playfully sprayed the water in Felicity's direction, staying clear of her at first but then slowly moving the stream of water closer and closer to her. Felicity tried using the corner of the house to shield herself, but it was no use. If she didn't move, she would be doused at any second.

Felicity burst out of the shrubs, coming to a stop about ten feet from the Russian. She was a mess—her gown was covered in mud and sticks and leaves and thorns and flower petals. She wanted to brush the mess away but was too afraid to move.

The Russian calmly turned off the faucet and took a long look at her. "Much better to see you in person." He then squinted his wide-set eyes. "How old are you?"

"Eighteen," Felicity lied.

"A child. I am old man of twenty."

Twenty! Felicity thought. *That's impossible! He looks older than my father does.* This close, she could see that his skin was weathered and creased. His eyes, although they sparkled in agreement with his devilish smile, also exhibited a slight weariness, as if pained by all that they had seen. *Twenty! Impossible.* She thought of all the young men she knew who were twenty—fresh-faced kids with ruddy cheeks and hints of acne.

"You do not believe me?" the Russian asked, clearly reading Felicity's skepticism.

"Well, you don't really look that young."

"Then you must take closer look." The Russian stepped toward her. Felicity instantly backed away, scared. "Relax. I not bite." Felicity almost chuckled and eased up a bit. The Russian moved toward her again, this time slower. Felicity allowed him to move to within almost a foot of her. "What you think now?" he asked.

Felicity studied his face. There were hints of his professed younger age—a touch of acne, a weak beard, even some slight baby fat just below his jawline. She nodded to him, signaling that she believed him.

"Good. I am Vitaly." He held out a large, leathery hand.

Felicity paused for a moment and then accepted it. Her soft, tiny hand completely disappeared in his. "I am Felicity."

They shook, and then their hands parted. Nothing was said, but Felicity found it hard to take her eyes off him. *Why is this?* she wondered. He was so ill mannered, so lacking in refinement. Yet the fact remained that she couldn't bring herself to look elsewhere. She always wondered why her sister's friends always had crushes on the stable boys at the club, but now, she thought she might understand. He was different, and that was exciting.

"Where are you from?" she found herself asking.

"My family is farmers. We grow potatoes to make for vodka." He reached out for Felicity, who again recoiled. "Sorry. Sorry." Then, moving much slower, he reached out again and plucked a thorny branch from Felicity's collar. He showed it to her, touching a fingertip to one of the sharp thorns. "I worried it would cut your skin. And your skin is so nice; it would be crime."

Felicity found herself blushing. "How long will you be in America?"

Vitaly reached out again—and this time Felicity did not recoil—and began removing more of the debris that had accumulated on her gown. "We head to New York today, for few days. Then we go to rest of your country."

"Are you on vacation?"

Vitaly laughed. "No. We are war heroes." He motioned toward the other two soldiers standing by the car. "We are here to raise money and goods for Mother Russia."

"Oh, right," Felicity said, suddenly remembering. "My mother is donating some old clothes for Russian war relief."

Vitaly bowed his head. "Thank you." As they talked, he continued removing pieces of vegetation from her gown. But instead of dropping it to the ground, he held the growing accumulation in his free hand. "There is big rally tomorrow in Manhattan."

Felicity nodded. "Yes, I know. My mother is going, along with my father."

"And what about you?"

"Oh, no. I can't go. They want a night away from the children."

Vitaly shook his head. "You are eighteen, right?"

Felicity found herself nodding in agreement. She was used to others mistaking her for someone older. For the last couple of years she'd become accustomed to her male classmates' shy stares, and her father's friends' more lingering glares.

"Eighteen is not children," Vitaly continued. "Eighteen is woman. You are woman. Beautiful woman."

Felicity stared at the ground. "Even if I could go, I don't like New York. It scares me." She wasn't making this up to mollify Vitaly. She really did dislike Manhattan. From a very early age, her parents had regularly dragged her the thirty miles into the city, and she found the place terrifying with its noise and traffic and haze and congestion. There was only one spot on the entire island that she liked—the northwest corner of 51st and Broadway. On that spot stood the Burke-Reese building, built in 1928 to house the Burke-Reese insurance company. The eagle was the company logo, and on the outside of the building at the eighteenth floor, four giant metallic eagles majestically stood guard, one on each corner of the building. On her very first trip into the city, when she was no more than four years old—and completely terrified by the overwhelming experience—she and her father had passed the building, and he'd pointed up, making sure she saw the gleaming eagles. He told her that, whenever she came in to Manhattan, they would always be there to protect her. It worked to soothe the young Felicity, if only a little bit. On every trip after that, her father and mother made sure that she saw them.

Vitaly smiled at her. "Not problem. You come see me in New York. I make it all right." Vitaly held out his closed hand and then opened it, revealing that his fingers had pressed all of the thorny branches and scratchy leaves and fallen flower petals that he had picked off Felicity into a sweet little bouquet. "See, I can take something quite bad and turn it into something quite wonderful."

Completely charmed, Felicity took it from him.

The front door to her house opened, and the small gaunt man exited, flanked by Felicity's father. The dark-haired soldier whistled, grabbing Vitaly's attention. "I must go," Vitaly said, full of regret, "but hopefully, this is not good-bye." He gave her a playful bow and hurried off to join the others at the car.

As Felicity watched the Russians disappear down the driveway, she twirled the tiny bouquet between her thumb and index finger.

The drive into the city took longer than it took Felicity to convince her parents to let her go with them. Maybe her mother felt a sense of guilt, or maybe her father was just indifferent, but either way, they had put up only token resistance to her pleas to not be alone in the house that night. There was some truth to her protestations. Since Kathryn had married and moved, the house had felt emptier and emptier to Felicity. Kathryn's new husband, Lieutenant August Grayson, had been sent to New Mexico by the army air corps so he could run a school for meteorologists—and Patricia was spending more and more of her time down in Old Greenwich, volunteering with her friends at the local train station. But the real truth was that most of the emptiness she was feeling was because she was missing out in the adventures they were having.

Kathryn was thriving as the wife of an army officer, and Patricia was in heaven, spending her days greeting the endless stream of troop trains that passed through Old Greenwich. Felicity was particularly tired of listening to Patricia and her friends talk about all the cute boys they were meeting, about how the soldiers would whistle and flirt with the girls as they passed cigarettes, cookies, and other treats up to them through the train car windows. And of course, each girl had her own special story of a private interaction with a soldier, which had almost led to a quick stolen kiss. Felicity could almost recite Patricia's story: "A beautiful, clear spring day with a perfect blue sky, filled with singing birds" was always in her endless retellings. One of the trains had to stop in Old Greenwich for two hours because of locomotive problems. The soldiers disembarked, and Patricia had allowed a strapping six-foot-four lumberjack from Oregon to talk her into going for a walk. As soon as they were out of view of the others, the lumberjack had tried to kiss Patricia, but she had demurred, explaining that she was a lady, not some common V-girl. They had finished the walk, and Patricia admitted that she had allowed their good-bye hug to linger a few seconds longer than she should have "because I might just be the last fair flesh he ever feels." That last pronouncement always elicited lovelorn sighs from her friends—and the urge to gag from Felicity.

But now, if everything went the way Felicity was planning it would, the next time the girls all got together to tell romantic stories, she would be able to join right in. And she would have the best story of all—better than any of Kathryn's tales of her husband's command, and certainly better than Patricia's mild flirtations. A romantic evening in New York City with a Russian war hero—no one could top that. And maybe, just maybe, her story would end with a kiss.

But as soon as they checked into their room at the Waldorf-Astoria, everything went awry. Her parents had planned to hire a babysitter to look after Felicity while they went out for dinner that night. Felicity was counting on this, as a babysitter would not be suspicious when Felicity decided to go to bed at eight o'clock, only to sneak out minutes later. But the hotel manager informed them that they could not find a babysitter; all of the girls they'd formerly had on call had gone off to better-paying jobs in war production. Her mother decided to skip the dinner and stay in the room with Felicity.

Felicity knew her plan now had zero chance of success. Her mother would be highly suspicious of her going to bed at eight, but even if she let that slide, Felicity could never sneak out past her.

"It's really not necessary. I can stay in the room myself. I'll be fine," Felicity offered, trying to hide her desperation.

"Nonsense," her mother answered. "We'll have a girl's night."

"No, no. You should go. I mean it." Felicity hoped she didn't sound panicky. But her mother didn't bother to answer. Instead, she left Felicity in the living room of the suite and went into the bedroom that they were sharing. Through the doorway, Felicity watched as her mother began to undress, preparing for their night in. She turned to her father. "I'm really fine on my own."

Her father threw up his arms. "When your mother makes a decision, she makes a decision."

"There must be something you can do. Maybe try the front desk again," Felicity said with as much optimism as she could muster. "You never know."

Her father shrugged. "You're right. You never know." He slumped into the other bedroom, not even trying to hide his lack of faith in the idea.

Alone, Felicity collapsed on the couch, defeated. It was over. The war had won. Again. There would be no night on the town with her Russian war hero. No crowded dance floor in a crazy club uptown. No late-night stroll through Central Park. No quick midnight kiss before she had to hurry off to beat her parents back to the room. Instead, she would spend the night with her mother, listening to her prattle on about one of her committees, and the next time Patricia and her friends got together, Felicity would have nothing to share with them.

No. This could not stand. She had to do something. Felicity pulled herself off the couch and hurried into the next room. Her mother had finished undressing and was cinching her robe over her nightgown.

"Mom, I'm almost sixteen. I don't need a babysitter anymore. I want you to go." Felicity knew she was pleading, but she was past the point of worrying about looking bad.

"Honey, that's very sweet of you. And I agree, you could stay here by yourself. Only I don't want you to be alone. I don't want you to be bored."

If she only knew, Felicity thought.

"Besides, I really want to tell you what happened at the steering committee meeting this afternoon. Bitsy Walker had the craziest idea—"

Felicity wanted to scream, but before she could even open her mouth, her father excitedly burst into the room. "Get dressed, Martha. You're going out!"

Martha shook her head, confused. "But who will stay with Felicity?"

Without saying a word, Scott led them into the common room of the suite, just as there was a knock at the door. "They called up from the front desk just a moment ago," Scott said as he opened the door. The hotel manager stepped past him, pushing a wooden box on wheels; the box had a dark glass plate affixed to its front.

"What's that?" Martha asked.

"It's called a television," Scott answered proudly.

"Yes," the manager said as he placed the set in the middle of the room and then searched for a socket to plug it in. "We've been experimenting with using this as a sort of electronic babysitter."

"I've always wanted to see television," Felicity said, hoping to sound excited; in truth, she really didn't know what it was.

The manager found a wall socket, plugged in the set, and turned it on. A soft hum, like a radio warming up, filled the room. Felicity and her parents stepped up to the screen and stared, their eyes as wide as saucers.

Nothing happened.

Scott turned to the hotel manager. "Is there something else—"

"Just give it a second."

The four of them continued to stare into the dark screen. Slowly, the screen began to glow, becoming brighter and brighter with a blue-white light. Then, just as slowly, from within the glow an image appeared—a man sitting at a desk, talking. The manager reached over and turned a knob below the screen and sound suddenly poured out of the television set, in sync with the moving lips of the man at the desk. He was a reporter, reading a newscast.

"Now what do you do?" Scott finally asked.

"You watch it," the manager answered brightly.

"Really?" Scott said, unsure.

Felicity quickly grabbed a chair, placed it directly in front of the screen, and sat down. She leaned forward, seemingly entranced. "I love it," she said, staring wistfully into the glowing screen.

Satisfied, her mother quickly dressed, tossed Felicity an offhand, "We'll be back around midnight," and left with her father.

The second the hotel room door clicked shut, Felicity was on her feet. She raced over to her suitcase, rummaged through, and pulled out the dress she had reworked from last year's fashion show. She would get a chance to wear the dress after all. Almost as excitedly, she pulled out a brand new pair of nylons that her mother had given her two years earlier when they first became scarce. She'd been saving them for a big occasion and was devastated when it turned out she wouldn't be able to wear them for the country club fashion show, but now they were going to an even better cause.

Moments later, she was dressed. She checked herself in the bathroom mirror. The dress hugged her figure even better than she had hoped, and her legs were smooth and sexy. She was ready. She grabbed a light coat, draped her purse over her arm, and headed for the door. She was about to leave, when she remembered the television. It was still playing.

On the screen, the newscaster was droning on about the war in Europe. The volume wasn't that loud, but it seemed strange to Felicity to leave it on. She looked around for an on/off switch but wasn't able to recognize one. Frustrated, she pulled the plug from the wall, and the screen instantly went dark, save for a small bright dot in the center of the screen. Felicity watched the tiny glowing spot for a moment, until it, too, faded away. With the sound gone and the screen safely blank, Felicity headed out.

Felicity had no trouble finding the Russians. On their way into the hotel, her father had stopped by the front desk to have a message sent to the Russian foreign minister about their dinner plans for the evening. In the ensuing conversation, the desk clerk had informed them that the Russian party had two rooms, one for the foreign minister and the other for the gentlemen who were traveling with him. Both room numbers were mentioned, with Felicity taking note of the one she was interested in.

Stepping off the elevator, she followed the room numbers toward the room she was looking for. As she drew closer and closer, the bombastic sound of Russian military music grew louder and louder. When she got to the correct door, the music was almost deafening.

Felicity straightened her dress, patted her hair, pinched her cheeks, and then knocked on the door. Nothing happened. The loud music played on and on. She knocked again. Again nothing happened. Finally, using the side of her fist, she pounded on the door. A moment later, it was pulled open.

A tall, lanky Russian with a smooth, baldhead peered down at her. He was wearing an off-white T-shirt with his uniform pants. His unexpected attire made Felicity uncomfortable, and it took a moment before she recognized him as the third Russian who had been waiting by the car in front of her house. It wasn't clear if he recognized her, but after scrutinizing her through narrowed eyes, he cracked a grin, showing bright, perfect teeth. Too perfect. They shimmered like polished piano keys, and Felicity could tell they were obviously fake. "Da?" the lanky Russian asked, clearly enjoying the sight of a pretty, young girl at his door.

Felicity tried to peer past him into the room, but his tall frame blocked her view. "I…well…I'm looking for Vitaly."

"Vitaly? You are looking for Vitaly?"

"Yes."

"Why are you not looking for me?" he said playfully. As he spoke, Felicity could see that his bottom teeth were also fake.

"Well, ah…"

"Sergei, what are you doing?" asked a familiar voice from within the room. The lanky Russian, Sergei, frowned and moved aside. Looking past him, Felicity spotted Vitaly sitting on the bed, his back against the wall, reading. A thick, choking haze of cigarette smoke filled the room as both he and the one-handed Russian, who was sitting at a table, feverishly smoked. When Vitaly spotted Felicity, he leaped off the bed, quickly buttoning his open uniform shirt. He stubbed out his cigarette in a nearby shot glass, turned down the record player, and hurried over to her. Sergei reluctantly gave up his spot at the door and returned to the table, slipping into the chair where his uniform shirt hung. He grabbed a cigarette and lit up, adding even more smoke to the haze.

"Hello," Vitally said, flashing a grin that Felicity was pleased to see contained all real teeth. "So you make it to New York."

"Yes."

"Now what shall we do?" Vitaly asked, clearly pleased.

Before Felicity could answer, shouting erupted from the table. Sergei and the wooden-handed Russian were arm wrestling while using their free hands to take shots of vodka.

Vitaly rubbed the back of his head, embarrassed. "Perhaps we will start by leaving."

On Park Avenue, cars hurled by, horns blared, cops yelled, and passersby pushed and shoved. It took all Felicity's strength not to turn around and run back into the hotel. But then she looked to Vitaly. His head craned back and forth in swooping arcs as his eyes darted from building to building to building to building. He was trying to take in everything, and his face lit up with delight at the sheer folly of the task. She could have sworn she heard him giggle. *How is it*, Felicity thought, *that this man from six thousand miles away, who lived on a farm in the middle of nowhere, should be so excited, while I am so scared?*

And why was she so scared?

It wasn't all bad. The heavy night air felt good and warm and comforting. The last streaks of red and gold sunlight hitting the very top of the tallest buildings had a certain majesty. The rumble of the nearby elevated train had a powerful but soothing vibration to it. Suddenly, she no longer felt overwhelmed by the city; she felt challenged by it. How was this possible? Was she really feeling this way? Then it occurred to her: it was Vitaly. He was right. He had taken something bad and made it good. Standing next to him, she felt safe—no, more than safe. Excited. Wonderfully overwhelmed by the moment, she took Vitaly's arm.

Pleased, he looked down at her. "Where you want to go?"

Felicity did her own swooping arc with her head. It was almost night, and the fading light felt like a preamble to the excitement the darkness would bring. She looked up at him, smiling. "Everywhere."

They started at 21, because, much to Felicity's astonishment, Vitaly had heard about the famous nightclub all the way over in Russia. She had been there a few times with her parents and always found the place loud and uncomfortable. But tonight, on Vitaly's arm, she found it a wonderland of excitement and glamour. She loved the way others did a double take when they saw Vitaly. Sure, the place was full of officers, but he was the only Russian officer, and she was the only woman on the arm of a Russian officer. They had a nice dinner, and Vitaly relished the generous amount of meat in his roast beef sandwich. But the meal came to an abrupt end when Vitaly practically gagged as he tasted his after-dinner vodka. "This is not vodka," he proclaimed. Disgusted, he grabbed Felicity's arm and dragged her out of the restaurant before she had a chance to finish her dessert.

After sliding into a cab, Vitaly produced a small glass pint from inside his uniform jacket. He unscrewed the top, took a drink, and then sighed happily. "Now that is drink." He held the pint out for Felicity. "Have some, Little."

"No, that's okay. I'm not really thirsty."

Vitaly showed her the label. The word "Kelechniko" was written in ornate Cyrillic over a drawing of a small village. "This is my family's brand. You must try."

Felicity was about to refuse again, but she stopped herself. Was she making a mistake? There was something incredibly romantic about this man's wanting to share a part of his world with her. She could imagine the envy-filled eyes of her sister and her friends as Felicity retold this part of her evening, of the longing on Vitaly's face for her to experience some part of his life in Russia. "Okay," Felicity said, reaching out for the pint.

She raised the small glass bottle to her mouth and took a small sip of the clear liquid. The tingle on the end of her tongue reminded her of mouthwash.

Vitaly laughed. "Do not be afraid. It is good stuff."

She took another sip, almost a mouthful. It burned on its way down.

"What you think?" Vitaly asked.

"It's good," Felicity said, with nothing to compare it to—this was her first taste of hard alcohol.

"That's because we grow best potatoes in all of Ukraine," Vitaly said proudly.

Felicity nodded, her head suddenly feeling a bit

Felicity took another drink, and this one went down a lot more smoothly, warming her on its way to her stomach. Much to her surprise, she liked it—she really did. At their next stop, the Copacabana, whenever Vitaly offered her another drink from the bottle, she happily took it. She found the more she drank, the more she felt like dancing and the more she enjoyed the tight feel of Vitaly's muscular arms around her as they moved about the dance floor…and the lower she would allow his hand to wander down her back. For the first time, she understood why her father always headed straight to the bar in the living room when he came through the door at the end of a long day.

But at their next stop, El Morocco, after another quick drink before hitting the dance floor, she found she was having trouble remembering things. She knew where she was and who she was with, but the details were starting to slip away. This upset her. She had to be able to tell Patricia and her friends all that had happened, but she feared it was all getting lost. So, despite Vitaly's protestations, she refused more vodka and forced herself to remember the way he led her into a room, as if presenting her as a great prize: the tickle of his stubble when he pulled her in close; the slashing scar she could see just below his shirt collar—sure it had come from whatever heroic deed he had done to win all those medals; the approving nods she got from other women as he led her across the crowded clubs.

Soon they were in another cab, heading toward Times Square. "I think I should get back to the hotel," Felicity said, as much tired as drunk.

"One more club, Little. We meet up with my friends."

Felicity thought for a moment. It was only eleven; she did have a little more time. "Okay. But no more drinking."

The cab let them off at Broadway and 44th Street, and they stepped out just as a cloud of smoke from the famous smoking Camel sign descended on them from above. Nearby, down 44th Street, Felicity could see a small line of soldiers waiting to go into a club that was below street level. From numerous articles and even a couple of movies, Felicity recognized it as the Stage Door Canteen, the famous club where celebrities worked as hostesses and waiters for soldiers headed overseas. As they walked toward it, her face lit up. This would be the perfect ending to her story. A first kiss while dancing in the arms of her Russian boyfriend in the Stage Door Canteen! Yes, that was how she would tell it to her sister Patricia and her friends. And yes, she would call Vitaly her Russian boyfriend, especially after he sent her letters. Or telegrams. Or flowers. These would all come from her Russian boyfriend. Felicity was flushed with excitement as they closed in on the Canteen. Could this night get any better? But about a hundred feet away from the club's entrance, Vitaly suddenly pulled her into an alley.

"We must have another drink before we go in," he said, as he once again pulled the bottle from inside his uniform jacket.

"Oh, no. No more for me. I've had enough," Felicity said, not exaggerating in the least.

"But they do not serve alcohol inside."

"Sounds good to me." She moved to head back out to 44th Street, but Vitaly grabbed her arm and pulled her back.

"Just one more drink," he said innocently. "There is very little left. This is the last bottle I have. I want to finish it with you."

Touched by his words, Felicity nodded. Vitaly handed her the bottle, and she lifted it to her mouth. There was actually quite a bit left, and with her mouth full of the burning liquid, she handed the bottle back to Vitaly. He didn't take it; instead, as she tried to swallow, he pushed his body against her, pressing his lips into hers.

They felt like two rough pillows—so much larger than her own petite features that they completely surrounded her mouth. With the last of the vodka finally down her throat, she returned the kiss, though when he tried to pry her lips open with his forceful tongue, she pushed him away.

"Okay, Vitaly, that was—"

He was on her again, and right away he forced the issue with his tongue. Felicity resisted for a moment. This was not exactly the romantic parting kiss that she knew she would be retelling for the next five years, but finally, she acquiesced. His rough, probing tongue found hers, and they slithered against one another until Felicity could take no more. She pushed hard to get him off her.

Surprised, Vitaly caught himself and quickly regained his balance. He turned to her, hurt. "What? You do not like me?"

"I like you, Vitaly. A lot. But I think you want something I cannot give you."

"Why can you not give it to me? You are woman."

"Yes, but not that kind of woman."

Vitaly held out the bottle for her. "Perhaps you need more drink."

"No, definitely not. I think I should go." Felicity stepped toward the alley entrance, but Vitaly grabbed her and pulled her back. He pushed her up against the alley wall, this time holding her in place with all his weight. Felicity fought to get away, but with one hand Vitaly held her flailing arms at bay, and with the other, he reached under her skirt and moved his calloused hand along her inner thigh.

"No! Vitaly, stop! Did you hear—"

Vitaly pulled out a handkerchief and pressed it against her mouth to shut her up. Felicity twisted under his weight, desperately looking toward the alley entrance in the hope of a passerby seeing her. Instead, she saw the wooden-handed Russian walking toward her, with Sergei lagging behind at the alley entrance, keeping guard. There was a ripping sound, as Felicity realized Vitaly had pulled down her underwear. She fought harder, which only made Vitaly lean into her more, pressing the rough brick into her back.

"Come now, Little, you must be good to me. We are allies." He unbuckled his pants and dropped them to the ground.

Felicity struggled again, fighting his hold on her arms and the weight of his body against her. It was pointless. Every time she pushed, he pushed back harder. She could feel the bricks cutting into her back. Suddenly, she felt a hard pressure inside her, and she closed her eyes as he began thrusting wildly. She tried to scream, but he held the handkerchief tightly against her mouth. Finally, her whole body went limp as she stopped fighting.

She lost track of time and felt herself losing consciousness. He finally paused but only for a moment, and then he started up again. As he forced himself into her, the hand clutching the handkerchief moved, coming within reach of her teeth. Felicity flexed her jaw and bit down hard. Instantly, pain shot through her mouth—she'd bitten into solid wood. Felicity opened her eyes; it was the wooden-handed Russian who was fucking her now. Ten minutes later, after Sergei's turn, it was over.

She stood motionless against the brick wall. Sergei and the wooden-handed Russian walked out of the alley, singing a Russian song. Vitaly gave her a lazy smile. "They do not allow dates inside Canteen, so this is good-bye, Little." Vitaly kissed her on the cheek. "You are good to soldiers." He finished off the bottle of vodka and threw it farther into the alley, where it shattered loudly. He pulled out another unopened pint of vodka with the same Kelechniko label from his coat. Drinking from it, he hurried off after his friends, joining with them in their song.

In a daze, with her dress still bunched up around her stomach, Felicity slid to the ground. Pain shot through her body as her bruised and naked rear hit the hard pavement. Less than a hundred feet away, she watched the three singing Russians walk out of sight. She wanted desperately to get the hell out of there, but her whole body hurt. Maybe if she just sat there for a little while, she'd feel better. Her thighs would stop throbbing, her back wouldn't be sore, her wrists wouldn't be numb. Maybe if she sat there long enough, she'd wake up back in Greenwich, and it would turn out that none of this ever happened.

She closed her eyes, willing it to be so. She was back home, in her room, safely under the covers on a warm summer night, with the cacophony of busy insects singing her to sleep. Yes. Yes. She was home. It had never happened. But when she opened her eyes, Greenwich disappeared. She was still in the dirty alley, with her ass on the cold, hard ground and the prying eyes of the Camel-smoking man watching her in the distance. Her thighs still throbbed, her back was still sore, and her wrists were still numb.

She forced herself to stand and pulled up her torn underwear. The elastic was hopelessly stretched, and there were spots of blood and several large tears, but Felicity barely noticed. She wandered out of the alley onto 44th Street, suddenly knowing exactly where she needed to go. Miraculously, it was only seven blocks away, and it was the one thing that just might save her.

She made it to Broadway and headed north, fighting through the miserably crowded sidewalks. People were everywhere, yelling and screaming. Cops blew loud whistles, horns screeched, the sky was black with evil, and the air was frigid and unforgiving. Somehow, she made it the seven blocks to 51st and Broadway. But when she got there, they were gone. The Burke-Reese building still occupied the northwest corner, and it still shot twenty-two stories up into the air, but the gleaming metal eagles—the ones that had protected her for the last twelve years whenever she came to Manhattan—were gone. Felicity walked back and forth, her head aimed straight up, searching the outside of the eighteenth floor where they had once lived. But they were nowhere to be seen.

They have to be there, Felicity thought. *Where could they have gone?* She backed up, stepping into the street to get a better angle, but still, no eagles. Maybe she had the wrong building.

A taxi horn screamed at her to get back on the sidewalk. She did, but the cabbie stopped anyway. Unshaven and with a head of greasy, sloppy hair piled under his cap, he rolled down his window and peered out at her. "They're gone, Toots," he said, gruffly, nodding in the direction of the top of the building. "Taken down and melted to make bombers." Then he sped away.

Felicity took the news without even a twitch. She finally turned and looked up, one last time, hoping he might be wrong. But he wasn't. They were truly gone. The war. The stupid war.

Now that she was definitely not safe, Felicity hurried back to the hotel. Once inside the room, she desperately wanted to take a shower, but she knew her parents would be back any moment. She pulled off what was left of her underwear and tossed it in the garbage can, careful to cover it with several layers of toilet paper. She removed her dress. Small bloodstains dotted the front and back around the waistline. The dress was too big to be thrown away, she realized, so she opened her mother's extra suitcase—the one stuffed with her donations for the Russian war relief rally—and shoved the dress inside, burying it as deep as possible.

Now naked, she caught a glimpse of herself in the mirror. Her inner thighs were badly bruised, as were her wrists. She carefully touched a series of small cuts above her breasts, which, she realized, were from the ribbons and medals on the front of the soldiers' uniforms. Her right shoulder was badly scraped where the wooden-handed Russian had held her down. It would take some work, but she'd find a way to hide all of it from her mother.

She slipped on her nightgown and checked the clock. It was nearly midnight. She should be in bed, but she didn't feel like it; she knew the darkness would only bring nightmares. But if she were awake when her parents returned, they would want to know why. And in her current state, she was afraid she would tell them.

She wandered into the living room. The television still sat in the center, the night maid having come and gone without moving it. Felicity eyed the blank screen. *Why not?* She plugged it in. Once again, slowly, the image faded up. When it came fully into view, the screen filled with a static shot of what looked like a target. The words "test pattern" were written below the series of concentric circles. Confused, Felicity played with the knobs, until another station flipped into view. On the screen, a man and woman sat at a restaurant table, talking. Their dialogue was light and airy, and Felicity realized they were performing a play. It wasn't particularly good, but she sat down anyway. Soon her face became a distant mask, and she watched as the show ended and the station went off the air for the night. She stared at the test pattern for a few minutes before noticing, and then unplugged the television and went to bed.

The rally the next day was a blur. All Felicity could remember by the time they got back to Greenwich was that it had been outdoors, and there had been some speeches, some singing, and some other performances. Over the next few weeks, as the cuts healed and the bruises faded, the entire trip had become so fuzzy, that Felicity began to question whether the rape had actually happened. Maybe she had gotten it mixed up with something she had watched that night in the hotel. Maybe it was all caused by television. It was the first time she had ever seen it; who knew what kind of effect it might have had on her. But four months later, when her clothes stopped fitting, and her period stopped coming, she knew it had all been real.

After the predictable histrionics, her mother switched into committee chairman mode in dealing with the pregnancy. Two goals were quickly established: 1. Keep any knowledge of it from Felicity's father. 2. Keep any knowledge of it from anyone else. Within days she had hatched a plan that would achieve both goals. Felicity's grandmother, her mother's mother, had been in failing health for the last few years. A story was concocted that she had taken a bad fall and needed someone to look after her. Felicity volunteered, after professing a sudden interest in nursing, to be the family member to look after her. So off Felicity went to Andover, New Hampshire—as far as her father and the rest of Greenwich society were concerned—to be nursemaid for her ailing grandmother.

In reality, Felicity was about sixty miles southeast of the city, buried deep within the New Hampshire countryside, at a home set up for women from well-to-do families who were in a similar situation. Safely hidden from prying eyes, Felicity and the rest of the girls finished their pregnancies. Upon giving birth, the administration immediately gave the babies over to prearranged adoptive parents. And after a suitable amount of time, the girls returned to their families, freed of their scandal.

Felicity passed the time by taking walks, reading, and trying her hardest not to think of what she was missing. The winter formal, the spring formal, the first crew races on the river, the parties after the surrender of Germany. She blocked all of it out of her mind, until finally the day came in mid-May 1945 when she headed home.

Viola picked her up at the train station, and upon reaching her home, Felicity walked into a house that was preparing for a large dinner party. For a brief moment, she thought it was for her homecoming, but when she spotted the "Good-bye, Adolf" banner hanging in the dining room, she realized who the real guest of honor was. Germany had surrendered just a week or so earlier, and even though soldiers were still fighting and dying in the Pacific, everyone knew it was just a matter of time before the war was over.

There were about twenty guests, about half in uniform, and Felicity was seated at the middle of the table, between the mayor's wife and her mother. It was a spirited occasion, with her father, his dress uniform covered with every ribbon and medal he had, standing to make toast after toast. But things ground to a sudden halt when the Canadian ambassador, who was seated next to her father, rose and proposed a toast to "our Russian allies." A brief, mostly friendly disagreement broke out. The ambassador stated emphatically that, with the new United Nations, there would be no more wars; her father was equally as convinced that the Russians could not be trusted, and it was just a matter of time before we would be at war with them.

Felicity sat listening until she couldn't just listen anymore. "My father's right!" she said loudly, silencing the rest of the room.

Everyone turned to look at her, including her father. He smiled, clearly pleased, and he looked at her as if for the first time in a long time, he really noticed she was in the room with him. "I'm glad to see the time with your grandmother has done some serious good," he said.

Felicity didn't notice the compliment, as she looked at the rest of the table with a gaze that was hard and focused. "My father's right," Felicity said again. "The Russians are devious and evil and will say and do whatever it takes to get what they want. They are not to be trusted."

...

Jonny cracked open an eye and looked around. *Where am I?* he wondered. All he could see was a blinding vision of gold. He sat up on the love seat and saw Felicity across from him, asleep under a blanket on the couch, and he remembered where he was—far away in a mythical land only read about in books and magazines and as alien to Jonny as the moon. He was in Greenwich, Connecticut.

The golden vision had been the sun, newly risen and blasting through the window to reflect off the giant gold leaf frame of an enormous painting of a president from the last century. *Either Polk or Arthur,* Jonny thought, his mind going back to third grade, when his classroom had been decorated with a series of portraits of all thirty-two presidents.

He took in the rest of the room, realizing that this was a home that one of the presidents, one of those gods that had adorned his classroom wall, might very well have been in at one time or another. He'd never been in a room where a president might have been—the thought was inconceivable to him. But as he looked across at the angelic figure of Felicity, the blanket rising and falling with her shallow breaths, he realized that she probably had been—and more than once. And seeing the face that was either Polk or Arthur repeated in at least two other paintings and a marble bust, Jonny also realized that she might very well be related to one.

The night before, after Felicity had finished her story and their lovemaking had begun anew, the storm had intensified, with blasts of lightning strobing the room in a frenzy. With each flash, piece by piece, snippets of the house appeared to him. The swooping staircase, the carved wooden ceiling, oil paintings in ornate frames, marble busts atop carved pedestals, an antique desk, a nineteenth-century fainting couch, an oaken table with four chairs, several painting-lined passageways leading to other parts of the house—each snap of light had been like flipping the pages of a photo book of a historical home. But now, in the light of day, seeing it all at once made it seem oddly calm. Stiff. Remote. Like being in a museum. Jonny felt that if he opened his mouth and said something, someone would come rushing into the room to tell him to be quiet. How could someone live in a place like this, day to day? He would be afraid to touch anything, to sit anywhere, to allow the dirt of his shoes to come in contact with the plentiful antique rugs or imported carpeting.

Felicity began to stir. Jonny wrapped his naked body with his own blanket, slowly stood up, and stepped over to the couch. Her eyelids fluttered open. "Hi," she said, her gaze sated with the laziness of morning.

"Hi," Jonny offered back.

Felicity sat up. "What time is it?"

"Well, according to George over there"—Jonny pointed to a bust of George Washington that contained a clock in its base—"it's just past six o'clock."

"Really? That early?"

Jonny shrugged. "Unless he's decided to tell his first lie, it would appear so."

Felicity chuckled. Then, suddenly aware that she was naked under her blanket, she shyly rearranged the soft wool to cover her bare shoulders. With his bare chest exposed to her and standing amid two hundred years of American history, Jonny suddenly felt like an exhibitionist. Carefully shifting his blanket, not wanting to make things worse, he, too, covered as much of his naked body as possible. Then, with both of them covered like pieces of furniture in a closed summer home, an awkward silence descended on them. Sheepishly, they both broke off eye contact as the reality of the night before slowly returned, seeping back into their minds like the creeping shafts of morning sunlight that had begun to crisscross the room.

"The power's back on," Jonny said awkwardly, while indicating the glowing bulb in a tiffany lamp next to Felicity.

"It is. That's great," Felicity answered, with the same level of discomfort. The silence returned.

"You hungry?" Jonny managed to ask.

"Starved," Felicity answered, her gaze now on the immaculate white rug.

"Should we…go out?" Jonny offered.

Felicity nodded. "I know the perfect place."

"Great."

Neither one of them moved, and their eyes were on anything but each other. "We should…uh…probably get dressed," Felicity finally suggested.

"Great idea," Jonny agreed. He turned away to give Felicity some privacy but also so he could step over to the love seat, where his pants and shirt had been hurriedly tossed the night before. He quickly put his shirt on, but when he lifted his pants, expecting to see his underwear underneath, it was not there.

"Ah, Felicity?" Jonny asked carefully, still turned away from her.

"Yes?"

"My underwear…I think it might be on your couch."

"Yep, here it is," Felicity answered after a quick search.

"You want to throw it to me?" Jonny asked, his eyes still safely averted.

Felicity laughed. "Jonny, it's okay; you can turn around."

Jonny also laughed, thinking he was joining her in enjoying the absurdity of the situation, but when he turned around, Felicity stood before him, completely naked. Jonny stopped laughing.

Behind Felicity, neatly folded on the couch, was her blanket. Next to it, also neatly folded, were her clothes, and next to them, also folded, was Jonny's underwear.

But Jonny wasn't looking at any of that. His eyes were busy going up and down Felicity's magnificent naked body, which the light of the rising sun was bathing in gold and revealing even more of what had been lost to him in the darkness. In his hands, her breasts had been wonderfully firm and fleshy, topped by hard, rigid nipples. But in the amber light they were downright spectacular - perfectly curved mounds of exquisitely rich skin, with perfectly placed bubble-gum pink areolas and nipples. Her body, certainly fantastic to the touch, now revealed smooth, creamy skin, with a stomach begging to be kissed and a belly button begging to be tongued. Her legs, though he had seen them before, were astonishingly well shaped, leading the way to the excitement of her upper thigh and what lay beyond.

Felicity calmly shifted on her feet, a bemused smile betraying her obvious pleasure at what she was doing. "There's something we need to do before we go," Felicity said matter-of-factly.

This time, the lovemaking was slow, smooth, and purposeful. Gone was the unbridled lust, the clumsy tearing away of clothes, the wild and chaotic passion. Two people, now comfortable with one another, each focused on the other's pleasure. Hands were clasped meaningfully; kisses were long, deep, and wet; two bodies moved as one. Even without the storm, their shared climax was ten times more intense.

As they finally dressed, long gone was the tension. Though nothing was said, Jonny felt this last orgasmic entanglement meant that, in the light of day, Felicity wasn't regretting what had happened in the dark of night. Nor was he. He had no idea where it would go from here—getting involved with someone he worked with certainly had the potential for all sorts of problems—but at least last night would not be tossed away as an accidental stew of fate, timing, and bad weather.

And that put him in the highest of spirits.

There was a short conversation about riding bikes to the restaurant, followed by an even shorter conversation about riding horses, and then they piled into Felicity's car. Like seeing Felicity's body for the first time in the light of day, Jonny finally saw what her world really looked like as they sped away from her house. It was just as enticing.

Large mansions, encircled by even larger lawns, flitted by, one after another, each demanding notice. In many yards, children played happily before school, awaiting one of several perfect yellow school buses they passed. Soon, the blooming spring foliage thinned out to make way for small brick stores and stucco markets, all overflowing with morning shoppers. They crossed the highway and made the slight descent down toward the shore, and finally, after passing through a stone tunnel that ran under the train tracks, they emerged into Old Greenwich.

Felicity eased them to the curb in the middle of a small business district, and they hopped out into a crisp world of salty air and the distant clang of ship's bells. This caught Jonny off guard, and he found himself, much to his surprise, filling his lungs with the rich air—something that was inconceivable in New York, for fear of inhaling exhaust or urine or worse. As he looked around at the stillness, the green, and the contentment, he found it almost in the realm of science fiction that they were a mere twenty-five miles from the city—not even a half hour from the minute-to-minute battle that was Manhattan. Even more surprising, he wasn't repulsed. Oh sure, he was probably surrounded by the very people who had made possible—with their complicity or at least their indifference—the suffering so many of his friends had experienced. But hadn't he learned just the night before, in Felicity's tearful story, that maybe their lives weren't so perfect? Maybe they had their own struggles and their own nightmares to survive, yet they were able to experience this—the calm, the contentment, the serenity of an easy life. Maybe they'd earned it. And maybe, so had he.

Felicity moved up next to Jonny, gave him a slight nod with possibly just a touch of a wink—he wasn't sure—and they started to walk. The sidewalk was clean, and there were no more than a scattering of pedestrians. With each easy stride, Jonny felt his shoulders ease back, his chest open up, and his arms swing back and forth freely. Was it actually happening? Was he actually relaxing?

It was a short, pleasant amble past quiet stores with smiling owners to the restaurant, and Jonny held the door for Felicity as they quickly went inside. The smell of fried fish hung in the air as they slipped into a white wooden booth. A few customers ate and chatted quietly; there was a charming laziness to the place. No one was in a hurry. No one was late for anything. A smiling waitress approached and slid two menus onto their table. "Wave when you're ready," she said happily and then returned to her perch at the nearby bar.

Jonny flipped through his menu, but Felicity slipped out of the booth. "If you'll excuse me, I have to go to the bathroom," she said with a smile and then walked away.

Jonny waved to the waitress. "What can I get you, honey?" she asked brightly. Jonny ordered two cups of coffee. Before walking away, she held out a newspaper. "While you wait, would you like a paper?"

"Sure," Jonny said. The waitress placed the morning's edition of the *Times* on the table and walked away. Jonny watched her walk to the kitchen, and then his gaze moved around the room. Everyone in the restaurant seemed so happy, so relaxed, so calm. Absent was the aggressive fight not even thirty minutes away. If the food took too long to come, no problem. What's the hurry? When it's ready, it's ready. There would be no shouting, no scenes, no fights emanating from the kitchen. Everything was serene and pleasant.

Even the headlines on the front page of the *Times* didn't seem as threatening. Yes, there was the ever-present threat of nuclear war, the stalled economy, the racial problems, even the bad start of the Giants, but it all seemed so far away. What was missing here was that feeling of malice, that creeping doom. It was as if all those things were someone else's problems.

Leaning back and inhaling deeply and contentedly, Jonny idly opened the paper. *I could really get used to this*, he thought, as he imagined himself a permanent figure in his fairy-tale world. But then, in the next instant, he shot up out of his seat as he stared at the paper. On the inside of the front page, near the top and below a short headline—"Home-front hero to receive medal"—was a small black-and-white picture of a man he knew all too well. Jonny's forehead broke beads of sweat. *It's him*, he thought. *It's definitely him.* Jonny was sure. He knew that face. He knew it well. Even though it had been ten years, there was no doubt in Jonny's mind. After all, he'd spent hours and hours of his youth studying it, and the passage of time had only accentuated the hideous features—the pinched, arrogant lips; the sharp, condescending nose; the droopy, "screw you" eyes; and the wise-ass brow that Jonny had dreamed of putting a bullet through.

Anderson Vleets was alive and well and, according to the newspaper article right there in front of him, about to receive a medal for his "distinguished and indispensable contribution to the war effort." The son of a bitch had murdered Jonny's sister, and now they were going to give him a medal! A medal! How could this be happening? Oh sure, Jonny had seen or heard his name over the years. Little had changed for Anderson, except the names of the girls who shared his latest scandal. But with each passing year, Jonny had experienced a miniscule level of satisfaction as Anderson had slowly come to be known as an old and pathetic playboy. His antics, while crazy and exciting when he was young and handsome, were now tired and sad. He was slowly but surely heading to a life of oblivion, one that Jonny hoped with every fiber of his being would end at the end of a self-hung rope or a self-fired gun. But now, suddenly, out of the blue, Anderson was being thrown a lifeline of respectability. They were going to legitimize that son of a bitch with a medal! The thought screamed through Jonny's head. From no less than President Eisenhower himself! Jonny seethed silently. *This cannot be happening. This cannot be happening. This cannot be happening.*

Felicity returned, and even before slipping back into the booth, she could see that something had happened while she was gone. "My God, your face is bright red. What's wrong, Jonny?"

His eyes stayed glued to the picture of Anderson inside the *Times*. "You need to take me to the train station," he said, looking up at her with eyes filled with fury. "Now."

...

In a complete panic, Felicity banged on the weathered wooden door. When there was no response, she banged again.

"Who is it?" a female voice yelled from the other side.

"It's Felicity! Open the door!"

After a concerto of locks, the door swung open to reveal Alexis in a frumpy housecoat, her bright red hair unkempt and hanging around her shoulders. "Darling, what's going on? Are you okay?"

"Please, can I come in?" Felicity pleaded.

Uncertainty flashed across Alexis's face for a second, but then she stepped aside. "Of course."

Felicity squeezed by her, and Alexis shut the door. Felicity opened her mouth to speak, but then stopped, taking in her surroundings for a moment. It was a dingy, one-bedroom apartment in desperate need of a paint job, new wallpaper, and some serious cleaning. On top of all that, the place was a mess, with books, papers, and take-out food containers scattered all over the beaten furniture.

Suddenly self-conscious, Alexis made a half-assed attempt to clean off a spot on the lopsided couch. "I wasn't really expecting anyone. Sit. Please."

"I can't sit." Felicity said, wound up again. She held out a disheveled script squeezed tightly in her quivering hand. "Jonny rewrote the entire script this afternoon, and we're going on the air with it tomorrow night. What am I going to do? What am I going to do?"

"Okay. Relax," Alexis said. "Let's start by having you sit down." Although Felicity almost thrashed against her, Alexis managed to get her over to the couch. "Okay. Good. Now, let's take it step by step. We'll concentrate on the scenes that have changed the most and—"

"No, you don't understand!" Felicity interrupted, leaping up off the couch. "He didn't just rewrite what was there. He wrote a whole new script! There's not a shred of the old story—top to bottom, it's brand new. Thirty-two new pages that are going out live tomorrow night!"

"Oh…" Alexis said, as the full reality of the situation flowed over her.

"I need your help if there's to be any chance of my being prepared on time! Please help me! Please!"

"Of course," Alexis said. "Tell me what the episode is about, in your words, and we'll work from that."

"Okay. Okay. Okay." Felicity took several breaths, feeling them flow in and out of her body. She forced herself to calm down. "I've only read it once, at the read-through about an hour ago, when we first got the new script, but here goes." Felicity closed her eyes and took another deep breath. "Everyone goes to the airport for a fashion shoot. There is a terrible accident as the tires on a passenger plane attempting to land suddenly blow out, and Justice Girl comes to the rescue, saving the passengers. An investigation reveals that the tires blew out, because the owner of the tire company was using out-of-date machinery to save money and made them improperly. In fact, a worker in his factory had died because of the inferior machinery, but it had been covered up." Felicity smiled, pleased that she had remembered that much of the story. "Oh, yeah. In the end, Chance gets kidnapped by the owner of the tire company, and Justice Girl has to rescue him."

Alexis thought through what she heard and then nodded. "Okay, let's go through it from the beginning. I'll read all the other parts."

Over the next two hours, they went through the brand new script, scene by scene. They would read each scene once. Discuss it. Dissect it. Break it down. And then they would read through it again. Alexis would make minor notes, adjust Felicity's performance, and then they would read through the scene a third and final time.

Upon finishing the last scene, which was the traditional end-of-episode wrap-up back in the offices of *Focus on Fashion*, Felicity exhaled loudly. "That didn't go so bad," she said, more than a little surprised.

"I agree. In fact, I think it went quite well," Alexis said, seeming pleased.

"It certainly helps when you have the right scene partner."

"The pleasure was all mine," Alexis said, accenting her words with an ostentatious bow and a roll of her hand.

"Especially that scene where you read the part of the passenger who helped Justice Girl with the rescue."

Alexis guffawed. "Not exactly a stretch, my dear—a middle-aged woman traveling all alone with her cat."

"Well, you nailed it," Felicity said, shaking her head, once again amazed by Alexis's acting ability. But then her eyes went wide. "You should play the role when we do it for real!"

Alexis's head snapped back at the thought. "Oh, don't be silly."

"No, I'm serious."

Alexis raised her eyebrows, giving the idea real thought. "It could be fun.... Is it even possible?"

"Sure. I told you this whole thing is being put together at the last minute. We're starting from scratch on everything, including casting. There's a run-through in about half an hour. Come with me, and I'll see what I can do."

Twenty minutes later, Felicity and Alexis stepped onto the crowded soundstage. Normally on a Saturday night, the studio was quiet, with the run-through for camera finished by six o'clock and everyone sent home so they could get a good night's sleep for show day. But not tonight.

Crew members ran around in every direction, redoing sets, rehanging lights, re-planning camera moves, with Jonny at the center of it all, directing the chaos. In a corner, the rest of the cast had returned from the break, and they were huddled together, running through their lines, with Jonny's freshly written script clutched tightly in their nervous hands. As they worked, costumers flitted about, holding up different costumes against the actors to see how they would look. Nearby, a pair of casting directors interviewed and auditioned newly arrived and bewildered actors for some of the smaller roles. Despite the seeming confusion, there was a palpable sense of focused tension to the endeavor, as if knowing that what they were trying to do was impossible was only making them want to do it more.

Felicity left Alexis and dashed across the studio toward the casting directors. A moment later, she was back, with a big smile. As Felicity had hoped, they had not cast the role of Mrs. Peters yet, so the harried casting directors readily agreed with her suggestion of Alexis, with more than a slight sense of relief, happy to have one less role to fill. "You've got the part!" Felicity happily informed Alexis. "Come on. I want to introduce you to the rest of the cast." Felicity led her across the studio, but halfway there, Alexis stopped and stood, wide-eyed, as the maelstrom of the hurrying crew swirled around her. "It's not as scary as it seems," Felicity said soothingly.

"No," Alexis said with a dreamy smile, "it's just so good to be back in this world. To be working again."

Hours later, when she finally left the studio, Felicity's eyes blinked in surprise at the rising sun. Their rehearsal had been so intense, so focused, so consuming that she had lost all track of time—she hadn't realized they had worked through the night.

But it had been worth it. The last run-through, completed just moments before, had gone exceedingly well. They were ready. Or at least as ready as was possible, considering the script they were doing hadn't even existed at this time the day before. She said a sleepy good-bye to Alexis and then hung around the front of the studio, waiting for Jonny. He had been a joy to watch, pulling together the exhausted cast and crew and inspiring them, despite the long hours. Sure, there was a director, but Jonny was clearly running the show. There was no question that this episode had a special meaning for him. There was some need being fulfilled that she didn't entirely understand.

Felicity desperately wanted to go home with Jonny. She knew she was betraying Braeden and maybe even her father, but in this moment, it didn't matter. She wanted to be near Jonny, to feel him again like she had the night before.

Denise was winning.

After another five minutes, when he still hadn't shown, she gave up, realizing he would probably be trapped inside the studio for some time, dealing with one issue or another. Reluctantly, Felicity headed off to her hotel room, alone. Despite the deep longing in both her heart and her body, she knew it was the right thing. She needed sleep; they were going on the air, live, in barely more than twelve hours.

But when she got back to her room, she found that she couldn't sleep. She just lay on her bed, tossing and turning and watching the reflections of the cars on Seventh Avenue streak across the ceiling. Her body pulsed; excitement overcame her. She couldn't wait to get back in the studio and do the show for real. It had been a thrill to work with Alexis. A mere three weeks earlier, Alexis had been Felicity's teacher; now, they were equals, acting in a show together. But it was more than that. Felicity could see and could feel—as if it were as tangible as a brick—the passion for work that oozed out of Alexis. And it was infectious. Alexis personified everything that Felicity was slowly realizing she wanted: the passion, the talent, the strength, the ability.

She finally managed about four hours of sleep and, by mid-afternoon, was back in the studio for the final dress rehearsal. It went smoothly, with the chemistry between her and Alexis even better than it had been the night before. Most of the cast headed off to an early dinner, but Felicity chose instead to go back to her dressing room to nap. She was awakened about two hours before showtime by a costumer dropping off her first outfit for the night; it had just been steamed and pressed. After she left, Felicity rose from the couch and ran through the preshow ritual, which Alexis had taught her, of stretching her arms, legs, torso, back, neck, and lips and repeating "I sell seashells by the shore" twenty times in the mirror. She dressed in her muted Sally Smalls costume for her first scene and then went to the makeup room. It took about a half hour to get her wig on and combed and her face painted just right, all the while listening in on the latest gossip about the cast and crew—such was the never-ceasing conversation between the two flamboyant makeup artists.

With about five minutes to air, Felicity left the makeup room to join the rest of the cast—Thomas, Benjamin, Veronica, and several other actors who had smaller parts specific to this episode—just inside the studio. There was a delicious tension in the air as the actors went through their last-minute preparations, knowing that they were about to go on the air live in just a few minutes. Felicity looked all around; everyone was there except Alexis.

Shaking off her nerves, Felicity eyed her costars and gave them all a confident nod before taking care of her own final preparations.

About a minute later, Alexis finally appeared from far down the hallway. Jonny was with her, showing her the way down the hall. As she approached, Felicity almost laughed at the sight of her acting teacher in the frumpy, middle-aged Mrs. Peters outfit. It was so strange to see Alexis out of her traditional all-black garb that if Felicity hadn't recognized the costume, she wouldn't have known it was Alexis—she appeared to be a completely different person. When "Mrs. Peters" and Jonny finally joined the tiny cabal of nervous actors, Felicity discovered exactly why Alexis looked so different—it wasn't Alexis. Same costume, different actress. *What is going on?* Felicity wondered. *Did they add another part? That's probably it.* In the previous two episodes before this one, minor roles had been added to the script at the last minute. Still, that didn't explain where Alexis was.

Felicity took a step toward Jonny to ask him, but before she could say anything, he had waded into the center of the group of anxious actors.

"If I could have everyone's attention..." Jonny said commandingly. "The part of Mrs. Peters will now be played by Mrs. Sylvia Laffert." Jonny indicated the woman with whom he had just walked down the hall.

"Hello," Sylvia said strongly, as a confused buzz swept through the group.

"She has memorized the scene and learned all the blocking. I realize this is highly unusual, this close to air, but I ask that all of you do the best you can. Thank you. And break a leg," Jonny said to the group as a whole. "Oh, and Denise, if I could have a word with you..."

When Jonny and Felicity stepped to the side of the group, she immediately asked, "What the hell is going on?"

Jonny sighed. "This is tough to say because Alexis is such a dear friend..." Jonny took a deep breath and steeled himself. "She got scared, Felicity. She choked."

"What?"

"It happens to some actors. I've seen it before. They become so overcome with panic that they can't go on. It happened to Alexis."

"Let me talk to her," Felicity said, stepping around Jonny to head down the hall to Alexis's dressing room.

Jonny grabbed her before she had taken two steps. "It won't do any good. She's already gone."

Felicity's mouth dropped open. "But…how could she? Why?"

"Sometimes when you've been away for so long, you can't handle it when you come back."

"But Alexis?"

Jonny nodded sadly. "Yes."

Felicity's entire body slumped; she felt defeated.

Jonny pulled her close, without the intimacy they had shared the night before. This was strictly business. "We go on the air in less than five minutes, and I need you to make this work," he said, staring right into her face.

"But I still can't believe Alexis would…. Not her."

"That doesn't matter now. *You* are the star of this show, and whether we sink or swim is on you. Everyone will feed off what you say and do. Understand?"

Felicity nodded. She was hesitant, but she understood. She moved away from Jonny and rejoined the rest of the cast. They were broken up into several small groups, all chatting away in quick bursts, clearly more than a little unsettled by this last-minute change. *So, it's all up to me,* Felicity thought. *Jonny knows I'm new to all this, yet he dumped it all on me.* As much as she hated the thought, she knew he was right. She was the star. She was the main character. She was the one, as Alexis would say when they broke a scene down, who was "driving the action forward." She had to show strength. She had to show power.

Felicity stepped over to Sylvia, who stood off to the side, alone, the only actor not engulfed in one of the circles of panic. "On behalf of the entire cast," Felicity said loudly, "I want to welcome you to the show."

"Thank you," Sylvia said, grateful that someone was talking to her.

Felicity then stepped away from her and returned to her preshow preparations, loosening up her face and body as if this were just another show. The rest of the cast watched Felicity and, one by one, followed suit. Minutes later,

Arnold came running up, yelling, "First positions! First positions!" And everyone hurried off to begin the show.

The episode of *Justice Girl* went off without a hitch. Jonny gathered everyone together on the stage afterward to proclaim it their best episode yet. He made a point of thanking them for rolling with the rather unusual last-minute change of script. Quite pleased with themselves, the cast and crew broke off, and Felicity practically sprinted to her dressing room. She dressed quickly, wanting to grab a cab and go find Alexis. But Jonny intercepted her and strongly suggested that she give Alexis some space. What had happened to her had not been easy, and she would need some time to come to terms with it on her own. Acknowledging Jonny's deeper knowledge of this strange world of actors, Felicity agreed; she would check in with Alexis in the next day or two, she decided.

An hour or so later, they were together at Jonny's new apartment, sitting on a brand new bare mattress, which, except for several suitcases of Jonny's clothes, was the only thing besides themselves in the empty home. They enjoyed some champagne that Jonny had demanded they stop to get on their way over. He was in a particularly good mood. Clearly, he hadn't just showered the cast with false praise when he proclaimed it their best episode yet. Felicity wasn't sure what to make of the wild swing of emotional changes Jonny had gone through since seeing the article in the paper the day before. But one thing was for sure: something transformative had been achieved by the creation of this week's episode.

"I read the article in the *Times*," Felicity said carefully, as Jonny refilled her Dixie cup of champagne. Immediately, she could see his mood darken, but she had to ask. "I remember the story from when it happened during the war. The accident at the plant. The girl who was killed. What's your connection to it?"

"Who says I have a connection?"

"Jonny, I think we're past the point of pretending with each other."

Jonny nodded solemnly. He took a long swallow of his champagne, draining his cup. Then he began to tell the story. By the time he had finished retelling the entire saga, the bottle of champagne was empty, as was a bottle of wine that Charles had given him as a housewarming gift.

"So that's what the episode was really about," Felicity said, flush with understanding.

"Yes."

"Do you really think it will make a difference?"

"I don't care. I had to do it."

Felicity considered his words, but she had other questions. *Do you think anyone will actually make the connection? Are you sure Vleets was behind it? What do you hope to get out of this?* But before she could ask anything, her thoughts drifted to Alexis. She turned to Jonny. "Are you sure I shouldn't check in on her?"

"Yes."

"To be honest, I'm feeling a bit guilty. After all, I was the one who suggested her for the part. I'm responsible for putting her in the situation she wasn't prepared for."

"Alexis is a big girl. She makes her own choices."

Felicity nodded, but she still was not completely mollified. "I still feel like I should reach out to her. If it wasn't for her, someone else would be playing Justice Girl right now."

"She'll be fine. Just give her a day or two. And I don't entirely agree with what you said about someone else playing Justice Girl." Jonny shifted himself on the mattress. "Sure, she's made you better, but there's something else going on when you play the role, some deeper connection. Maybe it's the whole Felicity/Denise thing." Jonny reached for the bottle for a refill, but it was empty. He shook it several times to extract a few final drops and then slipped off the bed. "I think I have another bottle in the kitchen."

Felicity lay back on the stiff mattress and removed her clothes. Jonny was correct; she did feel a connection, a closeness, to playing Justice Girl. And the more she thought about it, the more she realized it *was* the whole Felicity/Denise thing. The problem was, she didn't know which was the real identity and which was the secret one.

Episode Five

JUSTICE GIRL

"A WOLF IN SHEEP'S CLOTHING"

April 24, 1954

There were good numbers, there were great numbers, and then there were astounding numbers. *These are astounding numbers*, Hogart thought. At a few minutes after nine o'clock on Monday morning, he sat at his desk, sifting through the Trendex overnight ratings reports. *Justice Girl* had pulled in a phenomenal 28.7 rating and an incredible 74 share. The best part was that the *Percy Williams Show*, also preempted the week before, had gone on the air with its special guest star Bette Davis. Even without manufactured controversy and the subsequent sexy leg photo, *Justice Girl* had annihilated it in the ratings.

It was going to be a great day.

He leaned back in his chair and looked out his window across the East River to Brooklyn. The morning sun was eating away the cloud cover, and the vastly underrated skyline of the second-class borough gleamed in the yellow light. He was fewer than four hours away from lunch with Clinton Fortis, and oh boy, did he have a lot to tell him. Over fine food and, hopefully, some equally fine wine, he would lay out his exciting plans for the network, and then they would toast their good fortune and bright future. So what if Jonny had pulled another stunt, changing the script at the last minute and not even bothering to get Hogart's approval? With the contract still unresolved and with Jonny still holding all the rights, there was nothing he could do. It was a preachy story, fairly obvious in its target, and highly political. Anyone could tell. It had all the subtlety of a sledgehammer, hitting people over the head about an incident that was old news. But the ratings were huge, so if Jonny needed to go on his stupid political rants, so be it.

Justice Girl was just too damn popular. Nothing could stop her—or Hogart, for that matter. It was as clear as the sight of Brooklyn in his office window. The Regal Television Network was well on its way to being the powerhouse Hogart dreamed of.

His mind drifted to the several hours' worth of meetings he had in front of him before the lunch with Clinton. He was so giddy, he decided to cancel all of them. After the stunning victory in the boardroom, Hogart had done nothing to celebrate, even spending the entire weekend working up his plans for the network. Didn't he deserve a slight indulgence, a tiny reward for his victory? It was against everything he knew, but surely the network would survive if he took the morning off and treated himself to a shave and a hair-cut. In fact, wasn't making himself as presentable as possible to the chair-man of the board actually part of his job description? So, in a sense, with his plans done and the numbers ready to speak for themselves, pampering himself was the next best thing he could do.

Hogart reached for his intercom to buzz Mrs. Decosta to have her imple-ment his spontaneous plan, but before he could reach the button, it buzzed on its own.

"Mr. Daniels," Mrs. Decosta said, "I just received a call from Mr. Fortis's office. He has to cancel your lunch for today."

Hogart deflated into his chair, as his entire wonderful plan vanished before his eyes. He knew Clinton was a busy man, but did he really have to cancel? Today? There would be no haircut, no shave, no fine food, no fine wine. Just hours and hours of meetings with the executives he despised. "Very well, then," Hogart answered, not even trying to hide his disappoint-ment. "What day is it rescheduled for?"

"It's not. They said Mr. Fortis didn't have any openings in his schedule for the foreseeable future."

Immediately, Hogart knew something was wrong. If anyone else had brought him such an unusual message, he would have pressed further, as he'd have been positive that something had been mangled in translation. But not in the case of Mrs. Decosta. As far as Hogart was concerned, her talents as a secretary were unimpeachable.

Her veracity was further confirmed when Hogart called up Clinton's office himself, making Clinton's secretary well aware that he himself was calling, only to be told the same unexpected tale: "Mr. Fortis doesn't have any openings in his schedule for the foreseeable future." Hiding his frustration, Hogart playfully cajoled Clinton's secretary into telling him where her boss had now decided to have lunch.

So four hours later, after suffering through the meetings, Hogart found himself standing rather uncomfortably in front of the famous Union Club. Because the club prided itself on providing extreme privacy for its rich and successful members, Hogart had to endure the concerned stares of the uniformed doorman. Fortunately, it was only a few minutes before a limousine pulled up, and out stepped Clinton Fortis.

"Clinton!" Hogart said as he walked toward him, his hand outstretched.

Clinton showed his surprise for a split second before regaining his composure. "Hogart," he said coolly as they shook hands.

"I apologize for my forwardness," Hogart said, a sincere smile on his face. "But I was a little surprised that you canceled our lunch."

"You know how it is; something came up."

"And your secretary said you couldn't reschedule."

"I've become quite busy," Clinton said as he walked toward the front entrance. The doorman eagerly opened the ornate glass and gold door for him. "If you'll excuse me…"

Hogart watched him go, confused. What was happening? Why the cold shoulder? Clinton was almost through the door when Hogart stepped after him. "Clinton, again, I apologize for being so forward, but please help me out here. Did I do something to offend you?"

The doorman moved to block Hogart's approach, but Clinton waved him off, and he met Hogart head on. "What do you think won the Second World War?" Clinton asked firmly.

"Excuse me?" Hogart was clueless as to where this was going.

"What do you think won the Second World War?" Clinton repeated.

Hogart searched his mind, looking for something besides the obvious. He didn't find it. "Ah…intelligence. Daring. Heroism."

"Really?" Clinton snapped. "You think it was intelligence that won the war? You think it was daring and heroism that crushed the Nazis?"

Hogart shrugged. "Yeah. Sure."

Clinton raised an angry finger. "Bullshit. It was iron. It was steel. It was oil. It was munitions. It was textiles." Clinton jabbed the finger at Hogart. "And it was tires."

Hogart flinched as an inkling of what was coming crept up his spine.

"I don't seem to recall any stories of a German soldier cut down by intelligence," Clinton continued. "Pi is 3.1415926. Boom—he's dead. No, never heard that. But I did hear about a nice, sharp, American-made bullet fired from a precision American-made gun piercing a Kraut heart. Or an American-made bomb dropped from an American-made bomber leveling town after town in Germany. The industrial might of the United States that won the war. The true heroes were not those fools who ran around with guns or bazookas or flew around in planes. No, it wasn't them. It was people like Ford, Carnegie, Rockefeller, Kaiser"—Clinton took another step closer to Hogart—"and Vleets."

Hogart nodded painfully, his fear confirmed.

"I knew Eustice Vleets, Anderson's father," Clinton continued, no longer withholding his fury. "We were in the same class at Yale. He was a good man. He took a small company and turned it into a giant. A giant that helped win a war. He was also a good friend. Our families vacationed together. You probably don't know this, but I have five children. All daughters. I always wanted a son. Just before Eustice died, he asked me to watch over Anderson. And I did. I now have six children. I now have a son." Clinton leaned into Hogart's face. "So what if he made a little on the side? He's entitled to it! Without people like Eustice and Anderson, we'd all be speaking German and Japanese right now. You might tell that to the pissant writers on that little show of yours. How dare they impugn someone like Anderson Vleets!"

Knocked back by the tirade, Hogart didn't know what to do. Before he had a chance to come up with anything, another limousine pulled up in front of the club. He immediately recognized the occupant as Anderson Vleets stepped out.

Clinton tossed a parting comment at Hogart. "This whole thing has made me realize that I don't think television is a business I want to be in anymore. I think the people at Worthington have a much better idea of what to do with the network. Now, if you'll excuse me, I have an important lunch." Clinton turned his back on Hogart and greeted Anderson warmly, his strong affection obvious.

Hogart watched, his body almost doubling over, as if he'd been punched in the stomach. It hadn't even been a threat, just a simple statement. Clinton was going to change his vote. The network would be sold and that would be the end of all of it. Hogart became furious. He should have trusted his instincts! He had been right in the very beginning—it would be Jonny who, in the end, would screw the whole thing up. But it wasn't over. There had to be something he could do. But what?

Hogart stepped in front of Anderson before he could disappear inside the club. "Anderson, my name is Hogart Daniels. I am the president of the Regal Television Network, and I want to personally apologize to you for last night's episode of *Justice Girl*."

Anderson shrugged. His eyes were bleary, and his breath stank. He was clearly hungover. "Okay," he said, with a tone that inferred he wasn't entirely sure what Hogart was talking about.

"And I also want you to know," Hogart continued, "that the person responsible for that episode has been severely reprimanded and no long is in control of the show."

Clinton nodded approvingly. "That sounds like a step in the right direction," he said, more than a little impressed.

"Yes. That was one of the reasons I was looking forward to having lunch with you today. The Regal Television Network now has complete control of all rights pertaining to the show and the character Justice Girl."

Clinton took a step back, reappraising Hogart. "I am very pleased to hear that," he said firmly.

"Yes, it is good news. I also wanted to tell you about some of the upcoming episodes that we are planning—episodes about the industrial heartland of this country and how it has made all of our lives better," Hogart said.

Clinton nodded, pleased. "Good. I think I would like to hear them." Clinton thought for a moment. "I'm sure we can add another person to our table. Would you like to join us?"

Two hours later, after Hogart, Clinton, and Anderson had said their good-byes, Hogart fought the urge to jump and scream like a triumphant five-year-old. He had just completed the greatest lunch of his life—and in the Union Club, no less! Over the best trout amandine he'd ever tasted, the three of them had discovered they had a lot in common, both in their personal lives and—more important—in business. Soon, suggested schemes turned into serious discussions. They made plans—grand, ambitious plans that went well beyond just saving the network; plans that led to Clinton shaking Hogart's hand firmly just before they parted and saying, "We will do great things together."

Hogart knew it was all within his grasp, but getting it would not come without a price. There was a line he had to cross, and that made him pause. Fortunately, he'd been here before. He knew what he had to do.

The euphoria was fading as he walked down the street, scheming. The afternoon suddenly turned cold. His leg stiffened, and his limp returned.

...

"It's called television."

"Tele-what?"

"Television. It's gonna be big. Bigger than radio."

"What is it again?"

Hogart rolled his eyes. He'd been stuck in the front seat of this smelly '34 Packard for the last three hours, and out of sheer boredom, he had put down the magazine he had read cover to cover, twice, and decided to strike up a conversation, which he was now regretting. It wasn't that his partner and fellow military policeman, Yardley Tipton, was dumb. Hogart glanced at the hulking figure next to him on the car seat. It was rather more a product of where he'd grown up—the southeastern corner of Texas. Hogart had worked on an oil rig down there, and Yardley was like everyone else he had met that hot, sticky summer. He was just a good ol' boy, in no particular hurry, not interested in anything he wasn't interested in already, and just as happy to sit in the front seat of a Packard for hours on end as he was to stroll around Times Square, twirling his baton. Hogart was clearly the brains of the partnership, and at six foot two, Yardley was clearly the muscle. "It's like being at a movie theatre, only it's in your house," Hogart said, pleased with the analogy.

Yardley looked at him strangely. "My house ain't big enough for a movie theatre."

"It doesn't need to be. It's small. About the size of a cabinet."

"But you said it was like being at a movie theatre."

"It is, only smaller."

"Why would I want it to be smaller? I like big movie theatres—you know, the kinds that have big ceilings and organs and shit."

"So you can watch it from the comfort of your own home," Hogart explained.

"But my home don't have big ceilings and organs and shit."

"I never said it did."

"Then why would I wanna watch television?"

Hogart shook his head, regretting not reading his magazine for a third time. "Never mind," he said, throwing up his hands. It was times like this when it was almost not worth it to be an MP.

Almost.

The truth was, from the moment Hogart had enlisted just days after Pearl Harbor, he'd been angling for the job. No fool in basic training, while others wasted their time learning how to march well or shoot guns with greater proficiency, Hogart decided to focus on the most important thing— keeping himself alive. He figured out really fast that military policemen stayed far away from danger. Up to this point, they'd been stationed exclusively in the States, and when things did finally move overseas, they would either be in England or well behind the front lines.

Now based in New York City, his job consisted of keeping the tens of thousands of servicemen who were passing through the port city in line before they were shipped overseas. Drunkenness, fighting, gambling, prostitution, some petty theft—that was about as bad as it got. But now, with 1942 coming to a close and the first head-to-head confrontation with the Nazis in North Africa on the horizon, something new had been added to the list.

Desertion.

The visceral anger over Pearl Harbor had subsided, but it was replaced by the determined reality of the long slog ahead. Thousands and thousands of men were being shipped overseas every single day, but as the inevitable first encounter with the Nazis drew closer, more and more of them were deciding they didn't want to go, and dozens were deserting. Even though Hogart couldn't blame them—no way in hell he was going to get his ass blown off on some godforsaken African beach—he dutifully cruised around the city, picking them up, and dragging them back to their bases, where they were held under guard until they were safely loaded on to a troop ship and sent overseas.

Hogart's current case—the reason he had had to endure his thickheaded partner in such close quarters for the last three hours—was typical. Stewart Kowalski, a Polish kid from Milwaukee, just eighteen and just starting to shave, had decided that the military no longer fit in with his immediate plans. Whenever an AWOL report floated across Hogart's desk, the first thing he did was check the local whorehouses. Most of these kids had never been with a woman before, and that, combined with their having a little bit of cash, made their destinations fairly easy to figure out. In return for not raiding them, most of the brothels in Manhattan would cooperate when the MPs called to inquire about any soldiers who had taken up temporary residence at their place. Someone fitting Stewart Kowalski's description matched a soldier who was on his third day and fifteenth woman at a well-known establishment in Chelsea. Part of the unwritten, yet specific deal, was that the military police would wait outside for the AWOL soldiers to come out before apprehending them.

"You ever been in there?" Yardley asked, indicating with his muscled elbow in the direction of the whorehouse.

"No!" Hogart answered in his best incredulous tone.

"I have. A bunch of times. Best selection of girls in town. I met a real sweetie from Baton Rouge. Kinda fell for her something bad." Yardley sighed. "I gotta piss." He reached for the door.

"Where do you think you're going?" Hogart asked nervously.

"You heard what I said. I gotta drain the lizard. I'm sure Uncle Sam don't want me staining his seats."

Hogart handed him an empty Coke bottle. "Use this."

Yardley stared at it. "You ain't serious."

"Yes, I am. He could come out any minute, and I don't want you gone when he does."

Yardley sighed and took the bottle. He pissed in it then dropped it out the window, where it landed in the gutter with a wet crash. "Happy?"

"Yes. Thank you," Hogart said with a smirk. "Look, this being my...you know...last one, I don't want anything going wrong."

Yardley looked at him closely. "You really think this television thing is going to be a big deal?"

"Yep," Hogart said brightly. "That's why, for the rest of the war, I want to be the army liaison with the networks for the informational shows they're transmitting, and I'm very lucky they approved my transfer." Luck had nothing to do with it, Hogart knew. He'd been angling for this assignment pretty much every waking hour after that first time he had seen television. He'd only been in the city a few days when his captain told him to report to station WXPY to appear in a show about civil defense. Hogart showed up, figuring he was going to be in a newsreel; instead, what he saw changed the direction of the rest of his life.

Exactly on time, he arrived at the studios of the Regal Television Network, which were crammed into a corner of the fourteenth floor of an ornate office building in the middle of the 500 block of Madison Avenue. Several rooms had been gutted, including two from the fifteenth floor, to create the small cluster of offices and the oversized black-walled space where the actual filming was done—or "televising," as the pinch-nosed, bespectacled floor manager had called it as he immediately placed Hogart in front of a bulky rectangle of metal called a TV camera. The room was ice cold, his breath a puffy cloud of hazy white, and Hogart was glad he had his heavy wool uniform to keep him warm. As various people darted about in a hurry, a short, skinny, older man, wearing a heavy overcoat, joined him. After a brief introduction and even briefer run-through of what they would be doing "on the air," as it was called, the older man took off his coat—now he wore only a thin shirt and light pants—and suggested that Hogart might want to do the same. Hogart's bones were practically shaking from the piercing cold, so he declined, even as he wondered if this man had some sort of mental illness.

The bespectacled floor manager was back, informing them that they had thirty seconds. He stepped away, and suddenly a large bank of the whitest lights Hogart had ever seen burst alive all around him. Almost knocked back by the intensity, he held a hand up to block his eyes. The older man told him if he looked downward, in a few minutes, he'd get used to it.

But before he had a chance to try out the theory, the heat hit him.

Hogart had dug water canals in the Mojave Desert in August; he'd worked on an oil derrick in the Gulf of Mexico in July; and before he'd been smart enough to get transferred, he'd even been within twenty feet of an exploding 50 mm mortar shell. But he'd never in his life felt anything as hot as this. The wave hit him, searing his eyes and throat, and instantly, his uniform became a thick, suffocating skin. As his brow began to drip, a menacing, red light lit atop the camera, and they were on the air. The older man asked Hogart a series of questions about the duties and challenges of an MP, and Hogart answered them to the best of his knowledge. It was only a fifteen-minute broadcast, but by the end, he was soaked, head to toe, in his own sweat, and his voice was little more than a gasping wheeze. Then, mercifully, the lights went off, and the cool returned.

They did the broadcast five more times that afternoon, going on the air once an hour, and even though Hogart removed his undershirt and dress shirt, leaving on only his wool outer uniform, by the time they were done, he was a spent mess. *So that was television,* he thought as he rode down in the elevator. Once he reached the lobby, he propped himself against one of the cool marble walls, gathering his strength to make the journey back to the Times Square station house. But before he could carry out that plan, the bespectacled floor manager appeared and, seeing Hogart, offered to give him a ride across town. Hogart eagerly took it.

Inside the car, the bespectacled man finally gave his name as Paul and informed Hogart that he had to make one stop. They pulled over in front of an apartment building off Lexington Avenue in Murray Hill. As exhausted as Hogart was, given the choice of sitting in the car and freezing or going inside with Paul, Hogart chose the latter.

Three exhausting flights of creaky steps later, they entered the apartment of a stoop-shouldered older man, who was, Hogart realized from the shiny white pith helmet hanging on the wall, emblazoned with the bright red letters CD, a civil defense volunteer. Sitting on a cabinet in his cramped one-room apartment was a strange wooden box with a curved glass plate attached to the front of it. It took a moment for Hogart to realize it was a television. During the course of a brief conversation between the two men, Hogart gleaned that the man was complaining that the device didn't work. Paul reached behind the cabinet and plugged it in.

As the television slowly came to life, the screen steadily brightening, the man sheepishly teetered on his feet. Hogart realized the image on the screen was that of a man sitting at the same small desk and chair that he had seen in the studio. As soon as sound began to flow from the set, several excited neighbors flowed into the apartment. Seeing that the screen was alive again, they pulsed with excitement. The man on the screen was reading the news, and the gathered crowd hung on his every word. The day before, the cruise ship *Normandie* mysteriously had caught fire while sitting in its berth in New York Harbor. Because of the massive amounts of water sprayed on her to put out the fire, she had first flooded and then partially capsized. When the man on the screen finished reading about the disaster, the image on the screen suddenly cut to footage taken from an airplane flying overhead as the doomed luxury liner lay on its side. It was an impressive shot, slowly arcing over the dying beast.

Everyone in the room gasped at the stunning image.

So did Hogart—but not for the same reason. Sure, the picture on the screen was impressive, but what was even more impressive was seeing what it made everyone do. The *Normandie* had sunk over twenty-four hours earlier. News of its demise had dominated the radio waves, and pictures were splashed all over special-edition newspapers sold on every corner of Manhattan Island. Yet the chance to see it as a moving image, in the comfort of someone's home, had empted almost every apartment in the building.

Suddenly, Hogart wasn't tired anymore. Calculations shot through his brain, then ideas and schemes, and then finally, a clear plan. He would get himself transferred out of the MPs over to the army liaison office for the New York zone of homeland defense, with a special emphasis on televised communication. When the fighting ended, and the GIs came streaming home, Hogart would be well positioned with the Regal Network, just as the wartime restrictions on luxury items were lifted and television sales exploded.

Yardley suddenly shot forward in his seat. His eyes wide, he pointed through the windshield at a soldier happily trundling down the front steps of the brownstone. "Look, I think that's him." Yardley reached for the door handle, but Hogart stopped him.

"He came down the front steps. The entrance to the whorehouse is below street level," Hogart said authoritatively.

"Oh, yeah," Yardley answered, releasing his hold on the door handle. The serviceman crossed the street and walked right past them as they sat in their car. Yardley got a better look at the man's face, and he shook his head. "Nope, that's not him. You got it right, Hoag." But then he turned and looked at Hogart with a raised eyebrow. "How do you know where the entrance to the whorehouse is?"

Hogart started to say something but then looked away. Finally, he said, "Well, maybe I've been in there once or twice."

Yardley slapped him on the back of the head. "Son of a gun, you *are* human." Then he proceeded to pester Hogart in the dominating way only a larger man can harass a smaller man.

"Stop it. Leave me alone!" Hogart said, fending off Yardley's pokes and jabs.

Yardley stopped suddenly but not because of anything Hogart said. "There he is," Yardley said, pointing through the window again.

This time he was right.

A young soldier stepped up the small staircase and onto the sidewalk. Hogart and Yardley exchanged a nod and then slipped out of the Packard. As they had done several dozen times before, they split up, each heading in a different direction. Moments later, they nonchalantly approached the soldier from opposite directions. The soldier was walking toward Hogart, and Hogart could see Yardley coming up quickly from behind him. As he got closer to Hogart, his face looked all too familiar, and Hogart recognized another scared young boy, with blotches of acne, a caterpillar of peach fuzz, and wide, terrified eyes. But it was more than that; there was something familiar about this boy.

"Hogart?" the young solider asked, peering closely at him.

"Yeah?" Hogart answered, stopping just a few feet in front of him. Then his eyes went wide with recognition. "*Frenchy?*"

"Yeah, it's me!"

The two men spontaneously hugged, but it didn't last long. Yardley rushed up from behind, pulled Frenchy off Hogart, and wrestled him to the ground.

"It's okay; it's okay," Hogart said. "I know him."

Hearing that, Yardley relaxed and stood up. Hogart held out a hand and helped the stunned Frenchy to his feet. As his mind began to clear, Frenchy looked at Hogart with a mask of confusion.

Hogart smiled sheepishly. "I hate to tell you this, old friend, but we're MPs." He held open his hands, as if to say, *What are you gonna do?*

The realization hit Frenchy hard. For a moment, it looked like he might faint. "Any chance you might…you know…for old time's sake…" Frenchy tried, knowing how lame it sounded.

Hogart shook his head reluctantly. "I'm afraid I can't." He nodded to Yardley, who whipped out a pair of handcuffs and slapped them on Frenchy.

On the ride back to the station house, Hogart and Frenchy regaled Yardley with stories of how they'd met in basic training, and Frenchy filled in Hogart on what had happened with their unit since Hogart had become an MP. Almost the entire unit had been kept together, intact, sent through advanced infantry training, and now were stationed at Camp Shanks, just outside New York City, awaiting orders to go overseas.

It wasn't until they were inside the station house, with Frenchy handcuffed to Hogart's beaten wooden desk, that Frenchy gave Hogart an especially relevant bit of news.

"Gastwick!" Hogart responded, totally shocked. "Gastwick is the one they made squad commander?"

Frenchy nodded, the pain clear on his face. "Now, do you see why I deserted?"

Hogart nodded rapidly. Indeed, he did. Howston Gastwick was the joke of the unit, a snotty, effete brat from a long-serving military family, who had obviously signed up because that had been expected of him. He was utterly incompetent in every aspect of basic training and had the shortest odds in the company pool as to who would be the first to die. The only real question was whether he would get shot by an enemy soldier or shoot himself first. Hogart didn't have to ask how or why Gastwick was given a command—his father was currently a full colonel, serving at the Pentagon.

"Son of a bitch," Hogart said. Howston Gastwick in command? He felt terrible for his old friend, but there was nothing he could do. The situation Frenchy was in was precisely why Hogart had carefully plotted to get himself the hell out of the infantry. He knew the longer he stayed around, the more likely he could end up like Frenchy: shipped overseas, with an idiot as a commanding officer, with little more to look forward to than becoming target practice for the Nazis.

Hogart finished the rest of the paperwork in silence—he couldn't look Frenchy in the face. When he was done, he waved Yardley over from the other side of the room, where he had been chatting with a couple of other MPs.

"What's going to happen now?" Frenchy asked.

Hogart couldn't meet his friend's eyes. "You're going to be taken back to your unit. They're going overseas in a couple of days. You'll be confined to the base until then."

"Can't you do...something?" Frenchy pleaded.

Hogart shook his head. "I don't make the decisions."

"But don't you understand? If I go back, I *will* get killed. You know Gastwick; with him in charge, we don't have a prayer over there…" His pleading had turned into begging.

"I'm sorry," was all Hogart could say.

Yardley pulled out his keys to unlock Frenchy from the desk. Frenchy stood up, his agitation growing. He began to shake and cry. "I will be killed. I will die," he said.

Hogart backed off a couple of steps, signaling for Yardley to do the same. He wanted to give Frenchy a moment to gather himself.

Frenchy suddenly reached out with his free hand and pulled open Hogart's top desk drawer. Then he shoved that hand into the open drawer and, using his entire body, slammed it shut.

The horrific sound of bones crushing filled the room, followed by Frenchy's agonized screams. He collapsed, the cuffed hand stopping his fall, and dangled like an empty potato sack just above the tile floor.

Two hours later, Hogart checked on Frenchy, who was now handcuffed to a hospital bed in the small infirmary inside the station house. He was sedated and drifting in and out of consciousness. A huge bandage ran halfway up his arm. When Hogart asked the doctor for a prognosis, the news was not good. "I don't know if he'll ever be able to use the hand again," the doctor said wearily. "But one thing's for sure—the war's over for him."

Sedated or not, at that moment, Hogart could have sworn he saw his old friend smile.

For the rest of his shift and well into the next day, Hogart found himself extremely aware of his hands. Each movement, whether he was sewing a button or picking up a phone, became a world unto itself. He studied his movements obsessively, wondering what it would be like to not be able to make this object attached to himself do what he wanted it to. The thought terrified him. He found himself hyper-observant and, ultimately, hypercareful when closing the door to a cab or a refrigerator or an apartment. Mostly, though, Hogart was thankful he had figured out a way to stay alive that didn't involve maiming a body part.

On his way to work the next day, Hogart stopped in to see Frenchy again, but he was gone, transferred to a military prison hospital at a base in New Jersey, where he would serve out his sentence for desertion and rehab his damaged hand. Even though Hogart was early, he lingered for only a moment, staring at the empty, freshly made bed, before heading to the main room of the station house.

It was a Friday night, and the weekends were his busy season.

The normally rowdy soldiers, combined with a large uptick in the population of locals looking to blow off some steam, made for a long, long night. He knew that around 3:00 a.m., when he and Yardley would inevitably be breaking up a fight between a bunch of drunken sailors over a girl or pulling passed-out soldiers down from a Times Square lamppost, he would long for the excruciating boredom of a stakeout with his simple-minded partner.

Before reaching his desk, his immediate superior, Sergeant Pearson, beckoned him over with a simple, "Daniels!" Hogart found Pearson an odd mix of amusing and intimidating. Though a comically small five feet tall, Pearson somehow still managed to appear to peer down at Hogart, even though Hogart had almost a full foot on him. All of Pearson's features were small—piney nose, thin lips, and beady eyes, all accentuated by a reedy moustache that ended in waxed tips.

"Yeah?" Hogart answered. He joined Pearson in his small office at the far end of the room, hiding his annoyance at what would no doubt be a waste of time on a very busy day.

"You knew that kid from yesterday? The one that smashed his fingers in your desk?"

"Yeah, we were in basic together. Why?"

"I just wanted to make sure." Pearson tossed a slip of paper across the desk at him and then said with a chuckle, "The army has been known to get things wrong from time to time."

Hogart wearily picked up the paper. "What is this?"

"A transfer order. They're sending you back to your unit."

Hogart's jaw dropped. *"Excuse me?"*

"Yeah," Pearson said. "You're taking your friend's place. Since you trained with that unit, Division thought you would be an easy fit."

"But I'm supposed to be transferred over to communications," Hogart said, waving his arms frantically, "not sent to a combat unit. This doesn't make any sense."

Pearson nodded knowingly. "Making sense—that's what the army is known for."

Hogart stared at the transfer order in his shaking hand. "This...this is wrong. I'm gonna bring this up with Simms."

"Be my guest."

Hogart hurried away. This was a mistake—a big, grade-A, made-in-America, as only the armed forces could do it SNAFU. He had planned everything out precisely, and he knew he hadn't missed a thing. He had gotten all the right approvals, obtained all the necessary signatures on all the correct forms. Some stupid-ass pencil pusher clearly had fucked up somewhere down the line.

He climbed the stairs to the top floor, relaxing with each step. Ultimately, there was nothing to worry about. Whatever it was, Simms would fix it. After all, Major Simms had been his ace in the hole, his trump card, since about the second week of basic training. During the endless sweaty marches or clumpy mess-hall meals, Hogart had overheard a steady stream of joking rumors and sly comments about one of the base officer's "being a little light in his combat boots." While the rest of the idiots around him moved on to questioning each other's own sexuality or describing what they would do to each other's sisters, Hogart quickly realized that this information could be just what he was looking for—his ticket to staying far away from Nazi bullets.

It only took a couple of days of careful snooping to devise his plan. Finally, on a day when almost the entire base had leave and swarmed into Biloxi, taking over the entire town, Hogart put his plan into action. It was very simple, to the point of being foolproof. Hogart "accidentally" ran into Major Simms at an out-of-the-way all-male bar in a less-than-respectable part of town. Simms was seated at a dark booth, accompanied by a young, local boy who couldn't have been more than a year out of high school, if at all. Hogart sauntered in, feigning surprise at seeing Major Simms. The major was so thrown off guard he completely bought Hogart's excuse that he was there helping a friend in town deliver to the bar. Hogart played dumb as they engaged in useless chitchat, save for a few strategic, knowing glances in the direction of the young boy. The entire interaction lasted less than two minutes, but it continued to pay off for Hogart for the next nine months.

When Hogart wanted to be transferred into the MP division that Major Simms was heading up, he was greeted with open arms. Once they were assigned to New York, he had the pick of shifts, and if he needed the occasional day off, that was easily arranged. And finally, when Hogart wanted to be transferred to the communications core, Major Simms signed the order without a single question.

Yes, Major Simms would get it all sorted out. But when Hogart reached the major's office, the room was an empty shell, with nothing more than a deserted desk and blank walls. Gone were the carefully framed family photos of his wife and three kids, the cattle horns from one of the steers on his ranch, and most notably, the big flag of Montana that had hung directly behind him when he was at his desk. Panicked, Hogart chased down one of the young soldiers that he recognized as one of the series of young soldiers that were Major Simms's assistants.

"Have you seen Major Simms today?" Hogart asked, trying to seem calm.

"Nope."

"Any idea where he might be?"

"Yeah, California," the young soldier answered matter-of-factly.

"Excuse me?"

"Got transferred a couple of days ago. They sent him out to head MP operations in San Francisco."

"But he was running things here in New York," Hogart exclaimed, as if this young soldier could somehow change what had happened.

The answer was obvious and all too familiar. "That's the army."

The next morning Hogart was on the train, making the one-hour trip upstate to Camp Shanks, the ramshackle collection of quickly assembled barracks used as the final embarkation point before soldiers were shipped overseas. By noon, he had reunited with both his old unit and the Browning M1 rifle. Sadly, what Frenchy had told him was true. Howston Gastwick was their squad commander. And if anything, he was more incompetent than before, with his men openly expressing their contempt for him. Furthering the nightmare was the fact that Gastwick didn't seem to care. He happily ignored their mutinous behavior, content to sit in his small, private room at the head of the barracks and polish his boots.

For the next two days, Hogart shot, marched, and drilled, reliving the drudgery he had worked so hard to leave behind. At night, he dragged his sore and beaten body around the base, searching for an angle to get himself transferred to the communications group or at least back to the MP corps. But this base was much different from what he had experienced back in basic training. Back then, the war was just gearing up, and there was a sense of blossoming chaos that had worked to his advantage, even before he made his important discovery about Major Simms. Now, he was in the center of a well-oiled machine, finely tuned and running on all cylinders, processing thousands of men at a time. After two nights of probing and prodding, he had yet to find out whom he would need to convince to make the transfer happen. On the third day, the soldiers were granted leave, and Hogart planned to use the time back in New York City to attack the problem from a different angle. He would go to the communications office and MP station house and see if he could arrange for a transfer by having one of them make the request.

But just as he and the other soldiers were about to leave, with everyone dressed in their dress uniforms and bragging about how many dames they were gonna fuck, the leave was canceled. No explanation was given for the cancellation, but none was needed. They all knew what was about to happen.

They were heading overseas.

For the next several hours, they sat around the barracks, cleaning their guns, stuffing their duffel bags, and packing their packs. The mood was tense—no one questioned another's sexuality, or insulted someone's mother, or even proclaimed what they would do to each other's sisters. Night came, and still they sat in their barracks, waiting. As the moon-inspired shadows stretched across the floor, the men lay back on their cots; some even dozed off. Hogart finally gave in around 10:00 p.m. and nestled on a scratchy army blanket between his duffel bag and pack. Sleep wasn't possible for him, as his mind continued to run different scenarios of how he could still get out of this nightmare. His thoughts kept detouring into the realm of disbelief, still in shock that he was even in this position. He was about to go overseas, to die just like the rest of these idiots. How was this possible? He had thought things out. He had carefully planned. Yet, here he was, just hours or minutes or even seconds from embarkation to God knows where.

The hours ticked by. Finally, Hogart's eyes grew heavy, and they slowly closed, daring him to dream he wasn't destined to ship out that night.

The dream came to a shattering end just after 2:00 a.m., when the sound of two metal pots crashing together filled the barracks, accompanied by a jolting flash of white as every light came on.

"Moving out! Moving out!" the transportation commander boomed in his well-practiced baritone, all the while continuing to smash the pots together. Five minutes later, the barracks were empty. Howston Gastwick, still fumbling with his gun and pack, was the last to exit.

In silence but at attention, they assembled in a small square between the buildings. Chalk was handed out, a single stick to each soldier at the head of each row. Passing it down the line, one by one, they each scrawled the number of a train car and a seat on their helmets. Hogart still could not believe this was happening; with a damp hand, he wrote 3-24 on his olive-drab helmet. Ten minutes later, after a quick, silent march through the dark base, he was seated in seat number twenty-four in train car number three.

Thumpa-thumpa-thumpa of the hurrying train was the only sound he heard on the one-hour trip from upstate to the docks. Hogart stared straight ahead, like most of the other men, silently contemplating. Occasionally, a whimper or soft cry would cut through the silence as the reality became too much for some of the soldiers. But at this point, there was nothing any of them could do. All they knew was that, from now on, there would be no more stopping. The train would lead to a dock, which would lead to a ship, which would cross an ocean and deliver them to a battlefield.

As the train rounded a bend, a collective gasp shot through the car as the magnificent illuminated jumble of the Manhattan skyline filled their windows. They stared across the East River, all thinking the same thing: would they ever see it again, or would this be their final view of the city—or any American city? The thrusting arm of the Empire State Building drew Hogart's eyes. Though he couldn't see it from this distance, he knew that a television transmitter was among the metal tangle at the very top of the epically tall structure. A few hours from now, the Regal Television Network would begin sending images to the three or four thousand television sets scattered around Manhattan. Hogart became sick to his stomach, realizing that, instead of being a part of that broadcast and beginning his journey with this technological wonder, he would be several hundred miles out into the Atlantic Ocean.

With a painful sigh, he allowed his mind to wander as his eyes stared blankly at the deceitful peacefulness of the colorful skyline. He found himself daydreaming of a Nazi soldier a thousand miles away, watching the splendor of some great German city in the dead of night and wondering if he would ever see it again as he rode his own train. He thought about this Nazi's gun, riding above him on an overhead rack, just like Hogart's. He thought about the bullets in this Nazi's gun. Gold. Shiny. Sharp. He fixated on the one already chambered and ready to fire. Polished to perfection. Gleaming. Bright. Destined to pierce Hogart's skull and turn his brains into a pile of useless mush.

The train crunched to a jittery halt.

Looking out the window, not a hundred feet away, Hogart saw a massive troop ship moored to a dock. Thousands of soldiers, split into dozens of squads, milled about in the near darkness, awaiting their turn to head up the gangway to the ship. There was another collective gasp in Hogart's train car as each soldier realized this was his immediate destination. This was real. It was happening. Sergeants suddenly appeared outside the train, one to each car, and began shouting at the men. "Let's go! Fall out! Your mommas aren't here to carry your bags, so grab 'em and move your asses!" It jolted them out of their dazes, and in a flurry of activity, they piled out of the train with their massive packs on their backs and heavy duffel bags in their hands.

Immediately, they lined up in their battalion and joined the huge flow from other cars and other trains, all inching close and closer to the troop ship. Hogart crept along, still filled with disbelief. Not three days earlier, his plan had been working. He had everything set for his transfer out of the MPs and into the world of television. Now, he was heading overseas, where he was sure he would die. And stupid, unthinking, goof-off Frenchy would live. Frenchy had no plan, no clever plot; he hadn't been shrewd and cunning. *Yet he will live, and I will die*, Hogart thought, *all because of a smashed hand.* Then, slowly—and rather surprisingly—Hogart began to grin. *All because of a smashed hand.* The thought kept dancing around Hogart's head, and his grin reached from ear to ear. Smart, intelligent, brilliant Frenchy. He knew the truth. It wasn't about planning; it wasn't about thinking ahead. It wasn't even about being shrewd and cunning.

It was about being willing to do whatever it took to get what you wanted.

There was very little time to act on his epiphany, as his battalion had now moved to within twenty feet of the gangway. There was only one more unit in front of them before they would board. Hogart looked around desperately for the necessary accomplice to his plan. He spotted it just outside the waiting group—the perfect distance; it would affect him and no one else. Nearby, waiting patiently to be craned onto the ship was a ten-by-ten shipping palate piled about five feet high with big round drums full of diesel fuel. The heavy gray metal cylinders were on their sides, stacked like a pyramid and held together by thick rope. Hogart sauntered over, leaned against them, and fished a cigarette out of a pack of Lucky Strikes. He popped it in his mouth, lit it with a rusty Zippo lighter, and took a deep drag. He leaned back farther, seemingly relaxed and enjoying this moment of calm before they would be marched onto the boat. Out of view from everyone, however, Hogart removed his bayonet from his pack and very precisely yet surreptitiously began to slice at one of the ropes that held the pyramid of diesel drums in place. Hogart could feel the blade cutting deeper and deeper into the rope. He worked at it for a few more minutes as he continued to puff on his cigarette. Finally, there was little more than a few strands holding the rope together.

Perfect.

He couldn't slice all the way through, because in the ensuing chaos, his bayonet would end up God knows where—most dangerously, it would not be in his backpack where it belonged, and that would be a dead giveaway. He safely stowed the bayonet in its proper place in his pack. Hogart took one last drag and then dropped his cigarette on the dock. He stubbed it out with his boot and then leaned back one last time, sighing. Hidden from view, his hand slid down, found the thinned part of the rope, and tugged—hard. There was a horrible screeching sound of grinding metal, followed by pressure on Hogart's left leg. And then blackness.

He awoke three days later in a hospital bed, his left leg wrapped in a cast up to his crotch and suspended above the covers. He soon learned that, beneath his bandaged head, he had a severe concussion, and his leg had been broken in about a dozen places. Six months of rehabilitation followed, with Hogart eventually learning to walk again so well that a limp only showed itself occasionally. By the time of the Normandy landing, instead of floating ashore with the rest of the suckers, Hogart was at his job in the nice, warm studio of the Regal Television Network as the news trickled in.

Collecting the printouts as they poured out of the teletype machine, Hogart knew it wasn't planning that had put him in this fortunate position, and it certainly wasn't luck. It was his willingness to do whatever it took to get what he wanted.

...

Horns honked. Buses ground gears. Brakes screeched. Felicity, fully clothed and splayed atop a made bed, cracked open an eye. Through a wavering eyelid, she looked around. *Where am I?* she wondered. *Where am I?* As if answering her question, something rolled off the bed and landed on the ground with a dull thud. Felicity leaned over and picked it up; it was an empty bottle of champagne. "Oh, yeah," she said, as everything came flooding back. She was in Alexis's bedroom and had been in the apartment with Alexis since early last night. They had begun drinking early and had drunk all night, with Alexis finally telling Felicity around 3:00 a.m. that she could have her bedroom. Felicity took it, falling asleep before she could take off her clothes, leaving Alexis to fare for herself on the couch. With the mystery solved, and light from the unfortunately open window blasting her in the eyes, Felicity collapsed back onto the bed. This lifestyle was new to her, and she really didn't know how the others did it; she had been at it only a short while, and it already was killing her. She closed her eyes in the hope that the next time she awoke she would feel better. But sleep didn't come, as Felicity found herself trying to remember when it was that she'd last awakened without a hang-over. It was four days earlier, the morning of the broadcast of Jonny's special episode. From then on, everything was an alcohol-induced blur.

There was the champagne and wine the night of the broadcast, along with the mad lovemaking back at Jonny's—on a mattress on the floor, no less! They'd celebrated the next day and on into the night when they read the great reviews of the episode in the papers. Celebrating yet again the next morning, Jonny had been overjoyed that the *Times* had picked up on what he was really writing about and had run an article retelling the story of the actual accident involving Anderson Vleets. She remembered going with Jonny to a black-tie dinner party at some agent's apartment that night, and then the next day, finally sobering up enough to drop in and see Alexis.

Much to Felicity's surprise, it wasn't easy to leave Jonny behind. They'd been together almost every moment of the last four days, and despite everything playing out through a haze of drinking and celebrating, something powerful was developing between them. It was very different from what she felt around Braeden. The expectations of that relationship were so high, it felt like it belonged not only to them but also to her mother, her father, her sisters, their neighborhood, Braeden's parents and brothers, the city of Greenwich, and even the state of Connecticut.

But what was happening between her and Jonny was strictly about her and Jonny. "Do you think it could really work out between you and me?" she had asked in a playful tone just before she left, belying the deadly seriousness of the question.

"I think Jonny Dirby and Denise Yarnell could do just fine. Jacob Drabinowitz and Felicity Kensington? Well, that's a whole other question," Jonny said flatly. Then he smiled. "But it looks like we're going to find out."

Finally, after a lingering kiss in his apartment doorway and fighting the urge to begin another wild night with him on his now well-worn mattress, Felicity went to check in on Alexis.

She arrived around 8:00 p.m. and found her friend in relatively good spirits. They engaged in mindless chitchat at first—Felicity wanted to wait for the right moment to bring up the real reason she had come over, but Alexis beat her to it.

"I saw the episode the other night. I thought it went pretty well," Alexis offered off-handedly.

"Yes. But not as well as it would have if you had been in it."

"The same could be said for almost any show on Broadway, my dear, but that doesn't mean I'm opening tomorrow as Blanche in *Street Car.*"

Felicity chuckled. So that was how Alexis wanted to play it. Felicity thought about trying to dig down deep to find out why Alexis had run away scared, as it was clear Alexis wouldn't be forthcoming—there would be no sob-filled admission of her failure, just more jokes. So Felicity let it go and moved on to some gossip she had heard about other members of Alexis's class. Soon enough, a bottle of wine came out and the drinking began.

The liquid loosened up Felicity, but it transformed Alexis into a completely different person. She was always the possessor of a sharp tongue, but where sober Alexis's thoughts, words, and movements were tight and controlled, plied-with-alcohol Alexis had wild gestures, expansive body language, and a nonexistent editing mechanism. She regaled Felicity with the story of her career.

She had broken in as a model, armed with a fake birth certificate at the age of sixteen, doing magazine and calendar work. She headed west to Hollywood in her early twenties, where she was a background beauty, wearing a bathing suit, chorus girl outfit, or flapper gown in a series of silent films. Her one talkie was *The Cocoanuts* with the Marx Brothers, where she had a tiny part playing one of the hotel guests. Her scene, however, was cut. Tired of sleeping with casting directors for one line, she moved back east, where at least when she slept with a Broadway casting director, she got a nice scene or sometimes even a decent part. In the early thirties, she fell in with the Group Theatre crowd, and after discovering method acting, everything changed for her. For the next two decades, she sustained a successful career, performing in a series of their shows, as well as other shows on Broadway. But as she grew older, and the 1940s became the 1950s, good roles became scarcer and scarcer. She never went back to movies, but she did try to transition into television and was cast as the sarcastic, seen-it-all mother in the pilot of an NBC family sitcom *The Miltons*. She was replaced after one episode and had to endure the show's becoming a minor hit and running for four years. Finally, she turned to teaching, where she had been able to make just enough to scrape by for the last five years.

Felicity was transfixed, but one thought careened around in her head. With all these performances, over so many years, in front of thousands and thousands of people, how could she have suddenly gotten too scared to perform? The thought was incompatible—and inconceivable—when placed in the context of the fearless woman before her. But as incongruous as it was, the reality of the situation was unchanged. It had happened. It must have been the cameras, Felicity finally concluded. She understood how unforgiving the electronic eye could be and just how daunting the thought was of performing in front of millions of unseen people.

Something Alexis said later in the evening, when they were quite drunk, now came back to Felicity. After detailing her career, Alexis had moved on to her love life. She'd had a series of affairs, mostly with other actors and a few directors, but also the occasional "civilian," as she liked to refer to anyone not in entertainment. All of them ended—some easily, most poorly. Now, she was done with love, and everything else in between, because "in the end, you can't run away from your past."

In the end, you can't run away from your past. Alexis's words struck Felicity like a slap across the face. That's what Felicity had been doing. That's what all her drinking and smoking and fucking really had been about. She was trying to run away from her past, even if it had only been five days.

Felicity had tried calling home several times but always felt relieved to get a busy signal. It was a half-hearted effort—she always called at a time when there was a good chance no one would be home, as she dreaded hearing about how awful the barbecue had been. She also knew, once she made the call, everything would be over. She would be asked to come home, and there, in the presence of her mother, father, and two hundred years of Kensingtons, she would come forth with the names.

And that would be that.

No more rehearsals, no more broadcasts, no more smoky parties, no more overflowing empty-beer-bottle ashtrays, no more crazed conversations with cigarette smoke pouring out. And no more Jonny.

The thought of the loss made her sad, a slow sinking pain that became so intense it shocked her. This was the first time she had really thought about what coming forth with the names would really mean—not so much for the people named but for herself. She would be forever altering her life, too, steering it away from this new course she was being blown down by gale force winds.

With unbelievable heaviness, she reached for the phone on the night table next to Alexis's bed. But just as she was about to grab the handle, she stopped.

Why did it have to end?

What if she told her father that she'd found nothing? She had been wrong; there were no Communist or subversive writers working on the show. She'd looked long and hard but found nothing. He would be mad, saying that she had wasted all of their time and, in fact, had made things worse, but he'd eventually get over it. His political career might be over, but he'd find other ways, as he had, to keep the cause alive.

But most important, she would be able to stay right where she was, in the thick of it all, with Jonny at her side.

Steeled with this new determination, she reached for the phone and dialed. The sooner she told them, the sooner they'd rip into her, and the sooner they would get over it.

"Kensington residence," Viola answered officiously.

"Hi, Viola. It's Felicity."

"Oh, Miss Kensington, we've been wondering about you."

"Yes, I assumed that." She swallowed hard, steeling herself. "Is anyone home?"

"Yes, both your mother and father. But they're in the backyard, supervising the construction."

"Construction?"

"Yes. For the event this Sunday."

Felicity's eyes tightened, confused. "You mean, it's happening?"

"Very much so. In fact, it's sold out."

Alarm bells went off in Felicity's head. Something was wrong. "Viola, please ask my father to come to the phone."

"Yes, miss."

How is this possible? Felicity wondered. Her father had been dreading the barbecue, sure that the fund-raiser would be canceled, but now it was on—and sold out. What was happening?

Felicity heard rustling through the earpiece. "Miss Kensington, I'm afraid he can't come to the phone right now," Viola said. "But he wanted me to thank you."

"Thank me? For what?"

"I'm afraid he didn't say."

"Well, could you go—"

"Miss Felicity, if you'll excuse me, another delivery truck has just arrived, and I need to greet them."

Another truck? What the hell is going on there? Felicity wondered. "Oh. Okay. Thank you, Viola. Tell them I'll try—" Viola hung up before she could finish.

Felicity held the receiver, stunned. Her mind reeled. *He thanked me? Why in the world would my father thank me? What possibly could have happened? What could have changed?* As if answering her questions, a gust of wind blew through the open window, rifling the pages of several magazines on the nightstand before knocking them to the floor. Felicity reached down to pick them up but then paused.

The wind.

What if she hadn't dropped the list of investigated names in the trash, as she thought she had. After all, Jonny had startled her, so she'd done it in a hurry. What if she had missed the garbage can and the list had landed on the floor, only to be discovered by her father when he came home later in the day? He would have figured Felicity left the list on his desk and the breeze from an open window must have blown it onto the floor. It had to be that. Why else would they be setting up for the fund-raiser? Her father must have leaked word that he was about to make a big splash—the story of a show written entirely by blacklisted writers was probably going to hit the papers any day, and that made everyone buy up the tickets. He had just what he needed to become the party's choice, and the names on the list were his ammunition.

Felicity leaped out of bed. She was scheduled to meet up with Jonny later in the afternoon in the furniture department at Gimbels to help him buy everything he needed for his empty apartment. But as she quickly made herself presentable, she realized she needed to get to him as soon as possible. She had to warn him, which meant she had to come clean. Yes, she would tell him the truth. It wouldn't be easy, but she had to do it. And she had no idea how he would take the news.

Felicity turned the knob on the bedroom door, but when she tried to push it open, it didn't budge. She stepped back to see that a bright red blanket was shoved under the door from the other side. "Alexis!" she yelled, but no answer came back.

Perplexed, Felicity threw her body weight against the door, and slowly it inched open, the red blanket scraping along the cheap linoleum. Before Felicity stepped into the living room, a strong, overwhelming, acrid smell hit her. She knew right away what it was.

Gas.

...

"Perhaps at some point, when you make the skirts long enough," Jonny said, finishing his tale.

Across the table, Rod Serling burst out laughing. "That's vintage Blanche all right. You gotta love her."

"I guess, Rod," Jonny said with a playful weariness, though inside he still did not quite believe he had reached the point that he could call Rod Serling "Rod." They'd been at lunch for a little over an hour, and the two of them had clicked from the start. Amid the chaos of the previous week, Jonny had reached out to Blanche Gaines, hoping she was ready to read some of his less "kiddie" stuff. His entreaties had gone ignored until two nights earlier, when she had invited him to a viewing party at her Park Avenue apartment. It was to celebrate an episode of *Studio One* written by Gore Vidal. Besides Gore Vidal being there, that night Jonny had met Reginald Rose, Paddy Chayefsky, Arnold Schulman, and several other great writers of television but not Rod. He was supposed to be there but had called at the last minute to cancel, claiming he had a deadline. Taking pity on a disappointed Jonny, Blanche had arranged the lunch. Two days later, here they were in the world-famous Marimba Room, just two writers talking shop.

"But I'd love her a lot more if she would show some interest in my work," Jonny continued with a sigh.

"Give it time. She can be a tough nut to crack. With me, she was waiting for me to do something dramatic to show her I was serious. So I moved to New York from Ohio."

Jonny's eyes brightened. "I just moved out of my parents' place in Washington Heights."

Rod shot out a short laugh. "I'm afraid you need to at least change area codes."

Jonny glowered and lowered his head into his hands. "I don't want to spend the rest of my life writing kiddie stuff."

"Is that what you're doing?" Serling asked, leading, as he sipped his post-lunch coffee. "Sometimes the best punch is the one no one sees coming."

Jonny flinched. "But 'Patterns'—that was a shot straight to the gut of the American dream."

Serling nodded. "Yes. But think of how I went about doing it. If I'd written something about how capitalism is a monstrous machine that spits people out and has no regard for anything human, they'd simply dismiss it by calling me a Communist, and that would be the end of that. But if I disguise it as a battle of youth versus age, the old way of doing things compared to the new, then all they see is a great drama, while the rest of it slips in unnoticed." Serling raised a playful eyebrow. "Kind of like what you've been doing with *Justice Girl*."

Jonny wanted to act cool, but Rod Serling had just complimented him. He cracked a broad and uncontained smile. "Thank you," he said, with an appreciative nod, even as he fought the urge to get up and dance.

Serling shrugged, taking another sip of his coffee. "What are you thanking me for? It's only the truth."

Jonny's smile got even bigger. "If you'll excuse me, I have to use the bathroom." He dropped his napkin on the table as he stood.

"By all means, and have fun," Rod said after him.

As Jonny walked away, his pace quickened. The truth was, he'd had to go to the bathroom for the last half hour but just didn't want to leave the table for fear that when he came back, Serling would be gone. But now his bladder was on the verge of bursting, so he hurried down the sweeping staircase that led from the exclusive second-floor dining area of the Marimba Room and down to the main level. Despite the slight pain from his condition, this had to be the greatest day of his life. Not only was he having lunch with Rod Serling, but in reading the *New York Times* before Rod arrived, Jonny had noticed a small article buried several pages inside the paper. "White House delays medal ceremony," the average-sized headline read. The story was short: "Today the White House announced it would postpone the medal ceremony to honor Anderson Vleets. No future date has been scheduled."

It had worked. It had actually worked.

Not that Jonny could have envisioned three days earlier that his quickly written and slapped-together episode would lead to all this. He had created it from a place of pain, of desperation, of the deep need to find some way to strike back at Anderson now that he was about to be cleansed of his patheticness and legitimized. Jonny was too old to seriously consider shooting him again, not to mention that both Eddie Kubinski and Frankie Zannis were serving time in Sing-Sing, so finding a gun wouldn't be so easy this time around. The good reviews of the episode had led to an article in the *Times* that revisited the original accident during the war and the persistent rumors of a cover-up. Then there was the follow-up story, with the presidential press pool pressing Eisenhower's press secretary to comment, and then finally the article this morning. It had happened. His stupid television show had actually brought about some justice. Rachel was still dead, and Anderson was still alive. But for once, and probably the only time in his life, Anderson Vleets had been denied something. It wasn't quite what Jonny had once wanted— Anderson crumpled on the ground in a pool of his own blood with a hole in his chest—but it still felt pretty darn good.

As he reached the bottom of the staircase, he walked briskly across the giant black-and-white marimba keys painted on the floor, passing the tables of the mere mortals who came to the restaurant in hope of catching a glimpse of the famous who dined above them. Jonny found the long corridor that led to the bathroom. The walls were bright and colorful, painted to look like a South American jungle, and when Jonny passed the telephone room, a man in a drab suit slipped out and started following him. Not that he was famous, but over the last two weeks, since the profiles started appearing in the newspaper and magazines, Jonny had been noticed on a few occasions and had even signed a few autographs.

So when Jonny went to the sink after using the urinal, he wasn't surprised to see the same man standing there, holding a piece of paper. Jonny gave the rather dour man a warm smile. "It would be my pleasure," Jonny said, searching for a pen. Finding one, he reached out to sign the light blue slip of paper.

"That's not necessary," the man said, waving him off. "You don't need to sign for it."

Jonny looked at him confused. "Sign for it?"

"Yeah, for your subpoena," the man said. He quickly stuffed the blue slip into Jonny's breast pocket and walked out.

Stunned and almost afraid to touch it, Jonny carefully pulled the paper out of his pocket and unfolded it. *You are hereby ordered to appear* was as far as Jonny got before he threw up in the sink.

"I've been fuckin' subpoenaed by the House Un-American Activities Committee!" Jonny shouted at Hogart, slamming the blue slip down on the fancy coffee table. Both Hogart and Charles jumped, shocked by the action. The three of them were assembled in the gleaming showroom of the Pacific Mercury Electronics Company, one of several companies scattered around Manhattan that specialized in developing and selling the latest broadcast equipment to high-end buyers. Jonny had tracked down Hogart and Charles right after mumbling a hasty good-bye to Rod and hurrying out of the restaurant.

Hogart's visit to Pacific Mercury made sense with what Jonny had been hearing over the last few days. Though boardroom battles were entirely the purview of the management of the network, some word had leaked out to Jonny, most of it by way of Charles, that there had been some sort of a vote, and that it had gone entirely Hogart's way. Ever since then, there had been a noticeable sense of reinvigoration to the operations of the network—from a redesigned on-air logo, to plans to fill in some of the empty spots in the schedule with new shows, to talk of switching over to more advanced broadcasting technologies in order to deliver a higher-quality image.

Now, Jonny watched Hogart and Charles for a reaction. Though he hated to deal with them alone, Jonny didn't really have a choice. Mitchell was still upstate, relaxing, and wouldn't be back in the city for a few more days, and there was no way he would bring a fool like Marty into a situation like this. Besides, Jonny figured at this point, in spite of the numerous disagreements with Hogart and Charles, they would all be on the same side of this issue. Jonny certainly wanted no part of it, and he knew the network didn't either. This was exactly the kind of thing that could bring *Justice Girl* to a quick and sudden end.

"Let me see that," Hogart said, grabbing the subpoena off the glass coffee table. He looked at it quickly, shook his head, and then passed it over to Charles, who reacted in the same way.

"What do we do?" Jonny asked.

Hogart closed his eyes as he pinched the bridge of his nose between his thumb and forefinger. "Well, this is a bit of a problem. Let me think about it."

Jonny paced. "What do you think they want from me?"

"What they want from everyone," Charles said flatly. "To know if you are now, or have ever been, a member of the Communist Party."

"I haven't been, and I'm certainly not now," Jonny answered, almost defiantly.

"And they'll want to know if you've ever known anyone who was a member—acquaintances, friends, someone you've worked with in the past or... now," Charles continued.

Jonny's face fell. "Oh..." he said glumly.

"This is quite a mess you've gotten yourself into," Hogart finally concluded.

"*Me?*" Jonny said incredulously.

"Yes, *you,*" Hogart shot back. "Did you really think you could get away with using blacklisted writers? I tried to warn you, but now you're going to pay for the mistakes of others."

Jonny clenched his teeth and quietly seethed. He wanted to scream at Hogart and tell him to go fuck himself, but he didn't. He knew there was a kernel of truth in what he had said. In the end, it was Jonny who'd chosen to bring the other three in on the show. And yes, now he was paying for it. *No good deed goes unpunished,* he thought. He exhaled loudly and said plaintively, "There must be something that can be done to make this go away."

"There might be," Hogart offered optimistically. "The network does have a certain amount of power in these kinds of situations—when it chooses to use it. But on the other hand, you're asking us to get involved with something that has real potential to blow up into a disaster."

"But isn't it worth it to protect one of your assets? Me?" Jonny countered.

"Yes, but it would be nice to get something in return for the risk."

Jonny eyed Hogart suspiciously. "Why do I have a feeling I know what's coming?"

"Because you're a smart man," Hogart said cheerfully. "And that's why I'm betting you'll take my offer."

Was he a smart man? Jonny wondered as he rode in the back of a cab, making his way across town to meet Felicity. Swaying back and forth as the cab swerved through traffic, Jonny thought through Hogart's offer. As much as it sickened him, he returned to the same position: Hogart was right; he should take the deal. "Sign all rights to the character over to the network, and then we can help you," Hogart had said. "See how all of this is wearing you down? All of it—the limelight, the pressure, the fame. There are some writers that want it, but not you. I can tell you're serious. You just want to write. Sign the character over to us, we'll make the subpoena go away, and you can write without all the distractions."

Jonny fought the urge to throw up again. Just two hours earlier, he'd been having lunch with Rod Serling at a reserved seat on the famed upper level of the Marimba Room, listening to his idol heap praise on *Justice Girl*. And now, he was actually contemplating letting go of his creation forever. As Jonny saw it, he had three options before him. His first option would be to appear in front of the committee, take the fifth, refuse to answer their questions, retain the rights to Justice *Girl*, and effectively end his career.

He would be blacklisted.

His second option would be to appear in front of the committee, give them the names Annie, Shel, and Burton, claiming that he'd just found out about their subversive pasts. They were already blacklisted, so what difference would it make to them? And besides, he wasn't really on speaking terms with any of them at the moment.

But Jonny knew if he did that, he couldn't live with himself. He'd still have *Justice Girl*, but he'd lose his soul.

The third option—the easiest and cleanest—would be to take the deal from Hogart. He could see it all laid before him, so simple, so clear. Sign his name on the dotted line, the subpoena would vanish, and *Justice Girl* would be gone.

And then he could stop giving a shit.

He'd take one of the deals Marty had lined up for him. Hell, he'd take all of them. They were just stupid kiddie shows after all, right? He could whip out a script for one of those in an afternoon. An afternoon? Hell, he could turn one around in an hour! Who cares if they were any good? Quality didn't matter. They'd come up with a gimmick to get people to watch—a few planted items, some fake controversies. Piece of cake. The money would come pouring in, and before he knew it, he would be able to afford a house like Felicity's. And a girl like Felicity, with a sexy B-movie actress on the side, and maybe even a waitress named Larraine, too! Yes, it was all laid out for him—his for the taking. And in the end, it was the only real option. But as he climbed out of the cab, the question danced in front of him again. Was he a smart man?

Why not?

...

Where is he? Felicity wondered as she completed yet another orbit of the furniture department at Gimbels. It was almost three-thirty. She needed to see Jonny, now, and he was late. She had called the Marimba Room and had just missed him, and after that, she had no idea where he had gone. She even tried the writers' room, but it was deserted, and no one in the studio or the production offices had a clue. *Of all the times to go missing!* Originally, she had planned to arrive early, to scope out some furniture sets that she liked, so that when Jonny arrived, she would have winnowed down the choices to a nice, tight list. But with all that had happened in the last couple of hours, she found it impossible to concentrate and instead just walked in circles around the ample display of home furnishings.

Finally, she saw Jonny's face emerge as he rode the escalator up to where she was on the third floor. She steeled herself against a wall of cabinets as he stepped off and came ambling toward her. There was lightness to his gait and a strange look on his face. It was a smile. Felicity's head jerked back; she'd never seen Jonny smile before. He strode toward her, absent-mindedly running his fingers across several of the desks that were on display. He stopped to look at a lamp, pulling on the drawstring several times, seemingly enjoying the staccato bursts of light. Clearly, he hadn't heard.

"Hello," Jonny said breezily when he reached her. "Sorry I'm a little late. I stopped by the stamp department on the second floor. I thought I might start collecting stamps again. I haven't done it since I was about twelve years old and—"

"Alexis killed herself," Felicity stated flatly.

Jonny's lightness disappeared. "Wh...what?"

"This morning, when I woke up, I found her on the couch. She turned on the gas last night after I went to bed." Felicity collapsed on Jonny. "Why did she do it? *Why did she do it?*"

Jonny's face went white. Felicity was in his arms, but he was not aware of holding her. "Acting...was her life," he finally said, struggling to comprehend what she had just told him.

"But it would have come back. She would have gotten over her stage fright. There would have been other shows. She could have been in another episode."

Jonny eased Felicity away from him. "Felicity, she didn't quit the show because of stage fright. She quit the show because of you," Jonny said, letting go of a burden. Felicity looked up at him, bewildered. "To protect you."

"What are you talking about?" Felicity asked, breaking away from Jonny's hold.

Jonny ran his hands through his hair, frustrated. "Alexis had been blacklisted years ago. That's why her part was recast in *The Miltons* and why she had never appeared on television since then. When the casting director sent her name in, the network wouldn't clear her. About two hours before air, they made it quite clear they wouldn't let her go on. I was ready to fight them to the bitter end. But Alexis stopped me. She was afraid it would all come back on you, since you were the one who had vouched for her and brought her in the first place. She didn't want to see your career snuffed out at the very start. So, we concocted the story about her stage fright. I was against it, but Alexis made me swear to go along with it." Jonny looked off into the distance, his whole body seeming sunken. "I think she got tired of fighting."

"Oh, my God," Felicity said, almost falling to her knees. "So, I killed her."

Jonny put a reassuring hand on her shoulder. "It's a little more complicated than that."

"No, it's not," Felicity said, as she collapsed into the armchair of a staged living room, complete with faux walls, windows, and a television. *This is it; this is the moment I tell him*, Felicity thought, as Jonny fell into the armchair next to her, completing the image of the happy domestic future they might have had. She carefully reached across the armchair to squeeze Jonny's hand. "Jonny..." she began tremulously, "there's...something I have to tell you. Do me one favor and let me get through it all before you say anything." With that, Felicity came clean, leaving nothing out—why she had first auditioned for *Hermie's Henhouse*, the anti-Communist pamphlet her father published, his political ambitions. She kept her gaze locked on the floor beneath her feet, but noticed from the corner of her eye that Jonny's face was turning a horrific shade of red. But when she finished her story and finally found the courage to hold her head up and look at him, she found him eerily calm. His skin had lost its crimson hue, and his eyes had lost their fury.

"Thank you," Jonny said.

"For...what?"

"For reminding me which side I'm on." With that, he stood up and walked away. Felicity watched him go, almost trembling. But then, when he was about twenty feet away, he suddenly stopped and turned back. Felicity's eyes brightened, and she moved toward him, hopeful.

"No," he said flatly.

Felicity stopped in her tracks. "No?"

"No, I don't think it could work out between you and me." He turned back around and continued moving away.

Her eyes darkened and the trembling returned. Desperate, Felicity called after him, but he didn't stop, not hearing—or not listening. But it didn't matter. Either way, he was gone.

...

As per their last conversation, Jonny found Hogart and Charles waiting at the assigned time in Hogart's office. Four copies of Hogart's offer splayed neatly in front of Hogart, fanned on his desk, with a pen at the ready. "I'm sorry to make you waste paper," Jonny said as he burst in. "I'm turning down your offer."

Hogart and Charles both turned and looked at each other, but oddly, they didn't seem surprised.

"It looks like the writer and creator of your number one show is about to go in front of a congressional committee and be labeled a Communist," Jonny said, with all the pleasantness of a wedding announcement.

"Actually, what it looks like," Hogart said, "is that Charles owes me dinner." Hogart then turned to Charles. "I told you he'd never go for the offer."

"Very well. So be it," Charles said dismissively.

Jonny took another step forward. "You're damn right I wouldn't go for the offer. And I never will. *Justice Girl* is mine—forever."

But Hogart was unfazed. "You see, Charles, it's just like I told you: to some men, there is something worth more than money. Not you, not me, but there are some. And Johnny is one of them. It's called integrity." He turned to Jonny. "But fortunately for Charles and me, there is something even more important to you than integrity. Shame. The shame that you might bring to your family."

Jonny smiled. "That's it? That's your ace in the hole? That I'm afraid of bringing shame on my family by being accused of being a Communist?" Jonny laughed. "I'm in entertainment; in their eyes, I was lost years ago. Being a Communist would almost be a relief to them, compared to what I could be in their worst nightmares. You're the ones who have to worry, because my parents couldn't care less what I say to the committee."

"It's not what you'll say, Jonny," Charles said, taking a step closer. "It's what *I'll* say. You're not the only one who was subpoenaed."

Jonny's head jerked back, stunned.

Charles nodded for emphasis. "Yep, that's right. I got served several months ago. In fact, I'm the one who named you."

Jonny felt the wind go out of his lungs. He stared across the desk at Charles in disbelief. "You?"

"Yep," Charles said, nodding at his own reasonableness. "When you're the son of a famous man, and you meet a girl who shows interest in you without knowing your last name, you'll follow her to the ends of the earth. Or to a couple of Communist Party meetings, in this case. So when they asked if I knew any Communists or Communist sympathizers, naturally I named you."

"You son of a bitch," Jonny said, more resigned than angry. "Not that I should be surprised." Jonny glared at Hogart. "That still doesn't solve your problem. I'm still not going to sign over *Justice Girl*. As I said, I'm happy to talk to the committee."

"As am I," Charles continued. "You see, I'm not done with my testimony. I have another session in a day or two, and I can say one of two things. I can say I misspoke about Jonny Dirby, that I got him confused with someone else—you know how it is with those Communists; they all look alike. Or I can tell them another tale. About a soldier in Germany after the war ended who let—or perhaps it was *helped*—a top nuclear scientist escape to Russia. Talk about Communist sympathizers!"

Jonny lunged at Charles. "You bastard!"

Hogart flew out from behind his desk and caught Jonny just inches from Charles. He pushed Jonny away. "I don't think you need to add assault to your problems," Hogart said matter-of-factly. To his relief, Jonny didn't go after Charles again; instead, with his chest heaving, he held his ground. "Good," Hogart said, satisfied. "Now that you know what's at stake, I know you'll be signing whatever deal we put in front of you."

Jonny flinched, just enough to make Charles jump back. But Hogart was unfazed. Finally, Jonny's shoulders melted, his chest sank, and his eyes found the floor. "Yes," Jonny answered with a whole-body sigh, knowing there was no point in ruminating over it any further. It was true that his parents could handle any bad press concerning him—not that they would particularly like it, but it just wouldn't come entirely as a surprise. *Anything and everything is expected from those entertainment types.* But Mitchell was a whole other story. His mother's recovery from Rachel's death and her entire status in the neighborhood was linked to Mitchell's greatness. If Charles named Mitchell and the story got out—which of course it would—it would ruin his mother. It had taken her years to recover from the loss of Rachel; this, she never would. "Yes," he said again, thoroughly defeated.

Emotionless and without a word, Jonny signed all four copies of the agreement. Done, he dropped the pen back on the desk.

Hogart grabbed it and eagerly countersigned the contracts. Pleased, he scooped up the executed documents and eyed them happily. "MGM Pictures has Leo the Lion; Walt Disney Productions has Mickey Mouse." Hogart paused as his grin broadened. "And now, the Regal-Vleets Broadcasting Corporation has Justice Girl."

...

The spring tease of the warm summer to come was gone by the time Felicity's cab made its way up the long drive of her house in the fading sunlight. Clogging the top of the driveway were several work trucks, confirming what Viola had said over the phone—preparations were in full swing for the fundraiser in just a few days. Felicity quickly paid her driver and headed inside. She hurried into her father's empty study, dug out a copy of "Fight Back," flipped through it and, finding what she was looking for, nodded knowingly.

She found her father in the backyard, talking with the crew foreman who was overseeing the construction of a large stage amid the loud clatter of hammers and saws. Felicity hurried toward him, darting between the forest of several dozen dinner tables that had already been put in place for the event.

Seeing Felicity approach, her father smiled. "There she is—the woman of the hour."

"You have to stop this. Now," Felicity said. "You can't go forward with it."

Her father turned to the foreman. "If you'll excuse me..." He then pulled Felicity off to the side. "What has gotten into you?" he asked sharply.

"You can't just destroy people for your own personal gain. If you throw a name out into the public, it does more than keep that person from working. It can ruin his entire life." Felicity felt her father's glare burning into her, but she couldn't back down. Not now. Searching for strength, she imagined herself as Justice Girl, stopping a foe from a dastardly crime. "I forbid you from using the names."

Her father looked at her, somewhat bemused. Then he shook his head. "I'm not using anybody's name, and I'm certainly not throwing anything wildly out to the public. I don't need to, when I've got you." He turned around and pointed toward the stage as a huge banner was unfurled, featuring an enormous image of one of the publicity shots of Felicity dressed as Justice Girl.

Felicity stared in shock at the twenty-foot-tall visage of herself, standing proudly in her tight blouse, short skirt, and flowing cape. For good measure, it had an American flag behind her. "But the names of the writers…" Felicity said, trying to piece together what was happening.

Her father beamed. "You're worth a thousand shows written by blacklisted writers." He took hold of Felicity. "I wish you had been there, Felicity, at the barbecue last weekend. All anyone wanted to talk about was you as Justice Girl. They were thrilled! They wanted to know everything about you, and everyone wanted to meet you. When I told everyone that you would be here this weekend, we sold out our remaining tickets in half an hour. Half an hour! No one cared about what's-his-name with his war-hero son; all they wanted to hear about was you!" Her father hugged her deeply. "Do you realize what this means? The nomination's mine, and it's all because of you!"

Felicity's knees buckled, and she struggled to stay on her feet as she broke free from her father's embrace. "But you can't do this. Justice Girl is about fighting for what's good, for what's right, for what's just."

"That's why it's so perfect for my campaign. I fight for it in the Senate, while my daughter fights for it on television."

"But what you do isn't right," Felicity blurted out. "What you do isn't good, and it certainly isn't justice."

Her father looked at her strangely. "What's gotten into you?"

Felicity took a moment to calm herself. "I used to have this friend…" she began firmly, her emotions in check. "She was talented, passionate, inspiring. But she's dead now. She killed herself because she couldn't work. And you know why she couldn't work? Because you named her in your goddamn pamphlet!" Felicity practically shoved the pamphlet in his face. "That's all it took. No chance for her to defend herself; just no more work."

"The guilty have to pay for what they did," her father said through gritted teeth.

"Do you know what her crime was?" Felicity asked pointedly as she flipped the pamphlet open to the right page. "She attended a Russian war relief rally during the war." She held it up for her father to see it.

Her father threw open his hands. "Well, there you have it. Can you imagine helping out those godless Communists?"

Felicity stepped forward, and her father almost stumbled back, unaccustomed to her aggressiveness. "It was the same Russian war relief rally that *we* attended!"

"Nonsense," her father said dismissively. "We did no such thing."

"Yes, we did. And do you know why I remember? I got raped the night before."

"Martha!" her father yelled, backing away from Felicity and again almost stumbling to the ground. "Martha!"

"Yes, I was raped," Felicity said, pursuing her father, "and I got pregnant. All this time I've been helping you because I was convinced that what you were doing and what you believed in was going to make us all safer. But I realize now, you were never interested in making anyone safe, not then—leaving a fifteen-year-old girl alone in a hotel room in New York—and certainly not now."

"Martha!" her father yelled again as Felicity's mother finally came into view, rushing to join them.

"What is it?" her mother said, catching her breath.

"Talk to your daughter; she's lost her mind," her father said before stepping away, relieved.

"What's wrong, Felicity?" her mother asked, moving to block Felicity from going after her father.

"All of this. It has to end. The calls, the lists, the innuendos—his political career. It has to end. People are getting hurt."

"Stop it," her mother said, alarmed by Felicity's intensity.

"Innocent people."

"I said stop it."

"Good people."

Her mother gently pushed her back. "Enough, Felicity. Do you really think I don't understand what's happening to you?"

"How could you possibly understand?"

"Because your father was not my first fiancé."

Felicity looked at her mother, stunned. The story of their courtship and marriage had always been portrayed as something of a fairy tale. Love at first sight, leading to an extravagant wedding not even three months later.

"His name was Ernesto Gomez," her mother said. "Yes, he was from Spain. At least, that was what I was going to tell your grandmother. The truth was that he was from Mexico. Spain, Cuba—there was a chance they could handle that, especially if he came from a wealthy family. But Mexico? I don't think that even if he'd owned the Baja Peninsula they would have gone for that. But he wasn't rich; he was a musician. He played saxophone in a big band, and one year after they played the winter carnival, I ran off with him. For two months, I rode in the band bus with him, all over the South. About a week into the trip, the band's ukulele player announced that she was pregnant and getting married and quitting the band. How perfect was that? I would simply learn the ukulele and take her place. And I did. It was like a dream, a fantasy, the perfect life. There I was, touring with the man I loved. By day we played in the band, and by night we played together. We were going to get married. Then we arrived in Charlotte, and my mother and father were waiting there to meet me. They demanded that I come home. And I did."

"I'm sorry," Felicity said, seeing her mother as slightly human for the first time.

"No. Don't be. It was the best thing that ever happened to me. It's one thing when you're a wide-eyed eighteen-year-old, but another thing altogether when you're finally grown up. Can you imagine what my life would be like today? Married to a saxophonist and playing the ukulele in a band?"

Felicity thought of her own feelings. "But it's the first time I've ever felt like this. Like I belong, like it's where I should be. Like it's who I should be with—not because it's what's expected, but because it's what I want."

Her mother slowly shook her head. "It won't last. What you see all around you—this is real. This is what will still be here when the newness and the passion have gone away. Your father may not be the nicest man, but he's a steady man." She looked Felicity straight in the face. "Do what you have to do. Be with whom you have to be with. Just make sure in the end, you come home."

...

Stepping off the elevator just after 7:00 a.m., Jonny headed down the hall to the writers' office. All he wanted to do was sleep, but now that *Justice Girl* was no longer his, he wanted to clear out his things before the network stopped paying the bill and they were all evicted. Even though he was still the executive producer for the episode on Sunday, with the deal signed, he wouldn't put it past Hogart to lock them out today. Because of his exhaustion and general weariness, each step was a bigger ordeal than the last. But as he closed in on the door and the slumped figure of a woman sleeping against it, he knew his dream of collapsing onto one of the couches was temporarily on hold. Seeing Felicity lying there, he knew he should be furious, but he was just too damn tired.

Felicity stirred at the sound of Jonny's footsteps. She opened her eyes and sat up. "I was hoping you would be the earliest."

Jonny managed a slight chuckle. "Actually, it's late for me. I haven't been to sleep yet." He unlocked the door and walked inside.

Felicity pulled herself up to her feet and followed him into the room.

Jonny ignored her and collapsed on one of the couches. Felicity sat down on the one directly across from him. While Jonny stretched out, too exhausted for any pretense, Felicity sat rigidly upright, her hands stiffly in her lap.

"You can relax," Jonny said, lying flat on his back with closed eyes. "I'm too beat to scream at you."

But Felicity didn't move. "Where have you been?" she finally asked.

"Here, there, everywhere," Jonny said, moving his hands. And he wasn't lying. Since leaving Hogart and Charles, Jonny had wandered the city, a haunted man, the words "the Regal-Vleets Broadcasting Corporation" playing over and over in his head. With the large cash infusion from Anderson that came with the new name, the sky was the limit, with *Justice Girl* leading the way. It was bad enough to lose his creation, but now it was going to grow to unparalleled heights, with all of Jonny's hard work profiting not only Hogart but Anderson Vleets himself. It had taken all of his strength not to collapse into the gutter and vomit.

So Jonny had walked on, trying to outrun the nightmare, but it hadn't work. He walked streets he had walked hundreds of times before, but nothing had seemed familiar. The world had become a strange place, inhabited by people scheming to take advantage of him, to use him. Eventually, he found himself in an odd, negative-image re-creation of the day that Jonny, Annie, Shel, and Burton first had fleshed out *Justice Girl*. He retraced their steps backward from the Automat to the post office, down Fifth Avenue to Washington Square Park, and then over to Veleska, as if hoping to go all the way back to square one, back to the moment before he created *Justice Girl*. Back to a world where his greatest creation did not exist and was yet to be lost to the evil hands of the person he hated most in life. But it didn't work. The character was still gone. Only Jonny himself had regressed; in three days, he would be just another unemployed writer. And the only reason he wasn't one now was because this Sunday's script was the one he had written that had been bumped off the air for the last two weeks in a row.

His wandering went on for hours. He took buses, ferries, trains—anything to distract him from the reality of what had happened. The temperature dropped; his sport coat was ill suited to give him the protection he needed, but still he kept going. It was as if by staying on the move, there might still be a chance it wasn't real.

But it was.

By midnight he was cold and hungry, and his legs ached from his feet up to his shins. He found himself just down the street from his new apartment. Inside were shelter and sustenance and a nice warm bed. But when he reached the front entrance, he kept on going. His mission had changed. Somewhere over the last few blocks, he realized there just might be one more way out of this. It was a long shot, but what did he have to lose?

Thirty minutes later, he was deep in the Bronx, in an unusually nice section, where the stubby tenement buildings gave way to large, single-family homes left over from when this was a pastoral, unincorporated part of the city. Jonny crept down the block, eyeing each one closely, searching for the one he wanted. It wasn't easy; he'd only been here once before, when he was a young boy. At that time, his father had been in charge of directions, and being one in the morning didn't help things either.

Finally, reaching a sagging, three-story, vaguely Victorian structure, he stopped. *This must be the place*, he thought. For final confirmation, he snuck around to the side and saw the familiar sagging doorway surrounded by several windows. *This is the place*, Jonny concluded, and to his delight, though he couldn't see any detail through the opaque windows, the lights were definitely on.

Jonny knocked. No answer. Jonny knocked again. Still no answer.

Regrettably, he walked away, realizing he would have to take a more direct approach. He slipped around to the front of the house, walked up the dark front walk, and knocked on the heavy wooden door. Through the inlaid glass he saw lights come on. "Who is it?" an edgy, elderly female voice asked.

"My name is Jacob Drabinowitz. I would like to see Clarence Regal," Jonny said, hoping his voice sounded unthreatening.

"It's very late. Come back tomorrow."

"I can't. I really need to see him now."

"Well, it's not possible."

"Will you do this for me? Will you tell him I've come to see him, and I have a beautiful C14 plate block to show him? Would you do that for me?" Jonny asked, fully prepared to move on to begging if this didn't work.

There was no answer. Jonny took this as a good sign. As he waited, he thought of the only other time he had been to this house. It was many years ago, just before the war. Clarence Regal was an avid stamp collector and one of his father's most loyal customers. Once a week he would travel up to the Bronx to meet Regal and bring him a fresh round of approvals. Inevitably, Regal was satisfied, usually purchasing everything Jonny's father brought. Regal collected airmails from around the world, with a special emphasis on Zeppelin Post. The one time Jonny had come along, he and his father had immediately gone around to the side of the house, knocking on the sagging side door. Regal himself had answered, happily ushering Jonny and his father inside. Though their business was transacted just inside the door, Jonny could see farther into the room and marveled at all the test tubes, wires, meters, and electrical equipment on display. This was Regal's home laboratory. Years later, Jonny was to learn this was where the practical home use of television was born.

"Go around to the side," the elderly voice finally called out. "He'll see you."

"Thank you," Jonny said happily. He scurried back around to the side. This time, as it had been on that night all those years ago, a small ornate light fixture above the sagging doorway was ablaze, inviting company. Standing under it, basking in its glow, Jonny knocked.

Clarence Regal pulled open the door and stood before Jonny. "Hello," Regal said, clearly a little surprised. "I...I was expecting someone a little older."

"I'm Jonny...er, Jacob Drabinowitz. I'm Samuel's son. We met once, many years ago."

"I'm sorry; I don't remember. Your father, is he okay?"

"He's fine. That's not why I'm here. May I come in?"

"Of course," Regal said, stepping aside and letting Jonny enter.

Once inside, Regal shut the door behind him. Jonny got his first good look at Clarence Regal in over fifteen years. He was still incredibly tall, but age had given him a slight stoop, and his once average frame had withered, making him almost as skinny as Jonny. His gray hair had gone all white, and his face was a weathered road map of wrinkles, emanating like ripples from his pronounced nose. But a far bigger change had occurred to his home laboratory. Gone was the chaotic menagerie of tubes and wires and electrical equipment. The soothing presence of a well-cultivated greenhouse replaced it. Where television had once transformed from an experimental technology into a consumer product, hundreds of flowers and plants now grew in a variety of boxes, planters, and bowls.

"So I'm guessing you don't really have a choice C14 plate block for me to purchase?" Regal asked bemusedly.

"No," Jonny said sheepishly.

"Then what can I help you with?"

Jonny took a deep breath and then proceeded to tell Regal the entire story of *Justice Girl*—the strange way she was created, the ongoing power struggle with Hogart, and finally, his signing over all of the rights to the network.

Regal listened to all of it, absorbing all the details. When Jonny was finished, Regal simply shook his head. "Even more proof I did the right thing, leaving the television business years ago."

"But you haven't left entirely. I know you're still on the board of the network."

"Yes, but it's mostly ceremonial. I do get a vote, but that's it. I have no say in day-to-day operations."

Jonny sunk. "I was hoping there might be something you could do. You know, for old time's sake, since you know my father and all. Maybe get Hogart to back off a bit."

"I'm sorry," Regal said, shaking his head. "There's nothing I can do. Besides, your father already asked for his one favor concerning you."

Jonny was startled. "What are you talking about?"

"He asked me if I would send someone from the network to see one of your plays. So I did." Regal smiled. "However, I certainly didn't ask them to hire you. I'm afraid that happened because of your talent."

Jonny guffawed. "Son of a bitch…"

"I'm sorry to hear you won't be in charge of *Justice Girl* anymore. It's a good show. One of the better ones on my network."

"Thank you."

Regal suddenly sighed and then looked away from Jonny, seemingly into the distance. "You know, and it's going to sound silly, but I thought television would change the world. I really did. I thought it would be a tool for learning—news, culture, the arts. I thought a person would come home at the end of a long day and maybe watch an opera or a symphony. Or maybe wake up in the morning and learn something over morning breakfast. Something about current events or maybe a new language. Oh, sure, there's some good stuff on the air—your show, some of the dramas. But the rest of it? Wrestling and game shows."

Jonny sighed. "And the way things are going, that's all you're going to see."

Regal nodded knowingly.

Jonny sighed again. He knew he was out of options. "The hardest part is going to be watching what they do to my own creation," Jonny said, almost choking up.

"Darn it!" Regal suddenly exclaimed, causing Jonny to jump in surprise. "Sorry," Regal said as he bent down and lifted a potted plant off the floor. "These days, the only experimenting I like to do is with crossbreeding plants. You know, to make a stronger, more beautiful, more robust plant. I always hope for the best, but sometimes things don't turn out the way I want them to." He held the withered and bent plant for Jonny to see. Clearly one of his failures, Regal found a pair of scissors, snipped the plant off just above the roots, and threw it into the garbage.

Now, lying on the couch, Jonny turned to Felicity. "After that, I left and somehow made it here." Jonny's body relaxed as he began to drift off to sleep.

"If only our problem were as simple as Regal's," Felicity said, exhaustion beginning to overwhelm her too.

Jonny stirred, awake again. "What's that?"

"You know, being able to kill off our creation because it's turned into something other than what we wanted."

Jonny's eyes flashed open, and he quickly sat up on the couch, no longer tired.

...

"So we're just supposed to forget everything that happened and help you?" Annie asked incredulously.

"Yes," Jonny answered hopefully.

"Just like that?" Annie snapped her fingers for emphasis.

"Look, I've apologized for being an asshole."

"A complete asshole," Burton added.

"Fine," Jonny said, fighting not to show his irritation.

"Say it," Shel said.

"A complete asshole," Jonny said, forcing himself to mean it.

Jonny, Annie, Shel, and Burton were seated at their familiar table at Veleska, being served the familiar heavy food with the familiar disdain by Mrs. Belinski. But unlike their previous gatherings at their favorite lunch spot, everyone sat stiffly in their chairs, and a painful tension hung in the air. Jonny hadn't seen them in a couple of weeks, not since he had written the last episode all by himself—something he had expected would upset them, which their hostile glares confirmed. But as uncomfortable as it was, Jonny knew he was lucky they were even there. It had taken longer than he had wished to track them down, and all of them, to a person, had resisted his overtures. It was only when he suggested meeting at Veleska that, one by one, they all had agreed. That gave him hope and made him realize that underneath the animus, they, too, longed for the camaraderie they all had shared in that distant long ago of four weeks earlier.

"Why should we help?" Burton asked, still not sold.

"Because if you don't, they will have won. Just like they always do, they will have won. They will have divided us and then conquered us and won. But we have a chance to keep that from happening. Together, we can stop them."

Burton, Shel, and Annie just stared at him blankly, his words having made as much impact on them as a misty rain on a humid summer day.

Exasperated, Jonny threw his hands in the air. "Look, we can't just sit by and see them destroy our work!"

Shel crooked his neck and raised an eyebrow. "What did you just say?"

"I said, we can't sit by and see them destroy our work."

Annie's head snapped back. "My God, he said it."

"Hard to believe," Burton added, shaking his head in mild disbelief.

"Finally," Shel said, exhaling with relief.

Jonny shook his head, confused. "What in the hell are you guys talking about?"

"You finally said it," Annie repeated with a slight smile. "'Our.' You finally acknowledged *our* work."

"Well, of course I said 'our.' We all did it. Together. *Justice Girl* belongs to all of us," Jonny shot right back, as if it were the truest statement in the world.

It was as if Jonny had untied a balloon and let all of the air slowly seep out. The tension among the four old friends dissipated, so much so that they all sank into their chairs, their bodies relaxing, allowing them to assume their usual comfortable positions.

Jonny's three partners exchanged a series of perfunctory nods with each other before Annie turned and looked right at him. "We're in," Annie said with finality.

...

As the image faded up on the translucent screen, everyone in the studio gasped. The pack of actors, technicians, costumers, grips, gaffers, and other personnel who made up the entire production crew of *Justice Girl* fanned around a brand new television that had just been set up at Arnold's floor manager station. Hogart stood at the edge of the crowd, pleased by their stunned reaction.

Color.

For the first time, they were seeing color television. Oh sure, there was a chance one or two of them might have seen a demonstration in the window of some tony department store or perhaps in the living room of a very wealthy friend, but outside of that, this was a first time for almost all of them. Enjoying the amazement on their faces, Hogart looked across to the cameraman on the other side of the studio who was controlling the color television camera that was supplying the image—the camera firmly aimed at the set of the Focus on Fashion offices. With the flair of a proud showman, Hogart waved, and the cameraman panned away from the relatively bland set to the nearby Amazon jungle set. The television screen exploded with a crayon box menagerie of rich colors, and the studio filled with another round of gasps.

Color.

Hogart was enjoying this. And why shouldn't he? He was in control, finally. With great fanfare, the other networks had aired a handful of color programs, but this was a first for the Regal Television Network. Hogart knew it was an audacious and gimmicky move, but what better way to announce that the network was here to stay! Instead of dying and going the way of the dodo, the network was going to be reborn, rising from the ashes like a newly born phoenix. But a bed of red and orange flame was not enough for this miraculous rebirth; Hogart threw in blues and greens and purples.

Color.

Just an hour earlier, he had burst into the rehearsal and announced that tomorrow night's episode would be broadcast in color. As everyone stared at him, astonished by his pronouncement, a legion of workmen had flooded the studio with the latest color equipment. Hogart had expected some pushback—after all, Jonny was still technically in charge for this last episode, but when he looked to him, all he got back was the same stunned, open-mouthed expression that matched the rest of the crew. It really wasn't that surprising, Hogart reasoned. Hogart had beaten him, and Jonny knew it.

"Isn't it fantastic?" Hogart said from the back of the crowd. Most nodded in agreement; some just stared back in disbelief. "Just think: tomorrow night, for the first time, America will see the golden yellow of Justice Girl's blonde hair, the rich blue of the sky as she flies into danger, and the vengeful purple of the bruises she plants on the faces of the evil!"

More nodding and stunned silence. But as the amazement finally wore off, the questions began—slow at first. "Is this really a good idea? You've got one camera running, but can the studio really be ready in twenty-four hours for a full broadcast?" Then fast and furious: "You can't be serious. None of the sets have been built for color!" "Should we really do it this week?" "Do we get paid more?"

Slowly and methodically, Hogart answered them all. "Yes, it's a good idea." "Yes, the studio can be ready in time for tomorrow night's broadcast." "Yes, we should do it this week." "No, you don't get paid any more."

The questions kept coming, and to Hogart's surprise, Jonny never said a word and just stood off to the side, watching him get attacked verbally. Perhaps he was enjoying it, as if to say, "You wanted the show. Well, now you've got the show!" The truth was Hogart was enjoying it, because he knew it was the right thing to do. Difficult, chancy, ballsy, but definitely the right thing to do.

Whether it was his commanding presence or unflappable demeanor, or that everyone just finally ran out of things to ask him, after almost an hour, the questions finally stopped. "Good," Hogart said, taking the silence to mean they were all mollified. But as much as he wanted to hang around and make sure things moved forward as he needed them to, Hogart headed for the door. "I'll leave you all to it," he said as he dodged in and around the throng of technicians who, despite the volley of skeptical questions, had never stopped their work setting up the studio for color, "as I'm sure you've got plenty to do. I know I do."

Hogart did, indeed, have plenty to do—press releases to approve, affiliates to inform, executives instructed to stay out of the way—but that didn't mean he was taking anything for granted when it came to what was happening in the studio.

Almost to the studio door, Hogart passed Schmitty, who was huddled with his sound team, discussing what this new technology would mean to their part of the production. With Charles in Washington finishing his testimony to HUAC, Schmitty was his man on the inside, and Hogart caught his eye just long enough for them to exchange a nod—a nod that made Hogart secure that he had a secret set of eyes and ears keeping a close eye on Jonny.

Confident that he—and his new possession, *Justice Girl*—had seen the last of black-and-white, Hogart left, bursting out onto the bright street as streaking yellow cabs, flashing red lights, and patrolling, blue-uniformed cops moved about. Color. As he slipped into his waiting limo, he smiled at the sight. By the end of the month, every show of every genre on at every hour would broadcast in full, exciting color. The Regal Television Network: the "Color Network."

Color. Color. Color.

...

Color?

That was unexpected, Jonny thought, as he stood near the bright, glowing television. The word kept dancing in his head. Color. Color. Color. But as beautiful as it was, seeing their sets imbued with every color of the rainbow, his thoughts became darker. Almost paranoid. What was Hogart up to? The thought froze him in his tracks, long after everyone else in the studio had split off into small groups to discuss what this unexpected turn of events meant for their part of the production. *Could Hogart be on to what I've planned?* he mused, as his eyes swept the studio as if searching for the answer. But none was coming. Everything seemed normal, just a professional crew deciding how to deal with a major change thrown at them at the last minute.

And maybe that was all there was to it. Hogart was a tricky character, capable of almost anything, as Jonny had painfully learned the day before. But try as he might, Jonny couldn't find a link to what he was going to do and the sudden decision to broadcast in color. In fact, when he thought about it, it might actually help him.

Satisfied that he could proceed, confident for the moment that all was well, Jonny stepped over to Arnold. "I think we should get back to it," Jonny said. Arnold broke off his animated conversation with a few of his PAs and nodded at Jonny. "Yes, sir."

In a matter of moments, thanks to the commanding image of Arnold's large mass and his bellowing voice, the studio returned to the state it had been in before Hogart's unexpected entrance and subsequent bombshell. Everyone went back to rehearsing for the next day's live show.

They started with the second scene of the first act and, with no interruptions, made it all the way to the midpoint of the episode, stopping to take a fifteen-minute break where the commercial would fall on show night. Then, moving over to the jungle sets, they proceeded to tackle the second act. Jonny stood at Arnold's stage manager station, his eyes glued to the wondrous world of color pouring forth from the newly arrived television. As much as he hated to admit it, he had to hand it to Hogart. *Justice Girl* in color was a wondrous sight. Freed from the confines of a black-and-white world, she shone anew in wondrous color. But as the act went on, Jonny found it harder and harder to concentrate. They were rapidly approaching a crucial moment, a major linchpin in their plan. His heart began to pound, and his upper lip moistened. If it didn't work, then everything else they had schemed was for naught. His forehead dampened, but when he went to wipe it with his hands, they were wet too. Soon, he found he couldn't even focus on the actors' dialogue and performances. Fortunately, this being the episode that had been twice preempted, the actors and crew were well versed in how Jonny wanted the script performed, so even without his guidance, everything went well.

When the loud crash finally came, it still startled Jonny.

"Let's hold!" Arnold yelled, as everything in the studio came to a sudden stop. Jonny sprinted from behind the color television, straight toward the source of the horrifying metallic crunch. Just in front of the jungle set where they were filming, the dolly that held the long metal sound boom was on its side, its driver and operator sprawled on the ground. Jonny, along with a couple other crew members, helped them to their feet. "Are you okay?"

Jonny asked them in earnest. Though clearly shaken, they both nodded that they were okay.

Schmitty, having hurried out of the control both, raced by them and knelt down on the ground next to the end of the boom arm. Carefully cradling several pieces of shattered metal in his hands, he lifted what was left of the microphone. "It's gone," he said, as if announcing the death of a grandparent.

"Where can we get another one?" Jonny asked, anxious to get the re-hearsal going again.

"There are several in the tech closet," Arnold said, turning toward the equipment storage room at the far end of the studio.

"No. No. No," Schmitty said, stopping him. "All there is in there are cheap industrial microphones. Unless you want the show sounding like mud, I'll have to hit one of our studios uptown, but that will take a half hour, at least."

Jonny's eyes twitched as he thought, and then he turned to Arnold. "Let's break early for lunch, and then pick it up where we left off in an hour." Arnold nodded his agreement. Jonny turned to Schmitty. "Go! Go!"

Schmitty nodded and hurried away. "That's lunch, everyone!" Arnold bellowed. Everyone dropped what they were doing and headed for the studio exit.

Now carrying his jacket, Schmitty raced through the departing pack and out the door. As soon as he was gone, everyone stopped moving and stood motionless.

A moment later, Annie hurried into the studio. "I saw him get into a cab and drive away. He's gone!" she yelled excitedly.

Everyone instantly hurried back to previous positions, the sound dolly was put upright, cameras were moved into position and focused, and Arnold suddenly appeared with a stack of blue script pages and hurriedly handed them out to the cast.

Jonny looked around, watching the crazed activity. He tried not to giggle, realizing that with both of Hogart's spies gone, they could rehearse, which meant they had a really good chance of getting away with it. *Yes,*

Jonny thought. This just might work. Almost everything was in place, but there was still one thing missing. One very important thing.

"Hi, Jonny," a voice said from behind.

Jonny turned around to see Mitchell. It had been only two weeks, but the rest upstate had done his brother a world of good. He looked tanned and rested and stood proudly before Jonny—tall, straight, and powerful.

Now Jonny was sure their plan would work.

...

Felicity hurriedly stepped out of the station as the 7:15 from Penn Station rumbled away down the tracks and deeper into Connecticut. She rushed to the curb in search of a taxi. Of course, on this night, not one was around. Fighting exhaustion, she peered into the distance, but the lights in the parking lot had yet to come on, so she could see very little in the fading twilight. Seeing an empty bench next to her, she collapsed onto it.

She was beat. Tired. Worn out.

It had been a brutal thirty-six hours since they had hatched their scheme, and that had meant very little sleep. All she wanted to do was turn off the lights in her hotel room, fall onto the bed, and not wake up until the next day. Show day. But in spite of her complete exhaustion, that simply wasn't an option. She still had work to do.

Summoning her strength, she climbed back to her feet and continued her search for a taxi. But before she could spot one, a speeding car drove up and stopped right in front of her at the curb.

"Felicity!" Braeden said excitedly as he hopped out from behind the wheel of his coupe without bothering to open the door.

Felicity sighed; this was the last person she wanted to see right now. All she wanted to do was get to her house, do what she needed to do, and then catch the next train back into the city, where her warm, inviting bed awaited her. So when Braeden excitedly leaned in to kiss her on the mouth, Felicity turned her head, and his lips landed on her cheek. To hide the obviousness of the move, she pulled him into a hug, doing her best to hide the discomfort of having her arms around someone other than Jonny. Just four weeks earlier, this had been the most normal and comfortable feeling in the world. She loved having Braeden's big brawny arms encircling her. But now, she felt strange in his arms, as if it were an overly intimate move by a distant friend.

"Viola?" she asked, breaking the hug after an acceptable amount of time.

Braden didn't even attempt a false front. "Don't be mad at the girl," he said earnestly. "I was very persistent. I happened to have called again, just after you had inquired about your dad's whereabouts and then said you were on your way home."

"She still should have kept her mouth shut."

"It's good to see you too," Braden said, seemingly hurt.

Felicity grumbled before sighing again. "I'm sorry. It's nice to see you Braeden." Then, thinking it might not be enough, she added, "I've missed you."

He nodded, satisfied. "That's a little more like a wife should talk to her husband."

Felicity hid her flinch and just grinned. "Would you mind giving me a ride home?"

"It would be my pleasure." He opened the passenger door and elegantly motioned for Felicity to enter. Felicity slid onto the crunchy leather seat, and a moment later, Braeden landed next to her behind the steering wheel and dropped the idling car into gear. "But first, there's something I want you to see."

They sped away from the station, through town, over the thruway, and onto Lark Avenue, winding out of Greenwich and into the countryside. They passed the Brixton place, with its solemn, proud white gazebo dominating the front yard. Then the Simpson place, with its gray, stone walls and pseudo-parapets topping the almost movie-set-fake castle-style home. It was when they came to the overgrown front drive of Mumford Place, completely hidden from the street, that Felicity realized where he was taking her—to one of her favorite places on earth: Hughes Church.

Sure enough, five minutes later, he pulled to a stop in front of the termite-riddled tree stump that only a lucky handful knew marked the beginning of the short trail that led to the abandoned church.

Stepping out of the car, memories flooded back to Felicity: discovering the place for the first time when she'd wandered away from a boring party at the Mumfords'; coming back to it again and again over the years, always on a seemingly perfect afternoon; and finally, taking Braeden to see it on one of their first dates. They hadn't been back in years.

Then she remembered why.

"What about Old Man Hughes?" Felicity asked, her nostalgic reverie fading.

Braeden flashed a bright smile. "He's not going to bother us."

"But it's on his property. He'll chase us away. Remember? Last time?"

"He's not going to bother us. I promise." Braeden playfully pushed her toward the weathered spot in the grass that was the start of the trail, and together they followed it.

The walk was short and pleasant, and Felicity thought how little had changed since she had last been here. After five minutes, during which Felicity and Braeden didn't say a word to each other, they came out into a clearing.

Sitting in the center, as if having willed away all of the vegetation, save for the expanse of bright green grass that it stood on, was the decaying remains of the old Hughes Church. It was a two-story, sagging stone structure, with its ramshackle innards exposed to the outside world. Seeing it, with the familiar sight of its overgrown pews and collapsing altar still surviving and still as she remembered it, Felicity smiled.

Forgetting Braden, Felicity quickened her pace, and stepping gingerly over the pile of collapsed rocks that seemingly guarded the place, she climbed into the abandoned structure. Spring was in full display amid the assorted wild flowers, vines, and plants that had slowly but steadily taken over. A piercing shaft of yellow-red light added an almost otherworldly glow, pouring down from above through the remnants of a shattered stained-glass window. Felicity was speechless as she tried to take it all in. She took a deep breath of the sugary scent of wild honeysuckle.

"It's really something," Braeden said, moving up next to her.

A nod was all Felicity could manage as the scent began to trigger something. Suddenly, her insides were in an uproar as her stomach turned, her pulse quickened, and her heart slapped against her chest like a broken fan. It all came back—the life she lived, the people, the sense of history, the sense of purpose, the sense of "this is ours; we earned it, all of it." The feeling of this ancient place had always made her flushed, excited, but now it was something much more. She felt...she felt...she felt that maybe this was where she belonged after all.

"A great place for a wedding? Don't you think?" Braeden asked teasingly.

"You wish. Old Man Hughes will never let us use it."

"Sure he will. We can use it any time we want."

"I doubt that."

"It's true." Braeden flashed a cocky smile. "'Cause I own it."

"You bought the church?"

"No. No. No..." Braeden said, shaking his head. "His entire estate. He was in foreclosure, so I got it for a song. He'll be gone by the end of the week. Any time after that, we can be married."

Felicity took a deep breath, the reminder of how this world worked almost knocking the wind out of her. Her resolve fully revived—and quite possibly doubled—she turned to Braeden. "I really need to see my father. Now."

The driveway to her house was even more crowded with delivery trucks and vans. After a quick good-bye to Braeden, having once again succeeded in not agreeing to a wedding date, Felicity strode inside. The backyard buzzed with activity. With the stage completed, workers placed chairs around the wooden dinner tables and constructed several outdoor bars. After a short search, she found her father next to the stage, locked in a fierce conversation with Roland Graves. Felicity took a deep breath and headed for them, thinking of all that had happened over the last four weeks, especially Alexis's suicide.

Her father had his back to her as she approached, and Roland saw her first. Judging by his somewhat surprised reaction, it was clear that her father had informed him of their previous encounter. Seeing Roland's expression, her father turned around, just as Felicity stepped up to him.

Instantly, his eyes narrowed as he glowered and asked flatly, "Yes?"

"I…I've…" Felicity began, her gaze on the green grass at her feet. Finally, she looked up and right at him. "I've come to apologize for my behavior the other day."

Instantly, her father's face lightened, all the sternness fading away.

"What I did was uncalled for, and I'm sorry," Felicity continued.

"That's all right."

"No, it's not," Felicity said, shaking her head. "And I've come to help, any way I can."

"Thank you," he said, a father basking in the appreciation of his daughter. He then caught Roland's eye as if to say, *See? She did come around.* But Roland's gaze was cool, and this did not go unnoticed by Felicity.

"If there's anything I can do," Felicity offered, powering forward as much for her father as for Roland.

"Just go on being the best Justice Girl you can be."

"Oh, I will," Felicity said, enjoying the personal irony. "Wait until you see tomorrow night's episode. It's our best one yet. And it will be in color."

"Really?" her father asked, intrigued.

"Yes. It's a shame our studio is so small. I bet it would be fun for all your guests to watch it together." Felicity shook her head, disappointed. "It's really too bad. That would have been so good for you, having everyone watch it together." Then Felicity's eyes brightened. "But hopefully, they'll all make it home in time to watch. It's a really good episode. Fun, wholesome, family entertainment. When does the fund-raiser end?"

But Felicity's father didn't answer. His mind was elsewhere as something was clearly turning over in his head. Finally, he turned to Roland. "What if we ended the event with a giant viewing party? What if we—all of the guests—all watched the latest episode of *Justice Girl* together?"

Roland eyed Scott closely, considering his words. Then he turned and looked straight at Felicity. Felicity looked back, a mask of pleasant surprise on her face. But inside, her heart was racing, and she felt her throat tightening up. She knew her father had bought it, but she wasn't sure about Roland. He was studying her, clearly worried that he was missing something—something important. Finally, Roland moved his gaze back to Scott. "It's not the worst idea I've ever heard," he said thoughtfully.

Scott Kensington beamed. "What better way to permanently brand me to *Justice Girl*?" Then he reached out and hugged Felicity. "It's so good to have you back."

After he released her, Felicity smiled brightly and turned away. As she walked off, her father and Roland discussed where they could find enough televisions.

"Justice is served," Felicity said quietly to herself, smiling.

...

Hogart's knees buckled slightly as the elevator doors shut and the car began its rapid ascent. He was used to the sinking sensation of riding the express elevator up to the executive offices, but this being a Sunday, instead of reaching the fortieth floor and then stopping at every floor thereafter, it just kept rising, streaking toward the sixty-seventh floor. And despite having to come into the office on yet another Sunday, the rapid rise perfectly fit his ebullient mood. He was overjoyed—practically giddy—because in just a couple of hours, after this latest episode of *Justice Girl* went off the air, he would be done with Jonny, once and for all.

Not that he was taking anything for granted; he'd kept in constant contact with Schmitty, and everything was going along just fine. Jonny and the rest of the cast and crew were dutifully working together to get the episode on the air. Still, he would be glad when it was all over, and *Justice Girl* was his.

Relishing this thought, Hogart leaped out of the elevator and bounded down the deserted hall, breezing past Mrs. Decosta, who had been awaiting his arrival. She fell in behind him, and without a word, they hurried past his own office, heading for the conference room. Hogart's mood further brightened at the thought of what he was about to do. Everything was falling into place. They'd wanted to meet on a Sunday, and Hogart was more than happy to oblige them.

Ever since word had leaked out—first of the board's turning down Worthington's offer and then of the stunning partnership news with the well-moneyed Vleets—Hogart had been barraged with calls from acquaintances, associates, business friends, personal friends, and even enemies. But the most voracious, naturally, had come from within the network itself. His previously uninterested executives were now baying at the door, demanding to know what was going to happen with this new company—or more important, where they all fit in. Hogart enjoyed keeping them in the dark, which only made them more aggressive in their quest. The inquiries had reached a crescendo the night before, with Affiliates and Programming calling him at home under the guise of some other sort of business at the network that supposedly needed his immediate attention. Hogart had Trudy politely explain that he was unavailable to come to the phone, but by early evening, the calls started coming in more frequently, with Personnel, Advertising, and Legal joining the fray, and all pretense of other network business dropped. The one that put it all over the edge was when Mrs. Decosta called Hogart—it was the one call he did take—to tell him that his executives were now hounding her. At home. That was all Hogart needed to hear. It was time to act—as soon as possible. He asked her to set up the meeting for the next afternoon, and the executives couldn't agree fast enough. For once, not one of them complained about having to come in on a Sunday.

Pulling the conference room door open, Hogart strutted into the room. As expected, Programming, Affiliates, Advertising, Personnel, and Legal were all assembled around the rectangular conference table, leaving one spot open at the head. As Hogart stopped at the top of their man-made U, they all jumped to their feet and began peppering him with questions. Hogart had prepared himself for an attack, but this was much more than he'd expected, and it almost knocked him off his feet. Regaining his composure, he swatted at the air. "Sit down!" he yelled over them. "I will clear everything up shortly. I promise."

It took about thirty more seconds until they were all mollified, and one by one, they finally sat down.

"Good," Hogart said, pleased. "I know you all have a lot of questions. So I'll get right to it." Hogart paused for a moment to consider his thoughts, and then he took a deep breath and exhaled slowly. "You're all fired."

The entire room flinched in disbelief and then once again exploded with questions.

"Every...last...one of you," Hogart said slowly, for emphasis, before turning and walking for the door. Leaving behind the raucous scene, he exited into the hallway. Mrs. Decosta was right where he'd left her and once again fell in line as he briskly headed back toward the elevator.

He felt like he was floating on air.

He was done with them, and in just a few hours, he'd be done with Jonny. It was a clean sweep that would lead to a new beginning. He'd rebuild the network from the top down, starting with new, talented, obedient executives who would be loyal to him, work hard, and not spend their time thinking of their next job. With him as their leader, they'd build the Regal-Vleets company into a powerhouse to rival the other networks and, down the line, the movie studios. And he'd take the time to learn their names.

It was going to be a great future.

Reaching the elevator, he excitedly punched the button. Now there was nothing left to do but head downtown to the studio and watch the final episode before *Justice Girl* was all his.

But nothing happened.

He tried the button again. Still nothing—it remained dark. He looked up at the floor indicator numbers above the brass doors. Every one of them was dark.

"Oh!" Mrs. Decosta said, suddenly remembering. "They're doing some work on the elevators. There were a couple of workmen here earlier. They said they should have the elevators up and running again in just a few minutes."

Hogart frowned. He didn't like this at all. He wanted to get to the studio right away. Everything was under control; everything was just the way it should be. But still, he wanted to be there. Just to be sure.

He half-heartedly hit the brass elevator door with his fist and then stepped back to wait, which was all he could do. It wasn't like he could run down sixty-seven flights of stairs.

...

The spontaneous, tight bunching of five bodies finally broke off, and Jonny and the four actors separated from their group hug. They were gathered in their traditional "pre-first places" spot, just inside the studio, costumes on, makeup and hair done. Jonny had joined Veronica, Reginald, Thomas, and Felicity moments earlier, wanting to give them one last thank-you for all their hard work, but before he could say anything, they had all simply come together en masse, arms outstretched. No words were necessary. They were sad to do what they were about to do, but they all agreed it had to be done.

"Two minutes to air. First positions! First Positions!" Arnold yelled in the distance.

With a final nod to one another and a few weak smiles, they parted, somberly heading off to their first positions.

"Felicity, hold on," Jonny said, stopping her. "Thank you for doing this."

Felicity gave him a quick set of short nods. "It's for Alexis," she said softly. "And everyone else who was hurt by their ilk."

Jonny nodded back. "Yes."

"And I may owe you one," Felicity said, with a slight smile.

She turned to go, but Jonny stopped her again. "Break a jaw," he said, with his own slight smile.

They shared a quiet moment and then parted.

Jonny crossed the studio as actors and technicians scurried about with their usual last-minute preparations. Jonny marveled as the chaotic room crackled with the usual pre-show energy, in spite of what they were about to do.

With each step heavier than the last, Jonny climbed the short flight of stairs off the floor and quietly slipped into the VIP viewing room. So far, the plan was working, and the room was deserted. As the opening credits played on the newly installed color monitor, Jonny took a seat dead center in the front row. He had thought about staying on the floor, but for this episode, the last one, he wanted to watch it the way it was meant to be seen, the way the rest of the country saw it—on a TV screen.

Johnny sat back in the chair. It was hard for him to believe that this would be the last episode he would ever work on or, for that matter, that *anyone* would ever work on. But as the episode began, his mind drifted. There wasn't much to watch in the first part, just the usual story set-up resulting in all of the characters flying down to the Amazon in search of a hot story for the magazine. It was full of the usual fun lines and witty repartee at which he and the other writers had gotten particularly efficient, but all of the changes—all of the really good stuff—were in the second half, after the midpoint commercial.

Taking in the temporary calmness, an odd serenity filled him, as if his subconscious was confirming to him that he had made the right choice. And their plan received yet another lucky break, as if fate had agreed too, when they found out that Hogart was going to a meeting at the network's offices just before the show aired. It took some quick thinking; after all, they had designed their plan around cutting all his communications to the studio and keeping him from physically entering the building. But that was fraught with all kinds of uncertainty and the fear that they might not have thought of every entrance. Keeping him temporarily locked up two miles away— that was easy. Shel came up with the idea of shutting down the elevators, and he and Burton had thrown themselves enthusiastically into the role of repairmen.

Another thing added to Jonny's confidence. Charles had finished his testimony to HUAC the day before, informing them that he had been mistaken when he had named Jonny to the committee, and Jonny already had notification that his subpoena had been vacated. Now, instead of coming back to New York to oversee the broadcast, Charles had chosen to stay in DC for another couple of days. Jonny wanted to think that Charles might feel some shame over what he had done and thusly didn't want to show his face, but he knew better. Charles wanted to enjoy the best of Washington before returning home to his new, powerful position with the new company. This made Jonny's serenity melt into deep satisfaction because he knew that Charles would never attain the position he so dearly coveted.

The first half of the episode was ending, and Jonny focused his attention back to the television. With the commercial break just moments away, things were reaching a fever pitch, with the entire gang—Sally, Chance, Margaret, and Benjamin—caught by Amazonian natives and tied to stakes.

Jonny settled back; now things were about to get interesting.

Instead of the typical commercial extolling the virtues of Consolidated Oil and Gas, the earnest and confused faces of Mr. and Mrs. Belinski popped onto the screen, and they began a stiff recitation of the virtues of their restaurant, Veleska. Jonny laughed. It wasn't just their stiff performance or the absurdity of a small East Village restaurant getting a national commercial that he found so funny. It was the thought of what was going through Hogart's head at this very moment. Hogart was trapped two miles away on the sixty-seventh floor of his building. And the realization that his network was about to be hijacked for the next eight minutes would just be sinking in. Jonny could imagine Hogart sitting in his office, watching on one of his televisions—no, on all four—with rage and fury pulsing through his body. He could imagine Hogart seething and screaming. And his face! What would his face look like at this very instant?

Loud pounding startled Jonny. He turned around and instantly got the answer to his question.

His suit rumpled and his hair slick with sweat, Hogart stood behind the rear glass door of the VIP booth, looking very much like a man who had just run down sixty-seven flights of stairs. His face was aflame, his features pursed and tight, and his voice shrill as he continued his pounding. "Did you really think you could get away with this? Did you really think you could do this to me? Hogart Daniels, the head of Regal-Vleets Company!" With one last pound on the glass, Hogart rushed away.

Jonny leaped out of his seat and streaked across the VIP room. He knew exactly where Hogart was headed. At the far end of the hallway, just outside the VIP booth, was the control booth.

And no one was guarding it.

If Hogart made it inside, Sal would instantly cut the transmission when faced with the enraged visage of Hogart, even though Sal was one of the co-conspirators. Their plan would fail—*Justice Girl* would live and, most horrifyingly, would no longer belong to Jonny.

Taking the steps three at a time, Jonny reached the glass door, ripped it open, and burst into the hallway. Hogart was about thirty feet down the hallway, hurrying toward the entrance to the control booth, above which *Justice Girl* played on a mounted color television. Fortunately for Jonny, Hogart's limp was slowing him down. So, as Justice Girl fought to save everyone from the angry Amazonian natives, Jonny ran after Hogart and, leaping at the last possible moment, was able to grab Hogart's ankle with his outstretched hand. Hogart sprawled onto the gleaming white floor, coming to a stop just short of the control room door. Jonny leaped over him, spun around, and took up position, blocking entry into the control booth.

Jonny tensed in an almost comical defensive position, a distant memory from some Chinese fighting arts manual purchased from an ad in the back of a comic book. Hogart hurriedly climbed back to his feet and, seeing Jonny, hunched into his own fighting position.

But there was nothing comical about this one. Hogart tightened his body, ready to attack. Jonny was scared, remembering that he'd heard that Hogart had been in the army—a distinct advantage when it came to physical altercations.

Hogart held his ground for a moment, staring at Jonny. Buoyed by what he took as fear on Hogart's part, Jonny gained some confidence and flexed his wrists threateningly. Then Hogart moved at Jonny, and it was over in mere seconds. Hogart slipped behind Jonny, sliding his left arm around Jonny's neck and trapping him in a choke hold. Hogart closed his right hand into a fist and then lifted his right arm, ready to unleash a sharp blow.

Jonny closed his eyes and flinched, ready for the punch that would surely break his nose or, at the very least, split his lip. He tightened his face in a pathetic attempt to ease the blow. But a few seconds passed, and it never came.

Slowly, Jonny peeled open his eyes. Hogart's head still hovered just inches above him, his breath jabbing hot and angry across Jonny's face. But Hogart's confused eyes were looking upward and past Jonny, at something above both of their heads. Jonny almost chuckled. He was safe.

It had begun.

Utterly perplexed but still holding Jonny tightly, Hogart stared up at the monitor anchored high up on the wall. Jonny twisted his neck around as far as he could so he could also see.

On the screen, Justice Girl and a freshly freed Chance, Margaret, and Benjamin, were joined by Mitchell, who stood proudly before them, dressed as Superman, complete with tights, boots, cape, and giant "S" on his chest. Jonny shook his head, beaming. As impressive as Mitchell had looked in rehearsal, on screen in full, glorious color—piercing reds, saturated blues, shimmering yellows—he looked astonishing. There was no question about it; his brother made an incredible Man of Steel. Jonny broke into a wide smile at the sight of Hogart's eyes, blinking like the wings of a frightened hummingbird as he tried to comprehend what he was seeing on the screen.

Mitchell as Superman, striding heroically, approached the group. Stopping in front of them and thrusting out his chest, he addressed them, noticeably ignoring Justice Girl and looking directly at all the others. "Beware, good folks, for she is not who she claims to be." Superman turned and looked directly at Justice Girl. "There is no good here, only evil." He jabbed a finger straight at her. "For Justice Girl is nothing more than a lie."

Justice Girl stood her ground, defiant. "He knows not what he says. I am all that is good. I am all that is right. I am all that will protect you from the evil that is everywhere," Justice Girl said firmly.

"Ignore her lying words," Superman said dismissively. "Behold and watch what happens when I focus my inviso-vision in a way that allows you to see who she really is."

Superman jutted his neck out, squinted his determined eyes, and aimed his mighty gaze at Justice Girl. Complemented by a high-pitched, throbbing sound effect, Justice Girl's costume suddenly changed, slowly dissolving into a tight-fitting, bright red body suit with a bright yellow sickle and hammer on her chest. Her face also transformed, changing from the blonde, all-American good looks of Justice Girl into a dark-haired, dark-eyed, dark-lipped, sinister pout. With a dramatic flair, Superman swept his arm at her. "Behold Red Menace, a diabolical superhero working for the Soviet Union."

Everyone gasped.

But Red Menace was unfazed. Her eyes quickly shrunk into a dark squint, and she seethed in Superman's direction. "Exposing me will do nothing, Superman. I am Red Menace, and you cannot stop me. Nothing can, for I have the power and strength of the workers' state behind me—fifty million strong!"

Superman laughed. "That is nothing compared to the will and might of freedom and democracy!" Superman proudly retorted.

"Ha!" Justice Girl, now completely transformed into Red Menace, spat back. "I will destroy you!" Red Menace leaped at Superman, and a mighty battle began between the two superheroes.

Though the episode was far from over, Jonny felt the grip on his body loosen. In seconds, Jonny was free, and Hogart stepped away from him and sighed. His eyes landed firmly on Jonny, no longer interested in the action on the screen. Jonny could see that Hogart knew it didn't matter how the fight on screen came out; he had already lost. Whether Justice Girl lived or died, she was forever tainted. Who would want to watch a show about a Communist superhero? What parents would let their children tune in?

She was blacklisted.

Hogart eyed Jonny with a cocktail of anger, envy, admiration, and finally, resignation. Jonny could almost feel Hogart's thoughts: *I've been defeated, and by this little bastard, no less.* As if confirming what Jonny felt, Hogart straightened up and adjusted his clothes. "You know I'll land somewhere good," Hogart said defiantly.

Jonny nodded. "I know you will." And Jonny meant it, feeling in his gut that he and Hogart had not seen the last of each other.

Without another word, Hogart walked away from the control booth, just as Superman landed the final, defeating blow, and Red Menace crumpled to the ground, dead.

Catching his breath, Jonny turned back to the television to see Superman lift the limp body of Red Menace into his massive arms.

"Remember, Americans, always be vigilant," Superman said. "We face a crafty foe. The more one appears to be good, the more we must look for the evil that may lie underneath." With a final reinforcing nod at the camera and with the vanquished Red Menace in his mighty arms, Superman flew off into the distance. The image froze on the screen, and the closing credits slowly crawled across the screen. Through a window in the hall, Jonny could see the studio floor. They were off the air, and everyone relaxed—the actors, the cameramen, the stage hands, the costumers...the entire studio.

But gone was the usual explosion of shouts and applause that greeted the end of another successful broadcast. None of it. Just heaviness. Perhaps it was appropriate, Jonny thought; after all, they had just witnessed an execution. But in spite of the gray cloud in front of him, he couldn't help but feel excited, as well as feel overcome with a deeper sense of accomplishment than he had ever felt before. His eyes moved back to the screen as the last of the credits played over the triumphant silhouette of the mighty Superman and his vanquished foe.

It was a perfect image.

Clean, precise, to the point, and just what Jonny had wanted to say about those claiming the moral high ground. But the best part was much more personal. Mitchell had made a good Superman.

A perfect Superman.

A true Superman, who had finally brought about some small manner of justice for Rachel.

...

Felicity yanked open the door of her dressing room and rushed inside. She dropped into the chair in front of her dressing mirror and pushed three bright flower bouquets out of the way so that she could see the black phone at the center of her makeup table. A wave of pungent honeysuckle hit her. Braeden had sent them; two had arrived before the show, and the third,

Felicity surmised, had arrived while she was on the air, live. *He is really laying it on thick*, she thought, *sending three bouquets just to celebrate that they had decided on a place to get married.*

Or at least he had decided.

But none of that interested her now as she swiped her hand in front of her face, fanning away the rich odor and staring at the telephone. Her entire face tightened as she focused her eyes, willing it to ring. After an endless moment, it finally did.

Felicity ripped the receiver off the cradle. "Hello," she shot urgently into the phone.

"I only have a moment, Miss Kensington," Viola said haltingly—she sounded a bit overwhelmed herself.

"That's okay. Thank you for doing this. Now, tell me what you see."

"Well, the party has gotten awfully quiet. During the show, everyone was laughing and cheering—we served a lot of wine—right up until the end. They went crazy when Superman came on, but then it got awful quiet when you turned out to be that bad lady."

Felicity smiled. It was oddly reassuring to know that even Viola had understood what they were trying to say. "More. More," Felicity urged.

"Well, some people are starting to leave and—"

"Do you see my father?"

"Yes."

"What's he doing?"

"He's talking to your mother. They're smiling to everyone, but they don't seem very happy."

Felicity took a deep breath. "Now, I want you to look very closely. Do you see a heavy-set man, with a fringe of gray hair around a bald head, sitting anywhere near my father?"

"Umm…well, I did. He was sitting right next to your father, but he got up and moved right after the show ended."

Felicity let out a sharp breath. "Thank you, Viola." She hung up the phone, holding the receiver down on the cradle for a long moment. *My God, it actually seems to have worked.* Leaning back in the chair, she flushed and laughed to herself. She really couldn't have asked for more. Clearly, it had gone as well as she had hoped it would. Better. Her father was finished—at least in terms of a political career. No matter what he did going forward, from now on, whenever someone in the Connecticut political circle saw him, they wouldn't think of all the money he had helped raise for the party. They wouldn't think of his influential publication. No, they wouldn't think of any of that. Their first—probably their only—thought would be "It's the father of that actress who played that superhero who turned out to be a Commie." He'd hitched himself to her train, and that train had just gone off the track.

A quick knock at the door startled Felicity, but before she could answer, it opened, and one of the young female costume assistants stepped in. Without saying a word, she began gathering up all of Felicity's costumes, draping them across an arm so she could haul them off to be washed. Felicity watched her. Instead of the usual sprightliness to her work, she was slow and methodical, clearly aware that there was really no point to what she was doing—there would be no more episodes. With the bundle over her arm, she headed for the door.

"Would you like this?" Felicity asked, stopping the young girl. The costume assistant turned around, and Felicity pointed to one of the flower bouquets Braeden had sent her.

Through her rimmed cat-eye glasses, the young girl's eyes bulged. "Yes. Please."

"Take it."

The young girl hurried over and grabbed the bouquet with her free arm.

"In fact," Felicity continued, "take all three of them."

The young girl's eyes got even wider, and after a bit of juggling, she managed to make it out of the room with all three bouquets and the costumes.

As the door slammed shut, Felicity sank back in her chair, relieved as the smell of the flowers slowly dissipated. After a moment, the sweet honeysuckle scent was gone, and Felicity took several deep breaths, reveling in the damp, musty air of the tiny, cramped, and decrepit dressing room.

She had never been in a more beautiful room in her life.

EPILOGUE

In the ensuing craziness after the last episode of *Justice Girl* aired, Jonny stayed hunkered down in his apartment. He declined all interviews and refused any phone calls from anyone in the business, except for Blanche Gaines, who finally asked to read some of his work. Six months later, on the night the Regal Television Network gave its last broadcast—fittingly, one final episode of *Hermie's Henhouse*—before going off the air for good, Jonny had planned to sit alone in his apartment and watch. But instead, he found himself in a tiny rehearsal space just down the street from Rockefeller Center, locked in a feverish casting session for his upcoming episode of *Kraft Television Playhouse*. Within weeks of Blanche's signing Jonny, she had been able to sell his teleplay "The Road to Damascus" to Kraft, and they had promptly scheduled it as their sixth show of the 1955–56 season. But with just over a week to go before the show went on the air, they had yet to cast the female lead.

Jonny had not seen Felicity since the night they had killed off Justice Girl, though on two occasions since then, he thought he might have. Once, when he was trying to solve a script problem by taking a walk in the East Village, he thought he saw her climbing up the steps from a basement apartment. And another time, when he was driving to New Hampshire for a long weekend with some friends and stopped off in Old Greenwich to get some gas, he thought he saw her in a nearby park, riding a horse. But in both cases, by the time he tried to get a closer look, the person who might have been Felicity was gone.

But now, even though she wasn't on the list, as each actress came in, Jonny couldn't help hoping it would be Felicity, reading for the lead. Or even a small supporting role. He knew it was a long shot, but then again, this was live television, and anything could happen.

AUTHOR'S NOTE

To those of you who were incredibly generous with your help along the way—Marna Poole, Marc May, Ellen Stratton, Sadie Stratton, David Hoggan, David Teitelbaum, Andrew McCullough, Craig Koller, Jenny Thompson, Paul Canter, Greg Szimonisz, Dolores Stone, Nelson Stone, and Summer Ramsey—my heartfelt thanks..

CPSIA information can be obtained at www.ICGtesting.com
Printed in the USA
LVOW04s2146260515

440026LV00013B/215/P